ANN MOORE

Leaving Ireland

2002

FICTION FOR THE WAY WE LIVE

NAL Accent
Published by New American Library, a division of
Penguin Putnam Inc., 375 Hudson Street,
New York, New York 10014, U.S.A.
Penguin Books Ltd, 80 Strand,
London WC2R 0RL, England
Penguin Books Australia Ltd, Ringwood,
Victoria, Australia
Penguin Books Canada Ltd, 10 Alcorn Avenue,
Toronto, Ontario, Canada M4V 3B2
Penguin Books (N.Z.) Ltd, 182–190 Wairau Road,
Auckland 10, New Zealand

Penguin Books Ltd, Registered Offices:
Harmondsworth, Middlesex, England

Published by New American Library, a division of Penguin Putnam Inc.

First Printing, November 2002
10 9 8 7 6 5 4 3 2

FICTION FOR THE WAY WE LIVE

REGISTERED TRADEMARK—MARCA REGISTRADA

LIBRARY OF CONGRESS CATALOGING-IN-PUBLICATION DATA:

Moore, Ann, 1959–
Leaving Ireland / Ann Moore.
p. cm.
ISBN 0-451-20707-6 (trade pbk. : alk. paper)
1. Irish American women—Fiction. 2. Women immigrants—Fiction. I. Title.

PS3563.05695 L43 2002
813'.6—dc21   2002069590

Printed in the United States of America
Set in New Caledonia
Designed by Ginger Legato

Printed in the United States of America

For Rick,
Who makes everything possible

And for Nigel and Gracelin—
O, how I love you

ACKNOWLEDGMENTS

Thanks to the Bellingham Public Library and Western Washington University's Wilson Library for resource materials; to the many excellent historians of this time, including Cecil Woodham-Smith, Thomas Keneally, Tyler Anbinder, Edwin G. Burroughs, Mike Wallace; to U2 for the inspiration of their music and their politics; to the hardworking staff at Jean V. Naggar Literary Agency; to my editor, Genny Ostertag, for her dedication and excellent advice on this manuscript; to Teri Smith, Yolanda Calderon, Tony Robles, Sarah Vautaux—your unbelievable support means more to me than you'll ever know; to Randall Reinders, Peter Smith, and the late Walt Sheldon for sharing their love of good books and the sea; and to my husband, Rick, who continues to clear the road ahead so that I might have this life.

For I was hungry and you gave me food, thirsty and you gave me drink, a stranger and you took me in, naked and you clothed me, sick and you cared for me, in prison and you visited me there. . . . Whatever you do for the least of these, saith the King, you do also for me.

—Matt. 25:35–36

One

THE Irish Sea was behind them now. Thick fog rolled over the deck as the small ship made its way slowly up the river Mersey, the only sound that of the sharp crack of canvas sail, trimmed by the crew to catch any little wind. Only three miles to port, and all the passengers had come to the rail, wordless and watchful, readying themselves for whatever might emerge when they passed out of this world and into the next.

A glimmer of torchlight pierced the fog, and a murmur rippled through the crowd. Now they could see the riverbanks in the distance, the row of torches along the waterfront, the shadowy hulk of warehouses behind, as slowly the small vessel made her way toward the looming docks.

Ghostly figures shrouded in swirling mist drifted into view and out again; loaded wagons and men on horseback were momentarily illuminated as they passed through pools of flickering light; and the mingled shouts of sailors, vendors, immigrants, and runners were muted and fragmented as if this were a teeming city of apparitions. Gracelin O'Malley bent down to look in her young daughter's wide eyes.

"Liverpool," she whispered.

Everyone crowded to the rail, bags and satchels clutched

anxiously in cold hands, mothers and fathers counting heads, wrapping children more tightly against the damp chill of this November night. Almost all were country folk already overwhelmed by the cities of Ireland, completely unprepared for what they would find here.

Grace looked at them, her countrymen, and knew them well: the old, whose faces belied a struggle of bewilderment, exhaustion, and grief; the families—eight, nine, ten huddled together, older ones holding fast to younger; mothers come alone with babes in arms, toddlers on hips, children clutching fistfuls of skirt. There were the eager young colleens, arm-in-arm with their dreams of employment in big houses, a half-day once a month, marriages to good lads with steady pay, babies that lived. The spinsters linked arms with no one—a factory job, a shared room, a meal each day was all they asked; they went unnoticed by the young men with faces full of false bravado who shoved and punched one another, all the while stealing anxious glances at the rough mob waiting on the docks below. Older men, grimfaced and wary, collars turned up and caps pulled low, stuffed rough working hands deep into pockets worn thin.

Grace looked at all these ragged people and knew them to be the fortunate ones—those who had somehow escaped the terrible hunger and suffering. They knew it, too; there was a measure of guarded relief in the way they held themselves, along with the guilt and—for the older ones, the men—humiliation. They were dependent now on the very country that had brought them to their knees; here they were, crawling into England for food, lodging, and passage to a better life—crawling like pathetic beggars when, in their hearts, they knew they were kings.

But kings did not abandon their countries, nor their countrymen, and so they kept their eyes lowered and didn't speak unless spoken to. Some would make the long journey to Australia, hoping to reunite with family deported to Van Diemen's Land. Others would buy a cheap passage to Canada, though more than half of these would eventually make the brutal walk down through the back country, crossing the border into the

United States of America. Those with a little more money could pay their way directly to Boston or New York City, where they would be absorbed into the Irish Quarters, but those who had spent every penny just to cross the Irish Sea would find themselves battling for any menial job and a space on any floor of any room in the swelling, squalid Irish slums that now existed in every major city in England. A few might venture further inland—young men who had hired themselves out every summer as farmhands and knew the lay of the land—or travel the northern roads to Scotland, but for many of them at the ship's rail tonight, Liverpool was the end of the line.

"Hold fast to Mary Kate now, and stay right with me when we go ashore." Julia Martin's voice was grim as she surveyed the docks with the eye of a general about to engage in battle. "Watch out for those boys, there, the runners. They'll try to snatch your bag or Mary Kate, and force you to follow them God-knows-where."

"It's how they make their living," Grace said, remembering her brother's letter about the docks in New York.

"Let them make it off of someone else, I say." Julia eyed them menacingly. "We know where we're going, after all."

"Can we walk to it, then?" Grace asked, tying Mary Kate's scarf securely under her chin.

Julia hesitated. She had an address and directions that now seemed quite vague, considering the enormous warehouses and tall buildings that allowed only a glimpse of the street maze beyond.

"I don't know that, exactly," she admitted. "But we'd better not stand around looking lost or those thieves will be on us in a minute." She felt for the coin purse tied inside her skirt. "I see carriages moving out in that main road beyond, but first we'll have to get past this crowd and down over there." She pointed to a street barely visible through the fog. "Once we're on the main road, we'll hire the first carriage we see and I'll give the address to the driver as if I know exactly where it is. He'll be less likely to take advantage of us that way."

Grace frowned. "Should I not know the name of the place myself? In case we're parted?"

"We're not going to be parted," Julia said resolutely. "Just stick close to me."

Grace shook her head. "Much as I trust you, I'm not getting off this ship until you tell me where it is we're going."

Julia looked at the thin, weary young woman who was her charge and realized that she had been parted from everyone except the girl who stood by her side fiercely gripping her arm. *It's a wonder she's got any fight left at all,* Julia thought.

"It's in Prince Edwin Street. Number four. A Mistress Brookshire is holding the room for us."

Grace's face relaxed and she nodded. "Thank you. Thank you," she said again and—not for the first time—Julia found herself moved by this woman, moved by all she'd been through and by how bravely she bore it when Julia herself could hardly bear to think of all that had been lost. But she had only herself to blame—when William Smith O'Brien had broken the news of McDonagh's death, Julia had insisted she be the one to get Morgan's widow safely out of Ireland, and now here she was, faced with the reality of those words.

"Right," she said, shaking off her reverie. "I'll carry these bags. You take that one, Grace, over your shoulder. And hold on to Mary Kate with both hands."

Grace did as she was told, looking down into her daughter's eyes before giving her fingers a gentle squeeze.

"C'mon, then." Grace winked. "Off on another adventure with your old mam."

Mary Kate nodded soberly, but said nothing. She was too quiet for a three-year-old, and Grace promised herself for the hundredth time that one day soon her daughter's steady companion would be joy instead of sorrow. Holding tightly to one another, they followed the column of figures disembarking and entered the throng of confusion on the docks.

"This way," Julia shouted, pulling Grace and Mary Kate through the crowd to the side street that would take them to their carriage.

A sudden yank on Grace's bag nearly pulled her off her feet, but at the same time Mary Kate was being pulled in the opposite direction. Grace hung on to both desperately as Mary Kate screamed and kicked at the boy who had her other arm.

"Ouch, bloody hell!" The little ruffian clutched his shin. "Only trying to help, missus! Takes you to good lodgings, I will! Gets yer ticket squared! Finds you good eats! I'm yer man, missus!" he insisted, trying gingerly to reapproach Mary Kate, who kicked at him again.

The other boy shouted much the same thing—he, too, could be of good service, better service!—refusing to let go of Grace's bag. She followed Mary Kate's example and kicked him off, her heart pounding as he fell to his knees, howling as if she had attacked him. They were tough boys and leathery, but so thin, and dressed in tattered clothing, one with rags tied round his feet instead of boots.

"Sorry," Grace said, backing away. "I'm sorry . . . I . . ."

"Sod off, you cheeky bastards, or I'll have the guards on you!" Julia swung her bags at them, then locked arms with Grace and hurried her toward the street.

The curses of the boys behind them stopped abruptly; Grace glanced over her shoulder and saw the two swarm a group of timid young girls huddled together under a lamp. With sudden clarity, she realized that runners—boys and men—were everywhere, first cajoling, then bullying immigrants into following them wherever they might lead. Overwhelmed, many immigrants were easily taken up and led away down alleys and narrow streets, away from the docks, away from friends and even family members. There was no one to stop it, and Grace's heart pounded with anxiety.

They emerged from the side street onto a wide boulevard; Julia spied a carriage for hire and raised her arm, signaling to the driver that they would cross over. Realizing that the street was ill-lit and that horses, carriages, and wagons were everywhere, bolting suddenly out of the fog, Grace instinctively swung Mary Kate up into her arms, then let out a gasp of pain.

"Down!" Julia demanded instantly. "You're not to lift anything heavy—doctor's orders. It's too soon after the baby!"

Grace lowered her child carefully, breathing out in a steady stream of vapor against the sharp pain in her abdomen. Blinking away tears, she gripped Mary Kate's hand and held her close as they attempted to cross the street.

"All right, then?" Julia asked more gently. She handed their bags to the driver, then lifted Mary Kate into the carriage.

Grace nodded, not trusting herself to speak, and took up the hand Julia offered, sliding gingerly across the bench to make room. She pressed her hands across her belly, willing the pain to subside, hoping there would be no blood.

"Prince Edwin Street, please, driver," Julia commanded.

The driver twisted around in his seat to have a good look at them. He eyed especially Julia's good cloak and hat, the quality of the luggage, the expensive boots; then he nodded as if he'd come to a decision.

"Beggin' your pardon, miss," he said, doffing his hat. "But you'll pay more for the price of riding to Prince Edwin Street than you will to lodge there."

"That is our business." Julia straightened her spine. "Drive on, please."

The driver frowned and chewed the end of his cigar. "Beggin' your pardon again, miss," he said firmly. "But you don't look like the kind of ladies what lodge in that there street."

"And why is that?" Julia asked haughtily.

"Well, you see, miss, they sleeps 'em ten to a floor there, maybe you gets blankets, maybe you don't, but you're still sharing the place with strangers and you being ladies and all, and I see you got a young one."

"We've made prior arrangements," Julia assured him. "There is a *private* room waiting for us."

"Well, I'm sure that's right." The cigar worked its way over to the other side of his mouth. "All's I'm saying to you—respectfully, of course, miss—is that your room'll be full of others cut from different cloth, if you get my meaning. And I don't like to say but for your own good, the lodgings in Prince Edwin Street's known for the spreading of things, not to mention those what bring in the fever."

"Spreading of things," Julia repeated. "You mean, lice?"

"Them what gets all up in your hair and such, miss, is what I'm saying. Most of these Irish coming off the boats is a different class from you and they don't notice, but they leave them little buggers—pardon me, miss—and other things beside, and not a few die before they ever get to where they're going. Plus all the drink and rough talk and . . . well, it's not proper lodging for ladies like yourselves, is all I'm saying."

"I see." Julia frowned ever so slightly. "And what would you suggest instead?"

"Well," he said, his foot in the door. "My wife's cousin's husband runs a nice little inn, he does, not too far from here. The King George. It's clean—I'll promise you that on my mother's grave—and you'll have your own room with fresh water in the morning and a cup of tea, nice and hot, to go with your breakfast, which'll be more'n a hard roll. Very reasonable, though it'll be more'n you'd pay in Prince Edwin Street, I'll give you that, as well." He puffed the cigar, proud of his own virtue.

Julia eyed Grace, who glanced at the spot where Julia's purse was hidden behind folds of cloth. Julia nodded imperceptibly; they had enough.

"All right, then," Julia announced. "You've made a good case and we'll trust that you're an honest man simply looking out for our—and your cousin's husband's—best interests. You may deliver us to the King George Hotel."

The driver replaced his cap, grinning around the cigar. "At once, ladies," he said, and moved the horse out into traffic.

It wasn't a long ride, but enough for Grace to realize that they had probably been saved from a miserable night. The carriage moved slowly down the cobbled streets, wheels clattering, hooves clopping, faces appearing, then disappearing in the foggy gloom. Here and there, she caught sight of a door opening to groups of travelers and, on the floor, ragged bundles she realized were sleeping bodies.

Through grimy lighted windows, some beneath street level, she saw the same scene over and over again—cheap lodging for immigrants who were probably grateful, most of them. Somewhere a fiddler played, and gangs of young men huddled in the alleyways, passing a bottle. Now and then a girl—young or old, hard to tell with the white powder and red lip paint—stepped out into the streetlight as the carriage approached, only to slip back into the shadows as the carriage passed. Then the buildings began to change. Gas lamps were more frequent and more frequently lit, doorways were cleaner, the occasional guard turned a corner, and at last they stopped in front of a small, well-lit and clean-looking establishment over which hung a crown-shaped sign proclaiming KING GEORGE HOTEL.

The driver escorted them inside, carrying their bags up to the desk, where he proudly introduced his wife's cousin's husband, Albert Wood. Mister Wood welcomed them heartily to the King George and urged them to settle themselves in the comfortable chairs by the fire while he made sure a clean room was readied for them. Grace sank into hers with relief, and Mary Kate crawled into her lap. They watched as the two men shook hands, Mister Wood passing the driver a handful of coins, which were immediately pocketed—a share of the night's good fortune.

"Enterprising family," Julia murmured wryly, observing the same scene. "I think we're in good hands, though."

"God's hands." Grace dropped a kiss onto Mary Kate's head.

They were shown to a cozy room with a bed big enough for the two women and a trundle pulled out for Mary Kate. It was over the great room below and plenty warm from the chimney running along their wall. They undressed quickly and slipped under the covers, Julia snoring softly before the lamp was turned down, Mary Kate slipping quickly into a light, uneasy sleep. Though fatigue throbbed deep within her bones, Grace's mind was flooded with images and sleep eluded her.

Was it just last night, she thought, *that I looked down upon Dublin town from the hotel window? Only a week since I bore my wee boy, and a day beyond that I learned of his father's death?* She turned her face into the pillow, willing sleep to come, begging it to relieve her heart of its heavy burden, but instead the faces of her beloved family flickered before her—

dead or gone, all of them: all but Sean, who waited in America; all but her father and the baby left behind in Cork. She had to leave him—she knew she did—there was no other way. And yet, and yet . . .

Again she turned in the bed, wincing, her body sore, her heart heavy, her mind aching. How could she have done it? In the night, in the dark, there was no convincing herself that a mother is ever right in abandoning her own child. But she had and—in the night, in the dark—she wondered how on earth she'd find the strength to live with it.

"How, Father?" she moaned, and His answer came in a tender vision that took her breath away: For there—down the long road of her memory—were the tinkers, driving their horse caravan on the lane past her cabin. And there she was—that must be her, that happy young thing with dark hair streaming and cheeks gleaming from the spring air—running in the woods, down to the bog with Morgan and Sean to squish the mud between their toes, behind them the sound of Mam's teasing laughter and sweet singing; the gentle, practical voice of her gran telling the old stories; the smell of her da's tobacco as he swept her up into the air; the sight of his strong back as he worked the field behind their cabin.

And then the cabin itself—the wooden table around which they all sat each day, a turf fire to keep them warm, her mam's picture cards on the walls, a rug on the floor, curtains at the windows, fresh and sweet, happy and safe, the lane outside so lushly green and dear with flowers in spring, berries in summer, nests of birds filled with song from morning till night, the river nearby rushing, tumbling, flashing with salmon, the woods behind full of game. And Gracelin running barefoot through it all, eating her fill, laughing out loud at the sheer beauty of her world, the joy in her heart.

And then she was falling asleep at last, drawing deeply from the well of a childhood sustained by love. Her hand fell down beside the bed, seeking the warm shape of her own daughter, stroking the cropped, tangled hair before coming to rest protectively on the child's shoulder.

The tension in Mary Kate's little arms and legs washed away with this touch; she sighed and sank into a deep and restful sleep—her mother was there, guarding over her, and guarding over them both, she knew, was the ever-wakeful countenance of the Lord.

Two

THE world Grace occupied in her sleep was shattered by the sound of a morning well under way. Horse carts clattered noisily in the street below the hotel window as deliveries were made, foods and sundries bought and sold, directives given, orders placed. Doors swung open with a bang, windows creaked, dogs barked, and servants called to one another as they emptied bedpans in the lane, shook out cloths, argued with the baker over the price of buns. Grace listened to it all, remembering where she was and what she was doing there, then prayed quickly for protection through another day.

"Wake up, wee girl." She leaned over and stroked Mary Kate's cheek with the back of her fingers. " 'Tis morning time."

The girl's eyes opened immediately. "Will we eat?" she asked midst an enormous yawn.

"Aye," Grace reassured, even as her heart ached for a child whose first thought on waking would always be for food.

The door opened then, and Julia—fully dressed and marshaled—pushed her way in with a tray.

"I thought we'd have something up here before facing the world." She kicked the door closed behind her, then set the tray down on a little table by the window. "Who's for tea, then?"

"I," Mary Kate said shyly, sitting up.

"Of course, I!" Julia smiled warmly at her, took a cup of milk, and put in a generous spoonful of sugar before adding the tea. "And a warm bun, I should think, as we've got another long day ahead of us. Come sit here at the table, Mary Kate. Put that blanket round your shoulders."

Mary Kate did as she was told, bowing her head quickly in prayer before biting into the bun, her eyes wide at the sweetness of it.

Julia brought two cups of tea and two buns on a plate over to the bed, handing one to Grace, then sitting down gingerly beside her.

"I'm afraid I've got bad news," she said quietly. "I've been to confirm your passage on the *Eliza J*, but departure has been delayed. They had a stormy crossing and the ship needed repairs. It's taken longer than expected. We've got to wait four more days."

"Doesn't sound promising." Grace looked at the window and the cold, dark sky outside.

"No," Julia admitted. "It doesn't. But of all the ships departing to America, this one's the most reputable. William's contact here booked your passage and the captain comes highly recommended. He's part owner, and American—they say Americans run the tightest ships—so we know he's making proper repair. I've heard stories of these captains who simply patch up and sail off, unwilling to lose even one voyage in a year for the cash of it. Plenty of those go down only God-knows-where—they get lost and run out of provisions, or hit an iceberg this time of year, or sink in a storm and no one ever really knows what happened."

Grace stared at her, aghast, cup partway to her lips.

Julia winced. "Sorry. My father always says I'm as tactful as a hurricane. Never mind me."

They sat for a moment, not looking at one another.

"All right, then." Grace rested her cup in its saucer. "Four days. Maybe longer. And winter's coming on, so crossing will be risky, at best, and of course, there'll be fewer boats making the trip."

Julia nodded.

"So will we find room on another that's leaving right away then, or will we wait for this one to be repaired? And is there money to be had for lodging if we decide to wait?"

Julia bit her lip. "There's the money to buy extra provisions and clothing," she said. "And it's generous—William contributed and so did . . . the others."

"Meaning you?" Grace asked.

Julia ignored the question. "You could probably stay here for a week and still have enough to buy extra provisions for the two of you, maybe warmer cloaks and boots, a blanket."

"And if the boat's not ready in a week?"

"I don't know. If you stay on here, you'll run out of money eventually, of course, though it's one less mouth to feed as I'll have gone back to Ireland." Julia frowned, thinking. "I could send someone back with more. But the longer you stay, the riskier it is."

Grace glanced at Mary Kate, who was absorbed in watching the street life below their window. "Aye," she said quietly. " 'Tis the lion's den here."

Julia nodded soberly. "We'll keep an eye on the sailings this week so that if the *Eliza J* isn't ready, you can book passage on something else and we'll get word to Sean."

Grace was silent, considering. "Or Mary Kate and I simply get on another boat today."

"No," Julia said, firmly. "The *Eliza J* is seaworthy and well-captained, and it's common knowledge that any yahoo with a boat these days is in the immigrant business. It's best to bide our time a while longer. Boarding the *Eliza J* is our first choice. Our best choice."

Grace looked around the small room and took a deep breath. "I'm trusting you to know what you're talking about here, Julia, though Lord knows you're not getting on that boat with us."

Julia understood, but didn't waver. "We wait. That's the right decision."

"All right, then," Grace said. "And what is it you want me to do while we're waiting?"

Julia stood and began gathering up the breakfast dishes. "I want you to rest here while I go out and round up a few things for the trip. You'll need a small trunk to store your things, with room for food."

"Does not the cost of passage include our board?" Grace handed over her teacup.

"It does. We've booked you a private cabin and you'll take your meals with the other passengers in first. The rest of the passengers get weekly rations, which they prepare themselves. But rations run out if the ship is overbooked, or if you hit foul weather and the trip takes longer than expected, or if the captain is not as honest as we've been led to believe. . . ." She caught herself. "Sorry. There I go again. I don't mean to make you more anxious than you already are, but from all accounts, the crossing is not an easy one in any weather, and extra food and drink, a blanket or two—it's winter at sea after all—medicines . . . all will most likely be put to good use."

"Aye, you've convinced me," Grace said. "Get whatever you think we might need to survive this and I'll thank you for it every time we open that trunk, sure and that's the truth."

"Let's hope you won't have to," Julia said, and left the room with her cloak over her arm.

"Grace." A hand shook her shoulder gently, but insistently. "Grace, wake up. You've got a visitor."

Grace opened her eyes and saw that Mary Kate was still napping beside her on the bed; outside it had begun to snow. She turned over and looked up.

"You've got a visitor," Julia repeated and stood aside, revealing a woman dressed in a long velvet cape, her face hidden deep within the hood.

Grace swung her legs carefully off the bed and moved up, wiping her eyes and mouth with the back of her hand, and smoothing her skirt, self-conscious in front of this well-dressed woman and more than a little put out at Julia's lack of discretion.

"How do you do?" she said quietly, putting out her hand.

The hand that clasped hers was smooth and white, its long

fingers decorated with several beautiful rings. With the other hand, the woman lowered her hood.

"Do you not know me, then, Gracelin O'Malley?" she asked with the hint of a smile.

Grace gasped. "Aislinn!" Her eyes flew to Julia's face, then back again. "I can hardly believe 'tis you standing in front of me! 'Tis Aislinn McDonagh!" she said to Julia. "Morgan's sister!"

Julia laughed quietly. "I know who it is, or why do you think I've brought her here?"

"Well, where on earth did you find her?" Grace asked, astonished. "Where did she find you?" she asked Aislinn, and then began to cry.

Both women came to Grace immediately, but it was Aislinn who held her and whispered in Irish, calling her "sister."

"You know, then?" Grace asked. "About . . . everything?"

Aislinn nodded sorrowfully, her own eyes filled with tears.

"Mam." Mary Kate was awake and sitting. "Who's that, Mam?"

"Your mam was a dear friend of my brother, of all my family," Aislinn said gently. "I wanted to see her before you went away."

"To America," Mary Kate said gravely.

"Aye, 'tis a wondrous place and you will like it there very much." She let go of Grace and came toward the little girl. "May I give you a present?" she asked. "Something for luck?"

Mary Kate looked at Grace, who nodded.

Aislinn slipped a ring off her little finger and held it out to the girl. "The silver is in the pattern of a sacred knot," she said. "And do you see the green stone in the center?"

Mary Kate nodded, eyes riveted to the ring.

"It's from Connemara, in the west of Ireland," she explained. "I had that ring made to remind me of home, and now I want to give it to you to remind you of home when you are far away. Will you have it?"

"Oh, aye." Mary Kate's eyes were wide and she took the ring reverently. "Thank you."

"You're most welcome." Aislinn touched the girl's thick hair.

"You remind me of my little sister. Fiona was a pretty maid, as well."

Mary Kate ducked her head shyly, but they could see her smile.

"Come, little miss." Julia picked her up off the bed. "Let's you and I go down and have our tea by the great fire, shall we? We'll leave your mam and her friend to talk together, and then we'll come up to say good-bye. What do you say?"

Mary Kate nodded her head, always happy for the chance of a meal. She waved at them as Julia carried her out of the room, the door closing softly behind them.

"I can't stay long, but I wanted to see you before you left."

"How did you find us?" Grace went to the little window and sat beside it. Outside, snow fell softly, clinging to the leaded glass.

"Julia." Aislinn took the other chair. "Morgan asked her to find me, and last summer she did. But after I explained my situation, she agreed it was better I stay . . . missing. She sent word ahead that you would be here, but kept it from you in case I was unable to come."

"Unable?"

"I am the mistress of a very powerful man. A man who saved my life, actually, or what was left of it. He agreed to let me come, as long as I am discreet." She hesitated. "You're shocked."

"Ah, no, Aislinn, no," Grace insisted. "I just can't get over seeing you alive, is all."

Aislinn reached out and took Grace's hand. "I know," she said. "About Mam and Da. And the girls. Julia told all."

"Barbara's still alive. She's called Sister John Paul at the convent."

"Of course she is! Always the saint, Barbara." Aislinn scowled, revealing a bit of the girl she'd been before leaving home.

"I've nothing but love for your sister," Grace said. "She delivered me of my son, called John Paul Morgan after the two of them."

"Julia says you wed." Aislinn shook her head. "I could hardly believe it true."

"Father Brown married us in secret seven months ago. Another man was there, as well." She smiled wanly. "He gave Morgan the ring off his own finger. I wear your mam's." She held her hand out.

Aislinn took it, kissed the ring, and smiled. "Ah, Mammie. I did love her." She looked up at Grace. "She'd be so happy to know you wear this, Grace, so happy you and Morgan were wed. And that you have a son of your own."

"We had only the one night together, but 'twas enough."

"Did he know?"

"Aye." Grace closed her eyes briefly, and there was Henry's face. "An English soldier helped us. He smuggled Morgan's letter out of prison, but was killed in bringing it to me." She pulled the letter out of its place behind her vest and offered it to Aislinn.

"I can't read, Grace," the young woman admitted. "Morgan and Barbara both tried to teach me my letters, but . . ." She shrugged and smiled wryly. "Always had my mind on boys and the like, didn't I now?"

Grace slipped the letter securely back into its place near her heart. "He says he's glad for our baby, but knows he won't live to see it, to make a life for myself and our children, and not to mourn forever as he'll see me again one day. In Heaven."

"And so he will, Grace. So he will."

"I never knew he loved me all that time." Grace's face twisted in anguish. "Or it's him I would've wed first. I married Bram in good faith, the Lord knows I did. 'Twas worth everything to have our Mary Kate. But . . ." She paused, shaking her head. "It ended badly."

"There was news of the murder over here," Aislinn said. "The Donnellys, you know, and their fine society. They say your own brother did it at your bidding, but I didn't believe a word."

Grace hesitated. " 'Twas Moira."

"Moira Sullivan?" Aislinn wasn't surprised. "Having it off with him behind your back, was she?"

"Bram turned her head with promises he never meant to keep, and when he was through with her she couldn't bear it, her with a baby and all. She waited for him in the woods. And shot him."

"Good for her." Aislinn's voice was hard. "He was a bastard, Grace. She did you a favor." And then it dawned on her. "It was her baby you turned over to Bram's brother to raise! I knew something was wrong when I heard that story—the Gracelin O'Malley I knew would never give up her child without a fight. Hah!" She laughed delightedly. " 'Tis Moira Sullivan's boy those eejits are raising to be a young lord!"

Grace nodded, deciding in that moment not to tell Aislinn the entire truth—that the baby was not even Bram's, but a true Irish bastard the Donnellys had brought into their home.

Aislinn snorted gleefully. "I'm glad to hear it, Grace. That's a fine piece of work on them what treated you so poorly, and never you worry—your secret's safe with me. I knew you'd never give up your own son."

"I have, though," Grace confessed. "I'm going to America without him."

"That's not giving him up!" Aislinn insisted. "That's leaving him in safe hands till he's strong enough to come. 'Twould be the sure death of him to make this voyage, but you've no choice, Grace—they're looking for you in Ireland, Julia says, and you'd go to prison for sure."

"For shooting a guard that come to tumble our cabin." She paused and looked out the window. "And then, of course, I'm sister to Sean O'Malley, wanted for treason and murder, and rumored to be wife to the outlaw Morgan McDonagh. So I must know names and maps and the whereabouts of others, though truly I do not." She turned back to Aislinn. "I would've stayed in Ireland if the cost was my life only, but what will happen to my daughter and my wee son if I die in prison?"

"I knew it would torment you, and that's why I had to come—to tell you to go to America. And to make you this promise." She leaned forward. "I have money now. Plenty of it. I'll send some back with Julia to provide for your son, anything he and your da might need. Barbara can't know it's from me, though," she added. "She wouldn't take money from a whore."

"You don't know your sister, if you believe that," Grace said firmly. "And you're not a whore."

"What do you call it then—a woman who trades favors for food, shelter, and the protection of a man?"

Grace considered this. "Some would say 'wife,' " she offered.

Aislinn burst out laughing, then reached out and embraced her friend. "It's good to see you," she whispered. "A face from home."

Grace kissed her cheek, then leaned back. "The last I saw you was that night of the O'Flahertys' dinner party when Gerald wouldn't leave you alone. Did you run off with him, then? The serving maid eloping with the young master?" She winked.

Aislinn sighed in disgust, and shook her head. "What an eejit I was. I believed his lies of love, and a high life in London. But he only wanted me to bed, of course, and only when it suited him. I wanted to go out and see the world on his arm, as his wife, and after I fell with his child I thought sure we'd marry. But he was engaged to someone else, a distant cousin with a tidy sum each year, approved by his mother." She raised her eyebrow; they had both suffered Missus O'Flaherty. "I was furious, but he promised it would be a marriage of convenience only, that he'd arrange rooms for me and the child, and come to us there. I clung to that promise for a long time." She paused, remembering. "The landlord came twice to demand payment, which, of course, I didn't have, nor a single friend from whom to borrow it. He was nasty, the landlord, and that's when I realized I had been abandoned."

Grace leaned forward in her chair. "Why did you not come home, then?" she asked. "Your mam would've taken you in."

"Too proud for that, and of course it cost me dearly in the end." She glanced out the window, collecting herself. "I went to his rooms at the college, but he wouldn't see me and I . . . I fell into madness. I set fire to the place, and he put the guards on me, so I hid—moving from room to room, selling off my things." She looked directly into Grace's eyes. "I, too, bore a son. By myself, though the landlady come in with a knife to cut the cord, wipe him off, and hand him to me, saying to keep him

quiet so's the other girls could sleep, sharing a room as I was."
Her forehead creased with pain. "I tried to keep him warm and
fed, as best I could, but the money run out and I'd nothing left
to sell. We lost our place in the room, and took to sleeping in
the alleyways, begging at back doors. I've never been so feared
in all my life as I was then."

"And where is he now?" Grace asked gently.

Aislinn's eyes filled with tears, which she ignored. "He fell ill
and I couldn't bear to watch him die, so I took him to the nuns."
She wiped her eyes with the back of her hand. "I tried to forget
him, but I still had milk and my arms felt empty and I missed
the smell of him. So, I went back and begged to know where he
was. He was better off, they said, and so was I. I could repent,
and thank God my son would have a decent life." She lifted her
chin. "They were right. But not an hour passes I don't pray for
him."

"I'm sorry, Aislinn," Grace said, taking her hands. " 'Tis a terrible tale. And what of this man, then? Does he care for you?"

"Aye," Aislinn said without hesitation. "He saved my life. I
was low after the boy, and didn't care anymore. . . . When a
man offered me money to go with him, I did. He took me to a
house and I just stayed there—I had my own room, it was
warm and there was food, and every night I earned my keep
and more. But I was sick at heart. My gentleman took a special
interest in me, and after a time I agreed to an arrangement. I
have my own rooms—which are lovely—and he comes there as
he pleases. I entertain no friends, take no risks in public, and
bear no children."

"And in exchange?"

"Peace of mind," Aislinn said. "Title to my rooms in London
and clear ownership of everything he gives me, including a
small bank account into which he puts a monthly allowance.
You see, I have become a businesswoman," she said wryly. "I do
go out to entertainments in the company of my maid, though I
am careful."

"He's married?"

"Aye, and I believe he loves her, though she's older even than he. They have grown children. He's very wealthy and imposing, but I trust him. Even if he is an Englishman."

Grace nodded. "There are good ones," she allowed. "Henry Adams, and Lord Evans . . ."

"Lord *David* Evans?" Aislinn asked. "The Black Lord?"

"I never heard him called that, but aye—he's the one gave Morgan his own ring. They were great friends. Do you know him?"

"No, but he's all the talk in London! They call him the Black Lord because he sided with us. He's been brought here for trial."

Grace's heart fell. "I'd not heard."

"The magistrates are delaying his trial for fear of public rioting. He's ill, and they think he'll die soon. Then it will be out of their hands—no angry crowds or burning effigies."

London, Grace thought. How far away was that? "Is there any way to see him?" she asked. "Maybe your one could help?"

"I'd never dare ask," Aislinn admitted. "He's sympathetic to the cause, but he considers Lord Evans the worst kind of Englishman. And you certainly can't just go strolling in . . ." She stopped.

"What?" Grace leaned forward.

"Well, there *are* women who go strolling into prison. But only after midnight, and no one the wiser."

Grace understood at once. "I could be one of those women."

Aislinn looked her up and down with a practiced eye. "Aye." She grinned. "I believe you could."

Three

SEAN O'MALLEY sat in the very back of Mighty Dugan Ogue's saloon, the Harp and Hound, sipping the publican's famous dark ale and working his way through the New York papers in front of him. He'd already covered the endless headlines of the *Sun* and the *Herald*, along with several sheets of extras bought from the newsboy on the way in. There was little point in perusing the others—the old-fashioned *Journal of Commerce, Courier and Enquirer,* the *Express,* although he might have a look at the *Tribune*—they had all banded together on wire service time during the Mexican War and now monopolized the most current information. Calling themselves the Associated Press, they had reporters in any town with access to wire service and received daily, sometimes hourly, reports from which they drew the next day's news. It made for exciting reading, though much was repeated throughout the various papers. The new telegraph lines now linked New York with the nation's capital, Boston, and Albany, and there was talk of trying an overseas line to England.

Sean still awoke most mornings with the dizzy feeling of having stumbled far into the future, into a fast-paced modern life that was a century away from the mud huts, potato fields, and backwoods warfare of Ireland. Adding to this displacement was the proliferation of paper plastered to every surface around every corner of nearly every street—advertisements for everything from Man About Town Hair Dye and True Liver Pills to Famous Gypsy Palm Readers and Circus Oddities from Around the World.

Every saloon, oyster house, melodeon, and museum had its name stuck to walls, fences, carriages, and sandwich boards. Bill-stickers made the rounds after midnight with buckets of paste and brushes, covering up yesterday's notices with today's, slapping new announcements over the minutes-old notices of their rivals so that each day the landscape was slightly altered and one could not remember which corner one had turned the previous day.

Men with sandwich boards walked up and down the streets, and trade cards promoting everything from cough remedies to prostitution were pushed into Sean's hands on every block. As if this weren't enough to overload a simple man's eye, the entire place seemed to be festooned with banners and ribbons to mark the latest political rally so that street signs were often masked. He had become lost so many times in his first month here—despite the maps and guide books he'd been given—that he'd learned this district by sheer foot travel. Even asking for directions had been problematic because so many people were foreigners with heavy accents and a great deal of gesturing that often led nowhere. When he did encounter Americans, they spoke so quickly and with such clipped enunciation that he had difficulty keeping up. Their speech was more nasal and less lyrical than the Irish to which he was accustomed, though not without colorful idiom that tickled him now he was beginning to understand it.

"Here you go, Sean—hot off the press, as they say!" Tara Ogue, Dugan's hardworking wife, set the current edition of the *Democratic Review* down on his table, along with a fresh pint. "That ought to hold you for a while, eh, boy?" She reached out and plucked the glasses from his nose, wiping the lenses carefully with the hem of her apron. "It's no wonder you're half blind," she scolded good-naturedly, "trying to read through the likes of these. There"—she handed them back—"that's better now, isn't it?"

"Aye, Tara, and what would I do without you?" He grinned and reached for her hand, then winced.

"It's that shoulder again," she pronounced, peering at it. "Mind what the doctor said, boy, and quit hunching yourself up like that! Are you not wearing that harness contraption?"

Sean stretched carefully, massaging the crippled arm. "I forgot, Tara. Truly I did."

"Well, you march right up to your rooms, then, and put that thing on," she ordered. "Haven't you been breathing so much easier since you got that, and not half so sick in the chest?"

"Aye," he agreed enthusiastically. "And isn't it a miracle? Me who's been weak with the cough most of my life, on death's door more times than I can count . . . and here I am, strutting around Manhattan in good health and with barely a limp, thanks to the special shoes. Life is good, Tara. Life is grand—there's always hope. If a man can dream it, he can achieve it here. Ah, Tara, isn't America wonderful?"

"Ah, go on with you now." She cuffed him gently. "Sure and there's nothing crippled about that silver tongue God or the Devil give you—I don't know which!"

"Tara!" Sean exclaimed in pretended offense. "How can you say such a thing? 'Tis the Lord's work I'm doing here, and you know that as well as anyone."

"Won't be doing much of it if you take ill again," she reminded him.

"Just let me finish up these papers, and I promise I'll go straight up and put that harness on."

"See that you do," she admonished, snapping at him with her towel before rejoining her husband at the front.

Sean watched Dugan slip an arm around the waist of his wife and draw her in for a kiss, which she playfully tried to resist; he thought again how lucky he was to have ended up here, as the lodging came with Mighty Ogue's street wisdom and Tara's motherly attention. They were the ones who found the German doctor, and arranged to have the shoe built and shoulder strap made so that Sean might move about the city more like a man than a cripple. He owed them so much; he raised his glass to them now, blowing them a kiss, which made them laugh.

"Back to work, boyo!" Dugan's massive voice boomed across the room, turning the heads of the old drinkers who smiled with pride at the young Irishman working so hard for the cause.

Sean laughed and returned with pleasure to the paper in front of him. The *Democratic Review* was edited by John O'Sullivan, one of the many new friends he'd made in New York. John had introduced him to Evert Duyckinck, who sponsored the magazine and served as mentor to a group of young businessmen interested in making money and creating a wholly American culture, not a subservient one that simply imitated Europe. They were loosely known as the Young Americans, and stood in opposition to the old guard, a group of prosperous gentlemen—Whigs and anglophiles mostly—who dined out more than in, and amused themselves by writing lightly ironical essays for *Knickerbocker Magazine*, currently the most influential literary review in America . . . something that disgusted Sean. But then, everything about the Knickerbockers disgusted him—they were overprivileged snobs, too narrowminded to embrace a new culture of political idealism and literary radicalism.

The Young Americans, however, put their money and their hearts into supporting Western expansion and European revolution, which Sean found thrilling as well as inspiring. They published *Arcturus*, which fostered American literature and essays, and they had formed a copyright club in order to force the Knickerbockers to pay for the European writings they so casually pilfered. O'Sullivan and Duyckinck had also made an ally of publisher George Putnam, and Duyckinck was general editor of the Library of American Books; they had just launched the *Literary World*, a magazine to which Sean was contributing even though he had not yet developed what the others called "an authentic American voice."

His Irish voice was strong enough and welcome in the *Dem-*

ocratic Review, and the issue he held in his hands contained an article he'd written on the failings of British government in Ireland and the detriment of the influence of that culture on a new America. It was not all his original thinking—he had allowed himself to be steered by O'Sullivan—but it was a start in making his own cause more broadly known.

He'd found himself in the protective hands of the Young Americans from the first day of his arrival, and had gladly let O'Sullivan shape his days with speaking engagements, rallies, dinner parties, and work at the magazine. They did not hide the fact that they were using him to further their own political agenda, nor did he hide the fact that they were of use to him only when they opened their bankbooks and wrote drafts for guns and ammunition, food and clothing—all to be shipped to Dublin on specially chartered packets. They respected him for being an inside man with the Young Irelanders and for fighting in the physical world when they had only ever fought with words.

But sometimes it occurred to him that he was being swept up so completely, he had trouble knowing where Young Ireland left off and Young America began. He'd begun to realize that what turned his head most was the excitement of democracy, and of the progress this excitement fueled, an excitement he could not translate—no matter how hard he tried—to weary, starving Ireland.

More and more, he found his attention turned to American politics. In the coming month, New York would hold its first election under the new Constitution, an election the Whigs faced with confidence, bragging that they would take every branch of state and city government. The circle in which Sean moved was working diligently to oppose them at every step, and the debates stimulated and moved him. He was meeting prominent, intelligent people every time he turned around—people like O'Sullivan, Putnam, and Duyckinck, Jay Livingston and his sister, Florence—and all of them walked in the larger world of ideas, dreamed the grander dreams of progress and the future. They included him so readily in this walk and in these dreams, he sometimes forgot that his life here was only temporary, that one day he would return to Ireland.

But more and more frequently, he wondered what was *really* happening in Ireland. Communication was sparse and unreliable, and though he was raising money and had sent two small ships laden with supplies, he knew not how they fared. William Smith O'Brien and John Mitchel had both been detained, though William was rumored to have been released, and the latest report from London said Captain Evans would be tried for treason. But what troubled him most was the report that Morgan had been captured during a raid. There had been nothing after that of his best friend, and no one off the boats sailing daily into the city had anything other than hearsay.

"Ah, there you are now, all hunched over those papers and scowling like bad weather. Don't mind if I sit, do you?" The handsome young Irishman pulled out a chair, not waiting for a reply.

"How are you, Danny?" Sean smiled at his colorful friend, poor as any man, but always sporting a clean vest and a silk tie around his neck.

"Well, now, myself is just fine, but I hear your Miss Osgoode is home in bed and isn't that a lovely thing to dwell upon?" His eyes twinkled mischievously.

"Shame on you, Danny." Sean tried not to smile. "That's no way to talk about a fine Christian woman like Marcy Osgoode."

"Certainly not round her father, mind you, but here between two friends such as us, what harm in being manly?" He laughed and picked up Sean's glass, downing half the ale in a single gulp. "Thanks, boyo. 'Tis warm in here."

"Not that warm." Sean retrieved his drink. "What're you doing here, anyway? Why are you not out working like an honest citizen?"

"I'm my own man, am I not?" Danny puffed out his chest. "I keep my own hours, don't I?" He glanced out the window. "Well and anyway, 'tis raining, sure enough, and no one stopping to get their boots shined in this lousy weather." He turned his attention back to Sean. "Are you coming to the meeting tonight, even without your sweet miss?"

Sean grimaced. "I forgot, to tell you the truth, but don't say that to her father. I'm speaking to a group of dockworkers tonight—mostly Irish—reminding them of their duty back home."

"Plenty don't want to be reminded, you know, boyo," Danny told him. "Plenty just want to get on with their lives, make the best of things here in the new land."

"I know that. But those who've gotten out alive owe it to those who've stayed behind to fight. When Ireland is free, they'll want to be able to say they did their part."

"They'll say that anyway, being Irish." Danny grinned.

Sean laughed. "Fair enough. But I'm still going."

"You really think we'll win this thing, Sean? Beat back the English, and reclaim our land?"

"I do," Sean said with more conviction than he felt. "But not without guns and ammunition, not without food and medicine."

Danny nodded. "Maybe I'll skip prayer meeting myself and come along with you tonight, then."

"And disappoint all those young women?" Sean teased.

"Ah, 'tis true, 'tis true," Danny sighed with mock humility. "Lord knows I love to inspire my sisters to greater heights of devotion." He grinned waggishly. "But I'm feeling the need to be with men—Irishmen. I'll stand in the crowd, and loudly agree with everything you're saying, like you've won me over with your fine persuasion. Inspire my brothers, for a change. Besides," he said, lowering his voice, "that bastard Callahan's bound to show up, him and his guards. Thinks he's the only Irishman good enough to live in this city, always looking for ways to run the rest of us out."

"That's the sorry truth of it." Sean rubbed his arm. "You'd think having an Irishman high up as he is in the police would work to our advantage, wouldn't you?"

"Naw," Danny said scornfully. "He's just like them land agents back home—English on the inside, but Irish on the out and hating anyone who knows it. That's it. I'm coming. You need a bodyguard, and I'm your man. Get you out of there quick-like if a scuffle breaks out."

"Ah, you're a true friend, Danny Young. Come round about seven then, and we'll go from here."

"Done!" Danny jumped up from his chair and clapped Sean on the shoulder. "And after, we'll be making the rounds, eh?"

"Who's buying?" Sean asked, suspiciously.

"You are, of course. To thank me for supporting you while you give another of your famously long-winded—I mean deeply stirring"—he winked—"speeches about Mother Ireland! See you at seven, boyo, and don't be holding me up!" He gave a jaunty salute, then worked his way to the front door, slapping the backs of all the old drinkers.

Sean watched him go and thought again how much Grace would like Danny—he was a lot like Quinn Sheehan back home, and Quinn had always been able to make Grace laugh. Grace. His smile faded. He could only hope that William had gotten his letter and had then managed to find Grace and Mary Kate in the midst of chaos. He could only hope they were even now on the ship, drawing closer every day.

He looked down at the papers spread on the table—none of it good news, really. Not about Ireland. "Please, Father," he silently prayed, "deliver them safely. And if it's not too much trouble, Lord, would You include McDonagh in that bargain, as well?"

He closed his eyes briefly and for a moment caught a glimpse of Grace dancing with Morgan at their brother's wedding a lifetime ago—fiddler in the corner, neighbors crowded up against the walls, glasses full of poteen and punch, children running in and out, tinkers leaning in at the windows—and he was filled with a longing so sharp that it made him wince and clutch his chest. He opened his eyes then and looked out the smeary window as he did a thousand times a day, hoping beyond hope to see her face but seeing instead only the dark, forbidding sky of winter.

Four

"ABSOLUTELY not! You're not going!" Julia paced the room angrily.

"Well, I'm not asking your permission now, am I?" Grace put her satchel on the bed and opened it up.

"It's madness—that's what it is!" Julia threw up her hands. "Sheer madness! You've had some kind of a breakdown."

"I feel better than I have in some time," Grace told her. "I'm awake now somehow."

"I should never have brought Aislinn here," Julia muttered, still pacing. "Damn her. Damn her! How could she even suggest this? You're not going, and that's final."

"I *am* going, and that's final. The question is, will you help me or not?" Grace put her hands on her hips.

"I won't," Julia said stubbornly. "I will not stay here and watch your child while you go off to prison—something I'm trying to keep you out of, by the way—to see Lord David Evans, the most carefully guarded man in bloody England!"

"Come along then, why don't you?" Grace winked at her daughter, who sat soberly on the bed, holding her doll and watching the exchange. "Mary Kate would like to see London, won't you, love?"

Mary Kate nodded obediently.

"Oh, bloody hell. Excuse me," Julia said to Mary Kate, whose eyes had gone wide. "Just tell me why, then. Why, in God's name, you'd take a risk like this after all we've been through."

"There is no risk," Grace said confidently. "If we're caught— and they've been doing this for years, mind you—it's a fine to pay, perhaps a night in jail."

"What if you're discovered?"

"The guards don't even know I've left Ireland," Grace said. "They're not looking for me here."

"Yet," Julia added.

"Aye. And that's why we've got to do it now. Besides, we sail in four days. That's barely enough time as it is."

"I'm fond of David, as well, you know. He's an old friend. I should go in your place. That's it!" Julia jabbed her finger in the air. "*I'm* going!"

Grace shook her head. "Not this time. You've got to look after Mary Kate. 'Tis my only chance."

"But why?"

"I'm not debating it with you, Julia, for sure and I'll lose. I've got my reasons. The dying are close to God, you know—they have things to tell us." She paused, then lowered her voice. "Morgan died all alone, with no thanks nor words of love from anyone. If he were here, he'd find a way to see the man who had saved his life more than once." She crossed her arms defiantly. "And so I'm going. With or without you."

Julia let out an exasperated sigh. "You're just like him, you know. So noble it makes me ill."

Grace smiled despite herself. "You'll come, then?"

"All right, all right." Julia pulled out the tidy notebook in which she kept her endless lists. "Where exactly are we going, by the way?"

"Number Twenty-seven St. Martin's Place," she said. "Molly's Dance Hall for Gentlemen."

"Oh, Lord," Julia groaned.

❖   ❖   ❖

London was far busier even than bustling Liverpool, and Julia—used to rubbing the occasional elbow in higher society—found herself intimidated by the sight of such handsome carriages, riders in full dress on horseback, gentlemen in afternoon clothes tipping their hats to magnificent ladies in flounced skirts and fitted jackets under warm woolen cloaks, their own hats sailing jauntily atop hair that had taken most of the morning to arrange. They were near Hyde Park, and despite the chill weather, ladies and gentlemen were out walking in anticipation of the lavish teas that awaited their return. Julia frowned and attempted to tame her own wild hair, which had been hastily pinned by candlelight the day before.

"Underneath all their finery, they've worries same as us," Grace said quietly, watching her friend.

"I somehow doubt that any of them are planning to break into prison tonight as prostitutes," Julia muttered.

Grace laughed and wrapped an arm around Mary Kate, giving her a squeeze. "Ah, well, you may be right about that. So what do you think of this great London Town, then, wee girl?"

Mary Kate pinched her nose and wrinkled her face so intensely that both women had to laugh.

"Too many carriages and not enough shovels." Grace dropped a kiss on the top of her daughter's head.

The smell of the bigger cities was something none of them was used to—the sulfurous bite of coal dust in the back of the throat; the sharp, earthy smell of horse manure piled along every street; the rank rot of offal from the butchers and fish slime from the market stalls; human waste from back-alley privies. All of this fouled the air when it was warm, or ran together in the streets when it rained, creating a dark, dank liquid that splashed up on the walkways and clung to carriage wheels, boot heels, and cloak hems. No one seemed to notice; no one seemed to care—it was simply the way things were.

Having at last reached the crowded station, they disembarked from the carriage, collected their bags, and ventured into the street to hire a cab. The driver gave them a curious look when Julia—not wanting to be dropped at a house of ill-repute—gave him instead the address of a place she hoped would be nearby, but he delivered them in short order. They sat for a moment and watched as finely dressed men passed through the doors of a stately building, nodding jovially to one another, pausing to place a gloved hand upon the arm of a friend, the shoulder of a colleague, exchanging polite greetings and the latest news. They suddenly understood the look of the driver—Number One was the West End Gentlemen's Club.

They paid him and waited until he was out of sight, then walked quickly up the avenue away from Number One. As they traveled the long blocks, hedges inside each wrought-iron fence grew sparse and the fences themselves showed a need of repair and paint. Grounds were not manicured and ornamented in a style that reflected the owners' good taste, but had become nearly anonymous—still tended, but not by personal gardeners. Draperies were more often drawn, adding to the blank look of the houses, and the houses themselves appeared to have been divided into smaller residences as evidenced by the numbering—10A, 10B, and even 10C. Darkness fell and flakes of snow clung to their cloaks.

Number 27 St. Martin's Place still remained whole and un-divided—at least from the outside—though its lower floor windows were covered and its entrance nondescript. The neighborhood, by this time, was most definitely questionable, and the women approached cautiously, pausing at the alley that separated 26 from 27.

"This way," Julia directed, eyeing the narrow, unlit passage that stank of garbage and human waste.

She led them carefully down the way until they reached a blue door with a small, black letter M on it. Julia knocked. It was a long minute before the peephole slid open and a blood-shot eye looked them over.

"We're expected," Julia said quickly. "Let us in."

The peephole slid closed and the door opened, held by a chain.

"Who be you?" growled the large, grizzled woman who guarded it.

Julia hesitated. Only Molly knew their names. "Old friends of Molly's from Liverpool," she said, affecting a poor Cockney accent.

A trio of men lingered at the entrance of the alley, silhouetted in the lamplight, nodding their heads at one another, then starting down.

"You don't look like no friends of the Mistress." The woman eyed them warily. "Maybe you be church folk or some such thing."

"Ha!" Julia forced a laugh. The men had quickened their pace. "By God, woman, open this door or Molly will have your head!"

That did it. The door slammed shut, the chain rattled, and in they slipped, chased by disgruntled catcalls.

Grace let out her breath and gripped Mary Kate's hand, unsure of what they might witness now they were inside. The room was lit with red lamps; on the walls were large portraits of reclining women in various stages of undress. For once, Grace was glad of Mary Kate's shyness and the eyes glued to the floor.

Their guide led them down a long hallway carpeted with a thick Turkish runner; flickering candles behind opaque sconces lit their way. On either side, heavy wooden doors barely muffled the sounds of guests at play—the bursts of laughter and mock shrieks of the ladies, the low commanding voices of the men. Grace stayed in the very center of the hallway, praying no one would exit as they passed.

"That way leads to the entertaining room, where the gentlemen and ladies meet one another," offered the guide. "Upstairs is more private rooms for cards and such."

"And such," Julia whispered, nudging Grace. They shared a wide-eyed look of disbelief—they were in one of London's most notorious whorehouses.

"And this be where the Mistress lives." Their guide rapped on a gilt paneled door before pushing it open, then leaving them on their own.

"At last!" A commanding woman dressed snugly in a low-cut green gown swept across the room to greet them. "Molly O'Brien. So glad you've arrived safely."

"Julia Martin."

"Welcome. And this must be our Missus McDonagh."

"Aye." Grace put out a hand, which Molly took in both of hers. "Thank you for agreeing to this."

" 'Tis an honor in a profession that rarely allows for such." Molly looked down at Mary Kate. "And how grand to have a wee one for company this evening. What're you called, then, child?"

"Mary Kate," came the brave answer.

"I am Miss Molly. And you must be starved. Let's go in by the fire and have our tea, shall we? Do you like buttered scones and jam?"

Mary Kate nodded and allowed herself to be led into the sitting room, where an old woman with ivory hair presided over the tea table.

"Here they are, Gran. This is young Miss Mary Kate."

"How do you do?" The old woman nodded her head formally.

"This is my grandmother, Mary Kate," Molly explained. "She's a lovely collection of dolls. You wouldn't be the kind of girl likes dollies, would you, now? Because I know she'd like to show them off."

Mary Kate nodded shyly, then spoke to the old woman. "I have one," she said softly.

"Do you, now? And what's she called?"

"Blossom. Gran made her."

"Is your gran in Ireland, then?"

Mary Kate shook her head. "Gran's in Heaven."

The old woman reached out and took the little hand, rubbing her thumb across the child's smooth skin. "I'll show you my dolls after tea, and you must introduce me to your Blossom."

They ate their buns and drank their tea—more hungry than they'd realized—and then the old woman took Mary Kate by the hand again and led her away, the girl smiling anxiously at Grace over her shoulder.

"We are contained here," Molly assured. "Gran never goes beyond these rooms."

"Does she know . . . ?"

"Oh, aye." Molly laughed. "I couldn't run the place without her. She's quite a head for numbers. Ran my grandda's dry goods shop in Limerick half her life."

"But how does she . . . isn't she . . . alarmed by it all?" Julia asked.

"The two of us have survived more than you'd think there was to survive. We find it peaceful here, to be honest."

"It's a hard living, though, isn't it?"

"Well, it's not as though I expect her to earn her keep each night." Molly laughed, but her eyes were serious. "Do I look that hard to you?"

"No," Grace put in quietly. "Forgive us, Missus O'Brien. We'd no idea what to expect, but sure and it wasn't a lovely woman, kind and well-spoken, living in comfortable rooms with her old granny!"

"I am sorry," Julia added. "We're ever so grateful to you, and here I've put my foot in my mouth as usual."

"Nice trick, that," Molly said with a straight face. "Popular with them come back from the Far East. You could make a nice wage here."

Julia's mouth fell open, but Molly had already turned to Grace.

"You should have no problem tonight. This won't be the first time Lord Evans has received a visit from one of my girls." She paused. "Does that change your opinion of him?"

"Nothing could do that."

"I don't suppose there's any chance you're going to get him out of there?" Molly asked, the smallest note of hope in her voice.

"No." Grace sighed. "Though I wish with all my heart I had a plan such as that."

Molly nodded, grimly. "So do we all. We even considered putting him in a dress—bringing him out that way—but the guards check the cells before they release the girls, and Lord Evans' escape would mean prison for us all."

"Aislinn said as much. She could only promise me a way to see him, not to save him."

"She's done well for herself. I'm glad of that. Her downfall wasn't much different from my own." Molly stood and poured out the last of the tea. "I'll have something stronger waiting for you when you get back," she said. "But best keep your wits about you till then."

Grace agreed, though the thought of a little courage was tempting.

"Who are the others going tonight?" Julia asked.

Molly shrugged. "All Irish, this bunch. Just regular girls. Down on their luck, one way or another." She sipped her tea. "There's the odd one or two comes to it by choice, for the free-dom of it more than anything else. They make a good wage, have a good time, live safer here than on the streets. If they're smart and put a bit by, they can 'retire,' as we say—go off where no one knows them and take up life as a widow woman of inde-pendent means. A few marry, though some would say that's still work." She winked. "Speaking of which, it's time to get you dressed, Missus McDonagh." She stood and crossed the room, calling over her shoulder, "This way, ladies. The night is young."

Grace and Julia exchanged a wide-eyed look, then set aside their teacups and followed their hostess toward the sound of clinking glasses and laughter.

An icy drizzle tore holes in the smoke and fog, chilling Grace to the bone when she stepped out of the cab. They had been driven around back of a low stone warehouse; the door stood ajar, and a man with a lantern motioned them to hurry. Grace covered her hair and face with her shawl, then followed the other girls into the cavernous room, where the guard looked them over thoroughly, lifting his lantern up and down, pausing to squint at Grace.

" 'Aven't seen this 'un 'ere afore," he said, stepping closer.

A girl called Big Red linked her arm through his and pulled him close to her.

"Sure and you have, Bill," she teased. "You've seen us all one way or another, haven't you, then?" She winked coyly and kissed his neck.

"Aye, Bill, 'tis Bridey the new girl, been down a while, but better now, aren't you, love?" A pale, dark-haired girl dressed in lush purple moved closer to Grace, rubbing her hands briskly. "We'll all be down if we stand here in this freezing warehouse any longer."

"Unless you want to warm us up yourself," Big Red offered, pushing her ample bosom against Bill's chest.

He grunted and pulled away, disconcerted by their flirting. "Maybe after," he said gruffly. "Time to go now. An't got all night."

He snaked them through the piles of wooden crates and bound trunks to the far end of the warehouse; there, a small door opened to reveal steps down to a delivery tunnel that would take them into the prison kitchens.

They followed him single file, skirts clutched in gaudily gloved hands, thinly shod feet stepping carefully around puddles and muck. In the enormous kitchen, they were turned over to another man, who held a long boning knife in his hand; Bill handed him the lantern, the light of which now spilled across a grimy white apron smeared with blood.

The girls knew the routine and nodded to the butcher as he, too, looked them over, thick lips moving as he counted them off. Satisfied, he motioned with the knife for them to fall in behind him.

Grace's heart was pounding and she felt exposed in the thin red dress that revealed all of her neck and shoulders, and most of her bosom. She had a shawl of brightly colored silk, but the feel of it against her bare skin only served to remind her of how uncovered she truly was. The other girls had done a good job dressing her, and glancing at them, she knew she looked the part—her hair was pinned so that strands fell down around her neck, her cheeks glowed with rouge over white powder, her eyes were lined with kohl, and a beauty patch had been placed just above the corner of her lip. Her teeth were white behind the red paint, and long earbobs had been screwed into her lobes. Over everything was splashed a heady perfume that renewed itself whenever Grace moved.

The butcher led them up and down stairways, through narrow passages, and in and out of heavy wooden doors until at last they came to a kind of underground courtyard with cells lining the walls.

"Here they be," he told the guards at the entrance, who nodded.

"Three in here tonight," one of them ordered.

When the first three women stepped away from the group, Grace had a moment of panic. Was Lord Evans here? Had she missed her chance? A look from Big Red, standing next to her, said no.

The party traveled on, making two more stops to deliver girls, before Big Red squeezed her hand quickly, then dropped it.

"One here," barked the butcher.

Grace stepped forward, her heart pounding wildly.

"Wake up, Evans. You got company." The guard licked his lower lip and slowly slid his hand along her backside before pushing her toward the cell at the end of the room. A man slowly pulled himself up by the bars.

"Stand back there," the guard commanded.

He found a key on his ring, opened the cell door, grabbed Grace by the arm, and thrust her in roughly. The door clanged shut, and the lock was turned.

"Make it quick." He laughed meanly. "If you can make it at all."

The guard walked away, leaving them alone except for the echo of his surly voice from down the hall, where he passed a bottle with the other guards.

The only light now came from a torch outside the cell, though Grace could see a candle in its holder on a small, rough table that also held pen and paper. She could not make out the face of the man who stood quietly in the middle of the cell.

"Good evening." His voice was low and hoarse, but instantly recognizable. "Kind of you to come, but I'm afraid I won't be such good company tonight."

"Ah, now, Lord Evans, haven't you always been good company?"

He paused and leaned forward slightly, his head cocked to one side. "Do I know you?"

She came forward and touched his arm. "You wouldn't know to look at me now," she whispered. "But you stood up at my wedding one early morning before dawn."

He leaned closer and squinted into her face, stunned. "Good Lord, Grace!" He hugged her fiercely, then looked again, laughed, and shook his head. "I can hardly believe it! Am I dreaming? Have I died?"

"If you have, then so have I, and I must tell you"—she glanced around the dark cell—"Heaven's a bit of a letdown, isn't it?"

He nodded in amazement and touched her face, concern coming into his eyes as he felt the greasy paint, smelled the cheap perfume, realized the implication of how she was dressed.

"What's happened, Grace?"

" 'Twas the only way to get in, you see."

"I don't see. But I'm glad you're here." He took her hand and led her to a stool. "Please sit." He saw her settled, then lowered himself gingerly onto the mound of straw that was his bed. "I'm sorry I can't entertain you properly. I remember how well you looked the first night we met, so beautiful in the candlelight, surrounded by food and drink and elegance, passionately defending the good name of McDonagh over Donnelly's scowls. I like to think of that now and then."

"We've a bit of candlelight now. Food and drink, as well." She reached under her skirt to untie the flat package hidden there. "Bread, cheese, sausages, and a little Irish whiskey from Missus O'Brien herself."

"It must be truly hopeless if Molly is sending me food and drink without a bill attached. Not to mention you." He reached for the flask, unscrewed the top, and offered it to her. "Ladies first."

She shook her head. "I'm nervous enough in this place," she admitted. "Can't go addling my wits now, can I?"

"Drink with me, Grace," he implored, the ache of loneliness in his voice.

She didn't hesitate then, but took the flask and raised it. "To you, Lord Evans," she saluted, tipping it into her mouth.

"I prefer 'Captain,' " he said when she handed it back. "That's the only title I've ever earned. Here's to you, my dear." He took one long swallow, and then another.

The whiskey warmed them both, and they regarded one another, eyes now more accustomed to the dim light.

"You haven't come to break me out of here, have you?" he asked, trying to make it a joke.

"Give me a way to do it, Captain, and I will," she answered soberly.

"I'm out of time, is the thing." He coughed and put a cloth to his lips; it came away with a dark stain.

"As long as you've got a breath of life in you, there's time. Anything could happen, Captain. A miracle, even."

"It would take a miracle," he said. "And I believe I've used up more than my share of those."

"Is it blood you're coughing up, then?"

He nodded, crumpling the cloth in his hand. "The miracle for me, Grace, would be to go quickly."

"Ah, no, Captain, no."

He leaned forward and took her hand. "I'm not afraid to die, you know. My Lord waits for me, and so does the only woman I ever loved. Living has often frightened me more than the thought of dying." He smiled ironically. "My only regret is that I won't live to see you and Morgan ruling the Emerald Isle with a brood of children tumbling from your cabin door."

Grace's eyes filled with tears, which she hoped he could not see in the dark.

"How is he, the old renegade?" Evans took another swig from the flask. "And what on earth possessed him to send you into the lion's den like this?"

Grace bit her lip.

The captain's arm dropped into his lap and he was quiet for what seemed like an eternity. "He's dead, then—is that it?"

"Aye." Grace choked out the word.

Evans flung the flask against the cold stone wall, where it clattered, leaving a trail of whiskey tears against the gray.

"Goddamn them to Hell," he spat. "Damn their eyes and all their children. And for what? For what?" He tried to stand, but began coughing and collapsed.

Grace helped him sit, handed him the bloody cloth, wiped the sweat from his forehead with her shawl.

" 'Twas fever took him, so you can damn that too while you're at it." She paused. "He was in prison, in Dublin, charged with treason. He knew he was dying and got a letter out to me. By the time I read it, he was already gone."

"Oh, Grace." He put his hand over hers.

"I bore our son that day."

"A son." He shook his head, trying to take it all in. "Are you quite sure he's dead?" he asked suddenly. "The rumors—so many rumors . . ."

She placed her fingers across his lips to stop the words, then reached down the front of her gown, pulling out a muslin sack that had been tucked low between her breasts. She opened it and poured into her lap Morgan's earrings and his wedding band; the latter she held out to Evans. "I'm sure," she said.

He took it and saw that it was his, then made a fist around it and held it against his chest. "McDonagh was the finest man I ever met," he said quietly. "I loved him like a brother."

"Aye, Captain, and he thought the world of you. I wanted you to know that, to hear from me what happened."

"Thank you." He paused, then handed back the ring. "I want you to keep it, Grace. Give it to your son when he grows up. Tell him the story of your secret wedding, the story of his father. He can be proud of the name McDonagh."

"He'll know your name, as well, Captain. My children and their children and the children after—they'll all know your name." She put her hand around his and he kissed it gently, then laid his cheek against it for just a moment.

"What will happen to you now?" he asked.

"They say I must go to my brother, to Sean, in America." She tried to keep the anxiety out of her voice.

"Who is 'they?' "

"Smith O'Brien, Meagher, your Mitchel—the voices of Young Ireland. 'Tis Julia Martin brought me to Liverpool . . . but the boat was delayed, you see. And I found out where you were and how could I leave England without seeing you one last time, without saying farewell?"

"It's ludicrous." He shook his head. "Absolutely ludicrous. How in God's name did you come upon this plan?"

"Ah, now," she teased. "I've a number of friends in low places, as well you know."

"Yes, but . . . prostitutes?"

" 'Tis a long story."

"And we've no time for long stories." He sighed. "Tell me then, when do you sail?"

"Two days, maybe three. I'll start back to Liverpool tonight."

"What about the boy and—you have a daughter, as well?"

"Mary Kate is with me, but I've left the baby and Da behind with Barbara at the convent—they'll come when they're strong enough."

"That was hard."

She nodded, struggling against her emotion.

"Don't be afraid to make hard choices, Grace. If that's what it takes to stay alive, you and your children. It's what Morgan would do." He paused. "It's what I would do, if I had any choice left."

She raised her eyes to his. "True enough, and I'm ashamed to sit before you pitying myself."

"I hope not." He squeezed her hands. "It has meant the world to me to see you here tonight. It is one last miracle."

"Is there anything I can do for you, Captain? Anything a'tall?"

"You could call me by my Christian name." He smiled wearily. "It's been a very long time since anyone did."

She nodded, and was about to speak when the first faint sound of clanging keys and heavy footsteps came down the hall.

"Time to go." He stood and pulled her to her feet, then touched a piece of her hair, tucking it up into place. "We must say good-bye now. Not in front of . . . the others."

She put her arms around him, lifting her lips to his ear. "Ireland will not forget you, David," she whispered. "Nor will I. Go with God."

He closed his eyes and let his head rest against hers until the footsteps stopped outside the hall, and the guard approached with his keys.

"Finished up, have you?" He laughed and unlocked the door. "Out, you."

"Good-bye." She held on tightly, unable to let go.

"That's enough now," the guard complained. "Out, I said."

"Don't be afraid," Evans whispered, kissing her cheek.

"Nor you," she answered and found the strength to step away from him, though it broke her heart all over again.

The guard locked up and herded Grace toward the hall, but she stopped, pushed him aside, and looked back to where Evans stood just inside the bars.

"Look down on me," she called to him, "when you get there."

He hesitated just a moment, then raised his hand to show he understood. "We will," he vowed, and that was all.

Five

SOME say a man is closer to God when he's at sea, but Captain Reinders had never found Him there; certainly not aboard the *Eliza J,* nor in the quarters where now he sat; a god capable of ordering an entire universe would never have left it to the mercy of something as random and chaotic as Nature. To well-meaning friends with the gleam of redemption in their eyes, Reinders professed a general belief in some world other than this one, but in his heart he knew there was only one life and one world in which to live it. His religion was the discipline of keeping chaos at bay, the difference between those subject to a mysterious universe and those who unravel its mysteries. If Captain Reinders had a god, its name was Logic, and the blessing it bestowed was the ability to reason without emotion.

It was reason that led him to consider a life at sea—he looked with satisfaction upon the orderly cabin, felt the familiar sway of the ship beneath his feet, and realized how differently he could have ended up as the youngest son of a bitter, unlucky farmer held hostage to the whims of nature through the guise of God's will. It had been fifteen years since Peter Reinders left upstate New York, though he dutifully wrote to his mother once a year at Christmas and received a letter from her in return, in

German, the handwriting painstakingly familiar. It always came a week before Christmas and so would be waiting for him at the fine house of his partner, Lars Darmstadt, where Reinders had an apartment of his own; Lars' lovely wife, Detra, would have placed it on the chest of drawers in his bedchamber, where he would be sure to see it first thing.

Reinders rubbed his temples, thinking of that. The letter would remind him that his father was dead now, and his sisters all married away. His two oldest brothers still worked the farm, but Hans had suffered a fall years ago and was often bedridden, and Josef, though hardworking, could get no more out of the fields and the pigs than their father had. He, his wife, and five children had their own small cabin on the same land and toiled endlessly to provide for everyone. Peter's mother never asked him to come home, but he read it there between the lines; he knew they struggled, and he struggled against that, but would not allow himself to be swayed by emotion. Returning home was not the logical choice. He was no farmer; he was a seaman, partner in one of the most magnificent ships he had ever sailed, a respected captain who made enough to see to his own needs and send a bank draft home once a year. The money bought medicine, tools, supplies, paid for the endless repairs, supported if the market was bad—it was his money that made sense, not his back. He sighed and shook his head.

"Dearest boy," his mother called him in her letters, but he was a man of thirty now, tall and rangy, with a seaman's weathered face and eyes permanently narrowed from squinting into the sun, wind, and rain. The brown hair of his youth had turned the color of straw, thick and matted with sea spray; he tamed it on land with liberal use of hair oil, kept himself clean-shaven, too, but at sea, he preferred a beard and mustache—it was warm in foul weather and lent an edge of fierceness to his command. He ran a hand over his jaw, felt the bristle and scruff; he'd made a point of not shaving while in Liverpool. He stood and stretched, glad he'd not become broken and bent as the plowman, but that he stood tall and straight, steady and surefooted as any seasoned captain—his

mother would not have recognized the boy who'd stormed off
to sea so long ago.

In the middle of one of his father's frequent rages, she had
quietly packed Peter's knapsack, and when he and his father
came to blows, it was she who separated them and led the old
man back into the house, pausing just once to look back at the
boy, who stood angry and confused in the middle of the road.
She had managed a quick smile for him and an encouraging
nod—permission to go. The letter she'd tucked into his pack
had said she knew his father was a hard man, harder on him because he was different from the others and didn't care about the
pigs, didn't want the land, or the way of life. She loved her husband, though, and always would, she'd written; she loved her
son, too, and told him to remember his duty before God. Reinders frowned, unwilling to dwell on the memory of a father who
had rammed duty down his throat—God had been a weapon in
his father's fists.

He was free of all that now, Reinders reminded himself, free
to chart his own course. When he'd learned that the ship of leg-
endary Norwegian Captain Erik Boe was in port, he'd begged
his way on board and had shown, under the captain's demanding tutelage, a natural affinity for the sea—rising from boy to ordinary seaman, to able seaman and then to second mate, from
second mate to first, and finally to captain, from which position
he had entered into the venture with Lars Darmstadt, leading
to partnership in the grand packet *Eliza J.* Every penny—and
he'd saved a lot, refusing to buy a house on the East River or
fine clothes despite the great percentages from ship profits—
had gone into the *Eliza J* and he knew every inch from stern to
prow, every mark on the masts, every gouge in the decks better
than he knew his own body; she was the very soul of him, and
when she soared, he soared as well. But she had taken a terrible beating in this last storm, and for the thousandth time, he
yearned to have her safely back in their home port.

"Balls," he muttered, raking his fingers through his hair. It
was three thousand miles back across the Atlantic Ocean to
America. Three thousand miles taken one short day and one

long night at a time in icy banshee winds, blinding snow, and mountainous seas . . . if they were lucky; in the bone-chilling fog of becalmed seas, if they were not. They might cross in as few as twenty-eight days, or they might limp along, running out of food and water, for as many as sixty. It happened more often than seamen cared to think about; ships got lost in dense fog, where celestial navigation was impossible, the sextant and chronometer little help; ships got turned around in terrible storms, could be blown hundreds of miles off course, could lose a mast and the power of a mainsail, could hit icebergs in the night and sink within minutes, the icy black water keeping their fate a secret forever. There were always risks in any ocean voyage, more when the voyage was undertaken in winter.

Reinders got up and paced the length of his small cabin. He did not like risks at sea. He did not like winter voyages or the burgeoning immigrant-timber trade route he witnessed in the Liverpool port. Nor did he like the thought of wintering in this former slavers' port with all the misery and desperation around its prosperous edges. He hungered for home, for the cocky optimism of Bostonians and Gothamites, the excitement of their shabby docks, the freedom. He thought of Lily, back home selling fish on the docks, waiting to hear from him—she must wonder what had happened to him, where he was, why he had not come home with enough money to make good on his promise to her, worrying that it was too late now, simply too late. He felt acutely the loss of each minute of every day they were stuck in this port, but it must be agony to her.

He'd run out of choices here and it had cost him. He pressed his forehead against the porthole glass, remembering the despair he'd felt as the *Eliza J* limped into port after escaping the hurricane. She didn't fly on the sea anyway—packets weren't built for high speed, but then they rarely sailed in the light wind latitudes—but her three square-rigged masts and single topsails were designed to carry a tremendous press of sail in heavy weather without straining, and her crew of twenty-five was handpicked from among the very best northeastern American seamen. They had weathered storms at sea before—many,

many storms—but never one so unrelenting nor one that claimed so many lives.

At midnight, he'd given the "All Hands," and two men held the wheel against waves twenty feet high that slammed against the stern and threatened to wash them overboard. Mister Cobbs, his second mate, took six men aloft to crawl out on the swaying yards and sea-slippery ropes, where they struggled to reef the sails. Small John, ship's boy and fearless, had followed them up. The sail had filled out like a balloon as the ship pitched and yawed mercilessly, and then the fiercest of winds had hit, snapping the yard and the topmast, flinging the men into the furious black sea.

There had been no way to save them—they'd not tied themselves off as he'd ordered, aware that every minute counted in such a brutal storm. He had watched it unfold helplessly, the yard and the men simply gone, the topmast snapping and slamming into the lower mast, which took the blow with a sickening crack. Sails had shredded before his eyes and two more of his crew had been swept over as the heavy canvas billowed across the deck. The rail had been crushed in three places and a hole punched in the deck over the forecastle. He and the rest of the crew battled on until dawn when, at last, the storm was spent and the sea grew calm. Exhausted, all sat stunned as the roll was called and the number of lost men grew. Cobbs had been with him for three years, despite offers of a first-mate position on other ships, and the lad, Small John, was a soft favorite of the crew, being high-spirited and tireless in his work.

Reinders had not allowed himself to feel grief—grief crippled a man and made him weak—but he acknowledged regret and a deep sense of loss. He shouldered full responsibility for their deaths and the deaths of the others, but he could not afford to sink into despair when there was so much work to be done.

Arriving in Liverpool, the remaining crew had flung themselves into the arms of the prostitutes and barkeeps who set up shop in dance halls along the docks. Sailors were a superstitious lot—even the tough New Englanders, whose veins ran with brine instead of blood—but despite the black cloud of doom that had followed the ship into port, most would return; those who did not would have no trouble signing on elsewhere. His crew was among the very best and crimps were waiting the minute they stepped ashore, courting possible defectors with false promises of better ships and luckier captains.

Cole Mackley, his first mate, despised crimps and spat upon the first one who approached him. He slept aboard each night, and made himself available to the captain each day. Reinders expected this kind of loyalty from his second-in-command, but privately he was relieved; Mackley had been with him from the start, and Reinders counted on his excellent seamanship and sound advice. It was Mackley who suggested naming Tom Dean as second mate; Dean was an able seaman with a solid reputation who'd showed great courage during the storm. Like Mackley, he was a true-spoken man with an undeterred sense of duty; Reinders knew instinctively he could trust him. Both men were well respected by the others; they would be able to control the crew and complete the voyage should anything incapacitate their captain.

This voyage would be different, however, because of passengers. Reinders had been forced to strike a deal with the Liverpool Trading Company in order to secure repair of the ship—they agreed to finance labor and materials, and in return, he'd carry passengers back to New York City. Company directors were well aware that the *Eliza J* was no luxury ship, though she could offer a few small private cabins on the upper deck to those willing to pay. Most would travel steerage, and the midlevel of the ship had been outfitted with additional bunks so that they rose three levels high, instead of two; they were also packed closer together than Reinders thought necessary, but he'd bowed to the judgment of those to whom he owed money.

Proper ventilation was a concern, and he planned on allowing as many passengers as possible up on deck in all fair weather. They would cook on deck, and he'd even rigged up a low tented structure where they could relieve themselves down a hole flushed clean with seawater. The standard was a toilet on the weather deck in the bow of the ship, which women were loath to use because of the presence of sailors who thought the situation hilarious—they themselves simply let fly off the stern with no thought to modesty or comfortable accommodation. That was why, he'd been told, women and children sought the privacy and convenience of the orlop deck, below steerage, despite the smell that would begin to rise in a matter of days. Others surreptitiously relieved themselves in buckets they brought up and slopped over the side; but too often these spilled or were not cleaned out properly and this, combined with fetid air and poor ventilation, encouraged the spread of typhus and cholera. Reinders was determined to avoid that. He knew all about the coffin ships that sailed into Canada with more dead than alive, and no ship of his would carry that shame.

But he was worried. The directors had oversold the ship—booking more than twice the number he'd expected to carry. Standard practice, they assured him, simply protecting their investment. Not everyone who bought passage would actually board the ship, they said. It was a lie and he knew it; he'd spent every day talking to sailors who'd made this voyage before.

He could expect every passenger to show up, they told him, so desperate were the poor beggars to get out—expect stowaways, as well. They advised him to make a thorough search after everyone was aboard, and they promised he'd find at least five, and as many as twenty, packed into trunks and cargo boxes down in the hold. These he could throw overboard or put ashore to be tried by the magistrate, as he saw fit. Some of the passengers would die at sea, they said matter-of-factly—infants rarely survived, especially if there was illness aboard. Same with the young, the old, the women. Childbirth was rough; women lost strength and hope, especially if they buried a child at sea. Men fared best, but they smuggled drink aboard and drink led to fight; men with wounds might live or die depending on the man and the weapon used. These experienced veterans told him all this and more. It was true—they'd seen it all before. Never trust the company men, they warned.

As the departure date neared, Reinders' dealings with the directors grew more heated; he could not be responsible for the safety and well-being of so many people, he insisted, but was told in no uncertain terms that the *Eliza J* would then be detained until full restitution for her repair was made. He was too involved, they soothed; he should focus on the ship and leave the passengers to them. They had even secured a ship's doctor, American like himself, returning home after study abroad. What more could he want?

What Reinders wanted—returning to his desk, reviewing again the impossible list—was what he had always wanted: more space, fewer bodies because each body required provision. He figured six pints of water daily per passenger, and a small weekly allotment of flour, oats, salt, molasses, and salt beef. The directors had assured him this was more than enough; he should keep in mind that these were Irish peasants, starving to death just days ago, happy for bread and water.

The veteran sailors just shook their heads—aye, they said, the starving would indeed be grateful for hard bread and stale water, but they'd eat the week's provisions in a single day, so desperate was their hunger, and then they'd have nothing. Some would bring extra food with them, but this they'd have to guard with their lives, especially at night. Doling out each day would take hands off the sailing, and who could spare that on a winter sea? The old hands advised telling passengers the way of it right off—rations came weekly and no more. Deal harshly with them that pay you no mind, they warned; set an example straightaway and carry a pistol for weight—you won't have to use it if they think you will.

He gritted his teeth, thinking of it all, trying to foresee every unforeseeable event. He hoped to make the voyage in four weeks, five at the outside; there was no room for extra provisions, no room for livestock of any kind, nor the larger tools of a man's trade—anvils, carpentry and farming tools, looms and spinning wheels. Each family would be allotted a small space in the hold for one trunk, crate, or barrel. Only one.

Reinders shoved the list away from him, the cabin suddenly too close. He left the room and took the steps two at a time, emerging on deck to survey the ship that was his whole life. He breathed deeply and admired her solid masts, the complex web of her rigging, her tightly bundled sails and blunt bow. Above him, heavy rolling clouds pushed the sky low over the murky river and a chill wind rattled the rigging. Not for the first time, he thought about slipping her lines and navigating her down-river to the open sea. She'd outrun the other tubs in this port; no one would catch him once he reached the sea. But he couldn't sail her alone, and he couldn't round up a crew without drawing attention and, in the end, he had given his word.

What pride he'd felt in striking this bargain! No need to write to Lars for money or to use up what little they'd made from the cotton and tobacco—ruined, most of it, in the storm. He'd congratulated himself for keeping a level head despite the catastrophe, for taking immediate action to minimize the loss of what had promised to be a lucrative deal. Lars was the ac-knowledged money man, but Reinders had wanted to prove his own financial sensibilities, as well.

He looked toward the dock, disgusted with himself and his pride, and saw the somber line of passengers boarding down-river—boarding small, tired ships run by apathetic captains and squirrelly crews who wanted only to get the best price and be done with it. They were mere cargo, those passengers, and they knew it. They shuffled slowly forward, heads bent, murmuring anxiously as they approached the gangway.

Dirty gray gulls circled the docks in their endless scavenging, but it was an enormous raven that landed heavily on the rail be-side him, opening its beak in a raspy caw, black eyes glittering. *Bad omen,* he thought, then corrected himself. There were no omens; it was a random and chaotic universe, nothing more. He had only himself to blame. In the beginning, he'd had many choices—in the end, too few. Today, there were none. Not for him, and not for those sorry bastards down the way who had al-ready disappeared into a dark hold.

Six

"HAVE you got it all, now?" Julia eyed the small trunk beside Mary Kate. "You've not forgotten anything?"

Grace shook her head.

"All right, then." Julia inspected her charges one last time, eyeing with grim satisfaction their stiff leather boots and heavy woolen cloaks. "You can cover yourselves with these if it gets too cold at night," she reminded them for the hundredth time. "And leave your boots on."

Grace took her hand. "We'll remember everything you've said, won't we, Mary Kate?"

"Aye." The little girl nodded. She moved closer and took Julia's other hand. "Please come?"

"Ah, darling girl." Julia scooped her up and held her in a hard embrace. "Don't I wish I could? I'll miss you ever so much." She squeezed her once more, then set her down, straightening the bonnet she'd knocked askew. "Take care of your mother, now. See she eats and stays warm. And that she eats."

"You said that." Mary Kate smiled shyly.

Julia stepped out of the slow-moving line to have a look at the front.

"All trunks and boxes go to one side," she reported. "The sailors are carrying them off. Over there." She pointed to another gangway at the other end of the ship, where crewmen bore the luggage up on their backs. "Look, they can't take everything."

Grace craned her neck and saw a growing pile of pots and pans, farm equipment, tradesman's tools, and spinning wheels; someone's goat had been left behind, and two crates of squawking hens.

"There's a man checking names at the head of the line," Julia relayed. "He's talking to everyone who boards. Whatever about, do you suppose?"

"Have you seen the outlaw Grace O'Malley? Do you know anything a'tall about Gracelin O'Malley?" Grace mimicked in a low voice.

"Not funny!" Julia hissed, glancing around. "Not a bit funny, that!"

Grace put her arm around Julia's shoulders, giving her a reassuring squeeze. "Just having a bit of fun, is all," she apologized. "Take our minds off things."

"Well, don't take your mind off who you're supposed to be!" Julia admonished. "You're Missus Bram Donnelly, remember, and that's risky enough as far as I'm concerned. I know, I know"—she held up her hand to silence her friend's explanation—"you want to make sure Sean can find you no matter what happens."

"And there must be a record of us for Mary Kathleen's sake," Grace added. "For her future."

"Fair enough," Julia allowed. "But no more jokes and no mention of any other names than those on your papers, agreed?"

"Agreed."

The line inched closer to the gangway and Grace looked up at the ship that would hold her life and Mary Kate's across the vast ocean. Its size and sturdiness reassured her, as did the professional manner of the crew working steadily under the watchful eye of a tall, commanding figure at the rail.

"What's he called, then? The captain?"

"Reinders," Julia told her, then spelled it. "German name—the 'i' is long—but he's an American. Ship's American, as well."

"Guess he knows the way, then." The two women traded guarded smiles over Mary Kate's head.

When it was nearly their turn, Grace got out her papers, gripping them tightly against the wind that gusted along the wharf. She looked down at Mary Kate, all bundled up, and gave her a wink of courage. Then she turned to Julia.

"I'm wanting to say something to you if you can hold your tongue for all of a minute."

Julia opened her mouth to protest, then caught herself and squeezed her lips together contritely.

"I want to thank you for all you've done, Julia. For coming with me to London, for getting us to Liverpool in the first place. Sure and I don't know what would've happened to me without you. I would've been lost, and that's the truth of it."

Julia shook her head.

"Aye," Grace insisted. "I couldn't . . ." She hesitated. " 'Twas killing me, you know."

Pain flooded Julia's eyes with tears.

Grace put her arms around those stalwart shoulders. "Ah, Julia, I know you loved him. I didn't see at first, but then I did."

"Forgive me," Julia whispered, her cheek wet against Grace's.

"There's nothing to forgive." Grace kissed her. "And I know you love me, as well, now, though I'm sure you've cursed me plenty."

Julia didn't know whether to laugh or cry, agree or deny, and so she just clung more tightly to her friend.

"On the strength of that—the love we have for Morgan and for one another—I'm asking you, Julia, will you look out for Da and the baby? Will you see to them until all this is settled? If Ireland wins out, I'll be home on the next wind . . . but if time is passing . . ." She pushed away the feeling of desperation. "Will you send them on to me? Will you help them the way you helped me? I've no one else to ask, you see, and I know that if you promise, it will be done."

Julia wiped her eyes. "I promise," she said, and then her heart began to pound as the group in front of them fell away.

"Papers?" Cole Mackley, the first mate, took the documents Grace handed him, then compared the information to the names on his passenger list.

"Missus Bram Donnelly, age twenty, widow, and Mary Kathleen Donnelly, age three, child, bound for New York City?"

"Aye," Grace confirmed.

"One trunk?"

"Aye."

He raised his hand and the wiry crewman at his side pulled it over. "Unlock it, please."

Grace hesitated and looked at Julia.

"Now," he insisted, not unkindly.

"Stowaways," Julia mouthed and Grace nodded, took out her key, and opened the trunk.

The crewman poked around among the few articles of clothing and extra foodstuffs, then stood up and nodded. Grace closed and re-locked the trunk.

"Any firearms or liquor on your person?" Mackley inquired.

"No, sir." No need to mention the boning knife sheathed in stiff leather, well hidden inside her boot.

"You may board," he ordered, and suddenly Grace was being directed toward the gangway, away from Julia.

"Wait!" she called, now caught in the flow of those ahead making their way up to the ship. "Wait—Julia!"

"All aboard!" The sailor at the top waved them on.

She struggled to disengage herself as another group closed in behind her. "Julia!" The panic in her voice unnerved the others, who shifted nervously and began to mumble.

"You there! Stop!" Mackley commanded as Julia tried to shove past him. "Back in line!"

A struggle ensued as passengers pressed forward, afraid suddenly of being left behind; and then a gap appeared with Julia elbowing her way through. She rushed to the gangway and met Grace at the bottom, throwing one arm around her, reaching down with the other to pull Mary Kate into the embrace.

"Farewell," she whispered to them, in Irish now. "Farewell, farewell. God bless you both and watch over you both and see you safely to the other side."

Tears streamed down her wind-reddened cheeks even as she tried to give them a confident smile, a nod of assurance that all would be well even in the face of the impossible voyage ahead. She set Mary Kate down, kissing her tenderly.

"You are brave and strong," she pronounced. "Remember that."

She embraced Grace one last time, the words pouring out of her. "I'm sorry we didn't keep Morgan safe, that he died . . . that he never saw his son. Ah, God, I'm sorry. I pray you'll forgive us. Me. Forgive me."

Grace pressed her cheek against Julia's. "I never blamed you," she whispered. "Never."

"I thought so highly of myself," Julia rushed on. "My brilliant mind, my brilliant work, blah, blah, blah." She shook her head in self-disgust. "But I'm ashamed of myself, Grace. I'm nothing next to you. You're the finest woman I've ever known—kind and strong and brave and honest. . . ."

"Ah, now, next you'll be asking me to buy you a drink," Grace teased through her own tears.

Julia laughed, fighting off the hopelessness that threatened to overwhelm her, clinging to Grace until the group behind them had had enough and pushed forward, separating them once and for all.

"We'll see you again," Grace shouted from the top, holding Mary Kate's hand, both now waving their arms.

"Aye!" Julia yelled and blew them a kiss. "God willing," she said quietly to herself, and stood there in the freezing rain until the ship was long gone out to sea.

"I'll see the captain, then," Grace insisted, pushing down the panic in her voice. "He'll right this, if you cannot."

Marcus Boardham's dark eyes narrowed, but he ran his finger down the list again, tapping it with finality halfway down the sheet.

"No cabin in that name," the steward said shortly. "Missus Bram Donnelly and child, two bunks steerage."

"We've paid for a private cabin. It's right here on the ticket." She held his gaze, ignoring the irritation he made no effort to disguise, and at last he sent someone to find the captain.

"Go below." He waved her off.

"No, thank you," she said firmly. "I'll wait right here."

The steward stepped past her, forcing Mary Kate and her up against the wall of the small passageway, quickly engaging himself with another group looking for their cabin—a group meant to have private accommodations, according to his list, and therefore rightfully deserving of his attention. They were English, all of them, and Grace gritted her teeth, refusing to be intimidated.

"Problem, Mister Boardham?"

Startled by the commanding voice, Grace found herself looking over Boardham's shoulder and into imposing blue eyes that meant nothing if not business.

"Captain Reinders." Holding firmly to Mary Kate's hand, she pushed past the steward. "A private cabin was booked well in advance for my daughter and myself, but your man here says it's not to be."

"Well?" The captain looked over her head at Boardham.

"There's no 'Missus Donnelly' in first class, Captain. Only steerage."

"You examined her papers?"

Boardham sidestepped Grace to be closer to the captain, whom he turned slightly so that they faced away from her hearing.

"Tickets are marked first," he admitted reluctantly in a low voice. "But first is full. Passenger list says steerage." He held out the proof.

Reinders swore under his breath, jaw clenched.

Damn those thieving bastards to Hell, he silently fumed. He saw instantly what had happened. The directors had put their American medical man and his family in first, probably in partial payment for his services; Missus Donnelly and her little

Irish daughter had been dumped to steerage. He glanced at the passenger list again; all of the others would be settled by now; no one was going to voluntarily give up their cabin. It didn't escape his notice that the only Irish passenger among them would have been Missus Donnelly. *Damn them,* he thought again, but there was nothing for it. Boardham pissed him off, as well—another one of the directors' stipulations though who in God's name knew why. There was something irritating about the man, a ratty smugness. Reinders shouldered him out of the way and turned to face the woman and her daughter.

"There has indeed been a mistake, Missus Donnelly. You are most certainly correct in that, and I apologize most humbly, as does my steward, Mister Boardham." He shot the man a warning look.

Boardham dipped his head, but there was nothing sincere or apologetic in the gesture.

"I'm sorry to say there's no way to remedy this situation unless you wish to disembark immediately and rebook passage on another vessel."

Grace's heart skipped a beat. "No, Captain, I will not." She looked him in the eye. " 'Tis not the ship I paid for, but your reputation for sailing her. Did you not bring her into port despite a nasty storm and the loss of half your crew? I've heard tell you did. I've heard you're an honorable man. God has led me to put my life and that of my daughter in your hands, Captain Reinders, and until He tells me otherwise I'm staying aboard."

Surprised by this speech, he regarded her more closely, seeing now beyond the timidity he associated with most women— and the gaunt frailty of this one in particular—to the determined set of her jaw and the quick light in her eyes. Were they gray or blue or green? he found himself wondering. And then he knew—they were the perfect changeable color of the sea. He made a decision.

"Are you willing to travel steerage, ma'am?"

"Have I any other choice, Captain?"

"No, Missus Donnelly, I'm afraid you don't." He glanced at the child beside her, equally still and pale, but silently trusting.

"You will, of course, be reimbursed for your entire passage, and I will do everything in my power to make sure you are comfortable." He turned to the steward. "Missus Donnelly and her daughter are to be given the two lower bunks nearest the door, which are to be curtained off for greater privacy. I want this done right away. You are to see to it personally, Boardham. Missus Donnelly, you will, of course, take your meals with the first-class passengers in the saloon." He paused and lowered his voice. "Better food for the child."

"Thank you, Captain." Grace squeezed Mary Kate's hand. "I'll be no more trouble to you, then."

"You've been no trouble, Missus Donnelly. Please ask for me if there's anything else I can do." He nodded curtly, then tossed a sharp glance at the steward before striding back down the hall.

Stung by the captain's attitude, Boardham barked at a young sailor, who quickly heaved Grace's trunk to his shoulder and headed off to the narrow stairwell. Grace and Mary Kate followed, falling farther behind as they picked their way carefully down.

The stairwell opened directly onto a great room divided into three sections with narrow walkways in between. Tiers of wooden slats three deep ran the length of the room, and there was no light save the smoky flicker of wall-mounted oil lamps. The ship rolled slightly as the sea sloshed against her; her timbers groaned and creaked. Grace felt the press of tense bodies before she saw their shapes huddled on bunks or sitting on battered trunks, guarding what little they had left, children included. Their eyes were furtive, their talk hushed.

"You there, you'll have to move." The sailor spoke gruffly to two older men who'd claimed the bunks by the door.

"Why's that, then?" the one asked, suspiciously.

"Set aside for this woman and her child," came the smart answer. "Move along now, Captain's orders."

"And if we don't?" The other spoke now in a low, menacing voice.

"You'll be put off the ship," the crewman warned. "Tossed

overboard most likely. Captain Reinders never asks twice. He's American."

Cursing the American captain and his smart-mouthed crew, the two men gathered the bundle of cloth that constituted their worldly belongings and moved off toward the back of the hold, shouldering past Grace more roughly than necessary.

The murmuring in the hold had ceased as the other passengers listened carefully to the exchange. They eyed Grace warily, unsure if the captain's attention to her made her someone worth knowing or someone to fear.

"Thank you for your help," Grace said quietly as the young sailor settled her trunk next to the bottom bunk.

"No problem, missus," he replied jauntily. "I'll be back shortly to rig a curtain for you."

Grace surveyed the scene and made her decision quickly. "No need for that." She spoke loudly enough for all to hear. "Aren't I a girl from the lane, then, well used to the good company of my neighbors? Never you mind a curtain."

The sailor cocked his head at her, puzzled. "It's Captain's orders, missus," he insisted. "I have to bring it down." He glanced around at the wary figures on their bunks. "But I guess I can just give it to you, and you can do whatever you like."

"Sure enough, I will." Grace gave him a quick wink.

It took him just a minute to understand, but then he returned the wink, nodded, and whistled up the stairs, leaving her with the others.

She removed her bonnet, then untied the ribbons of Mary Kate's, running her fingers through the child's short curls, warming the little red cheeks between gloved hands as the girl gazed up at her watchfully.

" 'Twill be all right, agra," she soothed. "We've come aboard this fine ship safely and here we are, a bed apiece, the promise of meals, a big adventure ahead. Why, we'll be seeing your uncle Sean in no time a'tall, and won't he be surprised at how very big you've grown?"

"Will he?" Mary Kate wondered, touching her mother's cheek.

"Oh, aye," Grace assured her. "He'll see me first, and then he'll look all around, asking, 'Where's my wee Mary Kate, and who's this giant of a person come all the way across the sea with you now?' He'll glower at you with his arms crossed, looking all fierce the way he tries, and demand to know what you've done with his favorite girl."

"Say I swallowed her." Mary Kate giggled, then covered her mouth.

Grace laughed as well, just to see her, and suddenly neither could stop. They gave in to it, laughing and laughing until tears rolled down their cheeks, and the taste of salt was upon their tongues, Grace pulling Mary Kate onto the bunk and tickling the life out of her. Those near them froze with uncertainty, then stole glances at one another as the infectious giggling continued, shaking their heads in pity for the poor lunatic friends of the American captain. But soon enough, their own lips began to twitch and the mirth that was so natural to them escaped from its confinement, so contagious was the giggling of the wee girl and the whoops of glee from her mother.

Laughter rippled slowly to the very back of the hold, to the last bunk in the darkest corner, giddiness a relief to those who felt sure their hearts would burst with the strain of leaving—it spread and grew until it reached the captain's ears on deck.

He cocked his head, listening, thinking it the scream of trailing gulls, but then recognizing its human quality. Laughter. Laughter from that desperate, ragged mass below. What on earth could they find so amusing about being packed like slaves in a dark, dank hold for a risky voyage across an endless, fickle sea to an unknown country?

"They really *are* crazy," he muttered and shook his head. But as the sound grew louder, his own lips began to twitch and a smile defeated the tension that lined his face, the unease in his heart began to give way, and he tasted again the confidence that had eluded him these many long weeks. The *Eliza J* felt solid beneath his feet, above his head her full sails pulled the ship through a bracing sea, in his face the wind was stinging and clean. He was master and commander, and the exhilaration that coursed through his veins burst forth in such bold laughter that every crewman on deck paused in his work and turned to look.

Spent, Mary Kate had fallen directly from laughter into sleep and Grace, too, had drowsed with her daughter in her arms. When she came fully awake the atmosphere in the hold had changed and she was surrounded by a hum of conversation as her fellow passengers settled into the place that was to be their home for the next month.

She eased her arm out from underneath Mary Kate, then sat up and straightened her clothing, glancing around in the flickering, smudgy light at unfamiliar faces. Now and then a baby cried, the sound followed by a mother's quick shushing and the rustle of cloth as the child was put to breast. Grace's own breasts still quickened at this sound, but the ache was less with each passing day. She saw that the sailor had returned during her sleep; a folded square of canvas had been left on her trunk along with a length of rope. As much as she longed to rig a curtain and hide behind it, she did not. Quietly, not wanting to wake Mary Kate, she slipped off the side of the hard bunk, realizing with sudden clarity that there would be no additional bedding and that the canvas might come in handy after all, providing an extra cushion between the bare boards, thin mat, and her back. She stretched and looked around more openly now, stepping into the main aisle that ran the length of the hold. As much as she hoped to see someone she knew, her freedom depended upon anonymity and already enough attention had been drawn.

She turned at the sound of footsteps coming down the stairs and watched as Boardham, attended by a lantern bearer, entered the hold. He stood for a moment, then knocked his gaff loudly against the wall.

"Attention." His voice boomed in the uneasy silence. "The cargo hold has been rid of stowaways, such as have been put off the ship and are now in the charge of the magistrate." He looked around boldly, daring anyone to dispute this action.

Some of those stowing away were bound to have friends or

family aboard, Grace thought, though no one would dare own them now for fear of joining them in jail.

"We've left the mouth of the river and are now at sea," he announced smugly. "Secure your belongings and come up in an orderly fashion to the main deck, where Captain Reinders will address you."

The passengers instinctively surged forward, and Boardham banged the wall again forcefully.

"One at a time, now, one at a time," he barked. "Secure your belongings first!"

He glared at them and then was gone, the light that followed him leaving deeper shadows in its wake. Grace sat down again and gently shook Mary Kate until her eyes opened.

"Are we there?" Her voice was high and hoarse.

"Ah, no, wee girl!" Grace smiled. " 'Tis a long way yet. But now the captain himself wants to see us all, so here's your bonnet and off we go!" She forced enthusiasm into her voice, resolving to speak always as if this were great fun and everything as it should be.

They were among the first on deck, but steadily others made their way up until they were surrounded by a sea of faces. As the ship surged across the waves, many passengers, unused to the motion, stumbled into neighbors barely able to keep balanced themselves.

"Stand like this." Grace spread her feet wide on the deck. "Let your body sway against the roll of the ship. Don't fight it," she added. "Just brace yourself."

Mary Kate did as she was told and others followed their example until their small space in the middle of the group was fairly secured. Grace turned her face into the wind, squinted, and breathed the fresh air.

"Welcome aboard the *Eliza J.*" The authoritative voice captured everyone's attention. "I am Captain Reinders. This is Mister Mackley, my first mate." He indicated a wiry, fierce-looking man to his right. "And this is Mister Dean, second mate." Dean was powerfully built with massive shoulders; his face, Grace thought, was kind. "You've all met Mister Boardham, ship's steward. And this is Doctor Draper, who will see to your medical needs should any arise." The overdressed doctor stood off to the side, examining his fingernails; he barely acknowledged the introduction.

Reinders frowned slightly, then continued. "There are rules aboard any ship—the *Eliza J* is no exception. You will follow these rules to the letter, or find yourself crossing the Atlantic in a small cell in the cargo hold." He placed one hand on his hip, edging his jacket back just enough to reveal the butt of a pistol.

"Number one. No drink. If you have any, get rid of it now. Number two—no weapons. Bring your pistols, knives, and clubs to Mister Mackley for safekeeping, to be returned when you disembark. Number three—no fire in the hold. This means no cooking, no smoking, no candles. You must police yourselves or suffer the consequence of being trapped aboard a burning ship in the middle of the ocean." He let the full weight of those words sink in. "And finally, there will be no fighting. Bring your disputes to Mister Boardham and he will settle them. His word is final."

"Please, sir," a woman asked. "How will we cook our food, then?"

"There are four cabooses up here on the main deck." Reinders pointed to the small fireplaces. "They will be lit each morning. You will come up in groups to cook once each day. Only once. So plan for this." He paused. "You will be given rations for the week tonight, then seven days hence. You must make this last seven days. No more before then. Water is allotted each morning. When Mister Mackley rings the bell, bring your pots and line up. This is your water for cooking, drinking, washing. Understood?" He eyed the group carefully.

They looked around at one another, nodding hesitantly.

"The privies are located on deck," Reinders continued. "You must take turns, so be hasty. Do not, under any circumstance, relieve yourselves anywhere else on this ship—even in buckets that you intend to clean out—or we risk the spread of disease."

This was going well, he told himself, pleased. No problems so far.

"The saloon on the main deck is for first-class passengers only, as is the foredeck. You may cook, clean up, and take the air aft. You may also smoke a pipe there."

He glanced at Mackley in case he'd overlooked anything; the first mate tipped his head discreetly toward the hold.

"Right. No one is allowed in the cargo hold. If you require something from that area, please see Mister Mackley, who will be in charge of it until we land." Mackley nodded curtly. "All right. These are the rules. They will be posted where all can see them. If you keep to them, it will go well for you. In all good weather we should reach New York City in thirty days. Thank you."

He turned briskly and strode up to the helm, Mackley close behind. Dean crossed to where two sailors were picking apart old ropes for the oakum, while Boardham slipped across the deck and into the first-class saloon to brief the passengers who waited for him there.

Grace felt a timid hand upon her arm.

"Is that Missus Donnelly?"

She turned and looked into the pale drawn face of a woman she barely recognized.

"Alice?" she asked. "Is it Alice, then? From the hotel?"

"Aye." Alice smiled and Grace saw she'd lost most of her teeth. " 'Twas your honeymoon, if I remember right. Did you not wear a velvet gown of midnight blue one evening, your hair all arranged with flowers?"

Grace nodded, her hand moving self-consciously to the strands escaping her bun. "Aye. 'Twas a lifetime ago, that." She nodded. "Dublin's changed since then."

"The whole world's changed," Alice said grimly. "Nothing's the same anymore."

"Have you lost your home, then? Is that why you've come away?"

"Aye, and my work. But thank God, no family." Alice crossed herself fervently. "My husband's gone out to America a year ago now, so it's just me and the two children." She smiled at the little girl by her side. "This is Siobahn, and over there's our Liam."

Standing apart from them was an equally thin, but determined-looking boy of nine or ten, hands jammed into his jacket pockets, collar up like the older toughs.

"They'll be happy to see their da."

"I only hope he'll be happy to see *them*." Alice frowned.

"Sure and he will. Here he's bringing you all over!"

Alice pulled Siobahn closer to her side. "To tell you true, we've not had a word from him in all this time. But he's alive," she insisted. "Tally McGarrity had a letter from her man who said our one was in a boardinghouse on Cross Street. Spoke to him, and all."

"Does he know you're coming?" Grace asked gently.

"Oh, aye." Alice's eyes were bright with hope. "I had a letter written, saying we were come away—there was nothing to be done for it, no way to make a living no more, and no food for the children."

"Then he'll be waiting for you," Grace reassured her, though her heart was heavy as she looked again at the wary face of the boy; she looked into the trusting face of her own child by her side. "This is my Mary Kate. She's a shy one, but happy for the company."

"Ah, but sure you're traveling first-class, missus?" Alice glanced over her shoulder at the cabins. "We'll not be seeing too much of you."

"As luck would have it, Alice, I've escaped first class and am traveling in the hold with all the other decent folk!" Grace laughed.

"That never can be—your squire's an Englishman!"

"*Was* an Englishman," Grace corrected. "He has died, and I have been turned out. No love lost for an Irish widow," she added wryly. "So, I'm going to my brother."

"Ah, missus, you've suffered hardship, then."

"We're none of us strangers to that, are we, Alice?"

"No, ma'am," Alice said gravely. "Not in these times."

Boardham eyed the two women still on deck with irritation. They should've gone down with the others long ago, but no—

typical Irish, they did whatever they wanted. He started toward them, then stopped, caught off guard by how much the older one resembled his mother, his stomach churning suddenly at the thought of that bitch who'd ripped him away from the father he'd loved. Bile rose in his throat, sour acidity flooded his mouth, and he spat viciously; she'd been nothing but a whore, his mother, an Irish whore who didn't know how good she'd had it. He remembered bitterly the day they sailed out of Liverpool, sailed without a word to anyone, leaving his father to come home from work and find nothing but a cold hearth and an empty home. His father—an Englishman, a gentleman with manners and an education. She'd run because he'd beaten her, but he beat her because she drank and whored; Boardham knew that, knew it and believed it true. He'd been only a boy and she'd lied to him, taking him back to Ireland, where everyone hated him because he was English and he hated everyone because they were not. It was two long years before he realized his father was not coming for him, had no idea where the boy even was, and so he'd run away, leaving the bitch drunk and on her back, only to find the old man had died. Died alone without the comfort of his son. Boardham never forgave her for that, and never would. He hoped she was dead, prayed for it, and the world well rid of her. As far as anyone else was concerned, he was an Englishman and nothing to do with all that trash in the hold.

Seven

LILY Free hurried down Cross Street, head lowered but eyes glancing left and right as she passed Murderer's Alley and then the Old Brewery itself. Chased by a pack of ragged boys, a large sow squealed past her, squirted its muck on the walk, then darted into the street and startled the horses, who reared and stomped, causing their drivers to curse the boys, who just laughed and yelled out their own curses. Lily kept moving, thanking God yet again for getting her out of that infamous tenement building and into rooms smaller, but windowed, over on Little Water Street. Despite its reputation for prostitutes and the bullies who kept them, Lily felt safer in Cow Bay, where blacks, whites, and mulattos mixed freely and didn't ask too many questions. The few desperate times Lily had been forced to prostitute herself had been at the Old Brewery, just around the corner in the alley. She walked faster, pushing that memory off; runaway slaves have few options.

The only good to come out of that time was Jakob Hesselbaum, a German Jew as different from other immigrants as herself—"We're the only ones who don't long for home," he'd said. He'd actually talked to her after their quick coupling in the alley and, learning of her children, brought her small gifts of food for

them, and finally the offer of a real job—selling fish from his
stand on the docks, now that he'd done well enough to buy a
horse and cart. She'd said yes, because there was no other
choice, and because sex with one man was safer than sex with
many. And so she had worked for him and he paid her a small
wage—enough to move to a room with a window, with light and
air and privacy—and she slept with him now and then and her
children never knew, although God knew and she prayed He
would forgive her.

One rainy day, Jakob asked her to be his wife, but she had
said no—no, because she had a husband, a good man who was
still a slave in Georgia. And because she had two older children,
also slaves, and would never rest until she had enough money to
buy them out. She shook her head, remembering Jakob's
shocked face when she told him this, and then his own story of
persecution, of a wife and children gone now, and what he'd
give to have them back. She thought of this as she crossed Mott
Street and ran down Pell to the Bowery, where she barely
caught the omnibus to the dock. She smelled—she knew she
did—of sweat and soot and grease and fish slime, but she didn't
care; everyone stank in the city, especially in the hot months.
Let them move away from her on the bus, she didn't care. Only
that she was late, and Jakob would worry.

After she told him about her husband, he no longer took
her to bed, and yet he treated her as gently as if they were
lovers, something she couldn't begin to understand but for
which she was grateful. It was he who insisted she take Captain Reinders up on his offer, he who advanced her his hard-
earned dollars so that she might be reunited with her family.
She frowned—she owed him so much, and it was almost more
than she could bear now that the end was in sight. When the
captain returned from Liverpool, he would sail down the coast
and find a slave broker. . . .

The bell clanged and Lily got off, pulling her shawl more
tightly around her shoulders. She would never get used to the
freezing cold of the North or the dark, bleak winter landscape,
the ceaseless clamor of the city or the brutal exhaustion of

scratching out a living; she would never get used to it, nor would she ever complain because now she was something she thought she'd never be, something she had only dreamed of for her children. The slave who had been Lillian was now Lily Free.

"There you are at last." Jakob's accent was always thicker when he was worried, all heavy Z's and V's. "I been watching for an hour and still you do not come. I think maybe something happen, maybe you have some trouble." He wiped his hands on his apron and looked her up and down. "Everything is all right, then?"

She nodded. "We had police. Somebody find a body in the alley behind Stookey's Saloon."

"That Stookey is a jackass, always waving that stupid knife, he is." He handed her a large, clean apron.

"I can do my own wash, Jakob," she said, taking it guiltily.

"I know." He turned her around and tied the back. "But then all the clothes, they smell like fish . . . and all mein clothes"— he shrugged his shoulders—"they *already* smell like fish!" He let his hands rest on her hips for a moment. "Anyway, I want to, and you should let me. Besides, you have made me late. You and Stookey."

She laughed.

"The police, they bother you?"

"No," she said, turning back. "But I didn't like leaving Samuel and Ruth by theyselves in case somebody come round, asking questions."

"That's right," Jakob agreed. "We don't want trouble, not with Captain Reinders here soon."

Lily looked out at the wharves and the ships coming in. "Has something gone wrong, Jakob, do you think?"

"Ach, no. He's fine. It's the wintertime. Storms happen, ships get delayed. All the time, they get delayed. He'll be here. I promise you."

"You can't promise that," Lily reminded him.

"Sure I can!" He grinned at her and waggled his fingers. "And now I am going, or that damned Moushevsky will take all my customers. So good-bye, and sell all that fish before I come back, Missus Free!"

He put the last of the buckets in the back of his cart, climbed up, and started off, tipping his hat to her before turning the corner that led out to the avenue. *What a good man,* she thought again.

"Are you buying, Lily?" A couple little boys stood before the stand, a sloshing bucket of mussels between the two of them.

"I might be," she said. "How fresh?"

"Just this morning, Lily! Honest!" The oldest one plunged his hand into the freezing water, then offered her a fistful.

She took one, looked it over, gave it a sniff, then nodded. "All right then, you two. Same bargain as before?"

They nodded simultaneously, and brought their bucket round the back, pouring out its contents into one of her tubs. She gave them some pennies and tried not to smile when their eyes went wide—it was two more than usual, but Hesselbaum had told her to do it; his mother had been a Polish Jew like these boys and he knew what kind of life they'd left behind.

"Ah, good morning to you, Lily!" Tara Ogue smiled as the little boys ran off. "If those are fresh mussels you've got there, I'll take them right off your hands, I will!"

Lily spread out a thickness of newspaper and wrapped up the order. "Fresh this morning, the boy says." She liked this Missus Ogue, but was wary of the Irish in general—they were the drinkers and brawlers in her neighborhood and had no love for the blacks, with whom they fought for the lowest rung on the economic ladder. She never went into their saloons and didn't ever talk to them if she didn't have to, but Missus Ogue was nice enough and a good customer, buying as she did for the place they had on Chatham Street.

"Sure and I'll make a nice stew with this. Something to fill up those old sods at the bar, eh, Lily?" Tara winked. "How are the children? Boy and a girl, isn't that right?"

"Yes, ma'am," Lily said, always caught off guard by the woman's ability to extract information.

"Mind you forget the 'ma'am'-ing me." Tara stuffed the parcel into her basket. "I was once a widow myself, you know."

Lily nodded, feeling guilty about the lie but not enough to correct it; as far as anyone was concerned—especially the bondsmen—she and her children were legally free, and she had the forged papers to prove it.

" 'Twasn't so long ago I was making my own way in the city, same as you. I know the hardship of it. I didn't have the worry of children, mind you, nor did I their comfort." She stepped closer and leaned over the buckets. "God will look out for you," she assured Lily. "Didn't He bring me my own dear Dugan Ogue, just when I thought there'd be nothing for it but grief and loneliness? He did," she said firmly. "And He'll do the same for you."

Tara's words, rare kindness in a city of strangers, took Lily by surprise. "Thank you," she said truthfully.

"*Tara.*" Missus Ogue smiled and stepped back, adjusting the basket on her arm. "And now I must be going, as our lodger— a fine boy, our Sean—he's expecting his sister any day now and I promised to check the boards. Bound in from Ireland, she is, and I hope soon or he'll die for the worry of it!"

Lily knew the feeling. "Good luck," she offered. "And"—she hesitated—"see you next time, Tara."

She watched Missus Ogue walk down toward the landing offices, and thought that it was good to know that life sometimes worked out, that this woman had suffered loss and felt despair, and yet she had survived it. Not only survived, but was living happily. It gave Lily hope, and she looked past Tara—now a figure among many on the wharf—down past the docks and out to the sea, where even now a ship was coming in.

Eight

"TARA says they weren't listed."

Sean's face fell. Ogue poured him a whiskey straight up, then slid it across the massive oak bar and into the young man's waiting hand.

"Ah, now, don't give up hope, boy," he urged. "She'll be turning up any day now, sure as the sun rises. 'Tis a hard crossing, you know, and nigh unpredictable with winter as it is."

Sean looked even worse.

"Ah, don't listen to me." Ogue shook his head, disgusted with himself. Then his face brightened. "Wait, now! There's a packet come for you, might be good news. Watch the counter for me, boyo, and I'll get it from the wife."

Sean barely heard him. The packet would be from O'Sullivan—notes for an article on English transportation of grain out of a starving Ireland, as well as a copy of Duyckinck's last speech; none of it seemingly important in light of Grace's predicament.

She simply had not arrived in time to sail, Captain Applegate reported when the *Lydia* docked in Manhattan. Sean had stood on the dock for hours, questioning passengers—sea-weary, gaunt, and hollow-eyed, already defeated by the swirl of activity that now surrounded them. Glad as they were to shake the hand of a landed Irishman, no one knew Grace Donnelly or her little daughter.

He went each day to the harbor to read through the passenger lists; ships docked by the hour, and his eyes burned with the strain of squinting at every female form that came down those ramps, afraid to blink for fear of missing her in the crowd of stunned immigrants. Only with great reluctance did he end his search in the dark of late afternoon, haunted by the thought that she was ill, possibly delirious, and had not been allowed to land but was lying in the marine hospital out on Staten Island. Landed immigrants could travel back out by ferry to be with detained family members, but the practice was not encouraged; typhus and cholera were real threats. He was now so desperate, however, that he resolved to make the trip at week's end if she had not arrived.

He also feared she would disembark moments after his departure, easy prey to the throngs of runners with their green neckties and thick accents, the shoulder men waiting to take advantage of confused and disoriented passengers. To him, the worst of these were the Irish who had come before and now waited in green hats and waistcoats, brogue spread thick no matter how many years they'd been in America, inviting their former countrymen to buy tickets for trains and boats that didn't exist, or taking a small fee to lead them to "friendly Irish boardinghouses" along Greenwich Street—houses that were little more than dilapidated, filthy, three-story tenement buildings just off the waterfront, often with a grog shop on the ground floor, where the newly arrived family was invited to partake after their long journey. They'd be shown a room that already housed two other families, urged to settle in and reassured that payment could come later, after work had been found. Relieved, the immigrant family would lay down their bundles and sleep on the floor, prayers of thanksgiving falling from their lips even after sleep had shut their eyes.

The truth would come out later—after one or more had found work through the Labor Exchange—that a tab had been running from the first sip of grog, through every meal of broth and hard bread, to the room they shared with as many as twenty others. By the time the rent was paid and food bought, there was nothing left for next week's rent and into debt they went once more, unable to square up and get out. Only then would they realize they'd merely traded one cheating landlord in Ireland for another in America. If Grace disappeared into the maze of tenements, it would be nearly impossible to find her. A man could walk the city streets for weeks without seeing the same face twice. He could only hope she would check the notice board in front of the Labor Exchange—he left his name and address there every day, repasting it over the others that had erased yesterday's desperate notes.

Scanning the passenger lists was an exercise in turmoil—as much as he longed to find her name, he did not want to find it crossed out. And there were so many of those. He could not bear to think that she and Mary Kate had not survived the voyage—even worse, that Mary Kate had been left to fend for herself with Grace dead. It would be terrible for the child; he'd seen the bodies of mothers sewn into sailcloth and dropped overboard or, if no cloth remained or the crew was too busy, dropped without even this last shred of dignity, watched as the body bobbed in the wake, food for sharks and whatever else lurked in the deep sea.

It was the horror of his own crossing that fed these nightmares, the reason he'd insisted she sail on an American ship with an American captain. The Americans were rough, but their reputation for cruelty was nothing compared to the English—the crews out of Liverpool were, by all accounts, the worst.

When he heard the rude bark of a Liverpool crew, it still gripped his belly like an iron hand, sent his mind screaming back to his own place in the dark hold, where his passage had bought him not the space of one six-by-six bunk as advertised, but a quarter of that space, the bunk shared with a man, his wife, and their child. He never slept. No liquor was allowed, but the captain himself sold spirits once a week to any who could pay, and Sean's bunkmate was a drunk who thought nothing of taking his wife despite close quarters and her helpless protests. Sean had turned his back to block the sound of her defeat—and the sound of the sharp slaps and vicious curses earned by their son, who tried in vain to push his father off his mother. Sean had liked the boy and, on days the captain sold his grog, sat with him on the stairs, telling stories of Irish kings until the only sound below was that of heavy snores.

The mother died when illness broke out, and it had been Sean who stood with his hand on the boy's shoulder as they dropped her body into the sea. Then the boy had sickened, and Sean's efforts to get medicine had proved futile; the ship's doctor sold instead of dispensed.

The water had been stale, tinged by the wine or salted meat previously stored in the barrels; the meat was rancid and so salty that passengers had to choose between drinking their water or rinsing their food; the biscuit was inedible. So it was no surprise to Sean, really, when the boy simply gave up and died, his body barely rippling the sea before it disappeared.

Terrified that he might not survive this voyage, Sean had hidden on deck to avoid the rank air below. When discovered, he'd been beaten with crown crackers and steel knuckles, but did not dare complain, having once witnessed the consequence of such action: an older fellow who'd threatened to report the crew if more water was not doled out had been knocked down with belaying pins and buckets, tied to the mainmast, and shaved with a rough razor before his cheeks and neck were coated with hot tar. The man had howled for hours as the crew spat grog in his face.

Sean had decided then to endure and stay alive, and in the end, he jumped ship when the captain threatened to skip the inconvenience of Staten Island by simply unloading all visibly sick and injured passengers on another boat headed for Grosse Isle, farther north in Canada; he had no intention of posting the two-thousand-dollar bond required for each passenger too ill to disembark in Manhattan. Later, Sean learned that captains frequently sailed back down the coast and dumped the ill in New Jersey, leaving them to walk back up to the city, but on that night he had no confidence that he was not bound for Canada.

He escaped as she lay anchored in the harbor, the water so icy it stopped his breath, and he'd grabbed the first thing that floated past—a log come untied from the boom—to keep himself from drowning. The tide brought him closer to shore, but he knew he'd not have the strength to swim in and the sea would be his grave after all. But as he prayed, he was spotted by a band of angels disguised as drunken American sailors, who rowed out to him, hauled him into their skiff, and good-naturedly slapped him on the back as he coughed up ice water. They took him to shore and dried him off, commiserating that there was nothing worse than bastard Liverpool tars, then filled him with whiskey and sent a runner to find one Dugan Ogue, who'd come right away in the dead of night to fetch the boy, asking was it so bad in Ireland that he'd had to swim all the way here, then?

Sean shook his head, and tossed back the whiskey.

"Here 'tis." Ogue returned to his place behind the bar, holding out a battered envelope, the ink smeared from dampness.

Sean stared at the handwriting, and his mind went blank.

"From home, looks like." Ogue pushed it across the bar. "News, maybe, about your one."

Sean looked up, suddenly afraid of what that news might be. Tentatively, he took the packet and tore open one end, seeing by the handwriting that it contained two letters in different hands.

"This one's from William," he said hoarsely, scanning the page. All color drained from his face.

Ogue immediately refilled his glass, then moved respectfully away.

The letter began with no formality:

O'Malley,
  Terrible news—McDonagh is dead. He was imprisoned in Dublin. Reports say fever, but we cannot know for sure as so many have died and his body thrown into the pit with

theirs. A prison priest confirmed it was him and that he had suffered torture but gave them nothing. He was a brave man, a spiritual man, and I have no doubt he faced death with courage. This has been a devastating blow. The whole country mourns him and I feared they would abandon any last shreds of hope, but they have rallied stronger than ever in his name, even in the midst of the terrible suffering which surrounds us still. Above one hundred a day are removed dead from the workhouses and thrown with no ceremony into the pits, a dusting of lime their only shroud. Fever is rampant among us and orphans made every hour. The starving continues. I thank God you are well out of it for entire villages in the countryside now lie quiet as the grave they have become.

I made haste to locate your sister, but found her not in time for Captain Applegate. She and her daughter sail in one week's time out of Liverpool on the American packet, Eliza J, captained by P. Reinders, American. She has borne McDonagh's son and was hard pressed to leave him, but fear of imprisonment and the loss of both children convinced her at last; the infant is with your father at Cork. Grace is wanted for the murder of a guard and dares not travel openly. Julia will accompany them as far as Liverpool and see them safely on. I send this out directly and with all good weather it should reach you before they do.

We Irish have always lifted high our heroes, and McDonagh's life is well sung by poets and balladeers. We are terribly crippled by all that besets Ireland, my friend, and my own trials are great, but the longing for freedom has not ebbed and I know we shall rise up stronger than ever. Redouble your efforts in his name. I await news.

It was signed in Smith O'Brien's neat hand, followed by a postscript.

This came today from Alroy. I send it on at his request.

Sean set William's letter down and picked up Abban's, but he could not focus, because his vision was blurred. He remembered the first time he'd laid eyes on Abban Alroy outside the small cabin in Macroom, how he'd convinced the man to join the cause; Morgan had needed someone he could trust, and Abban—his family lost to the hunger—became McDonagh's right-hand man. The two of them had become a force to be reckoned with. Abban was devoted to Morgan; they'd broken Sean out of jail and gotten him on the ship to America—that was the last time he'd seen them. Hand trembling, he picked up his glass and emptied it in one long, burning gulp, blinking hard to clear his vision.

Abban's letter was crumpled as if carried in many pockets before reaching William, the writing full of words hurriedly spelled and crossed out, the smudged and blotted ink of a barely literate warrior poet. At the very first word, he heard Abban's thick Connemara accent.

Sean, my brother,

Our one was taken in a raid and I not there to save him, tho you know I would have torn them all apart with my bare hands if given half a chance. I learnt of his dying by letter in his own hand, meant for Grace, and that she was with Barbara, but I could not take it to her myself as my foot was come off, the leg to follow. She's ever on my mind as the letter said she carried his child and we both know how he loved her. So, I come to Cork in the back of a cart but have missed her by the day for she's gone to Liverpool and then to you, Barbara says. Lord knows I'd go on if I could, but I'll stay here til I'm healed, looking after your da and the wee boy. It helps my heart to know he made Grace his wife and got this child—it's all he ever wanted in the world. Remember the night we come for you, you cursing the guards so it rang out the walls and Morgan laughing so hard he could barely think how to save your scrawny hide? He loved you like his own, he did. Now I'll do that for him. I'm sorry for us all.

Abban

This was the letter Sean crumpled to his chest as he let out a wounded roar. The others in the room fell instantly silent, staring at the gimpy lad who often sat at a back table, scheming with the mighty men. They knew he was here to fight for Ireland—him with his short leg and twisted arm, keen mind and quick tongue—and they looked out for him as best they could, but hearing the depth of that pain they knew there was nothing for it but to sit still. For in that roar was the sound of a man's heart ripping in two, the sound of a man's mind yearning to come apart in order to forget what he now must know forever, the sound of a loss so great that it would never be fully overcome, and now the man was crippled in more than just his body. They watched as Ogue come around the great bar to speak low to him, look at the letters laid out before him, then shelter him in his mighty arms, helping him across the floor and up the back stairs to the rooms above. They waited in silence, no one coming or going, lifting their glass nor speaking a word, until Ogue come back and told them the terrible black news that McDonagh was dead in Ireland. They sat, staring at his face as if the understanding of it was somewhere in the big man's eyes. He shook his head—that was all. Then he poured whiskey into Sean's glass, still on the bar, and lifted it high before him.

The men rose as one body, chairs and stools scraping the wooden floor, snatching off their caps, pulling themselves up tall and proud.

"Let us drink to him now," Ogue called.

"McDonagh!" the men roared, glasses thrust fiercely in the air.

"And to Ireland," came a lone voice from the back, and fifty pairs of eyes filled with the misty vision of home.

They drank their drinks quietly then—for Irishmen—clasping hands soberly with one another and telling stories of the Great One himself, though most had never met him, but sure they knew someone who had. His raids, his courage and compassion, his undying love for Ireland and for a beautiful Irish girl whose heart was as great as his own—the legends grew as hours passed and word spread through the neighborhoods, from the Fourth Ward into the Sixth, up Baxter Street and down Mulberry. The Irish emerged from dark cellars and freezing attics, filthy alleyways and twisted paths, drunk and sober both, filling the windows and doors of crowded tenements, spilling out onto the sidewalks, where they were swept up by the silent mob making its way down the long blocks to hear the truth from the big man himself—the unwonted truth, the terrible truth, the heartbreaking truth that Morgan McDonagh, the Great One, was lost to them all.

Nine

AFTER two weeks of freezing drizzle and stinging squalls, there came a morning when the clouds lifted and the sun shone brittle and hard, blinking off whitecaps that blinded any who dared to peer over the ship's rail. Sheltered from the biting December wind, Grace and Mary Kate ate some of the breakfast they had collected from the cook at dawn and then sat contentedly between two large coils of rope, faces tipped up to catch the light.

"Good morning, Missus . . . Donnelly. Enjoying the day?"

Grace opened her eyes and blinked away the sunspots.

"Aye, Captain Reinders, we are indeed. The light's a blessing after the dark days below."

"And how goes it in the hold?" he asked, realizing he'd not seen much of her since they set sail.

"Fine, thank you. Biscuit?" She offered him a piece.

"I ate hours ago."

"Ah, well, I've little doubt of that. Tell me, Captain," she asked, playfully, "do you ever sleep a'tall? I can't think of a time you've not been up here on this deck."

"Well, I . . . that is to say . . . " he stammered, caught off guard by her familiarity. "A good captain must keep an eye on every watch, so I sleep a few hours at a time, then get up and see to . . . things."

He'd noticed that the Irish did not exactly stand on formality; they plunged right in with the most intimate questions about a man's family and private thoughts. In fact, there seemed to be little they did not discuss and often with a great deal of mirth, which was doubly disconcerting for a man such as himself. Certainly, he was not going to review his sleeping habits with this young woman and her remarkable eyes. A captain should always appear interested while remaining detached— best not to get drawn in. He decided to change the subject.

"Missus Donnelly, why aren't you taking meals in the saloon with the other first-class passengers? Isn't the food better there?"

"Oh, aye, Captain, 'tis, and I'm grateful." She glanced down at the leftover biscuit, cheese, boiled bacon, and apple in her lap. "I prefer to eat in the open air, is all, and I hope it's no trouble to you, then?"

He eyed the little girl, who had stopped chewing, though her cheeks were stuffed full of food.

"No." He frowned. "It's no trouble to me. But we've had mostly rain the past two weeks. Don't tell me you sit up here in the rain."

Mary Kathleen, her eyes never leaving his, shook her head.

"We take our share below," Grace admitted.

"But why not eat in the saloon? It's pleasant enough, isn't it?"

Again Mary Kate shook her head.

He looked at her, surprised. "No?"

Grace bit her lip. "It's mostly English you got there, Captain," she explained, apologetically. "And you know they don't look upon us so well, especially those come up each day, smelling like . . . the hold."

"I'm very sorry to hear that." He frowned. "You know, I could eat in the saloon instead of my cabin."

"Ah, no, Captain." Grace shook her head. "Don't put yourself out. All those sour faces are bound to spoil *your* appetite, as well, and we can't have that now, can we? Besides," she said,

"Mary Kate and I are more than content, and your cook has been ever so kind in handing us our food off his kitchen each day."

"Galley," Reinders corrected absentmindedly. "A ship's kitchen is called the galley. But Missus Donnelly, you're entitled to all privileges of first class."

"And is not one of those being able to eat where I like?" she asked.

He nodded reluctantly.

"Well, then, Mary Kate and I choose to take our meals down below or out here in God's fresh air. Thank you very much for your concern, Captain, but don't trouble yourself over it."

"Well, I don't like it," he said, stubbornly. "And I'm not sure I should let those upper-crust snobs get away with it. But if this is the way you want it . . ."

" 'Tis," she said firmly.

"All right." He turned to go, then hesitated. "If I may say so, Missus Donnelly, you are certainly a very gracious person."

"Ah, no, Captain, just thankful." She looked him in the eye. "On this ship, we have food every day. Why should I care where we eat it?"

He had no reply for that, simply nodded and then took his leave.

"You can swallow what you've got in your mouth now, girl," Grace said softly. "There's no reason to be afraid. He's built like your da, but a different kind of man altogether."

Mary Kate did as she was told, then drank a cup of water, sitting practically on top of her mother as she always did. Grace pushed the last bite of bacon into the child's mouth, then brushed the crumbs from both their skirts.

"Shall we go find Missus Kelley, then? You can play with Siobahn and Liam while she and I clean the clothes."

Mary Kate nodded and Grace pulled her up, leading her by the hand across the deck to the open hatch. Down below, the air was noticeably more rank, even with the wind sweeping through. Some passengers still lay abed, or had gone back to bed, sick or uneasy with the journey, though the worst of the seasickness appeared to be over. Others, having finished their gruel or biscuit, were straightening beds and organizing belongings, shaking out clothing and blankets if they had them.

Grace found Alice sitting on the edge of her bunk, hands in her lap, staring blankly. Siobahn lay next to her.

"Alice?" Grace leaned down. "All right, then? Want to come up and take the air awhile?"

Alice's eyes cleared momentarily, then filled again with anxiety. "'Tis Siobahn," she whispered. "She tossed about all night."

Grace placed her hand on the girl's forehead. Not hot, but very warm; cheeks, as well, and her eyes—when she opened them—were glassy. The child had been unwell since she boarded, and Grace had noted her steady decline with growing alarm; she was plagued by random fevers, each leaving her more listless than before. This morning, her lips were dry and cracked.

"Has she had any water yet?"

Alice shook her head.

"Go on up, then, and get in line. I've some here, but she'll want more." Grace took the woman's hands and pulled her up. "Go on now," she admonished. "I'll sit with her. Go up into the air. 'Tis a fine morning and you'll feel better for it. Where's Liam, then?"

"Here." The boy's head popped out from the upper bunk.

"Come down from there at once, Liam Kelley," Grace scolded. "The owner of that bed eats naughty boys for his breakfast!"

Liam swung himself over and landed gracefully beside her; he was lithe and full of spirit, not nearly as sullen as she'd taken him for at first, and Grace had grown very fond of him.

"I've a job for you." She handed him his cap. "Take your mam up and wait with her in the water line. 'Tis lovely up there. I've just come back. Go on now, off with you both!"

He grabbed his mother's hand and towed her along, grinning back over his shoulder before they disappeared up the stairs.

Mary Kate remained by Grace's side, a firm grip on her mother's skirt. "Is she sick?"

"Aye." Grace met her daughter's eyes; the child was old beyond three years, and it was best to tell her the truth. "She has a fever."

"He's sick." Mary Kate pointed out a man lying on his bunk across the aisle. "And her." She pointed to another figure rolled on her side. "Them, as well." This last a family of four, all lying listlessly.

Grace looked from them to her daughter and back again. The child was right. These people lay too still, eyes staring, breathing quick and shallow. She felt Siobahn's forehead again. Had it grown warmer in the last few minutes?

"Ship fever, is all," she said, as much to reassure herself as Mary Kate. "Siobahn needs fresh air, water, a little broth if we can cook it." She bit her lip, thinking. "Come on, girl." She scooped up Siobahn, blanket and all. "Into the light with you now."

Mary Kate led the way, Grace right behind. Feeling Siobahn's arms go feebly around her neck, Grace smiled down into the little face, the heat of the child seeping through the rough blanket. Up on deck, they picked their way carefully back to the rope coils, which allowed full sun but sheltered them all from the biting gusts of wind.

"Sit here, Mary Kate, by Siobahn." She settled the girls into a space in front of a large wooden crate. "I'll find Alice and Liam, and see about getting up a broth."

Grace found Alice straightaway, nearly to the front of the line, and told her where the girls were. Liam begged to come when she said she was off to the kitchen—the galley, she corrected herself—and Alice was glad to let him go. He was a boy who insisted upon filling every moment of his life, who bristled with a kind of nervous energy even when lying still, perhaps in answer to living among the dead for so long, his mother supposed; but oh, he did wear on her.

He frisked along behind Grace, following her across the deck to the stair that led to the cook's galley when, unexpectedly, she veered off and approached the captain, who stood with a crewman at the wheel.

"Captain Reinders," she said, her voice lost in the sound of wet, slapping sails. "Captain!"

Startled, he turned. "Missus Donnelly!"

"This is Liam Kelley, Captain. I'm sure you've seen him scampering all over your boat like a wee squirrel, so I wanted you to know his name in case he gets himself into trouble."

Reinders regarded the young man seriously. "Like the *Eliza J,* do you, son?"

Liam's eyes went wide. "Oh, aye, Captain. She's a beauty, she is! And so fast! We must be nearly there, the way she flies over the sea. What a boat!"

The corners of Reinders' mouth twitched. "Ship," he corrected. "And we've still got a lot of sailing ahead of us. Hey!" He narrowed his eyes and leaned down. "You're not the boy my men shouted down out of the rigging yesterday, are you?"

Liam's shoulders slumped and he hung his head. "Aye, Captain." He peeked up meekly, eyes beseeching. "But I had a notion to see the view from way up there." He pointed to the crow's nest. "And my feet just moved on their own. I could do nothing to stop them!" He glared at the treacherous feet, then lifted his eyes again in wonder to the place high up the mast above the straining sails. "What do they see from up there, do you suppose, Captain? Do they see all round the world, from one side to the other?"

Grace and the captain exchanged a glance over the boy's head.

"Mostly, they see water," Reinders said, trying to remain serious despite Liam's infectious enthusiasm. "Water and more water."

"Oh." The boy's face fell.

"But sometimes they spy other ships on the horizon," the captain added. "Or schools of shark. Sometimes whales."

"Whales!"

"Around here we watch mainly for icebergs."

"Icebergs! I've never seen an iceberg! Are they grand, then?"

"Grand and deadly," Reinders cautioned. "They lie waiting like crystal castles. Seamen used to think they were floating islands of ice, and came in close with their ships, lured by the brilliance . . . but they're *not* islands," he said. "What you and I see is only the tip—they go deep, the icebergs, down to the very bottom of the sea. And just beneath the surface, they spread a skirt of jagged edges that can scrape the bottom off the sturdiest of ships or punch a hole right through her side. We stay well away from icebergs on this ship."

"Have you enough men looking out then, do you think?" Liam glanced around, anxiously.

"I do," Reinders assured him. "We'll be past them soon, and then it will be land the look spies out."

"Will they call us, Captain? When they see America?"

"Sure. But do you see that fella over there?" Reinders pointed to the bow, where an old man gripped the rail, jacket buttoned up tightly to his neck, hat tied down under his chin with a hank of rope.

Liam nodded.

"My money's on him to see it first." The captain winked. "He took up that place the first day we sailed, and except for a few hours' sleep each night, he stands there in all weather, never taking his eyes off the horizon. I tied him to that rail myself in the first storm, when I realized he'd only sneak back if I sent him below. He says he's got no family left in Ireland and no one waiting in America. What he thinks he's going to see, I can't begin to guess."

"I can," Grace offered. "It's his last hope. He thinks he's sailing to Tir nan Og—Land of the Young. A new life."

Reinders kept his eyes on her face for a moment, then looked back to where the old man stood. "Land of the Young," he repeated thoughtfully. "He's going to be sadly disappointed when we get there."

"Ah, no, Captain." Grace laughed. "Won't any of us be sad about that!"

"I will!" Liam insisted loudly. "I love this boat!"

"Ship, boy! Ship!" Reinders' voice was stern, but he liked the lad, liked his fire. "Tell you what, Master Kelley. You stay out of the rigging and off the deck in foul weather, and I'll give you a tour of the whole ship myself before we land—agreed?" He put out his hand.

"Oh, aye, Captain! Aye!" Liam pumped the hand up and down with both of his.

"And . . . ?" Grace prompted.

"Thank you, sir! Thank you very, very much, sir!"

"You're very welcome, and now if you'll excuse me, I must make sure we're headed for North America, not South."

Grace and Liam watched him stride away, Grace noting the firm set of his cap and the clean line of his jacket—a confident man.

"He's a fine one then, isn't he, missus?" Liam's eyes shone with admiration.

"Aye," she agreed. "But mind what he told you now—don't be getting in everyone's way, roaming like you do all over the boat."

"Ship," he corrected automatically, and she laughed.

The cook, a grizzled old sailor with milky eyes, was in a fairly good mood and produced a beef bone with shreds of meat still clinging to it. Grace thanked him gratefully as she did every morning after receiving her breakfast, making sure to stay on the good side of the one in charge of the food.

"Run down and fetch your mammie's pot," she ordered Liam. "I'll see to the girls and then we'll get a place at the fire to make Siobahn a good broth."

"Is she quite sick, then?" Liam asked. "She was always sick at home, and some days she never did get out of bed, mostly when there was nothing for it. No dinner, I mean. . . ." His voice trailed off.

"I know it's been hard for you." Grace put her hand on his head. "That's why you're going to a new life. And she'll be fine, not to worry." She ruffled his thick, tangled hair, then gave him a gentle swat on the bottom. "Run on, now, and find that pot."

She watched him make his way nimbly through the knots of

passengers who had come up on deck, and thought again what
a good boy he was. He reminded her of young Nolan Sullivan,
son of the housekeepers at Donnelly House; she pushed the
thought quickly away as she did any thoughts of the past these
days. Morgan's letter never left the inside of her vest and she
brought her hand up to press against it nearly every hour of the
waking day and many times in the night, but to dwell on him—
the loss of him—or on their child, who lay behind, would be to
invite a despair so deep that she might never rise from it again.
And so she kept busy.

She spied Alice's green shawl at the head of the line; reassured that they'd get water, Grace started back to the girls.
Rounding the corner, she saw a man bent over them, shaking his
fist in their faces—Mary Kate's eyes were wide, her mouth a
frightened O, but her arm was around the older girl's shoulders.

"What's going on here?"

Boardham turned around, eyes squinting in the sun that
shone over Grace's shoulder. "You can't just leave your brats
anywhere you like," he reprimanded. "They gets in the way of
the crew."

"I'm here now." Grace forced herself to be polite, not wanting to tangle with him. "You needn't worry yourself further."

He scowled. "If there's foul weather, the crew'll be needing
at these ropes. The brats is in the way. Get 'em out of here, I'm
telling you."

Grace glanced up at the sky. "We'll only be out a while
longer."

He took a step closer and now the sun was not directly in his
eyes. "I know you," he growled. "Irish trying to pass as decent
folk. Got sent down though, didn't you? To the hold. Where you
belong."

"I remember you, as well, Mister Boardham," she answered quietly. "Will you leave us in peace now, or will I call
the captain?"

Boardham's mean little eyes narrowed even more. "You
might have him fooled, but not me," he hissed. "Americans like
him don't understand you dirty Papists, sneaking bastard

Irish—but I do." Spittle formed at the corner of his mouth. "You can't get around me."

Grace's eyes flicked to the faces of the children; he followed her glance and the little girls drew back even further into the ropes. He glared at them, but then suddenly he smiled.

"She's sick, that one." He tipped his head in Siobahn's direction. "Fever, I can tell. She'll infect the crew. Fever stays below—that's captain's orders, and I'm only carrying them out." The grin spread. "Take her below and keep her below till she gets well . . . or till she dies." He spat the last word.

Grace stared at him, aghast, and he held up a hand to signal the end of their discourse.

"Got other duties to perform," he said smugly, "now I've checked the deck for vermin." He laughed hard at his own joke, then turned his back and left.

"Hush now, girls," Grace soothed, taking them both in her arms. "Don't let a great eejit like that ever see you cry—a man who threatens children is no man a'tall. Here's your mam coming now, Siobahn. Wipe your tears and don't let her know we've had trouble."

Alice set down the pail of water and pushed back her shawl, eyeing her daughter with surprise. "She looks better, she does. Color's back and all. You were right about the air. Just needed a change, I expect."

"I got this from the cook." Grace held up the beef bone. "And Liam's gone to fetch your pot."

"Ah, bless you, Grace." Alice picked up Siobahn's hand and caressed it. "Dear Mother of God and all the Saints, Heaven knows what we'd've done without you on this boat."

"*Ship*," Liam corrected, handing her the pot. "It's a *ship*."

Ten

BARBARA McDonagh's eyes were gritty with weariness, bruised from her night of watching over the fevered sleep of others. Her arms, resting on the desk in her study, felt stiff and heavy, and she listened to the sounds of the waking convent as if from far away. She knew she had entered that state of remove that veils the deeply tired, but that it would be pierced by a strong cup of tea and her acceptance that day had indeed come again. She pinched the bridge of her nose and blinked her dry eyes until a bit of moisture came forth to bathe each one, small relief for the desert they'd become.

Outside the study, a squalling wind continued to rattle the ill-fitting windowpanes, some of which had been broken in earlier storms and patched with whatever materials were at hand. Every crack and crevice that remained was an invitation to the biting wind, and the study was cold despite a brick of turf burning low in the grate; she was reluctant to add another—the plentiful pile cut early in summer had rapidly diminished with keeping the children's dormitory heated.

Thank God Abban had arrived when he did. Even with one leg gone, he hobbled about with his crutch, patching walls, mending windows, stopping leaks, and now going into the wood for fuel. The lash of winter storms had only just begun, and she had not known how they would keep warm through the long, dark months. None of the three sisters left were strong enough to drive the cart to the wood, cut down a tree, strip the limbs, cord, stack and load it, then drive it home, and she dared not leave them alone now their dear Mother herself had died. But God had provided Abban, and Abban had provided hope in the form of determined optimism.

She turned and looked out the small window on the bay side. Great slamming sheets of rain the night before had given way to spatters come only now and then in brief gusts against the glass. She could see that the clouds were higher in the sky and rode more lightly on the wind; soon the storm would pass and she'd go out with Abban to survey the damage. But first she'd go up to the little room on the third floor and check on her tiny nephew, who'd been frightened by the storm and made restless all night long. She'd gone in several times to quiet and rock him so that Patrick—who kept the baby in his own room—might get some rest. He'd been wakeful, and together they'd marked the hours of the long night; the words of their only conversation still echoed in her thoughts.

She pressed fingertips to eyelids and rubbed gently, until a solid rap on the door caused her to look up.

"I brung you a cup a tea, Sister."

Abban came into the room awkwardly, the saucer in one hand, his crutch in the other. He set it down on Barbara's desk, then fished a hard roll wrapped in a cloth out of his pocket.

"Thank you, Abban." Barbara took the tea gratefully and inhaled its fragrance, her stiff fingers warmed by the pottery, her face by the steam. "And thank God for Julia Martin."

Julia had sent a box of supplies that included the luxurious black tea, and Barbara had allotted each adult in the house one strong cup each morning, a welcome change from the hot water or weak teas they'd been brewing from dried berries and herbs.

"Eat your roll now, for I know you've not broken your fast yet this morning." Abban peeled away the cloth and waved it temptingly. " 'Tis a lovely roll, this—not two days old and still easy on the gums." When she failed to laugh, he took a closer look at her. "You look terrible worn-out, Sister. Rough night?"

"No more than usual." Barbara stifled a yawn. "More children came in the wee hours. True orphans in the storm, this lot."

"Oh, aye." Abban glanced out the window. "I saw them when they come for their oats—two wee girls and a boy. How come they, then?"

"An older brother. Their mam died giving birth—baby, as well, I suppose, though he didn't say. Their da brought them to the city with an eye on going out to Canada, but the soup kitchens along the way were Protestant and . . ." She shrugged helplessly.

"He wouldn't give up the faith." Abban finished the sentence. "Ah, God love him, the poor sot."

"Fell down in the road, made the boy swear to deliver them safely to us—not the workhouse, nor to any Protestants—and then he gave a great gasp and died." She sighed. "How the boy managed to get them all here, I can only guess. The little ones are still shocked out of their speech, and the boy wouldn't say more, just that here they were and thanks very much for taking them in."

"Would he not stay himself, then?"

Barbara shook her head. "Though I argued with him for over an hour. Can't have been more than ten, but determined to make his own way. Going across, he said—'tis what his da wanted and he'd promised, you see. He'll send for themselves once he's arrived and got himself a good job and big house." She smiled ruefully. "He let me put a little food in his pocket and he didn't say no to a blanket, God bless him."

"Poor boyo," Abban said. "We'll never hear from him again."

"We might," Barbara insisted. "Where's your faith, man?"

"I've plenty of that, Sister, but it's not blind. 'Tis a risky business making the crossing, let alone a small boy on his own with just a roll in his pocket and one blanket to keep him warm. Hard enough for grown men and women to survive a winter crossing."

"Don't remind me." Barbara frowned.

Abban thumped himself in the head. "Ah, what a daft eejit I am. Themselves will make it—I'm telling you that, and I know it in my heart."

"Do you, Abban?"

"Aye," he said firmly. "The Lord has too much work for our one to do, to let her go after all this."

Barbara's eyes could not mask her doubt.

"Where's your faith, girl?" he teased.

"It's in my other pocket," she said, guiltily. "I'll fetch it right after breakfast."

"You do that," he minded. "And keep it on you from now on. How's himself holding up?" He jerked a thumb at the ceiling.

"All right," she said, picturing Patrick sitting up in his little room with the baby in his arms. "God's working in him, as well, and it's not easy for him."

"He's a proud man," Abban allowed.

Barbara nodded. "We talked last night. He's been so worried about her, but I think he's coming into some peace about it now."

"Good. Worry'll kill a man slower than a bullet, but just as dead."

She looked at him. "Where in the world do you get those things?"

He grinned sheepishly. "Ah, well, I'm just an old farmer turned soldier turned convent handyman, you know. What wisdom I've got's a mess of this and that."

She smiled then, and he smiled even more to see it.

"Eat your roll now, and I'll go see to that broken glass in the kitchen." He pulled the crutch up under his arm and headed for the door.

"Thank you, Abban," she said quietly. "For everything."

"You're harboring a criminal here, Sister," he reminded her over his shoulder. "So let's just call it even."

"Done," she agreed, "though I'm getting the better part of the deal."

He threw his head back and laughed, and when the sound of

it had faded Barbara turned her attention to her meager meal, softening the roll over the fading steam of her tea. She savored each bite and, when done, moistened her fingertip to pick up the crumbs that had fallen, touching them delicately to her tongue for their last mite of nourishment.

Hunger was a steady companion, but her stomach had ceased its fiercest protests months ago as her body learned to function with less. She was grateful to be able to count upon some measure of food every day, even if only stale bread and tea, weak broth, a bit of dried fish or oats—that was bounty to most of the people in her land and she knew it. It was bounty to her, as well; she and Morgan, Aislinn, and the little girls having grown up where potatoes and buttermilk made the meal.

Each day, the food stretched to whoever was housed with them, and while the children weren't robust and thriving, they weren't dying in droves, as in the workhouses, hospitals, and fever tents. They were weak, true enough, and her heart ached at the sight of them sitting so still throughout each day, conserving their little bit of strength, moving slowly, never laughing, rarely crying—too weak even for the energy to muster grief. Almost any illness carried them off; so she spent time with them daily, watching for signs of cough or fever, making sure to quarantine them immediately until they were well or—most often—their pitiful life here had ended. She hated that, the shutting them out, especially when they had brothers and sisters, but she saw no other way.

And she knew Sister George would bathe them in love and comfort until it was over, for it was always Sister George who went into quarantine with the sick and who remained to attend them. She spent more days in that room than out of it, but never did her devotion to the children waver, nor her conviction that this was her place. Once, Barbara had ordered her to come away and rest for a day or two while others took over, but Sister George had said firmly and calmly that her orders came directly from Jesus Christ Himself. Hadn't He told her that she was needed to ease the passing of these children from this world into the next, and hadn't He given her the strong health and heart to do it? Aye—she'd answered herself—He had, and here she'd stay until He'd other work for her to do. Barbara never argued with her again about it, just added her to the growing list of those for whom she was thankful.

She could not, however, let go of her worry over the baby. Even though he nursed regularly at the full breast of Missus Keavy—the farm woman who'd lost her own infant within days of coming here—he was still thin and listless, his mewling pitiful to all who heard. Looking upon his face brought no reassurance as his eyes remained milky clouds, pale blue windows that let in no light; Barbara feared he was blind.

Patrick spoke little, sitting by the window in his room, holding and rocking the tiny thing, staring out over the tops of the bare, wind-stripped branches down the hill to the bay as if his watchful guard would bring news of Grace to him all the sooner.

"They're in the middle of the ocean now," he'd said last night when she'd slipped in to check on the boy. "Nobody knows where."

Startled by his voice, she'd lifted the lantern higher and there he lay, propped up on his elbow, eyes as tired as her own, face haggard with the burden of helplessness and despair.

"God does," she'd whispered, then set the light down on the small table near the door so that she might pick up the whimpering baby; he'd been dry, so she'd settled herself into the chair to rock him. "Can you not sleep, then, Patrick?"

He'd hesitated a moment, then spoke quietly. "I'm afraid of the dreams that come."

"Tell me, if it'll ease your mind."

Again, he'd hesitated, but the burden of the dreams was too great. "In one, she's lying upon a bed with Mary Kate beside. I wait for them to move, but they never do. I cannot see if they're asleep or . . ." He'd stopped and taken a deep breath. "In another, Mary Kate is eating bread and jam with a strange woman—she looks kindly, but 'tisn't a place for Mary Kate and I call to her from outside the window but she can't hear me. It's snowing, the glass fogs, and she disappears." He'd shaken his head, frowning. "Then I see Grace in a place full of shadows

where men are evil—a place where no one will ever find her—
and I wake up sure that death has come, so tight is my heart."

"Patrick . . ."

"Tonight," he'd rushed on, agitated. "Tonight, I saw her on
the boat, deep down in a dark place. There was a storm, Barbara, a terrible storm, waves as high as the mast, the sky black
and cut with lightning, men screaming and all those people
trapped in that pit below." His voice caught in his throat and he
stopped. "It's going to be the death of me, Barbara, these
dreams."

"You must have faith," she'd told him, the words sounding
small even to her.

"I've never had it. And I don't know how to find it now. I'm
sorry, Barbara—you a daughter of the Church and all—but
that's the truth of it. She's the one had all the faith. Just like her
mother before her."

"She's in God's hands, then."

"I never knew what that meant," he'd confessed. "It can't
mean He'll keep her safe, for aren't all the poor bastards out
there in His hands and just look at them—dying for want of a
potato and shelter at night."

"You're right," she'd admitted. "It doesn't mean He'll save
her, though He can and He does every day. How many times
are our lives spared before we finally die—hundreds? Thousands? Living through any day a'tall is miracle enough." She'd
felt herself a witness to this many times over, but how to explain
it? "What I believe, Patrick—and it's only me, mind you—is that
to be in His hands means He'll never abandon us, that He's at
our side through all the trials of our living. He sees us, knows
our pain and weeps for us, carries us in His own hands even as
we go to our death so that we might not be afraid, so that we
might meet any end with dignity."

"Are these dreams from God, then? Is He telling me the way
of it?"

"I don't know," she'd answered. "Dreams are a way of seeing,
true enough, and the Bible's full of dreams. But sure and the
devil himself knows how to play our simple minds and uses our

weaknesses to his own end, for won't he tell you a thousand truths to get you to believe the one great lie that God is not in charge? It may be God's voice reaching out to you, or it may be the Devil pretending to be God—the answer lies in the condition of your own soul."

Outside, the wind had raged as if in response—snapping branches, smashing windows, wreaking havoc across the already ravaged land.

"The condition of my soul," he'd said, his anguish apparent, "is nothing if not a raging battle between begging Him to keep her safe and cursing Him for what's happened to us. I can't bear that she's out there alone, at the mercy of cruel men, going to a strange land where her brother may or may not be." He'd gripped his forehead as if taken with a terrible pain. "I should never have let her go off alone. I'm her father for pity's sake, and 'tis my duty to protect her, for isn't her life worth a thousand of my own?"

"You'd die for her, then? Is that what you're saying?"

"In a heartbeat."

"If you've the courage to die for her, Patrick, can you not find the courage to live for her, as well?"

His eyes had sought hers.

"What she needs from you is the courage to fight despair, to battle hopelessness and worry the many months ahead, for won't it be spring or even summer before we know what's become of them? Do you have the courage to go on living for your child, and for the child of your child—this poor wee baby boy who has no one but us? Do you now, Patrick?" she'd demanded, suddenly angry. "Because I tell you, I will not write to her after she's survived a great voyage across a treacherous sea only to tell her that her father's dead of foolish dreams and the baby as well because I hadn't the strength of two people to care for him. I won't do it, Patrick! I tell you, I will not."

He'd raised his head then, chin jutting, back as straight as a younger man's, shoulders no longer hunched around a broken heart, and in that moment, Barbara remembered the fierce, proud man who was once Patrick O'Malley.

"You'll not have to write such a letter as that," he'd said then. "I've become old, true enough, mush and easy prey for bad dreams . . . but I'll not give in to them again, nor will I let myself be swayed from hope. You're right—'tis the Devil himself plants them there to weaken me, and I swear to you I'll fight him each night if that's the lay of it."

"Aye, Patrick. That *is* the lay of it."

"I've a great deal to learn, even at this late hour," he'd said, and his voice had been so tired. "Maybe that's why God has kept me here. For sure and I've been a trial to my wife and my children all my life, too proud to bend a knee before the Lord. I thought He'd give up and leave me in peace if I ignored Him long enough."

"He never gives up. I sometimes think He likes the stubborn ones best. Bit of a challenge, you know."

"I've been that, and more." He'd paused, considering. "We would've been lost without you here, Barbara, and that's the truth of it. I was wrong all those years ago when I frowned on my own Kathleen's friendship with your mam. She was a good woman, Mary was, and your da, as well. I was too harsh a judge when I had no right. I hope you can find it in your heart to forgive me."

She'd nodded immediately. "Mam was as good a woman as ever lived, but you and I both know himself was a rascally sort. He brought us ever more grief than comfort, and that's the truth of that. Morgan was the head of our family."

"Aye, and the very best of men."

She'd looked down at the baby sleeping in her arms, the weight of him nothing compared to the heaviness that still invaded her heart whenever she thought of her brother.

"He's asleep now." She'd risen and settled the baby gently in his cradle, then taken up the lantern. "Good night to you then, Patrick. Sleep well."

"God go with you, Barbara."

"He always does," she'd whispered before closing the door.

"You always do," she said to Him now, standing by the window in her study.

Bright morning sun flooded the yard, lit up the hills, and sparkled on the waves of the bay beyond, turning it into a moving body of light. They were out there somewhere, she thought, somewhere upon the vast, open sea, and there—on the knoll by the fence, facing the same way—was Abban on his only knee.

"We're all of us praying, Lord," she said aloud. "And I know You can hear us."

Eleven

SIOBAHN'S fever returned in the small hours of the morning, and there was no taking her up then. Not a single ray of weak December sun penetrated the low clouds, heavy as wet clay, clouds from which a thick, sleety rain had begun to fall, puddling icy slush on the deck. Rising at first light to take Mary Kate to the latrines, Grace watched others slip and slide, or lose their footing altogether as they navigated the treacherous deck on their way to fetch this day's water, or to relieve themselves of yesterday's. Only a few braved the terrible cold in an attempt to light the grates, so food for most was cold biscuit and hard cheese. Grace felt more guilty than usual about collecting her flask of hot tea, warm porridge, and salt pork from the cook. She did not allow these feelings to deter her, however, but quietly got her basket, slipped up the stairs, across the deck and to the door of the galley, where she covered the food with a cloth before retracing her steps.

Below again, she shared the meal with Mary Kate and Liam, and poured hot tea for Siobahn; Alice, she knew, would decline even a bite of Grace's rations, but would whisper her thanks for the feeding of her children, especially Liam, who ate anything and everything offered. The ship's rations for steerage were enough to sustain the body, Grace felt, especially starved bodies such as these, but there was nothing for the spirit. The regular food—dull though it was—had reawakened an appetite the existence of which many had forgotten, particularly the young. Mary Kate was eating more and more, the evidence in the way her face had begun to fill out; Liam, too, wolfed down his food, licking every morsel from his fingers, and while he never asked for more, his eyes swept the basket hungrily for crusts and rinds. Only Siobahn still nibbled and sipped, tiny portions placed on her tongue as if the weight of anything larger was simply too hard to consume.

"Her poor wee body's forgotten how to take its nourishment," Alice often lamented. "Not that we had ever so much in the way of a meal before the troubles," she'd confided once as she and Grace watched the two girls—Mary Kate ripping off great bites of bread with her little teeth, Siobahn picking at the edges of hers. "Our one's a drinking man—*was* a drinking man—afore he took the pledge and made for America. But many a time he drank up his own wages and most of mine, as well, and too often we were hard by."

Grace had taken Alice's hand, listening there in the gloomy hold.

" 'Twas a miracle, him taking the pledge and all, saving the drinking money for his passage. We were more peaceful with him gone," she'd admitted shyly. "But I missed him, true enough, and the worry's been terrible. I don't think he knew how bad it was or he'd've sent for us. I saved every penny, and one day I could see the choice was a few weeks' food out of it and then nothing, or passage to America. I'm sure we'll find him, I'm sure of it. . . ." she said, more to herself than to Grace. "I've sent ahead to the address, and there'll be others know how to find him."

Grace had agreed, but in her heart she had misgivings and vowed to keep the family with her until their future was more secure.

Alice herself was not faring well; she suffered aches of the stomach and head when the sea was rough, which was nearly always. Many had suffered seasickness at the start of the voyage, but this had seemed to ease a week into the trip. Not so for Alice.

In the evenings, though, spirits were lifted as they all gathered on their bunks to listen to the fiddlers play the old songs, sometimes singing along, the music a comfort to those who felt sick and afraid. And then, as they settled down to sleep, low voices told legends of kings and castles, and of battles fought over the land—always stories of the land, of estates handed down through family lines, divided and divided again until they were fields handed down from family to family, fields the English owned but that belonged truly to the Irish who worked them. They told tales of warriors and lovers, curses and charms, fairies and spirits and mischief and war—always war as far back as they could remember—and of great mystical journeys like this one here. The old told these to any who would listen, the young listened to any who would tell, and together they got through those first frightening days when the land disappeared altogether and they were the last living people on the face of the earth.

As Grace listened, she rested and ate and held her daughter in her arms, her strength returning; blood coursed through a quickening heart, and the fog in her head began to lift. She grieved when the ache stopped and her breasts grew soft with the absence of milk, but she did not allow grief to overwhelm her, and when the last of the spotting disappeared, she crept up to the deck in the middle of the night and threw the old rags overboard with relief. It had been hard to keep herself clean, though she'd rinsed the rags out in buckets of salt water and dried them covertly on the back of her trunk. They'd remained damp and stiff, which chilled and chafed her, and she'd worried that the bleeding would come on again strong, or that she'd fall ill.

She had little faith in the competency of the ship's doctor after meeting him at dinner in the saloon on their first night aboard. Draper, he was called—a stout, arrogant man with bushy side whiskers; he'd spouted on to his captive audience about the science of phrenology, which was revolutionizing the medical field. It was the shape of one's head, he said pompously, that indicated the difference in intellectual breeding between the races; the prominent protrusion of the Irish jaw, he pointed out, was evidence of their lesser intelligence as seen in their base way of life, their dependence upon the government of others, and their stubborn dependence upon a singular, though unreliable, crop. In fact—he'd gone on, warmed by his wine and the rapt attention of the other passengers—the Irish and the African savage had very similar head shapes, being at the lower end of intellectual development, and would most likely never be able to assimilate into civilized society. Which, he added, was as God intended as an advanced society was better enabled by the utilization of a servant class.

As everyone took advantage of the break in his speech to partake of their meal, Grace, annoyed no end, asked him in the heaviest Irish brogue she could muster to please pass the dish of singular crop unless he planned on finishing the entire thing himself. His cheeks burning—though not with embarrassment, she thought—the doctor regarded her for a full minute, eyes roaming the shape of her head, before replacing the serving spoon in the mashed potatoes. The meal ended in uncomfortable silence, and Grace had vowed then to eat elsewhere rather than expose Mary Kate to such nonsense. Now, though, she regretted baiting him as Siobahn lay quite sick with fever.

She was not the only one. By nightfall, the retching had begun in earnest; voices called out for water in their delirium, but there was no going up as the weather had worsened. Alice sat awake all night with Siobahn, trying to cool her with cloths dipped in a bucket of seawater. By morning, the child's lips moved but issued no sound; her eyes, when they opened but briefly, were glazed with pain and absent of recognition. Alice was desperate.

"Siobahn." She pulled the girl up by her shoulders and shook her. "Siobahn, open your eyes now, child, and speak to your mammie! Siobahn!" She shook her more roughly.

Grace came awake from a troubled sleep as if bidden, sat up

and went immediately back to the Kelleys' bunk. She took the girl gently out of Alice's hands, lowered her to the mattress, and felt her face and throat, relieved that the child still breathed.

"She's tired now, Alice. Let her rest."

"She's dying!" Alice gripped Grace's shirt. "I couldn't keep her warm enough, and now she's too hot and I can't cool her down. And it's so wet . . . it's so wet down here. She's soiled herself, but I can't clean her. For the love of God, Grace, do something. Get us off this boat! It's the boat that's killing her. Oh, God, I should never've taken us away."

"Alice." Grace kept her voice low, but firm. "Alice, stop. You know there's no getting off the boat. It's not the boat. She's sick, is all. She's been sick before. I'll help you now. We'll clean her up and get some tea in her, wrap her up in extra blankets. You're tired, Alice. We'll all tired. But we'll get through this."

She looked at the child, who was shivering now though beads of sweat clung to her brow. The air was foul, but when she moved her head away, she realized how many others were sick, as well. The stench of dysentery and vomitus filled the air, as did the groans of the old and the whimpers of the very young. As others awoke and realized that they, too, were ill, panicked cries for water joined the chorus.

"Liam," Grace commanded. "Liam, where are you?"

He appeared out of the gloom. "I'm sitting at the top of the stair," he said, wrinkling his nose. "The smell's awful down here."

"Aye. 'Tis real bad." She paused, thinking. "I want you to find Captain Reinders. Tell him we've got fever here. We need water brought down and the doctor. Can you do that, boy?"

He nodded.

"Be careful up there," she warned. "The deck is slippery and you could be knocked right off your feet. Go now, and come straight back."

He was away and pounding up the stairs before the words were out of her mouth.

"The doctor will come now," she reassured Alice. "He'll know what to do, and we'll get them to leave the hatch open, change out this bad air for fresh." She took her friend's hand. "I've got to check on Mary Kate. Then I'll be right back."

The air was a little fresher near the front as they caught every blast that came when someone went in or out; still, the smell of sickness clung to the blankets and clothes. She placed a hand on the warm bundle that lay peacefully on their bunk, rousing her gently.

"Wake up, child," she murmured. "Wake up now and come away from your dreams."

Mary Kate opened her eyes and sat up, blinking hard and reaching for her mother. She yawned, then coughed.

"Whoosh," she said, wrinkling her nose.

"Aye." Grace brushed the unruly hair back from her daughter's face, a face that was blessedly cool to the touch.

"Are folk sick?"

"They are," Grace told her. "And we'd do best to keep ourselves out of it."

"Is Siobahn dead, then?" she asked, and Grace's heart lurched that her daughter could ask that question so soberly.

"Ah, no, girl! Siobahn's sick, true enough, but her mother's with her and Liam's gone for the doctor. We must hope for the best in all things," Grace said, wondering what that might mean to a child who had grown up surrounded by misery, to whom illness, starvation, and death were everyday facts of life. "Get your cloak. And put on your boots. We'll get our food as soon as Liam comes back."

Mary Kate did as she was told, but when Liam came down the hold there was no doctor behind him and the boy's face registered his anger.

"Ah, he's a great eejit of a man." Liam snatched off his cap. "The captain orders him come right away, but he says he must have a good meal first! And after the meal, there's coffee to be had and then his pipe, and then his daily constitutional!" Here, the boy's curiosity got the better of his disgust. "What's a constitutional, then?"

Grace shrugged. "Another thing to keep him from coming down, sounds like. Where's the captain now?"

"In the bow with Mister Mackley, the first mate. They sent that Boardham to tell the doctor and I come along to show him the way." He glared, his anger fully returned.

"Did you tell the captain?"

"He wouldn't let me! Boardham, I mean. Said the doctor would come when he was ready, and I was to leave off the captain as he had enough to attend to what with the storm coming and all."

"Is there to be a storm then?" Grace asked, suddenly aware of the worsening pitch of the ship, the lanterns swaying on their hooks, the groans of the timber.

"Oh, aye!" Liam's eyes sparkled. "A terrific one! Just ahead is a great black cloud that swirls above the sea and the captain says we're in for it." He clapped his hands in excitement. "I'm going up to watch!"

Grace caught hold of his shirttail. "Oh, no, you're not!" she ordered. "You're going to stay right here with Mary Kate while I get our food and water. We may be stuck here awhile."

He crossed his arms and turned his head away in a huff.

"I'll tell you what," she bribed. "If the storm's not hit by the time I come back, we'll put on cloaks and go up into the air, the three of us. But you must do everything I say—do you hear me now, Liam?"

He nodded grudgingly.

"And if the doctor comes, you show him to your sister right away. Until then, you stay right here with Mary Kate. Understand me?"

Again he nodded stiffly, letting her know it was far beneath his dignity to be a mere baby minder; but by the time she'd prepared herself to go up, he was sitting cross-legged on the bunk across from Mary Kate and entertaining her with a hand-clapping game, his dignity set aside.

Stepping onto the deck, Grace was hit with a blast of wind; she wrestled the hatch closed behind her, then put her head down and pushed forward, moving from post to post to keep from being blown over. The sky was nearly as dark as night, but the thick, swirling mass of driving rain that lay just ahead was blacker still. Captain Reinders stood at the helm, hand to his mouth, shouting orders into the wind. Crewmen clambered down from the rigging, having reset and tied off the sails, while the rest moved quickly to secure the deck. There was a grim urgency to their work that chilled her heart, but she fought her way to the galley and pushed open the door.

"Yer late!" the cook yelled. "I've stowed it all away! Can't you see we're in for terrible heavy weather, you stupid woman?"

"Please," Grace shouted above the howl of the wind. "Anything!"

He untied a cupboard and pulled out a greasy packet. "Fried bread," he growled, shoving it at her. "Butter and cheese."

She stuffed it into her basket and thanked him profusely.

"Take these." He pushed three boiled eggs into her hands. "And this." He'd already filled a crock with tea. "Don't come up again if it's bad," he warned. "You'll go right overboard and no one to fish you out."

"Thank you!" Grace shouted. "Bless you!"

The wind was even worse now, and the rain pelted against her face, blinding her. She fought her way back to the steep stairwell, forced open the hatch, then climbed down into the hold, which was warm and dry for an instant, then close and overpowering.

"Come sit on the stair," she beckoned Liam and Mary Kate, and they followed her halfway up where the smell was not so bad.

She undid the parcel and gave them each a slice of fried bread, wiping the butter with it first. They practically inhaled it, and then the cheese and eggs, all washed down with tea.

"There'll be no going back up," she warned them, looking straight at Liam. "The wind is fierce. It's not safe."

"Where will we pee, then?" Liam asked. "And what about the water for Mam and Siobahn?"

"I've a little water left from yesterday," she said, thinking aloud. "If you can't hold on to yourself, then pee in the pot by our bunk. But don't miss!" she admonished. " 'Tis bad enough down here."

Mary Kate looked up at her wide-eyed and nodded solemnly. "You two stay," she ordered. "And don't move a'tall. I'm going to see to your mother, Liam, and get her to eat something."

The air was definitely worse as she worked her way into the back of the hold, and she wished there were some way to move the Kelleys closer to the stairwell. There was a time, not too long ago, when she would not have hesitated to bring them all into her own bunk; she recognized this and was ashamed, but could not alter the sorry truth of it. The need to survive made harsher judges of them all—the life of her own child was more important to her than the life of another, no matter how dear. And yet her heart was heavy, knowing how she'd changed.

"Here." Alice looked up at the sound of Grace's voice. "You must eat something now or you'll be no good to her a'tall." She handed the exhausted woman a boiled egg and a piece of bread, then poured out the rest of the tea in Siobahn's mug. "Eat and drink, Alice. You must."

Alice sighed, then nodded and began to peel the egg. Grace felt Siobahn's face and listened to her shallow breathing; her eyes remained closed and the breath rattled in her chest.

"Where's the doctor, then?" Alice asked at last.

"Liam says the captain ordered him down, but now a terrible storm is upon us and I don't know what's happening. I've been up myself," she said. " 'Tis bad—all the crew are making ready and the captain's busy with getting us safely through."

"Is he English, the doctor?"

"American," Grace told her. "But bringing home an English wife."

Alice's face fell. "We won't see himself down here, then," she said bitterly, picking up her daughter's hand.

"Ah, now, the captain won't abide that. If he has to drag the man down himself, you know he will."

Alice said nothing, but Grace knew she held little hope.

"I've set Liam and Mary Kate on the stair. The air's better there, less chance their falling sick. Why don't you go sit with them a while? I'll stay with Siobahn."

Alice shook her head. "She'll be wanting her mother when she wakes." She turned now away from Grace. "She'll want her mother," she said again, and lay down beside her sleeping child.

They fought the sea hard for two days and two nights, and when the clouds parted on the morning of the third, Captain Reinders' exhausted crew breathed a collective sigh of relief and thanked God that not one of them had been lost. When the damage had been assessed and as many as could be spared excused to sleep, the weary captain went down to tell the passengers himself that the worst was over and it was safe to come up.

He expected stink—the latrines had been impossible to use—and he expected grim, frightened faces. But he had not expected the horror of mothers keening over the bodies of dead children, the foul odor that stung his eyes and stifled his next breath, the baffled, gaping mouths of the dying and the bewildered, accusing eyes that met his own. And when he saw it—his eyes adjusting to the darkness—when he realized what had happened, it nearly broke him.

"Where the hell were you?" Reinders demanded, now back in his cabin.

Draper shifted uncomfortably from foot to foot as the ship bounced steadily through the sea.

"Secured in my cabin, Captain, looking out for the welfare of my own wife and children. And calming the others, as needed."

"What others?"

"My fellow passengers in the upper cabins, of course." Draper lifted his chin with an air of indignation. "Certainly you did not expect me to risk my safety by attempting to reach those in steerage? A responsible physician owes it to every passenger on board to keep himself alive and well in order to attend them."

"Every passenger includes those below," Reinders said, gritting his teeth. "That's where I sent you before the storm."

"My good man . . ."

Reinders brought his fist down on the desk. "How many dead?"

The doctor blinked and looked away, appearing to think. "Thirty-five," he reported, less indignation in his voice. "Mostly women and children, the elderly."

"How many ill?"

"About the same—though more men now, and still a number of children." He removed his spectacles and polished them with a handkerchief drawn from his vest pocket. "Some of these will die, of course," he added matter-of-factly. "But not all. And there shouldn't be too many more cases now that the weak have been culled."

Reinders winced. *You coldhearted son of a bitch*, he thought. "I want you down there every day, all day, until this is over. Is that understood?"

Draper replaced the spectacles on the bridge of his nose. "Surely, Captain, you don't require that I exhaust myself and so expose myself to illness. Where would you be then?"

"Exactly where I am now," Reinders spat. "You've proved yourself worthless so far. Let's see if you can't improve on that record, or I will report you to the hospital board when we arrive in New York."

Draper gave a dismissive flick of his handkerchief and turned as if to go. "I am a man of solid reputation, *Captain*."

"Times have changed in New York since you've been enjoying the fine life in London, *Doctor*." Reinders stood, rising to his full height. "There are medical boards now. Standards. Plenty of able doctors. No hospital is going to associate with a man who left hundreds of sick passengers to die in the hold of a ship simply because he didn't want to get his feet wet."

Draper eyed him warily.

"So you get your syrups and your pills and whatever else you've got in that bag, and you get yourself down there and save as many of those poor wretches as you can," Reinders ordered. "I'm holding you personally responsible for every death that occurs on my ship for the rest of this voyage. Got that?"

Draper opened his mouth, then closed it again, turned and huffed out of the room, but Reinders had no doubt he'd get his bag of tricks and make haste to the hold. Reinders sank

back into his chair again and allowed himself a moment of disbelief, head slumped into his hands. He'd been so proud of
the crew and the ship, pulling through that storm, on top of
the world this morning, despite his fatigue, when the last
cloud blew over and clear skies shone ahead. So proud. And
now so humbled.

There was a tight rap on the door.

"Come."

"Sorry to disturb you, Captain." Mackley closed the door behind him and handed Reinders a piece of paper. "Here's the
list."

Reinders sighed, looking it over. "You've confirmed it? The
names of the dead have been verified by someone else aboard?"

"Yes, sir." Mackley stood at attention.

Reinders ran down the list again, *Donnelly* catching his
eye—no mark; none by the daughter, either. He was relieved.
That was something anyway. And then he remembered the boy
and went farther down the list to *Kelley;* plenty of those and one
in the boy's group was marked: *Siobahn, age 5. Must've been
Liam's sister*, he thought, and rubbed his forehead wearily.

"Excuse me, Captain," Mackley broke in.

Reinders put the list down on his desk and looked up.

"I've got every man I can spare on sewing up the bodies. If
you'll say a few words, we'll bury them at sunset."

Reinders nodded. There was a service for burial at sea
printed in his captain's manual and he would read from that.
But these were very religious people.

"Any priests aboard?"

"I already thought of that, Captain, and there is one old fellow who's sick, but still on his feet. Should I ask him to pray or
something?"

"Yes." Reinders pinched the bridge of his nose. "When
everyone is up on deck for the burial, I want a detail sent down
into the hold. The place reeks. There'll still be sick passengers
down there, and that worm of a doctor had better be in attendance, but give him a few jobs anyway."

"Yes, sir. I'll see the hold is scrubbed down and the toilets, too. They flooded during the storm. And what about their bed-ding, Captain? A lot of it is shitty. Do we throw it overboard?"

It would be damn uncomfortable for those who did not have any extra blankets, but unless he wanted the illness to spread it would have to go. "Save what you can, but if there's any ques-tion, throw it over."

"Aye, aye, Captain." Mackley retrieved the list. "It's not your fault, sir," he offered. "Just bad luck, you know. Those damned medical officers in Liverpool barely run an eye over 'em before they board. And then the storm, and them all being shut up . . ." His voice trailed off. "Just bad luck," he finished weakly.

"Excused, Mackley," Reinders said, not unkindly.

When the first mate had gone, Reinders stood and looked out the porthole at the brisk but settled sea, whitecaps sparkling in the sunlight. He listened to the sound of the waves slapping against the hull, a sound that had always brought him great sat-isfaction, comfort even, if one were to think in those terms. But it gave him no satisfaction today, brought him not an ounce of comfort. Today, he would bury thirty-five men, women, and children in those waves, and tomorrow he would bury even more. He could only hope that none of his crew fell ill, but if they did, he would bury them as well. No, the sound of the sea and its very vastness were of no comfort today, only reminders of how small and alone each man truly was.

Twelve

SEAN sat at the long table in the Livingstons' beautiful dining room, each course growing cold until it was whisked away only to be replaced with another. Meat, fowl, fish—it all looked the same to him.

"You've not eaten a bite, Mister O'Malley," Florence murmured in her warm, deep voice. "I had the pheasant done especially for you, in the sauce you liked so well last time you were here."

"Forgive me, Miss Livingston," he apologized. "I shouldn't have come tonight. I'm not fit company for your lovely table."

"Is it your sister?" she inquired gently, her voice low so that others would not hear their private conversation. "You must be quite worried."

"I'm sick with it," he confessed. "It's all I think of night and day. The weather's been so bad, early snow and all, and her out there in it somewhere. Her and the little one."

"Is there nothing I can do?" She placed her hand surreptitiously on his arm, out of view of the others. "You know I'd like to help, Sean."

He shook his head. "There's nothing for it but to wait."

"I'm looking forward to meeting her, this great sister of

yours." She gave his arm a tender squeeze, then let go. "You must bring her to one of my afternoons as soon as she's settled in."

"Oh, aye. She'll like that." He glanced at the window, whose heavy curtains did little to muffle the sound of driving rain against the glass.

"Don't offer him any comfort, Florence," Jay chided his sister good-naturedly from across the table. "He's nothing but doom and gloom these days. Look here, my good man, ships sail safely from Ireland to this shore all the time and there's no reason to think your sister's won't. Now have some wine and tell us the news. No one's as entertaining as you on the subject of budding democracy."

Sean opened his mouth in an attempt to oblige, but his mind was a blank. He stood then, and bowed to his host and hostess. "Will you please forgive me, Jay, Miss Livingston? I'm in rare bad form tonight, and should not have wasted the prized place at your table."

"Oh, Sean, come on now," Jay complained. "Don't go."

The other guests had stopped talking and were watching the scene with interest. The Livingstons cultivated an interesting crowd at table, but this latest addition of the crippled Irishman had baffled most. And here he was, showing himself to be the boor they had suspected all along.

"Well, then, let me walk you out," Jay offered, quickly assessing the situation. He rose and came around, took Sean's arm companionably, and led him out into the great hall. "Really, O'Malley, this is most unlike you! I invited those people in there because of their checkbooks, just for you and your favorite cause."

"I don't know if I believe in the cause anymore." Sean allowed the butler to help him into his coat. "I don't know if there's a cause worth believing in."

"What!" Jay threw up his arms in disgust. "What about 'Ireland for the Irish?' What about 'Education for All' and 'Every Man a Voter?' " He eyed his friend suspiciously. "What about 'Freedom for the Freedom Fighters'—like your great pal, Mc-

Donagh, and that Lord Evans? Have you forgotten all about them?"

"McDonagh's dead," Sean said simply. "And Evans." His eyes searched Livingston's face. "Good night."

"For God's sake, O'Malley!" Jay grabbed Sean's good arm, shocked. "I hadn't heard. I didn't know. Dear God, no wonder you're so upset. I'm so sorry," he said, calming down. "Please don't leave like this. Come into the library. Let me give you a drink."

Sean shook his head. "I can't. One drink leads to the whole bottle for me these days. I've had to lay off."

"And your sister. You'll have to tell her. He was her friend, too, wasn't he?" Jay saw the anguish on his friend's face. "There's something else. You can tell me, Sean. I won't breathe a word, I swear."

The two men looked at one another.

"He was her husband," Sean revealed. "I don't know how— just that they married and she bore a son. A son she's had to leave behind."

"Why?"

"I think he must've been too weak, and she had to get out right away." Again, he hesitated. "She's wanted for murder, Jay."

Livingston drew back, shocked.

"She killed a guard. I'm sure 'twas self-defense, but they'd hang her anyway. And if they know she's Morgan's wife—and my sister . . ." He slumped, defeated. "I can't imagine how she's surviving this."

Jay took his arm, marching him firmly into the library and closing the doors behind them. He went straight to the sideboard and poured two very long drinks. "Here." He thrust a glass into Sean's hand. "Finish the bottle. I don't care. Finish all the damn bottles in the whole damn house, in the whole damn city for all I care."

He downed his in two gulps, waiting while Sean did the same, then poured out another measure for them both.

"My grandmother was Irish," Jay announced, eyes wet with the fire of the drink. "By God, my grandmother was *Irish!*

Toughest old woman I ever knew. Boxed my ears for thinking too highly of myself and then lectured me for hours about who I was and how I should think more highly of myself." He laughed, and took another drink. "I know one thing, O'Malley, one thing. . . ."

Sean nodded, his own eyes wet.

"If your sister is half the woman my grandmother was"—Jay eyed his friend, swaying slightly—"and I believe she is, being your sister, a contentious O'Malley—then not only will she survive this loss and this voyage, but she will triumph! Do you hear me, O'Malley? She will triumph!" He raised his second drink and downed it. "By God, I'm half in love with her already!"

Sean laughed then, and the bands around his heart eased just a little. Florence told them both in the morning that she'd had to usher the guests out past the unbridled, passionate singing emanating from behind the library doors as if she heard nothing at all, and she'd thank them to be more discreet in future. But when she heard Sean's news, and was told the whole of the story, she quit her scolding, put her arms around him, and held him for a long time.

Thirteen

GRACE kept her arm around Alice's waist throughout the short service and the long lowering of thirty-five bodies into the sea, tightening her grip when Siobahn's turn came near the end. Liam stood on the other side of his mother, holding her hand, his face creased with bewilderment and disbelief—how could they have been robbed like this and who was the thief? Mary Kate clung tightly to Grace's skirt with both hands, the regular tugs as the ship rolled reassuring to Grace, who thanked God with every breath that her child was alive and standing beside her.

Captain Reinders read in a clear, strong voice that belied the fatigue in his eyes; no one saw his hand tremble as he turned the page, his proud, broad shoulders braced against the icy wind. Finally, he closed the book and stepped aside for the old priest, who had robed himself and donned a large crucifix; when he kissed it and lifted it before the crowd of passengers, everyone sank silently to their knees and prayed with him for the mercy and forgiveness of their Father and for a quick passage to Heaven for their dead. The sight of this wretched group on their knees, heads bowed before their Lord and Savior, moved Captain Reinders and he turned his eyes away to rest them upon the endless sea.

When the priest had finished, Reinders again stepped forward and began reading out the names of the dead, pronouncing each full name clearly as the body to which it had belonged was hoisted carefully by his men, then lowered into the sea. As the priest blessed each one and made the sign of the cross over them, many of the passengers surrendered to their grief and began to weep openly. The list was long, but Reinders forced himself to go slowly, giving each name its moment of remembrance, looking up only once after Siobahn Kelley to search out the boy's eyes, red-rimmed and angry, and meet them with what he hoped was a measure of compassion.

The sun had not yet set when the last body was laid to rest, but the passengers lingered until dark and bitter cold drove them below. Grace and Liam helped Alice back down the narrow stairwell into the damp hold, pausing as their eyes adjusted to the fitful, sputtering light of the oil lamps. The hold had been washed down, but the stink of dying remained. Grace felt the limpness and despair in Alice's body, saw nothing of life left in her eyes, and was afraid for her—she could not survive the fever that was surely upon her now if she had no will to live.

"Come now," Grace murmured, guiding Alice firmly the few steps to her own bunk. "You're to lie here now. They've taken away Siobahn's mattress, and you can't rest on bare boards."

Alice did not reply, but closed her eyes the minute she laid her head down. Grace sat beside, touching her face, her hands. Warm. Very warm. Sweat glistening on her brow. Tomorrow morning then, Grace would move her to where the sick were now kept, but tonight Alice would remain with them.

There'd be no trouble from the doctor; he only looked busy when the captain or first mate appeared. Reinders had come down twice in the course of the long day to speak to all of them and say what would happen in the way of a burial. He had introduced Doctor Draper, pulling the man forward gruffly, reassuring them all that they could count upon medical attention around the clock until the fever had run its course. The second time, he asked them to reorganize their belongings so that the sick were together in a kind of ward in one quarter of the hold to ensure better attention from the doctor, and to spare the healthy. Grace and another fellow, a fisherman from Galway, had come forward at that moment and agreed to take over setting up the small hospital.

Once they'd begun the actual move, it went smoothly, many hands looking for work to take their minds off the fear that they too might die aboard this ship and never reach the promised land. It was agreed to move as many remaining mattresses as possible over to the ward so that the ill might be made more comfortable; there was grumbling, as well, and some who were afraid to lie among the sick, as though it were a sentence of death, but overall they had done as they were asked and by the time Mister Mackley announced the burial service on deck, the sick lay in one corner of the hold separated from the healthy by two rows of ominously empty bunks.

Grace looked up and saw that Liam now stood beside her, reeling from the strain, worried eyes on his mother's still face. She reached out and took his small hand.

"She's only sleeping," Grace promised. "Hasn't she been up day and night with Siobahn until there's nothing left to her? She'll be better in the morning, you'll see."

The eyes he wrenched away from Alice and turned toward hers were like his mother's in that they held out little hope, but were willing to be persuaded for now. She stood and put her arms around his stiff shoulders, pulling him to her, kissing his mess of salty hair. She felt his arms go round her waist, the weight of him leaning in against her.

"You must lay yourself down now, Liam, and try to rest," she insisted gently.

"What if she needs something in the night?" he asked, forlorn. "I'm all she has now."

"Are you forgetting the rest of us, then?" Grace scolded. "It's not up to you alone, you know."

His face was so very pale, she thought, and glanced down at her own little daughter standing off to one side, returning her gaze, bearing everything silently as though she understood the mysteries of life and death better than all of them.

"Mary Kate's so very tired," Grace whispered in Liam's ear. "Would you lie with her until she's asleep? I worry she'll roll off from up there, and I've something yet to do."

He nodded against her chest; he would do that for her. Moving away from her warmth, he hoisted himself up to the bunk above his mother, reaching over the edge as Grace lifted up Mary Kate. When the child had settled herself under the thin blanket, he curled up behind her, one arm wrapped protectively across her body, her soft hair nestled just under his chin, the way he had lain beside Siobahn nearly every night of his life. Mary Kate seemed to know that this brought him comfort and she snuggled close, gave a deep sigh, and closed her eyes. Grace prayed with them and said good night, pretending for Liam's sake not to see the tears he struggled to hide.

No fiddlers played tonight and no dancers danced, everyone too exhausted and desperate for dreams. As Grace made her way between the narrow bunks, she heard the groans of men shifting in their sleep, cramped and uncomfortable on hard boards, helpless to do anything for their wives and children. She saw a woman, alone now, sitting, rocking on the edge of her bunk, skirt bunched in fisted hands, shoved against her mouth to muffle the sobs. Grace rested a hand upon her head in passing. She listened for, and heard, the sound of mewling infants, the soft cluck of their tired mothers, and the satisfied suckling that followed—not all the babies had been lost, and this gave her heart. She moved carefully through the shadows and back into the dim light of the area where the sick lay and where the doctor stood, somewhat apart, squinting at his pocket watch.

"Evening, Doctor Draper." Her voice startled him and he jumped. "Will you be going up to your own family then, soon? After such a long day as this?"

"I will not!" Frustration burst the dam of his resolve not to engage in conversation with these beggars. "I dare not! I have now been thoroughly exposed to whatever it is you people have carried aboard, and I certainly cannot go back to my cabin, where young, innocent children sleep with their trusting mother!" He stared defiantly as if this were all her fault.

" 'Tis a shame, that," she consoled.

"Shame is the least of it! Captain Reinders clearly understood the implications of ordering me to remain in this . . . hole. But he didn't hesitate to consider the inconvenience, let alone risk, to my own family! What kind of man behaves that way?"

"Well, now, I'm sure I don't know," Grace answered, thoughtfully. "Captain Reinders seems a decent man, a man who cares about everyone on his ship."

Draper stuffed the watch back into his vest pocket, glaring down his nose at her. "What is it you want? Why are you bothering me? If you're sick, go lie down and I'll see to you later."

"Ah, no, I'm not sick, thanks for asking," Grace said, feigning thickheadedness. "But I'm wondering what it is you do for them that are. Can you cure them?" She glanced at the two leather medical bags lying partially open on an empty bunk. "Is there a remedy?"

He followed her eyes, then narrowed his own. "Why?"

Grace shrugged her shoulders in what she hoped was a casual manner. "Curious is all I am. My gran was a great one for cures; she made all sorts of remedies from what she gathered in the fields and from the wood around our cabin."

"A midwife," Draper dismissed.

"Ah, no! She didn't bring on the babies, just tended the sick or them with injuries. Folk medicine is all, but I used to help her some and I was wondering, is all."

The doctor refused to engage.

"You must know everything about healing," she flattered. "Been to university and all. Worked in the great hospitals in London and America. I'll bet there isn't anything you don't know."

His face reflected the struggle of conceit and stubbornness, finally giving way to pride, the compromised winner. He eyed Grace again, then flicked his finger in a gesture that gave her permission to follow him at a respectful distance.

"As you seem to have some base interest in medicine, I will grant you a look at my surgery." Draper opened the first bag with such flourish that all Grace saw at first was a flash of silver.

He lifted each instrument out as he spoke. "Forceps for difficult deliveries, saws and knives for amputating, of course. A Hey's saw, tourniquets . . ." He smiled condescendingly as the color drained from Grace's face. "I'm sure your old granny hadn't anything so modern as this. Used an old ax, I suppose, straight off the woodpile. Stitched with a quilting needle, most likely, leftover thread."

Warming to the show, he reached deeper into the bag and withdrew a smaller case of tooled leather, releasing its clasp and laying it open.

"This is a pocket dressing kit," he explained, overenunciating each word as if for a slow child. "Scalpel, gum lancet, tenaculum, scissors . . . This is called a bistoury." He held up a small, slender knife, turning it to catch the light. "Very sharp," he added, touching the tip gently, looking for her reaction. "Slices right through flesh and muscle."

Grace glanced at the row of curved needles, arranged by size, each held in place by tiny strips of leather.

"Stitching." He trailed a finger lovingly across them. "No wound too large or small. Very useful kit. One can manage all sorts of surgeries very successfully with only this. A good physician goes nowhere without it. Certainly I don't."

"Nor would I." Grace swallowed visibly, her mouth dry. "And . . . and in the other?"

"Prescriptives," he said importantly, pulling open the second bag and lifting out an assortment of small jars, thick bottles, tins, and paper twists. "Balsam of Capiri, castor oil, cream of tartar, calomel—for worms." He glanced at her, then continued, lifting up first one thing and then another. "Spirit of hartshorn, jalap in powder—a wonderful purgative; friar's balsam, Epsom salts, rhubarb in powder, peppermint, laudanum . . ." He paused, eyes narrowing with suspicion. "Familiar with laudanum, are you?"

"Ah, no," Grace said innocently, though she'd marked the blue bottle. "What's it for, then?"

"Toothache," he offered. "Nasty stuff, though. Makes one nauseous and delusional, but I fear I am plagued with toothache, and so must always carry a bottle for when the pain becomes unbearable."

"Sure and that's wise," Grace commended. "Can't have the doctor going out of his head, now, and all of us depending upon his wisdom. And what of that jar of pills just there?" She pointed to the last bottle.

"Ah!" Draper's eyes lit up. "Blue Pills! An example of modern medicine at its finest," he said warmly. "An excellent cure-all, and one that comes highly recommended by the physician to the royal family. My most popular remedy." He picked up the bottle lovingly.

"Is that what you give the ones with fever, then?" Grace matched his excited tone. "Blue Pills?"

The doctor quickly moderated any exuberance, tightening his grip possessively on the bottle. "Well—um, no. I mean, not always. Not unless they *really* need it."

"And how will you know, Doctor?"

"It requires precise assessment," he responded, puffing himself up all over again. "If patients are only slightly symptomatic, then they don't need it, and of course, if they are in the process of succumbing, then it will do them no good."

"Ah!" Grace nodded. "So the trick is to catch them right at the moment before they begin to die."

Draper frowned. "There's no *trick*, as you call it—the doctor watches his patient carefully, then administers the Blue Pill at exactly the right moment. Whereupon the patient recovers nicely."

"Have you enough, I wonder."

He glanced at the bottle, obviously full. "I suppose so."

"And how many have you given out?" she asked. "Today, I mean."

He hesitated. "None."

Grace glanced at the thirty or so people lying in the ward. "So what you're saying to me, then, is that those folk there are either well or as good as dead?"

He narrowed his eyes, nodding once.

She sighed as if it were all beyond her comprehension. "Well, you're a fine doctor, true enough, and isn't it a blessing to have you on board? Sure and you'll be tired staying up to watch for the right moment in each of those poor souls." She paused. "So I'll go now and leave you to it. And thanks for your time."

He nodded curtly, unwilling to say another word, not sure what had just taken place. As he watched her make her way across the dimly lit hold, he had the feeling he'd been toyed with, but it was always difficult to tell with women—such flighty creatures. Weak-minded, abstract. And of course, this one was Irish in the bargain and therefore completely incapable of carrying on any kind of meaningful discourse, let alone one that involved logical thinking. He disdained the Irish—they talked and talked and talked, and in the end little was said but the words themselves.

And now it came to him—who she was, where he'd seen her before. She was the woman who'd spoken so rudely to him that night at dinner in her effort to secure more potatoes for herself and her pale, watchful brat. That kind of greed turned his stomach, and he'd been pleased when she'd appeared no more, sensibly banned from decent society. He had assumed others had taken up the complaint of her ill manners and complete unsuitability for the first-class community and that the captain had acted with immediate good judgment. Further remembrance, however, reminded him that he'd seen the captain and that woman in close conversation on more than one occasion. A puzzle. He struck the pose he was most fond of, hand to chin, and recalled the stories of ship captains who occasionally kept a woman on board disguised as a passenger. Could be. He shrugged. It was certainly no concern of his if Reinders chose to dally with a pathetic common woman. Though perhaps this could work somehow to his benefit—exacting revenge, say, for this posting to Hell.

He sat down on the edge of the bunk and began packing away his jars and bottles, warmed by the thought of ruining Reinders once they landed in New York. But how to do it, how to do it? He picked up the laudanum, pausing for a moment before easing out the cork and taking a swallow. Thinking hard, he replaced the stopper and packed the bottle carefully away in a piece of cloth, savoring the first sweep of the drug as it began to take effect. It would come to him with a little help, and he lay back, drifting off into a most satisfying fantasy that spun out a web of disgrace for the captain and praise for the honorable doctor, who might even, in the course of this plot, enjoy some private time of his own with that young woman who needed only a firm hand to set her on the right moral course. He closed his eyes and licked his lips, the sticky residue now tingling on the tip of his tongue as he indulged himself in glorious visions of redemption.

Grace picked her way carefully around boxes and trunks on her way back to bed, the sounds of restless sleep following her as closely as did the eyes of those still awake. She passed them, unaware, her mind on her plans. The doctor would sleep eventually, she knew, and his slumber would be accompanied by great deep snores. She would lie awake all night if need be so that at the right moment she could slip over to that bag, undo the clasp and shake out a fistful of those Blue Pills. And if Blue Pills weren't enough to keep Alice alive, well then, she'd have the laudanum, as well; Siobahn had died in terrible pain, and Liam was not going to watch his mother go the same way. If there was nothing for it and all was lost, she'd give Alice enough laudanum to cross over in peace. She did not allow herself to think that these things might be needed for herself, or for Mary Kathleen, though she paused long beside the bunk to measure the rise and fall of her daughter's chest, lay the back of a hand upon her cheek, smooth the tangled hair.

She settled the blanket around Liam's thin shoulders, felt his face, too, and fought off the wave of helplessness that threatened to overwhelm her. She sat down then, on the cold, hard stairs, pulled her shawl tightly around, and kept a watch on the far corner of the hold until the light dimmed and the doctor's snores told her it was time at last.

Fourteen

"*December 23, 1847,*" Reinders wrote in his log. *Becalmed.* And then, because there was nothing more to say, he closed the book.

It was freezing. The heavy fog into which they had sailed muffled even the sound of the sailors' voices as they called to one another from bow to stern, lookout to deck. Mist clung to the sails and masts, forming thick, sluggish drops that froze suspended, becoming icy, then pieces of ice, icicles. The deck was treacherous despite buckets of seawater thrown across it. Sailors wrapped rags around their palms, fingers free to handle ropes and rigging, warmed them by hot breath when they stiffened with cold. The *Eliza J* rolled gently in the placid sea, ropes and pulleys knocking against the swaying masts, her lone sail flapping listlessly as she turned this way and that, seeking any small gust that might pull her from this mire.

There was food enough, though they were now five days behind schedule with no wind in sight. He could not yet in good conscience issue a ration order on the water—not with so many still sick—though this would have to happen in another twenty-four hours as they'd lost barrels in the storm. Not everyone was claiming their food rations, even after he'd sent Mackley down to insist that every able body do so in order to keep up their strength. It was quiet below, Mackley had reported. No singing or music making. Those who ventured above deck were also quiet—eyes downturned, faces grim.

Reinders took a deep breath and exhaled loudly; he'd had a nightmare last night, and it plagued him still. He was in Georgia, at the market, and there were Lily's children in chains. The auctioneer set a starting bid and Reinders opened his mouth, but nothing came out; he tried to raise his arm, but realized he was wound tightly in rope. He struggled helplessly as the bidding went on around him, and then the children were gone and he himself was on the block, staring out at a sea of white faces, desperate for someone to realize that a mistake had been made. No one did and he was sold, and when the owner's cart started out of town, Reinders looked out and saw his mother standing at the edge of the crowd, weeping and calling his name while the hands of strangers held her back. He had awakened in a terrible state of panic, and with a piercing need to see her one last time.

"Mackley," he called, standing and pulling on his coat.

"Here, sir." Mackley appeared in the doorway, dark circles under eyes that were merry despite the lack of sleep.

"Any wind?"

"None but what comes out of the backsides of your crew, Captain."

Reinders laughed despite himself. "Assemble them, would you? I'm coming up."

Mackley handed him his cap. "Aye, aye, Captain. Everyone?"

"Morning watch only. Let the others sleep while they can."

"Weather might change, sir."

"Let's hope so," Reinders said, and closed the door behind him.

It was a morning that brought no relief from the bone-chilling air permeating the hold. Grace stood by Alice, covered now in two blankets but shivering despite the heat that radiated from her face. At dawn, Grace had forced one of the Blue Pills between her chattering teeth and made her swallow it, but it had not helped and Grace cursed herself for not asking the doctor how many pills to give in a day and how long before the patient began to get better. She decided not to wait, but to give Alice another one now.

Liam and Mary Kate sat huddled together under a blanket and a shawl at the top of the steps, right in the path of the icy air, but free from the rankness below. Grace checked on them, then returned to Alice's side to sit and watch. She was weary—there had been no rest last night—and troubled, lest the light-headedness she felt was the onset of fever instead of fatigue. She had tried, in the early morning hours, to weigh her duty to Alice against the duty of staying alive, but found she could not make the necessary decision—not with Liam's frightened, worried eyes searching hers whenever he came to see if his mother was better.

"Grace." Alice's voice was hoarse and ragged, her eyes bloodshot; she struggled to sit, but had not the strength and fell back.

"Here I am, Alice. Here I am." Grace pulled the blanket back up. "Rest now. You'll feel better if you sleep. We'll talk later."

Alice watched Grace's lips move and then smiled what Grace had come to know as the spirit's smile.

"Now," Alice whispered.

Grace nodded, letting the lie of soon-to-be-well fall away.

Alice coughed, then took a labored breath. "Siobahn," she wheezed, "is still so little. Liam"—she took a breath—"can stay . . . with you."

Grace listened, steeling her heart.

"His da." Alice grimaced. "I . . . don't know. . . ."

Grace reached under the blanket and found Alice's hand. "He'll not leave my side unless I know all's well," she vowed. "I'll keep him safe. I promise you that."

Tears of relief flooded Alice's exhausted eyes; her mouth trembled. "Thank you," she breathed. "Don't let him . . . see."

"I'll help," Grace whispered close to her ear. " 'Twill be like sleeping."

Alice understood and nodded gratefully. "Where is he?"

Grace left her and went to the stairs, climbing up to the children, telling Liam he was wanted and she would sit with Mary Kate. His eyes went wide but he said not a word, just nodded and went down like the good boy he was.

Grace pulled her daughter close, kissing the small head, resting her lips against the child's hair. They sat that way for nearly an hour until Liam returned, eyes swollen from crying, but dry from the fierce rubbing of his fists. In the time he was gone—Grace could see it in the way he now held himself apart from them—he had come to understand that he would no longer be his mother's beloved son, but the son of a world that did not value him. She saw that he was afraid of what lay ahead, but determined to deny that fear, and her heart ached for him.

They kept watch over Alice through the night and into the next day as the pain grew steadily worse and she slipped away from them into delirium. Grace was able to ease her discomfort with sips of laudanum from the flask into which she'd poured half the doctor's bottle, filling it back up with water. After, Alice slept more peacefully, and Grace took the children up for the air and to escape the gloom. Many others were sick as well, and as each one began to die, then died at last, the heaviness of mourning and grief threatened to crush even the heartiest spirit among them. Far better, went the whispering, to have died back home—to have been buried in Irish soil, the place marked and cherished—than to die aboard this ship and be swallowed whole by the sea; fear and regret were bitter pallbearers.

Finally, in the evening of a long and heavy day, and for the first time in weeks, someone brought out a fiddle. Grace stepped to the end of her row and saw an old man sitting on the edge of his bunk, tuning strings gone sour with dampness. Softly—so softly that at first Grace could barely hear—he began to play, just a few random notes; then the notes ran together as his fingers warmed up and the music came upon him. First he played a song from her childhood, and then another her mother had sung. Then there was a pause. And when he began to play again, it was "Silent Night, Holy Night," for this was Christmas Eve.

He played tenderly now, gallantly, and then another fiddler joined him, and a piper, and then a voice and then another, and finally all in the hold were singing loud enough to be heard despite their faltering voices, despite the tears that choked them, despite the misery in their souls. They sang because they believed with all their hearts that in Christ's birth was their Father's unwavering love for them and His compassion for their plight; they sang because their beloved dead were safely in His arms even now, and even now looked down upon them and heard their worship. And so they sang.

Grace sang and Liam sang and Mary Kate watched them both, touching her mother's tears with small fingers, then touching Liam's, too. They all sang—every man, woman, and child who still had breath—even the doctor who was stirred by the beauty of their voices, and the sound carried up to the captain, who stood at the top of the stairs, astounded by the power of their love for God even in the midst of death.

> *"Silent night, holy night,*
> *All is calm, all is bright . . ."*

With those words, he looked up and saw that the fog had lifted and the sky was hard and clear, full of stars by which to navigate, full of wind by which to sail, a full moon to guide the way. He looked up and was unable to find the words, could not move, could not speak, his reverie complete and unbroken, until he felt a brotherly hand on his shoulder.

"We're under sail, Captain," Mackley said. "Merry Christmas, sir."

There were burials on Christmas Day, including Alice Kelley. When it was over, and the few who had ventured up into the cold had gone down again, Captain Reinders made his way over to Grace and Mary Kate.

"I'm sorry about the boy's mother, Missus Donnelly." He stood there awkwardly, cap in hand. "Will you tell him for me?"

"You can tell him yourself, Captain." She stepped aside, and there was Liam behind her.

Reinders looked down at the boy, who seemed so familiar, yet could not possibly be. He took in the brave set of bony shoulders, the defiant chin, the mouth set tight against any sign of weakness, eyes that blamed and questioned and were so terribly hurt, yet would never admit it.

"Master Kelley," he said, gently, "I thought now would be a good time to show you the ship."

Liam said nothing, his eyes searching the captain's face. Behind him, Grace nodded imperceptibly.

"Come, then." Reinders adjusted his cap, then put an arm around the boy's shoulders, pulling him forward. "We'll start with the helm." He glanced over his shoulder at Grace. "He'll take his supper in my cabin, and then I'll return him, if that's all right."

"Aye," Grace said. "Thank you, Captain."

The two walked off, Liam silently and Reinders talking enough for both of them. Grace was relieved; if the captain cared in some small way about the boy, then her request might be granted.

"And you, my sweet." She scooped Mary Kate up into her arms. "Merry Christmas to you, sad day though it is."

Mary Kate nodded soberly.

"I've a present for you," Grace announced, setting her on a water barrel. "Close your eyes and open your mouth."

The little girl did as she was told, and Grace pulled a small, dark square out of her pocket, took off the paper and popped it into Mary Kate's mouth.

The child's eyes opened wide in astonishment, wider still as she worked her tongue around the marvelous thing in her mouth.

"It's chocolate." Grace smiled, pleased with the delight on Mary Kate's face. "Our friend the cook gave it to me with our breakfast this morning, and didn't I save it just for you? Is it good, then?"

Mary Kate nodded enthusiastically, then wrapped her arms around Grace's neck. " 'Tis," she said, leaving a sticky kiss on Grace's cheek. "Love, Mammie."

Grace covered the little face with kisses, fighting back tears she had not known were left. She was suddenly so very thankful that they were still here, she and her daughter, that they were surviving this and that they might actually make it all the way to America.

"Will Liam be ours now?" Mary Kate asked, returning to her sober self. "His mam told him so."

Grace bit her lip. "Does he want to be ours, do you think?"

Mary Kate considered that. "He says I'm his sister now and he'll take care of me, and then he cried a long time and fell asleep."

Grace nodded, as much in amazement at the length of her daughter's speech as at what she'd revealed.

"We'll have to look for his da," Grace told her. "But until then, you'll be brother and sister."

"And the baby, as well," Mary Kate said confidently.

Grace's heart made a great lurch at the thought of her wee baby and her old father, sitting in the convent this Christmas day, wondering where she was.

"Aye." She pushed away that pain. "And there'll be Uncle Sean and your grandda—all of us together in America."

"I hope there's room," Mary Kate said anxiously.

"There's always room for family." Grace kissed her again. "Blessed Christmas, my sweet girl."

"Blessed Christmas, Mam."

Fifteen

"YOU'RE late," Mister Martin announced when the front door banged open. "Missus Geelan has left us a roast of some sort, and I'm hungry!"

"Oh, Lord, you don't suppose it's the *cat,* do you, Father?" Julia swept into the room, unbuttoning her coat and tossing it aside. "She hated that cat. *You* hated that cat!" She slipped into her seat at the table and eyed the roast suspiciously.

"I most certainly did not," he declared. "I'm the one who brought the cat *home*—for *you,* my dear. To cheer you."

"And it did cheer me," she admitted. "Until it grew up. Really, Father, you must confess you never did get it from any conventional litter—you must have claimed it from a passing circus, or the gypsies!" Her eyes lit up. "They always have exotic beasts, lions and the like."

"It was *not* a lion."

"It was *not* a cat!" She picked up her fork and tentatively poked at the still-warm roast. "They say cat has a nice taste, actually."

"It is *not* a cat!" he insisted.

"My point exactly." She smiled and put down the fork. "Anyway, how was your morning, Father?"

"Lonely." He eyed her pointedly. "I know you don't hold much with convention, Julia, but most families do spend Christmas together."

She blinked. "Oh, Father, I'm so sorry. I completely forgot!"

"I know," he said sternly, but his eyes were warm with affection. "Off to that rag of a newspaper, I suppose. Was anyone even there on Christmas morning?"

"John, of course. They're setting his piece on Sir Grey's Crime and Outrage Bill, and you know he's got to oversee every period and comma."

Mister Martin smiled and poured them each a glass of wine. "Clarendon's gone a bit mad with power—there's no denying that. Any more arrests?"

"Too many to count." Julia took her glass. "Every time there's a murder—and you know how often that is—he immediately drafts a police force into the district and makes every man between the ages of sixteen and sixty join the hunt. If they refuse, it's two years in prison."

"Seems very hard."

"It's more than hard." Julia's eyes blazed with anger. "It's an insult! And what's more, after he sends his thugs into the district, he makes the villagers repay all costs of feeding and housing them! It's ridiculous." She shook her head in disgust. "No one's allowed to bear arms without a special license, except gamekeepers and households needing protection—read *English*—so how the hell . . . excuse me, Father . . . how are the farmers supposed to protect their own homes or hunt to feed their own families?"

"I suppose you have written your own piece about this, Mister Freeman?" He paused in slicing the roast, eyebrows arched.

"It'll be in next week's *Nation*."

"You and Mister Mitchel are neck-and-neck in the pursuit of English Aggravation, it seems. Pass me your plate, dear."

"Aggravating the English is just a bonus—this is about Irish Emancipation, as well you know." She took back her plate, sniffing the gray meat. "It's cat, I tell you."

"It's not. Have some potatoes and pass them along."

"Anyway, I think John's just about had it at the *Nation*." She tumbled a few potatoes onto her plate, then mashed them with a fork. "He and Duffy do nothing but argue these days. Repeal, repeal, repeal—Duffy says move slowly and cautiously, John says throw caution to the wind and attack."

"Oh, my." Mister Martin chewed his first bite of roast slowly, an odd look coming over his face. He swallowed, washing it down with a gulp of the claret. "Guess it's been a while since we had meat on the table," he said carefully. "Not used to the taste."

"It's not cat, Father," Julia assured him. "It's old mutton, actually. I got it myself yesterday from the butcher. I was only kidding."

"Did you actually see him cut it up?" Mister Martin was not convinced. "Are you quite sure?"

"No, I didn't see him, and yes, I'm sure. Watch." She put a bite in her mouth and chewed vigorously. "Definitely mutton," she confirmed. "Lovely old, chewy, dried-up mutton. Just the way you like it."

He laughed. "It's good to have the old Julia back again. I've missed you—bad jokes and all."

She reached across the table and squeezed his hand. "I'm sorry if it's been hard on you. I think it was just too much all at once—troops flooding the city, starving everywhere, all that illness. . . ."

"Morgan's death," he added gently.

She nodded.

"And then you took his widow all the way to Liverpool and put her on a ship to America and agreed to care for her infant and old father." He shook his head. "So much weight for those young shoulders."

"Not as much as she carries." Julia sat back in her chair. "Please God she's made it, and isn't still out there on the winter sea."

"Will you go down to Cork soon to see about the others?"

"As soon as I can get away. They're bound to need more food and supplies. Morgan's sister was running that convent single-handedly, and frankly I don't trust Father Sheehan not to close the doors now there's just a few of'them left."

"What would happen to the children?"

"Workhouse, most likely, or left to fend for themselves." She sighed and pushed her plate away.

"I know it's hard to sit in front of a good meal while others are starving," he told her. "But you do them no good in wasting it, either. Now eat up, and maybe I've a little gift for you."

"It's not another lion, is it?"

"No, my dear," he chuckled. "Actually . . ." He fished in his vest pocket, then handed her a small gold box. "Here. Merry Christmas, Julia dearest."

She opened it carefully, then took out a delicate cross on a gold chain. "It's Mother's," she said, and her eyes filled with tears.

"You know she nearly got us all excommunicated with those family-planning pamphlets of hers," Mister Martin reminded. "But she was a deeply religious woman, nonetheless, and every morning she slipped this around her neck—'putting on the armor of God,' she called it." He paused. "You've been through so very much, my dear," he said gently. "I thought you could use a little extra armor."

She came around to his side and knelt by his chair, her arms going round his waist.

"Now, now." He smoothed her hair. "You're so like her, you know. I've always admired the two of you tremendously."

She looked up at him. "I've something for you, as well." She put into his hand a framed miniature. "She had that done right before she died. It was to be a surprise for you, so she hid it in my drawer. I found it again after I came back from Liverpool."

"Oh, Julia." He could not take his eyes off it. "Look how very much alike the two of you are."

Julia shook her head wistfully. "No, Father, don't you remember how charmed everyone was by her? She was so very beautiful."

"Exactly." He held out the portrait, and for the first time, Julia really looked at the woman her mother had been, recognized the stubborn set of her jaw and the intelligent humor in her eyes, eyes that were exactly like Julia's own.

"I miss her," she said then.

"I miss her, as well, but oh, God, how grateful I am to have her daughter." Mister Martin kissed Julia's forehead. "Now get up and go finish your cat before it gets cold."

She laughed and he laughed, and they finished their dinner, then sat by the fire for the whole of the afternoon, enjoying one another's company and the rest of the claret, closing out—for a little while—the heavy weight of the world.

Sixteen

CAPTAIN Reinders found himself becoming very attached to the boy who now followed him everywhere, and he worried what would happen when they landed. Were orphans sent back to Ireland, he wondered, or taken to the asylum in the city, or simply left to fend for themselves? Reinders could not stand the thought of the boy locked away where he might languish for years unclaimed, nor could he bear to think of Liam begging for pennies on the corner of some low street, at the mercy of any thug who wanted to beat him out of his day's earnings. Missus Donnelly had clearly taken him under her wing for now, but would she keep him when they landed? Would she be able? Widows, he knew, were rarely in charge of their own lives.

And so he began to consider what it would be like to have Liam remain with him, sail, and learn the trade. Was it a proper life for a boy, the logical solution? The more he thought about it, the more he realized how much he wanted to do this—logical or no, Liam Kelley had come to mean something to him.

He looked now to the corner of his cabin where Liam sat, finishing his lunch and looking at the charts on the map table.

"Can you go anywhere in the world with these, sir?" he asked in his excited way.

"You can go anywhere with or without them." Reinders came over and had a look over the boy's shoulder. "But you might not always know where you are. Maps show you the lay of the land and the water around it; charts give you that and more—they show what the winds are like, how deep the water might be in a harbor or lagoon, which is the fastest route from one place to another."

"Are there places not on the maps, then?" Liam looked up, bread crumbs clinging to his lower lip.

"Plenty of places not charted yet, but we know they're out there."

"Ah, Captain," Liam breathed, his eyes wide. "That's what I want to do when I'm old enough. I want to find those places and draw them on the maps for sailors." He turned back to the intricate charts. "Aren't they the most beautiful things, then, sir?"

Reinders smiled and laid a hand on the boy's shoulder. "They are. They really are."

There was a knock. Then Boardham entered without waiting to be called. He eyed the tableau with such a lascivious sneer that Reinders let go of the boy's shoulder and stepped in front of the map table to shield him.

"What is it?" he asked sharply.

"First-class passengers are wondering why there's so little variety in their diet, sir."

Reinders crossed his arms. "Because we've been at sea nearly two weeks longer than expected—you know that. They're lucky to have any variety at all—most of steerage is down to stale water and hard tack."

"I did tell them, sir, but they wonder why you never take your meals in the saloon." He paused. "They feel very hard about the doctor," he added, a note of agreement in his voice.

"I don't give a damn *how* they feel about the doctor—he's got patients below, and that's where he stays until we land. As for my meals, I don't have time to waste an evening with that gabby bunch."

"Of course, sir." Boardham gave a little bow, then continued with seeming reluctance. "If I might say, sir, they do comment on how often you're with the boy there, and how you go below regular-like."

"That's no one's business but my own," Reinders said firmly.

"Oh, absolutely, sir, absolutely. Cabin boy's a right nice comfort on a long voyage. We all know that." Boardham winked.

Reinders crossed the room in two strides, grabbed the steward by the collar, and shoved him up against the wall. "You ever say that again, you bastard, I'll throw you in the brig and forget all about you."

"Beggin' your pardon, Captain." Boardham squirmed. "I meant nothing by it."

"Like hell you didn't." He let go, but muscled up close. "I've been watching you, Boardham, and I don't like you—I don't like the way you shirk your duties or the way you treat the passengers, especially the women. I don't like the way you sneak around or the way you gamble with the men—you cheat, Boardham, and I hate cheaters. I don't even like the way you look. If you don't want to spend the rest of this voyage in the bowels of my ship, then you keep your filthy talk to yourself and follow my orders to the letter, starting with this one—get out."

Red-faced, Boardham slunk out the door; Reinders found he could not look Liam in the eye, afraid the steward's venom had poisoned the boy's innocence and their friendship.

"I never did like him, either," Liam offered then, and Reinders snorted, relieved.

"I shouldn't have lost my temper. A good captain never lets scum get the best of him—remember that when you've got your own ship."

Liam flushed with pleasure at the thought.

"And stay out of his way," Reinders added, unable to shake the way Boardham had looked at the boy. "He's bad news."

Cold though it was, Reinders paced the main deck until he saw Grace come up to join the queue for the toilets. Boardham was nowhere in sight, which was too bad—Reinders would've liked an excuse to lock him away.

"Missus Donnelly." He caught her before she went back down. "I was hoping to see you—may I have a word?"

"Aye, Captain." Grace's teeth chattered. "I've been meaning to speak to you, as well."

"You're freezing." He had to raise his voice over the sound of the wind ripping across the deck. "Will you come to my cabin? I could give you some tea?"

Grace nodded, then followed him down to an unfamiliar door, which he held open for her. She passed through, glancing around quickly at the compact quarters, the mounted bunk and suspended lantern, map table secured to the floor, charts weighted with a flat stone, brass instruments lying to one side—some in their cases, some out—of the small desk, a trunk in one corner. He motioned for her to sit in the chair beside the trunk, then stuck his head back out into the hall.

"Fletcher," he called. "Bring a pot of tea and two cups, right away." He closed the door, then settled himself behind his desk. "I wanted to talk about Liam."

"As do I," Grace said, her shivering subsiding.

"Good. That's good. We're on the same course." He paused, wondering what to say next. *Better just to lay it on the table*, he decided. "Missus Donnelly, I'd like to adopt Liam Kelley."

"Captain!" Grace nearly fell off her chair. "That's very kind of you, but isn't he just nine years old, and what does a bachelor seaman like yourself know of nine-year-old boys?"

Reinders had expected this. "I was nine once," he replied confidently. "And a boy, of course."

"All right, then," Grace teased. "You can have him."

"I'm serious! The boy's an orphan, and clearly he loves the sea. I know it's not a traditional life, but I'd see that he got an education and I'd teach him everything there is to know about navigation. Can you imagine what a magnificent seaman he could become?"

"I've no doubt you'd do right by him, Captain, but he has a father—in America." She paused, sorry for the hurt now on his face.

"He never mentioned a father."

"Left the family over a year ago, and not a word from him since. Times being what they are in Ireland, the only thing for it was to come ahead."

"Did they think they would just get off the ship and there he'd be, waiting for them?" Reinders asked, incredulous.

"There's many think that. Family gone missing, and they've no idea how big America is. I don't know myself, but I suspect a man can simply vanish in it, and maybe that's the draw for some."

"Maybe he's dead."

"Maybe he is," she agreed. "Most likely he is. A drinking man by all accounts and not too reliable. But maybe sobered up, working, and waiting after all."

"They wrote ahead?"

"Aye, some time ago. I've an address where to look."

"What if you can't find him?" Reinders could hardly believe this.

"I've turned it over myself, many times since his mother died, Captain," Grace said, wearily. "I promised to watch over him, but will I be able to just take him off?"

"Are you related?"

"No," she admitted. "Though I think of him as mine."

Reinders smiled wryly. "Grows on a person, doesn't he?" He thought for a moment. "Would you be able to keep him with you until we found out about his father?"

"Oh, aye." She brightened. "I'm to live with my brother. He's a good man and won't mind one more. But will Liam be allowed to go with me?"

Reinders frowned. "I don't know. He'd have to be handed over to the authorities, and probably from there to the orphan asylum."

Grace shook her head. "Absolutely not, Captain."

"I agree. That'd be terrible for him."

The knob turned and Boardham stepped in bearing a tray.

"Your tea, sir." He kept his eyes lowered, contritely. "Two cups, as requested. Anything else, Captain?" He glanced up quickly, his eyes flicking from the captain to Grace and down again.

"No," Reinders said shortly, dismissing him.

"Will I say you're not to be disturbed, sir?" Boardham asked neutrally from the doorway.

"Yes." Reinders felt his face grow hot. "No. Get on with your work," he ordered.

"I don't like that one much," Grace said when the door was closed.

"No one does." He poured out a cup and handed it to her, pushing away his irritation with the steward. "Here's what I think," he resumed. "You're Liam's relative. I'll make a note of this on the passenger list and record in my log that on the day his mother died he was remanded to the custody of his aunt, Missus Gracelin Donnelly. Then, if any questions are asked upon landing, we're covered."

Grace set her tea down and looked at him. "Thank you, Captain. Ever so much. But is it against the rules?" She bit her lip. "Will you not get yourself in some trouble over this?"

"It's not regulations," he allowed. "A captain's log is gospel and not to be tampered with in hindsight. But in a case like this, well—what does it matter to anyone where he goes?"

"It matters to you, Captain," she said gently. "You made plans for him. Had it all worked out."

He looked down into his cup for a moment. "I only want what's best for the boy," he said. "But I would ask you one thing— if his father's dead and you find you can't provide for him, would you let him come to me? Or even in the future, if he still loves the sea, he could always crew for me. I'd teach him everything."

"He's lucky to have such a one as yourself interested in him."

"It's settled then." Reinders nodded. "We'll stay in touch."

"Might I ask you a question, Captain?" She leaned forward, cup resting on her knees. "Something about yourself?"

He eyed her, hesitant, then nodded.

"Have you any family of your own in this America?"

"My mother and brothers live on our farm in upstate New York," he told her. "I thought I'd send Liam there for a while if he proved too young to live aboard ship, and I'd see him whenever I could."

"Is it far, then?"

"A couple of days' ride," Reinders allowed. "But I haven't been back there in quite a while. Fifteen years to be exact." For the first time he felt how long that really was.

Grace blinked, surprised. "How do you know they're still living?"

"My mother writes once a year."

"If you don't mind my saying so, Captain, 'tis a strange way for a man to be with his very own mother. Have you done something awful, then, that she won't see you?"

"Of course not! She'd like to see me."

"Then why, in Heaven's name, have you not gone in all this time?"

He hesitated. "I'm not sure," he said, at last. "I think about it. I do miss her. Miss the place." He stopped, and shook his head firmly. "But I'm a sea captain. My life is different now."

"If you had Liam, you would've gone back," she reminded him. "Why can you not go on your own?"

He frowned, very uncomfortable under the scrutiny of those green eyes. "If I took Liam there, I'd be a father instead of a son. They couldn't expect me to stay. But if I go alone . . ." He sighed, exasperated. "They expect too much. She expects too much. And now she's old. I won't be able to walk away a second time."

"How did you in the first place?"

"She packed my bag, led me to the door, and pointed out the road," he recalled. "She made me go. Said she knew I was no farmer and would never be happy there."

"And you can't forgive her for that?"

"No!" he exclaimed. "I'm grateful to her."

"So grateful that you'd never let her see you again?" Grace gave him a look she saved for foolish children. "Ah, now, Captain, no one tells a man what to do—he does what he wants." She nodded. "Your mam is old and living with all the choices she did or didn't make. She doesn't want you to come home to stay, only to look upon you and see the man you've become, to look in your eyes and see if you're happy with your life. Because if you are, then, Captain, that's a choice she made right and her heart can be easy with it."

Reinders felt her words pierce his heart, and he replied defensively. "You don't look old enough to be dispensing wisdom about mothers and sons, Missus Donnelly."

"I am twenty years," she told him, the weight of her life rock steady in her gaze. "And I know about mothers because mine was the finest that ever walked the earth. She died young and *her* mother became my mother, the finest that ever walked the earth. And if either one of them were alive even now—sitting by a fire, waiting for me—I would go, no matter where on earth I was. I would go. I am who I am because of them." Her eye caught the unfurled charts on the table. "A man cannot navigate his life without understanding where he came from and where he might be headed. Oh, aye, Captain—if I had a mother still alive on this earth who had never done me a bit of wrong, I would not forsake her in her old age."

Guilty, he judged himself, *guilty as charged.*

"I'm not saying you're guilty," she continued. "But you are her son, and mothers love their sons. I know about that, as well, you see—I've buried two, and left one behind." The words were out of her mouth before she could stop them.

"Left one behind?" Reinders was surprised. "In Ireland?"

"He was newborn," she explained hesitantly. "And sickly. I was afraid to bring him. Afraid 'twould be the death of him."

"So you lecture me about abandoning my mother, but you see nothing wrong with abandoning your own son?" He heard the harshness in his voice, but was unable to temper it. She had wounded him.

"I see everything wrong with it," Grace amended quietly. "And every day, I curse myself for not having had the courage to stay behind."

"Where is he? In an orphan asylum?"

Grace winced. "He's with my da."

"So you abandoned both your son *and* your father?" Reinders shook his head. "So much for family loyalty."

"I love my family with all my heart." Grace lowered her eyes, refusing to let him see her pain.

"Well, Missus Donnelly, if that's the way you love your family—especially your son—maybe I'd better rethink putting Liam in your care."

Grace looked at the captain's hard face and wondered how she'd managed to anger him so quickly. Her eyes searched his, and she knew suddenly that she would have to tell him the truth.

"I had no choice when it came to leaving my son behind," she said resolutely. "A mother across the sea is better than a mother hanged."

That got his attention.

She leaned forward and lowered her voice. "I'm wanted in Ireland," she confessed. "For killing an English guard."

Reinders stared at her, stunned. "Did you do it?"

"Aye," she said evenly, though not without remorse.

"I'm speechless."

"I only hope you'll stay that way." She smiled, ruefully. "And that you'll not judge me so harshly. You've no idea what it's like, Captain—how many dead, how many turned out of their homes. 'Twas my own home about to be tumbled, my old da shot by a greedy land agent, and I did what I had to do," she said determinedly. "There's many of us did what we had to do to keep our families alive. There's no living to be had in Ireland, Captain, without a piece of ground to grow your food. The English want the land, all of it, and they're not about to feed those who occupy it. So we fight them, or we die. Or we leave."

"I'm sorry," he said, and he was.

"I'm not asking for your pity." Grace lifted her chin. "I've made my own choice and I'll live with it. I pray I'll see my son before his first year is out . . ." She bit her lip. "But anything could happen, and I only hope that even if he grows into a man without me, he won't hate me for my hard choice, but understand that it broke my heart. And I hope he'll seek me out so that I can tell him not an hour passed without my yearning to see his face."

Reinders let out a long, slow breath and regarded her anew. "This is why you took Liam—because he's a lost son."

Grace nodded, fighting back her tears. "I've told you more than I should have." Her hands trembled with the enormity of her confession.

"You risked it for the boy. And because you want me to go visit my mother," he added, wryly.

"Aye." She laughed a little, wiped her eyes. "Will you then?"

"I guess I'd better." He patted his pockets, hoping a hand-kerchief would magically appear. "I swear to you, Missus Donnelly," he offered instead. "What you told me today will never leave this room. You have my word on that."

Grace nodded, still shaken.

"I'll do everything I can for Liam," he assured her. "Tell him to start calling you *Aunt* so that it becomes natural."

"I will." She was embarrassed now, drained. She set her cup on his desk, stood and smoothed her skirt, her hair, resettled her shawl.

He stood, too, and came around. "I . . . I enjoyed our conversation," he said awkwardly. "And I'm glad we've come to a resolve."

Grace gave him a shaky smile and put out her hand, which he shook warmly. *What remarkable eyes,* he thought again.

"My da told me once they were the same as the great pirate queen Grainne O'Maille—though how he knew, I can't say. 'Twas for her he called me, and he never does tire of the story."

Reinders nodded, embarrassed to realize he'd spoken aloud.

"Anyway, I'm grateful to you, Captain." She let go of his hand. " 'Tis a hard thing for the boy, losing his mother."

"Good-bye, Missus Donnelly," he said gently.

"Good-bye, Captain. Thank you."

After Grace had gone, Reinders sat down again and took out his log. He wrote nothing, however, simply sat in his chair and stared at the wall—thinking, thinking. So caught up was he in thought, that he missed the creak of Boardham's stealthy tread as the steward disengaged himself from the shadows of the narrow hall and crept past the door to which his ear had been pressed until Missus Donnelly took her leave.

Seventeen

"YOU came!" Danny bounded across the room and shook Sean's good hand. "The lovely Miss Osgoode's here," he added confidentially.

Sean shoved him off. "Shut that great gob of yours, will you?" He glanced around self-consciously. "God forbid she should hear your blather and think me an eejit like yourself."

"Ah, now, boyo." Danny put his arm around Sean's shoulders and steered him into a corner. "You may have it all over me in the matter of brains and the like, but when it comes to matters of the heart"—he tapped his own chest—"I'm your man."

"Are you trying to tell me you love me, then, Danny?" Sean asked with a straight face. "Because you know I'm fond of you and all. I just don't think of you that way."

Danny laughed and punched him. "You're daft, man! You know you're not my kind!"

"I'm not anyone's kind." Sean glanced ruefully at Marcy standing in a circle of admirers. "Look at them—big, strapping Swedes and Germans. Who'd want a crippled Irishman can barely earn his keep?"

"It's true you've got an ugly mug," Danny allowed. "And you're not the mightiest of men, with your arm like that and your big shoe, you live above a saloon, your clothes are all patched—"

"I feel so much better now," Sean interrupted. "Hang on while I go over and ask her to marry me."

"As I was saying." Danny grinned. "You might not think you've got a lot to offer, but you're forgetting one thing."

"And what's that?"

"Your charm." Danny crossed his arms with satisfaction. "You're grand company, O'Malley—especially when you're buying." He winked. "A true gentleman is what you are, and folks feel a little sharper, a little brighter when they're around you."

"All right. How much do you want to borrow?" Sean pretended to pat his pockets, looking for money.

"Ah, now, you know 'tis true! You've a gift! Why I'll wager you could even charm Police Captain Callahan, that oily snake."

"I wouldn't want to get close enough to try," Sean told him. "That's one man whose notice I'd like to avoid."

"Wish I could—isn't he the new landlord, and our rent just gone up?" Danny shook his head, disgusted. "Sent over a couple of Bowery B'hoys to shake us up a little, let us know we'd best pay or get out. We'll have to take in another man to keep the room."

"You've already got six in there! Is the window still broken?"

Danny nodded. "Aye, and the rats are coming through the hole in the wall, but he won't be making repairs anytime soon—instead, he's adding on more rooms in the back."

"How does he get away with that?" Sean was indignant. "Aren't there inspectors? Isn't the city supposed to be trying to clean that place up, provide decent lodgings?"

"Ah, not really." Danny shrugged. "That's just talk for the papers. I been there two years now and it only gets worse, not better."

"Why don't the tenants speak up?"

"Who'd listen? Hundreds pour off those boats every day willing to rent a space on the cellar floor if that's all they can find—better to take it, then rent half to some other poor bastard and get ahead. It's all bribes and payoffs, anyway. No one wants to rock the boat, and get kicked out." He rolled his eyes, wearily. "Getting fed up with it myself. 'Tis no way for a man to live, scrambling over each other like the rats."

"It's beating you down, then."

"Aye, 'tis. I'm a rough man—not like you, with all your charm—and I'm only getting rougher." Danny glanced at the yellow-haired girl at the refreshment table. "Ellen LaVang, over there, she likes the thought of taming me, and I'm starting to like the thought of letting her."

"Must've been a hard day," Sean joked.

Danny didn't laugh. "They're all hard. And soon enough I'll be a hard-drinking man like those who share my room—just another poor, dumb Irishman came to the new land and made nothing of himself."

Sean drew back in surprise. "Danny, I . . ."

"Ah, never mind." Danny threw an arm around Sean's shoulders. "Just crying in my beer, is all. But I'm serious about Miss LeVang," he said. "And by the way, she's let me in on a little secret."

Sean eyed him suspiciously.

"Your Miss Osgoode hasn't a moment of care for those lunky farm boys. Seems she's got her heart set on a high-minded city boy—an Irishman, no less!" Danny squeezed him.

"I don't believe it." Sean pulled away. "It's not true. And even if it were—her father's a solicitor and an Elder of the church. He'd never allow it."

"You don't know that!" Danny insisted. "The man dotes on her, being motherless and all, and I'll wager what's important to her is important to him, as well."

Sean looked across the room just as Marcy turned to look at him; their eyes met and she smiled warmly, kindly, then excused herself from her companions and started toward him.

"Oh, my God," Sean muttered in alarm.

"Just talk to her," Danny advised. "If there's one thing you know how to do in spades, my friend, it's talk. Good evening, Miss Osgoode! You remember my pal Sean O'Malley?"

"Of course I do." She smiled again and Sean found he could not take his eyes off her.

"If you'll excuse me, I'd like to say hello to Miss LeVang before the meeting starts." Danny bowed politely, then turned and slid Sean an encouraging wink before he left.

"I'm glad you found your way back to us, Mister O'Malley. Danny told us at the last meeting that you'd had bad news from home." Marcy hesitated. "The death of your friend. And your sister's ship is still not in. We've been praying for you." She touched his hand briefly.

"Thank you," he said, gratefully. "It's been heavy on me, true enough. Morgan was like my own brother, and Grace . . ." He stopped; this was not the light conversation of courtship.

Marcy watched him intently. "You must be feeling quite alone, then. If it's any comfort, I hope you know you have a family here. With us." She blushed, and looked down.

"Are you sure there's room for an Irishman?" he asked pointedly. "We tend to be the odd men out in families such as this."

"Not at all!" she exclaimed. "We don't think like that! We're not Norwegians or Germans or Swedes or Poles or Irish . . . but Americans! All of us, American, coming together to worship as one body. One family in God." Her eyes glowed intensely, and she leaned closer to him. "And you are a welcome part of that family, Sean. If you want to be."

"I do," he said, caught up in her fervor, the intimacy of the moment, the closeness of her body to his.

"I'm so glad." She took his arm—his crippled arm—and this meant more to him than anything else. "Will you sit with me tonight while Father speaks?"

He nodded and allowed himself to be led across the room, oblivious to Ellen's satisfied nod and Danny's thumbs-up; he sat beside Marcy, breathed in the clean, soapy smell of her, and didn't hear a word her father said, but felt—for the first time in a long time—the unassailable comfort of belonging.

Eighteen

DOCTOR Draper found the arrangement more than satisfactory: a regular supply of good whiskey in return for providing Mister Boardham with a place to do his business—a brisk, stealthy trade in extra food, water, blankets, spirits, tobacco—thereby undermining the authority of the captain, a man he had come to loathe. Draper's wife and youngest son had fallen ill, and while the captain allowed him to tend them, the doctor was not permitted to leave off his other duties. His laudanum gone, he depended upon the whiskey to see him through each long night, and so found himself beholden to the steward, a hard little man true enough, but sympathetic to the doctor's plight.

He was a little drunker than usual tonight, but what did it matter? The patients—indeed, most of the passengers in the hold—were sound asleep; the only others still awake were Mister Boardham and his lady friend. *Lady friend.* Draper snorted. Not all those who wanted extras had the pennies or trinkets to trade and were, if men, out of luck. But if women . . . He listened to the sniggers, the sound of rustling clothes—oops, a tear! A gasp! Draper scooted his chair a little closer to the curtain that separated his private space from the rest of the ward, and cocked his head toward the sounds—more urgent now,

Boardham's low voice demanding, a girlish squeal. Aroused, the doctor swigged from his flask and closed his eyes to better imagine what was happening not five feet away. There was the undeniable rip of cloth and a yelp from the girl, followed by a fleshy thud—the back of Boardham's hand, most likely. A little slap and tickle, Draper told himself, that was all it was, all the steward wanted in return for a loaf of bread, nothing wrong with that. The girl had come willingly; she knew what was expected. Draper licked his lips and considered peeking around the end of the curtain; certainly things had progressed, the thrashing and moaning louder now.

"What's going on?" Grace's voice, rough with fatigue, startled the doctor, who opened his bleary eyes and frowned at her.

"Go away. This doesn't concern you." He took in her own rumpled state of undress, the loosened ties of her blouse. "Unless, of course, you're next."

She saw the flask in his hand, took in his drunkenness, the sounds of struggle, and stepped toward the curtain.

He stood, knocking the chair back, and blocked her way. "It's none of your business," he said sharply, recognizing her. "You."

There was a hard thump against the wall or floor, and the girl cried out, was slapped hard, and cursed viciously.

Grace looked at the doctor, then realized he would do nothing to help and stepped around him, flinging back the curtain. The girl was pinned beneath Boardham and turned a pleading face toward Grace—her lip split and bloody, eye swelling, the front of her dress torn open, the skirt pushed up. Boardham turned too, furious now, at the interruption.

"Get out," he hissed, spittle flying from his mouth.

The girl beneath him renewed her struggle, and he released her long enough to deliver a sound punch to her jaw.

"Let her go!" Grace moved forward, but Draper wrapped an arm around her waist and covered her mouth with his hand.

"Do it," Boardham urged. "You take her first."

Grace brought the heel of her boot down hard on the doctor's toes, causing him to loosen his grip; she drove her elbow into his gut, then shoved him off. Quickly, before he could recover, she pulled the boning knife out of its sheath in her boot and held it out, warding off the doctor.

"Let her go," she demanded, and to her surprise, Boardham rose off the girl, but kept his fingers twisted in her hair, pulling her with him.

"Drop the knife."

"Help!" Grace yelled.

"Shut up!" Boardham moved closer. "Drop it, or I'll tell. About the murder. About you being wanted for murder."

Grace's heart fell, but she tightened her grip on the knife.

"They'll be very interested in that when we land," he warned, eyes glittering. "They'll lock you up. Take away that little brat of yours. And the boy." He tongued the cut on his lower lip. "Drop the knife, and no one's the wiser."

Grace held steady, eyeing both the steward and Draper; she sensed that others were awake now, that some had risen and were standing just outside the circle of light, though none moved forward to help. Had they heard? she wondered. Did they know? Or were they simply too afraid of going up against the black marketeer and the ship's only physician?

"Let her go," Grace demanded fiercely. "And you can live."

His bluff called, Boardham angrily flung the girl to the floor and nodded to the doctor, who crept in from the side. Grace took two steps back, swinging her knife from man to man, but when Boardham suddenly lunged, she held her ground. He came in low, then let out an anguished howl that froze everyone in their tracks; bringing his hand away from his cheek, Boardham looked in amazement at the blood dripping from his fingers, then at Grace.

"You bitch," he snarled. "You fucking bitch."

He attacked and she slashed him again, opening his arm, then stuck him in the shoulder when he fell to his knees. The knife was part of her hand now, part of a rage so black, she could easily slaughter him where he knelt, and then the doctor, and anyone else who got in her way; she was so tired, so tired, so furious and angry and tired of all of this. She raised her hand, but it was caught in midair—caught, and held firmly while a strong arm went round her waist, and a familiar voice said in her ear, "Stop now, Missus Donnelly. Missus Donnelly, stop," it said. "I'm here now."

She did as he commanded. Her vision cleared and she saw Boardham cowering on the ground, covered in blood, so much blood; she saw the doctor wide-eyed in the corner, saw the other passengers come out of the shadows, their faces guarded. Saw Liam with his arms around Mary Kate, forbidding her to look, though he looked—looked and saw and was stunned. And that was when all the air went out of her body. She sagged against the captain, and he took the knife from her hand.

"What the hell is going on down here?" Reinders looked around the room, Mackley and Dean on either side of him. "Boardham?" The steward struggled to his feet, holding his arm and moaning. "Draper? I want an answer. Now!"

The doctor eyed the crowd, weighing the situation. "The Donnelly woman attacked him," he tried cautiously. "A case of jealousy, I believe, Captain. Your steward is a popular man with the ladies."

"Is he?" Reinders snapped.

"I was minding my own business when she come at me with that knife," Boardham complained, picking up the story. "I'm bleeding here, sir. I'm right hurt. Weren't nothing going on she had to cut me."

Reinders eyed the bloody knife that had fallen from Grace's hand. "What about that, Missus Donnelly? Anything to say?"

She heard him as if from far away and could not answer, only stare at the steward as if she'd forgotten who he was.

They had all forgotten the discarded girl, who now gathered herself up and stepped out of the dark corner. "Don't blame her," she said quietly, holding the torn dress together with one hand. " 'Twas my own doing and no one else's."

"Who are you?" Reinders asked, not ungently.

"Ada, sir. Ada Murphy." She hung her head. "I didn't think I'd have to . . . that he'd want . . ." She covered her face and began to weep. "He said he'd give us bread."

"Is that right?"

Boardham shrugged sullenly. "*She's* the one made the offer—I seen nothing wrong with taking her up on it."

"I'm sure you didn't." Reinders turned back to the girl. "What happened when Missus Donnelly tried to help?"

"They held her," Ada said through her tears. "Him there, and the doctor. They said she was next. She fought 'em off, though."

The captain's jaw tightened. "All right. I've heard enough. Are you with someone on the ship, Miss Murphy?"

"My sister." She cried harder now.

Reinders sighed. "Mister Dean, help her find her sister, please."

Dean stepped forward and took the now sobbing girl by the arm, shielding her as he led her through the crowd.

"The rest of you, back to bed now," Reinders ordered. "Not you, Draper," he added. "You come here."

Draper's eyes widened in surprise. "Me? Surely, Captain, you don't think I had anything to do with this? In my ignorance, I may have misread the situation, but my only crime is naivete."

"I'm not sure what your crime is yet," Reinders warned. "But yours"—he turned to Boardham—"is assault."

"Assault!" Boardham clenched his fist, then winced. "She's the one had the knife. What about her, then?"

Reinders and Mackley exchanged a quick glance.

"That's *your* knife, Boardham," the first mate said smoothly. "I've seen it on you a dozen times."

"She pulled it out of her boot!" Draper insisted. "Really, Captain, these charges are false."

"You charge me," Boardham threatened, "and I'll report *her* to the authorities the minute we land. For murder."

Reinders felt Grace tense against him, and kept his arm firmly around her waist.

"They'll throw her in prison right off," Boardham jeered. "Or ship her back home to hang."

"They lock up lunatics, too. Take him, Mister Mackley." The first mate grabbed Boardham's good arm.

"I mean it, Captain." The steward yanked his arm away. "I heard the whole thing. In your cabin. You're a party to it."

Grace was alert now—painfully alert, knowing Mary Kate and Liam were listening—and stood on her own two feet.

"What?" Draper narrowed his eyes. "Is this true, Captain? You were aware this woman is wanted for murder, and now she's nearly committed another?"

Reinders saw Liam's face out of the corner of his eye. "Boardham's a liar and a cheat—his word means nothing on my ship."

"Obviously not, but it may mean something on land, and I intend to take it up with the proper authorities."

"You do that," Reinders said evenly. "Ah, Mister Dean. Everything all right with the young woman?"

"Yes, sir." Dean crossed his massive arms and eyed the steward with disgust. "They say our Mister Boardham was running quite a trade down here, and that the good doctor—"

"I had nothing to do with it!" Draper held up his hands.

Dean nodded. "Too drunk, I guess. Boardham did as he pleased."

"Take him to the brig," Reinders ordered.

Mackley and Dean gripped the steward under each arm and hauled him toward the stairs.

"And you." Reinders turned to Draper. "Get your things together. Then go down and stitch him up. Mackley'll come for you."

"I say," Draper sputtered.

"You're in no position to say anything. Get going." He turned to Grace. "Can you walk?" he asked quietly. "Are you hurt?"

"No, Captain." Her voice was shaky. "I can walk."

"Good. Then follow me." She looked ghastly, he thought. "Liam." He put his hand on the boy's shoulder. "Good boy to run for help. I'm proud of you, son."

Liam smiled weakly.

"Take the little girl back to bed now, and I'll see you in the morning." He knelt down in front of Mary Kate. "I must speak to your mother, but I won't keep her long," he promised. "She did a very brave thing tonight. I'm sorry you were frightened."

Mary Kate nodded, then rushed to Grace and buried her

face in her mother's skirts. Grace hid her bloody hand behind her back and stroked Mary Kate's hair with the other.

"Go with Liam, agra," she murmured. " 'Tis over now, and I'll be back soon."

She kissed both children, then followed the captain up the stairs and across the deck—pausing to take in the hard, glittering night sky and breathe the cold air before entering his cabin.

"Sit down." He handed her a brandy. "Drink this. I know I'm having at least one."

She drank and felt steadier; they regarded one another in the dim lantern light of the cabin.

"What'll happen now?" she asked. "Now I've made a mess of things."

He laughed shortly. "Well, you probably saved Miss Murphy from bearing an unwanted bastard in nine months."

"He must've been listening at the door." Grace shook her head. "Now they all know. And the doctor. I'm afraid for the children." Her eyes filled with tears.

Reinders set his glass down. "I'll keep Boardham in the hold until we land and you're safely off. I have to take those who are still ill to the marine hospital, but I'll feign ignorance, unload the well passengers first, then sail back to Staten Island."

"Won't they speak to the doctor?"

"I believe he'll be tied up." He grinned wryly. "In surgery or something. Maybe I'll send him back to Boardham, forget he's there. His family can disembark—they'll understand about medical emergencies."

She nodded gratefully. "Thank you, Captain. I'm causing you a great deal of trouble."

He waved that off. "Will your brother meet you on the dock?"

"I don't know," she confessed. "He thinks we sailed on another ship out of Cork City, but I'll find him. He lives above a saloon run by Mighty Dugan Ogue."

"The boxer?" Reinders' eyebrows went up in surprise.

"I don't know him myself," she admitted. "But he's a cause man, and Sean's been there since he come."

"If you run into trouble, go to the Irish Emigrant Society. They have a good reputation for helping their own." Less tense now, the captain leaned back in his chair. "I, for one, will be glad to see you swallowed up by the city."

"Will there be trouble, then?"

Reinders shrugged. "I'll have Boardham beaten up and thrown overboard, and I'll let the doctor watch, then threaten him with the same. That ought to shut them both up long enough for me to lodge my own complaints and discredit them before I leave town."

"Another voyage so soon?"

"A short one," he said, casually. "Something important that's been waiting for me. But then I thought I'd take a trip upstate." Reinders smiled. "Time I did that, don't you think, Missus Donnelly?"

"Aye, Captain. I do."

They looked at one another for a long moment.

"Missus Donnelly." Reinders leaned forward again, hesitating before he spoke. "I want you to know I'm not a man who places much value on the regard of others—especially those idiots who roam the society pages—but I find that your regard, your good opinion, matters very much to me."

She looked at him in surprise. "Do you remember, Captain, what I said to you the very first day—when you asked me did I want to get off?"

He thought for a moment. "You said I had a good reputation for bringing ships through bad storms."

"And what else?"

He frowned. "That God told you to put your life in my hands."

"Well, then, Captain, if God has such high regard for you, how could I have anything less?" She smiled gently. "Was He right, then, do you think—to put my life in your hands?"

Reinders considered this under her steady gaze, considered it in light of her own considerable faith, and all she had been through. In one more day they would dock on Manhattan in the year 1848, to a country presided over by James Knox

Polk, the eleventh president of the United States. All of these passengers—all but the sixty-five who had died—would find lodgings and jobs, carve out a living, raise their families, and slowly, slowly, the tale of their voyage to the new land would change from one of trial to one of triumph. This was what he sorely hoped.

"Yes, Missus Donnelly," he said at last. "Yes, He was."

She didn't hear the call of "Land!" in the middle of the night, but in the morning when she went up on deck, there lay the coast in all its glory with its tall ships and taller buildings, clatter and commotion, clouds of dark coal dust, clouds of white steam; and up in the bow in the place that he'd claimed from the very first day—the weathered old man, his face alight with joy.

" 'Tis America, then?" She put a hand gently on his arm.

"Aye, 'tis!" He turned and hugged her fiercely. "We've made it, girleen! All the way across the bitter sea to the land of the free!"

He hooted gleefully and did a little jig, and she laughed to see it. She kissed him for luck, then went below again and said her good-byes to those she'd come to know—the fiddlers and pipers, the singles and couples and families, old folk and young runabout children. Liam and Mary Kate danced about her in excitement, begging, and at last they came up on deck to stay until the ship eased her way into the long quays of South Street, Manhattan, America.

The gangway went down, and passengers lined up to disembark, listening to the instructions about passing through the medical inspection building first. Grace, Mary Kate, and Liam were midway in the line when the captain approached in a clean jacket and brushed cap; he took Grace by the arm, drawing her aside.

"Get off right away," he directed quietly. "With the first-class passengers. I'll take you over myself."

"My trunk." Grace looked for it.

"Right here." He tipped his head toward Mister Dean,

who had hoisted it onto his shoulder and was waiting to follow.

He led her to the front of the line and turned her over to Mackley, who checked her off the list.

" 'Missus Gracelin Donnelly,' " the first mate read, a great grin upon his handsome face. " 'Mary Kathleen, daughter. Liam Kelley, cousin.' "

"Aye." Grace glanced surreptitiously at the captain.

"Welcome to America, Missus Donnelly." Mackley tipped his cap and stepped back to let her pass.

"Captain, I . . ."

Reinders held out his hand. "Missus Donnelly. I wish you well. And you, little miss." He bent down to look in Mary Kathleen's face. "You proved very seaworthy. As did you, young Master Kelley."

"Oh, Captain." Liam pulled himself up straight and threw a perfect salute. "I love the *Eliza J,* Captain!"

"Then you'll have to come back when you're older and learn to sail her yourself. That's an order."

"Oh, can I?" he breathed.

"I'll save you a place," Reinders promised. "Now off you go. You're holding up the line."

Grace looked over the boy's head at the captain, and an understanding passed between them.

"Come and see us," she said quietly and put out her hand.

"I will." He held it tightly. "I'll tell you all about my mother."

Her eyes sparkled and she laughed then, letting go of his hand and starting down the wooden ramp, hands on the ropes for guidance, the children behind her, Mary Kate holding Grace's skirt, Liam's hand on Mary Kate's shoulder. When they reached the wharf, they turned and waved up at the captain, who took off his cap and held it over his heart. *Good luck, Missus Donnelly,* he thought.

"Good luck, Captain!" she called, then stepped into a new world.

Grace held her breath as they passed through the immigration station and back out into the swarming confusion of the harborfront. She spotted the runners with their green neckties immediately and beat them off before they could say a word. She saw an Irishman in his bowler and green vest, but fought the urge to approach him and was glad when she witnessed him eyeing the crowd with professional objectivity, picking out a simple, exhausted-looking family and greeting them with the exuberance of a long-lost uncle before hustling them off. He was no uncle—he'd returned in fewer than ten minutes to choose yet another harried and confused victim.

It was the same as Liverpool and she fought off her disappointment; she'd hoped for better in America, but maybe this wasn't truly America—maybe America lay farther in, away from the docks. She sniffed the air, but it was much the same as anywhere—salt water, coal dust, fried meat, horse dung. She glanced around, but the people were no different either; different language perhaps, but the faces just as baffled, the children just as ragged as any she'd seen. The buildings along the wharf were newer and had a more modern look about them, but their intent was the same as any other building on any other wharf. It was the sound that was different, now that she listened: the English sharper and more buoyant, the slang unfamiliar but confident—coupled with winks and nods, tipping hats—the speech and manner of cocky optimists. Americans. She was surrounded by them.

"Stay close to me, now," she admonished the children. "Sit down on top of the trunk and don't move while I think what to do next."

She denied the feeling of complete exhaustion, forced herself to stand and take a good look around. They were in a vast area from which narrow streets led away from the waterfront to the boulevards beyond. There were many large buildings and a number of boardinghouses—she could see signs for rooms to let, but knew now that these would be expensive and dirty, and she pitied the weary groups that made their way to the first open door.

The trunk was heavy—she had packed everything from Alice's into this and two carpetbags she carried, one in each hand. The trick would be to get the trunk, the bags, the children, and herself into a carriage, but the carriages were out on the boulevard and that was too far. She was reluctant to ask anyone for help as now they all looked foreign when only moments ago they had seemed familiar. She had a sense of coming out of her body, of watching herself watching everyone else, and she shook her head vigorously. It was freezing now, and snowflakes settled on her head and shoulders. Her teeth chattered and she bit her lip to stop them, sending up a silent prayer to God.

"Gracelin!"

She turned and there was Sean, her beloved brother, running across the square as fast as his limp allowed, arms outstretched.

"Grace! Dear God! Grace!" He swept her into a tight embrace, covering her face with kisses, holding her out to drink in the sight of her, hugging her again and again, laughing in disbelief.

"Sean," was all she could whisper into the collar of his coat, the smell of him, the warmth and solidity of him all suddenly overwhelming. He was here. She clung tightly to him and began to cry.

"Ah, now, darling girl," he murmured, wiping her tears with his fingertips. "You're safe now. You made it, by God, you did." He looked over her shoulder, searching the crowd.

"He didn't . . ." She stopped. "He's dead."

Sean's eyes returned to hers, his face infinitely sad. "I know. William wrote. I'd hoped he'd got it wrong, is all."

She shook her head and he held her.

"Let's get you home now," he said gently. "We'll talk then."

She nodded, unable to speak, the tears blinding her, cascading down her cheeks. He wiped them away, then peered around her at the two children sitting on the trunk.

"And who is this you've brought along?" He pretended to be baffled. "Surely 'tis not our Mary Kathleen for she was but a wee thing, and this is a beautiful giantess! What have you done with her, you bold creature—don't you know I love no one but herself?"

Mary Kate ducked her head shyly. " 'Tis I," she said, then suddenly thrust up her arms.

He scooped her up and buried his face in her neck. "Ah, now, little one," he whispered in her ear. "I knew 'twas you all along, and aren't you a sight for lonely eyes? I missed you, Mary Kate. You're as pretty as your mam."

Liam sat silently, watching them all with downcast eyes, kicking his heel against the trunk.

"This is Liam Kelley," Grace told her brother. "His mam and sister died aboard ship. He's going to live with us until we find his da. Is that all right, Sean? Have you room for us all?"

Sean set Mary Kate down and extended his good hand to the boy. "Welcome to America, Liam, and sorry for your terrible misfortune. I'm glad to have you with us as otherwise I'd be outnumbered by the womenfolk, and you know what a burden that can be to a man."

Liam gave up a reluctant smile.

"Is this your trunk, then?" Sean asked. "Or are you just keeping it warm for someone of greater inheritance?"

The boy laughed. " 'Tis ours," he said, jumping off. "The bags, as well. I can carry the bags."

"Well, and I'll help you," Sean offered. "But first I'll see about a cab. The driver can fetch the trunk. Would you want to come with me on this bit of man's work?"

Liam nodded shyly.

Sean kissed his sister once more. "I can hardly bear to let you out of my sight, but I'll be right back."

She opened her mouth to speak, but faltered, fresh tears welling, mouth trembling all over again.

"I know." He placed his hand against her cheek. "Hold on."

They watched him walk off with Liam; then Grace sat down on the trunk next to Mary Kate and put her arm around the child.

"We made it," she said, wiping her eyes and stilling her heart.

"Aye," Mary Kate answered calmly. "God said."

Grace pulled her daughter close and held her as the snow

swirled round them both, and the barkers yelled from their stalls and the runners called out, and sailors rushed past, and ship after ship released holds of human cargo, and immigrants staggered off, fell to the ground, kissed it, and wept.

Nineteen

MIGHTY Ogue wasted no time in preparing the best party the saloon had seen since James "Yankee" Sullivan defeated William Bell in a bare-knuckle fight after twenty-four rounds, thirty-eight minutes. It was a great day for Irish pugilists everywhere, and Dugan had been happy to host the betting party as Sullivan himself had coached Ogue in his own heyday at the Sawdust House. That had been August five years past, an August hotter than any Ogue remembered.

The former boxer turned saloonkeeper paused in his work and gave a great sigh at the thought of Sullivan, up the river even now, sitting in Sing Sing Prison for having arranged the infamous fight between Thomas McCoy and Christopher Lilly, a fight that ended with McCoy—the Irishman—drowned in his own blood, and Lilly—the Englishman—smuggled out of the country. The trial that followed had been one of the most sensational the city had ever seen, and Sullivan was sent up for inciting riot and manslaughter.

Ogue shook his head and resumed polishing the bar. The city had seemed tame to him ever since, and he'd quit the boxing life while he still had a few teeth in his head, and the remains of a nose, and was not too ugly yet to win the heart of his own dear Tara.

But this was no hot August night filled to the rafters with Irishmen waxing poetic about somebody they knew personally, by God, who was the best fighter ever seen in the entire world undisputed by anyone anywhere who'd witnessed the last fight, and if you hadn't, then you didn't know what you were talking about and you'd best just shut your gob right now, Christ forgive you. No, it wasn't hot August, but freezing-cold January, and the saloon was filling quietly with those who'd watched Sean go out day after day, in all kinds of weather, in case his sister was waiting on the dock. And when he'd come back two mornings ago, themselves in tow, everyone was thankful, especially Ogue, who stepped quietly into the storeroom to thank God personally, and even took himself off to church to put an extra penny in the poor box.

Though no one had been told outright, most everyone seemed to know that O'Malley's sister was Morgan McDonagh's widow. She stood near the fire, and shyly, they came—the older ones who understood sacrifice and wanted to pay respect; the younger ones, the boys-just-men, because she was beautiful and because her husband was a legend even here, and because they wanted with all their hearts to be as noble as that man and win the love of such a woman; and the women, because they knew the pain of trying to breathe around the shards of a shattered heart—hadn't they all lost husbands, lovers, sons and daughters, friends and neighbors? This was what they tried to convey in words both English and Irish—old words of comfort, new ones of hope. And then they left her in peace, and set themselves about the room, greeting one another with grave respectability, settling in to exchange news and letters from home, word of jobs and where to buy bread, who was working and who was not, who lost a baby or had one newborn, why those two ever married and what of the terrible fights that one over there got into—letting the great ball of conversation roll on and on until it had covered the subjects nearest their hearts: Ireland and Irish politics, America and American politics, politics in general, God, and boxing.

The room was crowded now, fifty conversations all at once,

voices raised to be heard, cheeks flushed with passion and drink. When the tide turned to boxing, Ogue's own fights were taken out and dusted off, recalled blow-by-blow by the boys who had backed him, this leading, of course, to a discussion of Sullivan's brilliance in training boxers and the good old days at the Sawdust House. It was rumored that when Sullivan got out of prison, he would fight again, perhaps in Maryland as it wasn't legal anymore in New York. The sporting gentlemen in the crowd began placing bets on the fight even though it was a year from being set, even though no one knew whom Sullivan would fight, even though Sullivan himself might not even be alive by then. When this was pointed out—by a man of little faith, a man too soon off the boat, perhaps even a college man—the doubter found himself confronted by one who rolled up his sleeves and danced the challenge dance, fists up, jabs thrown. The doubter accepted the challenge, removed his jacket and cap, turned up his own sleeves, and entered in, feigning jabs of his own, grinning to the crowd and winking at the girls, as the circle of cheering enthusiasts widened around them.

The first blow wiped the grin off his face, and he looked at his opponent with real surprise, the same look as appeared on the other man's face, for who knew it would actually turn into a fight? But now they were mad—for a thousand small reasons besides the big one—and their surprise and mock jabs turned to focused determination and calculated blows. Money changed hands quickly as first one man fell down and then the other, only to be pushed back up and into the ring by the same hands that held the money; a nose was bloodied, an angry roar, an eyebrow split, a call for more, and then—before tables and chairs were broken—the fire was doused by the ringing of Ogue's bell and the announcement of "A drink on the house for everyone here and two for the boxers, let's give 'em a cheer!" The two fighting men shook hands and agreed that Sullivan—an Irishman, after all—would indeed live to fight another day, and Ogue himself would take all bets. Arms over shoulders, the two boxers staggered to the bar, held their whiskeys aloft, and accepted the cheers of the house, each one privately appropriating victory while loudly congratulating the other.

The crowd settled down then, and realized they had exhausted—only for the moment, mind you—the subjects of Ireland, America, politics, God, and boxing, and so they sat back in their chairs, ordered more to drink, and called for a song.

Tiny Tara Ogue obliged them by taking out her fiddle and setting up at the end of the big room. After plucking the strings and fine-tuning her instrument, she tapped her foot and began to play. Other feet joined hers, knees jiggled, hands clapped, heads bobbed, and finally a couple of the big boys—unable to contain themselves any longer and having missed out on the fight—got up to dance a vigorous jig. The mood grew merry and familiar, Ogue brought out more pickled eggs, ham, bread and butter to keep them all nourished and they danced until he threw them out at midnight.

When all had gone and bid farewell, the chairs turned right and the doors locked, the Great One's wife had come up to thank him—Missus Donnelly, she was to be called—and he told her it was an honor, a privilege, the very least he could do, and weren't they all so very grateful to have her there among them?

She stood on tiptoe and kissed his cheek, then thanked him again for all he'd done for her brother and herself, for the two little ones, for Ireland, and he'd been moved by that, by the well-spoken words and the way she looked right into him with eyes the color of the Irish sea. She reminded him of someone, of the old stories, of kings and queens and warrior poets—there was all that about her, in the way she carried herself and the wisdom in her eyes of years beyond her age. She made him remember his home in a way he had not since coming to America. There was a glimpse of his mother in her, his granny and all his aunties, all the strong women he'd ever known, including his own Tara, who'd come all this way from the islands in the North only to bear a great sorrow. There was a rare beauty in these women, a kind of shining nobility that years in the hard city dulled; but it was fresh in Grace—she was still a daughter of

Ireland, a daughter of the thousand kings who once ruled their island, a reminder of the majesty from which they'd sprung. He and Tara had never been blessed with children, but he'd come to feel fatherly about Sean, and now he took Grace into his heart, as well. It was nothing he'd ever say to them, nothing he'd admit even to Tara, but it was how he would look out for them, these children of home. It was how he would remember who he really was.

Twenty

ABBAN and Barbara finished filling in the last of the three graves, then gathered up the pick and shovel, and went into the warm kitchen.

"At least they all went together, bless their souls." Abban sank wearily onto a stool, leaning his crutch against the wall.

"I wonder if their brother made it, or if he died on the road." Barbara hung the kettle over the fire. "Worse for him, going alone."

"Aye." Abban kicked a chair away from the table. "Come sit down now, Sister, and have a rest. You've not slept a'tall these days past, caring for them."

"I miss Sister George." Barbara's eyes misted, and she pushed back her hair, leaving a smudge of dirt across her forehead. "Not just for her devotion to the children."

"That young one, Sister James, she'll do for them." Abban tapped the chair with his foot. "Come on now, sit."

Barbara crossed the room and settled herself heavily at the table, reaching out to pat Abban's knee. "I'm so grateful to you. So thankful to have you through all this."

"Ah, no," he scoffed. "I've a roof over my head and the protection of the great ladies in gray themselves, so don't go thanking me. Safer for me here than out in the world."

"Speaking of the world—" She pushed a long letter toward him. "Did you read this from Julia?"

"Not sure I wanted to," he confessed. "All the news these days is bad or worse."

Barbara nodded, sorrowfully. "She's been to Liverpool again, trying to help with relief for all the paupers pouring in. There's not room nor food enough for them all."

"Still running to stand still, are they?"

"Flooding the ports to get out, she says. Thousands each week."

"Thousands." Abban sighed. "I suppose it's the landlords paying their crossing."

Barbara nodded. "A few shillings and they're England's problem, not ours." She tapped the letter. "Julia says it's madness. The crews don't care—more money for them—they kick and curse, herd them onto any boat, decks are overcrowded and dangerous, folks fall down, get crushed or pushed overboard. Pigs everywhere, she says, but minded as they've some value. More than Irish emigrants, I guess."

"Poor bastards." Abban massaged the thigh of his good leg. "Will they stop them, then, from coming into the country?"

Barbara got up to get the kettle. "I don't think they can," she said. "If you've the fare, they must let you cross. But the parish is being ruined, from what Julia says. There's not enough money for more relief stations, and now our ones have broken back into boarded-up cellars to live. As many as forty to a room, Julia says—all of them hungry, many of them dying."

"So they're taking the fever with them, not escaping it." Abban took the cup she handed him, warming his hands around it.

"Aye, and Liverpool will have an epidemic as well. They're already threatening to round them up and send them back." She sat again, and sipped her tea. "Julia says they sneak off in the night and are spreading all through England, Scotland, and Wales. But they can't get work." She frowned. "The English laborers hate our boys, and now they've got the fear of fever as a good reason to shut them out."

"What about Manchester?" Abban asked. "Little Ireland?"

"Ah, 'tis a terrible place, I've heard, a slum town. Nothing but filth and sin, and already packed with Irish. No." She shook her head. "Won't many find shelter there. They'll go on to London, and if they live and manage to get any work—they'll try for America or Canada."

"Anything, just to eat," he said heavily. "Halfway round the world for a bowl of porridge and a straw bed."

"And for freedom. Freedom from all this." Her shoulders slumped. "Sometimes, Abban, I've half a mind to go down to those docks myself and board the first boat out. To get away from this endless misery and start a new life. Sometimes I hate it here. That's how weak I am." She covered her mouth, ashamed.

Abban reached out and pulled her hand away. "You've got mud all over your face, girl," he admonished gently. "Streaky like that, with your hair flying all round, you remind me of your brother."

She shook her head. "Now you shame me, for sure he never had a moment of weakness his whole life."

"Sure and he did." Abban looked her in the eye. "And that's what made him truly courageous. Times were he was bone-weary, hungry, dirty, and so heartsick for herself he could hardly put one foot in front of the other, let alone lead a band of rag-tag men to victory." He squeezed her hand. "But he did. Time and time over, he did."

She sat quietly for a moment. "Do you think he would've gone to America with her had he lived?"

"He would've gone to the moon and back, if that's where she was."

Her eyes filled with tears. "Poor Morgan."

"Ah, no." He squeezed her hand again. "Lucky Morgan. Lucky, lucky man to have known a love as great as that."

"Poor Grace, then."

"Aye. 'Tis those left behind suffer most. But his love'll carry her to the end. I've no doubt of that."

"Were you married, then, Abban?"

He let go of her hand, eyes lowered. "She died at the start of the hunger, she and my sons. I buried them. And then I moved on."

"You're a man of courage, as well."

"We're all of us, in our own quiet ways. Even the man who simply rises from his bed each morning in light of all this."

They looked at one another then—the tired, grizzled man with one leg and enough sorrow to fill three lifetimes, and the tired young woman who'd been caring for others and trying to survive for as long as she could remember—and each found comfort in the company of the other, a warmth that shed light into the corners of hearts that could remember only the duty of love, but not the joy. And they were able to go on.

Twenty-one

I<small>T</small> was the food that amazed Grace most of all. Even in the dead of winter, she found fruits and vegetables on every corner; windows filled with breads, cakes, pastries of all kinds; penny candies and something called ice cream; milk and cider and ale; so many cheeses; fresh fish; any cut of meat or fowl, as well as kidneys, livers, hearts and brains, bones, tails, sausages, and liver spreads. It was an incredible abundance, and the sight of it all left her feeling giddy and tearful and unable to make a purchase even though Sean had given her money. Just go out and look, he told her. Look around each day, and soon it will be real.

He took her himself in those first weeks, showed her the famous streets and the parks, the mansions and the tenement district, took her to the Irish Emigrant Society, where they registered Liam's name and posted that of his father, Seamus Kelley of Dublin. Sean taught her how to use the strange money, how to ride the omnibus. Soon enough, she could do it herself and out she went each day, adding block after block to her rounds, until she began to get used to sights and sounds and smells. Tara sent her on errands—for fish, for shoes, for pickles, for meat—and slowly she became oriented.

Karl Eberhardt, the butcher around the corner, was like

many Germans who'd decided to stay in the city rather than go north to Albany, west for farmland. They stayed and conducted their business in aprons streaked with bloody swipes, sons working alongside if they had them, wives or daughters if not. Karl's wife, Dagmar, worked beside him, weighing out meat, counting out money—every day but Sunday.

There were no Irish butchers that Grace had found; Irishmen were street peddlers selling buttons, thread, fiddle strings, suspenders, soap, matches, any little thing that could be easily bought and sold. They were carters, drivers, dockworkers, laborers, runners, bootblacks, saloon sweepers, muckrakers, beachcombers crying out "Fresh shad!" and "Rockaway clams!" in lyrical voices that took her instantly, heartbreakingly home. These were the men; the women were needle workers—either in dim, noisy factories that made them blind or deaf, or consumptive from breathing the fibrous air; or they worked at home doing piecework for pennies, often cheated by managers who paid a fraction of the price originally promised—if they paid at all. For who was there to represent the poor, ignorant Irishwoman, surrounded by her hungry children, stitching shirts by candlelight in a cold basement corner? They were the vulnerable, invisible behind the doors of dirty tenements. More visible were the maids of all work—scrubbing the floors of the wealthy, cooking meals, polishing silver, laying tables, washing dirty linens—their white faces, Papist though they might be, preferable to the dark ones who previously occupied these positions.

These dark faces fascinated Grace, and she'd been scolded by Sean on more than one occasion for staring as she watched them peddling their buttermilk and bedding straw. They were also the chimney sweeps and waiters, drivers and doormen, sailors and back-door errand boys. Were they all from Africa? she'd wondered aloud, and Sean had told her all about slavery and those states of the union where it was rigorously defended. Most of the blacks Grace saw were freemen, Sean said, but others were runaways who lived in constant fear of being picked up by the bondsmen who roamed the city looking for them; even freemen weren't safe from these thugs, who thought nothing of kidnapping a black man or woman, then transporting them down south to turn in for the reward or selling price. That was why they keep their eyes lowered, Grace thought, and why they moved quickly through the crowds. Like the Irish, they preferred the company of their own kind and mistrusted all others.

The Jews kept to themselves, as well, but she had come to know their differences—the Russian and Polish Jews through their cries of "Glass put in!" as they hawked their glazing skills, and the German Jews from romantic-sounding places like Bavaria, Bohemia, Moravia, and Posen, who haggled with customers in front of their used-clothing stores along Chatham and Baxter Streets.

The Italian men were laborers, their women ragpickers; they saved their money for fruit stands, like Mister Marconi, who hoped one day to operate a grocery. The French were more established—they owned restaurants and millinery shops, were dressmakers to the upper class, had wonderful bakeries like the favorite of Liam and Mary Kate, who always stopped in front of the glass to peer in at the tiny iced cakes, tall layer cakes, braided sweet breads, long crusty loaves of bread.

Her children were immigrant children, but they did not work yet like the other children who stood on the corners in summer and sold hot buttered corn, who swept the streets in winter when mud was at its worst, who peddled newspapers all year long. They had to work, these children, in order for their families to survive; and if they were orphaned, this was all that kept them alive.

America was the land of plenty, true enough, but there were plenty who had nothing, and most of them were Irish. Every immigrant group had its community, had found its place, and Grace had understood from her first day out that the place of the Irish was last, that the Irish and the blacks had been left to fight each other for the last rung on the slippery ladder of daily survival with no hand reaching down to pull them up. NO IRISH NEED APPLY was a common notice in shop windows and ads, and Grace had begun to worry. She could hire herself out as a serving girl, but only if they would let her go home at the end of the day, which was highly unlikely. She was further unnerved by the cartoons that abounded, poking fun at the assumed stupidity and incompetence of Irish household help. They were all called *Brigid,* these cartoon girls, and depicted as monkey-faced and ignorant of the basic civilities of sophisticated society. Grace cringed whenever she saw one of these, battling shame and anger.

There was shame and anger, too, over the reputation of the Irish as incorrigible drunkards. In Ireland, there had been too much daily labor and too little money for drunkenness to be a problem, but here liquor was cheap and plentiful, a balm to those who felt displaced and disoriented, disillusioned and disheartened, disliked and disappointed. There were saloons for the everyday man and grog shops in tenement housing for the boarders; porter houses for day laborers, carters, and sailors; taverns for the artisans, clerks, and tradesmen; pubs for newspaper men and the literati; corner whiskey sellers for those wanting a cheap bottle; and the private clubs, each of which had its gentlemen's lounge. There were the enormous German rooms—Duetsches Volksgarten, Atlantic Gardens, and Lindenmuller's Odean—where hundreds of people went at one time to hear music, dance, and drink. But not the Irish. They couldn't afford it, they were afraid, they stayed closer to home.

She knew they'd have a drink at the end of a day when no work was found, though plenty available, and soon enough they'd begin each day with a drink, as well—a drink to steady themselves against the blows to their pride. And then, the morning drink and the evening drink would blur into one long day of drink, for how could they return home to face those who depended upon them with nothing for it? No money nor bread nor promise of better lodgings; just manure on their feet and the stink of cheap whiskey and tobacco in their clothes, bitterness settling in as the look in their children's eyes turned from hopefulness to disappointment.

Grace understood that the consolation for disenchantment could be found in a penny shot, that like sought out like for

comfort and the reinstatement of pride, and that was why they
gathered in saloons and grog shops, one on every block, two on
the Irish streets. The lowest of these was no more than a board
across two barrels in the dank basement of an old building,
down a steep flight of steps rank with urine and vomit; if the
liquor itself didn't kill you, the man beside you might. This was
where the most desperate gathered, men and women who had
exhausted their money and their credit at better places like the
Harp, whose days had become nothing more than a search for
cheap drink—forget food, they couldn't stomach it; forget family, they had none left; forget pride, it was gone forever; forget
God, He couldn't see them in Hell.

Grace's heart bled each time she passed these holes and saw
an Irishman stagger out, barely alive for another worthless day.
She steeled her heart against the misery of the women, abandoned by husbands, taken in by lovers who later abandoned
them, with child more times than not. So many children on the
street alone: Italian and German children begging pennies for a
song; dark, tinker children running in packs, picking pockets,
disappearing into alleyways; fair English children eyeing each
passerby warily, sizing up the possibility of begging a coin or
stealing one. Grace had read the editorials deploring the ragged
and hopeless situation of those whose ranks seemed to swell
each day. Decent society could not be held accountable for the
beggar children of immigrants and slaves, it was said, but there
were others who pointed out that ignoring the problem now
only meant facing it later—later, when these children had
grown up and become menacing men and women, embittered
by a society less charitable to them than to its horses, who allowed them to be victimized by any degenerate with a lust for
children. Grace had never in her life imagined that children
might be prostituted, but it was among the many nightly vices
offered in this city. She agreed with the editor who said that for
want of examples of kindness, consideration, and morality, these
children would grow into a breed of predator unlike any other;
they would be the most cruel of adults, devoid of moral conscience, if something were not done for them now. She had

thought Dublin's poor the most desperate until she'd seen Liverpool; coming here, she'd realized man could sink even lower.

And yet, here in this city, she had seen the finest things man could accomplish—magnificent architecture, glorious art, radiant music, beautiful parks; schools, businesses, transportation, machines, advancements everywhere she looked. But she had also come to realize that the heights of man's achievement were equally matched by the depths of his degradation; the face was strong and confident, but it fed from an underbelly ripe with corruption. The Irish floundered in this environment, removed as they were from the influence of old parishes and generations of family. Men became distanced from wives and children, pulled down by drink and self-loathing, finding no relief in any quarter. The great irony to Grace was that the Irish—to whom land was everything, who had fought to the death for every inch—had settled so completely into the city; and not just into the city, but into the worst, most crowded slums. They were too lonely, Sean told her, too lonely and heartsick to move out west, where a day's pay might buy acres of land, but the closest neighbor was miles away.

Grace thought with longing of acres of land—room to breathe, privacy, the children running free out of doors—but she knew it was out of the question. Maybe when Patrick and the baby came, maybe by then she'd have saved enough to buy a farm for all of them. She hoarded what little of Aislinn's money was left, but knew she must find work. Sean earned some through writing and speaking engagements, and Ogue charged them next to nothing for their room and board, but Grace was mindful of the debt they already owed, though she did not for an instant begrudge her brother the medical expenses. He now wore a specially built shoe that added two inches to his leg, and a brace that held his knee steady, reducing the severity of his limp; his arm was slowly being straightened with the help of a leather shoulder harness that he wore at night, and the benefit of all this was that he had become a new man. He walked taller, moved confidently through a room, and conversed without self-deprecating remarks. He had filled out, was healthier—no long, chest-racking illness so far this winter. His skin glowed and his eyes shone; his hair had grown long and he wore better fitting clothes now, as well as boots for the first time in his life. He was thriving in America, and she was glad for that as she knew he could easily have died had he remained in Ireland. She worried that her arrival with not one, but two children would become a burden and so she lay awake in the small hours of the morning, considering her options.

It would have to be needlework, she decided. Her sewing skills had been among the most excellent in County Cork, but she had no idea what her value would be in a city full of skilled seamstresses. She did not want to leave the children for sixteen hours each day to work in the garment factories, not if she didn't have to, and was considering piecework—she'd seen advertisements in the paper; Daniel Devlin, an Irishman from Donegal, was paying seventy-five cents a week for out-work. She knew seventy-five cents wasn't much, not when in-house cutters and tailors—mainly men—made as much in a day, but it would be a start. Finally, after pacing the city for hours with the children in tow, she came back to the saloon and raised the question with Dugan.

"Ah, now, Grace, the home-men are all crooked thieves and the factory-men are slave-drivers!"

"I must do something," Grace insisted, shaking the snowflakes from her shawl. "We've got to earn a real living, Sean and I. We've got to save up and get a place ready for Da and the baby."

"You can all live here!" Ogue waved his arms expansively. "What's another old man and a wee one?"

Liam and Mary Kate nodded enthusiastically, and Grace sent them over to the fire to warm up.

"It's two more mouths to feed," Grace said. "And you've got your own to think of. How is she, today, by the way?"

Ogue's face clouded. "Not so well, darling. She's not young, Grace, you know. I was a sorry bachelor all my life, and thank God she married me when she did. I never minded us having no babies, never even thought of it! I was just happy to have her. And now . . ." He stopped, at a loss for words. "Well, 'tis a miracle, this. A true miracle. But I don't mind telling you, it scares me."

"Don't let it." Grace took his hand. "What can I do to help?"

"Well, that's just the thing, you see." His eyes shone again. "I know you're wanting work, and I've wanted to offer you some but"—he lowered his voice—"a woman like yourself, you know, you shouldn't be working in a place like this."

"Don't be a great eejit," Grace scolded. "Doesn't your very own wife work here?"

"Not anymore," he confessed. "She's got to stay abed, the doctor says. Because of the spots. She'll lose the baby otherwise, but it's not easy for her. She's been working all her life, you see."

"So you want someone to see to her, and do the kitchen chores?"

"Aye." He nodded, relieved. "I'd have to hire a girl anyway, Grace, and it'd drive herself mad having some flighty thing in and out of our rooms, messing in her kitchen. Do you see?"

"I do." Grace knew how proud Tara was.

"But she says to me, 'Ask our Grace if she'll do it. She's a good one,' she says to me, 'and I trust her.' " He put out his hands, begging. "So I'm asking you to please take the job, and I'm telling you that we'll make room for your da and the boy when they come."

"I could save then," Grace thought aloud. "Repay you, and when Tara's back on her feet, we'll get out of your hair."

"Live here as long as you like, darling, and I'll never care," he said honestly. "But will you do it, then?"

"Oh, aye, Dugan. Of course I will." She threw her arms around the big man, who patted her back shyly.

"Go up and tell her, then. Before she thumps on that floor one more time to ask me."

Grace grinned, fished a couple of pickled eggs out of the jar on the counter, and took them to Mary Kate and Liam, along with a thick slice of bread. She admonished the boy not to wolf it down in one bite, and warned the girl to eat all, no hiding any under her pillow for later. They nodded solemnly, but she knew neither one had yet come to count on a next meal, and she shook her head as she climbed the stairs.

Dugan and Tara lived over the kitchen at the back of the saloon; she knocked quietly, then pushed the door open and entered a parlor with lace curtains hung at the windows. Tara had a clean rug on the floor, her two good chairs, a settee, a sideboard, and an oval table with an oil lamp and a mantel clock; it was warm here above the kitchen, peaceful with the ticking.

"Is that you, Grace?" Tara called from down the hall. "Come here!" She smiled anxiously when Grace appeared in the bedroom door. "Has he asked you, then? About the work, and all?"

"Aye." Grace sat in a chair near the bed. "And I'm grateful to the both of you. You've been so kind to us."

"Ah, no—'tis God's will you're here for this, I believe that, Grace."

"Don't worry about a thing."

"I do, though," Tara admitted. "I keep thinking of my own mother. I come along late in her life, and she died of it, you see. Of having me. And I'm even older than she was."

"Well, but that was a long time ago, and don't you live in a great city with doctors nearby?" Grace smiled encouragingly. "Every time you worry, close your eyes and see yourself with a lovely baby in your arms. I've lived through it three times, myself," she assured her. "Three times and four babies."

"Four!"

Grace bit her lip, realizing her gaff. "Two died young, but I've two still living. Mary Kate you know, and my boy back in Ireland."

"I've wanted to ask you, but Dugan told me to leave it alone. The boy—he's Morgan's, then?"

Grace nodded, her vision suddenly blurred.

Tara picked up her rosary beads, thinking. "I had a husband before Dugan," she confided quietly. "Me and Caolon come over on the boat together a long time ago, full of plans for a new life in America. We grew up together—I never knew a time without him."

I know, Grace thought. *I know.*

"He was hit by a runaway carriage one night as we walked out to look at the shops. Not ten days after we come to the city. There was a commotion, and then he shoved me out of the way, but not in time for himself." Her face stilled, remembering. "One minute we were walking out, arm in arm, our whole lives before us—and the next he lay on the ground, his head cracked right open and all that blood spilling out . . ." She winced. " 'Twas a young gentleman in charge of the carriage, he in his fine clothes, more than a little drunk. Rushed off by other men in fine clothes, he was, but not before he give me a wallet full of money—for the doctor, he said, though 'twere a burial I paid for instead." Her eyes cleared and she searched Grace's face. "Since the day you come, with your terrible loss and all, the memory of himself has been strong upon me, and I guess I just wanted you to know."

"Some days I can hardly bear it." Grace's mouth trembled.

Tara nodded. "I thought I'd lay myself down and die when Caolon was killed. 'Twas ages before I knew I'd come alive again, and that was a sad day, as well. But God is good, and Dugan Ogue loves me, and I'm to have his baby. I survived the blackest days of my life," she said firmly. "And you will, too. Because he loved you."

"He did," Grace said, and dried her tears.

Twenty-two

"Sit down, Mister . . . Boardham, is it?" Callahan motioned him in with his lit cigar.

Boardham stayed in the doorway. "I done nothing wrong," he growled. "I come to report a wrong done to me."

"I heard that." Callahan leaned back in his chair. "Interesting story you told downstairs. I'd like to go over it with you."

"Why?"

"Curious." Callahan shrugged. "Like a cigar?"

Boardham licked his lips. "Don't mind if I do." He sidled over to the desk and took it, then sat gingerly in the chair.

"Now let me see if I've got this straight." Callahan puffed, the ember glowing. "You sailed an American ship out of Liverpool in November, correct?"

Boardham lit his own cigar. "The *Eliza J*, P. Reinders, Captain."

"And you say Captain Reinders illegally discharged passengers—including a known criminal—before going back out to Staten Island, still correct?" Callahan eyed him through the smoke.

"Aye."

"You and a Doctor"—he glanced at his notes—"Draper,

Doctor Draper—the two of you objected to this and were beaten up."

"Right." Boardham jabbed his cigar at the police captain. "I never seen Draper after that, but they took me to Boston, they did, and dumped me in the harbor! I had to make my way back on my own, no money nor nothing!"

"Why did you wait until now to report this?"

Boardham tensed again. "Well, I was afraid for my life, wasn't I?" he whined. "Said they'd come after me if I told, and they will. I'm not happy about sitting here."

Callahan leaned forward. "Then why are you?"

"Got myself in a bit of trouble, I guess," Boardham mumbled.

"You got in a knife fight and slit a man's throat."

"It's what I'm telling you! He's one of the crew done me over! Not the one I'd like to get, mind you." Boardham glowered. "But he's a start."

Callahan regarded him with interest. "Do you realize you're sitting in a police captain's office, talking about the murders you'd like to commit?"

"Not murder," Boardham corrected. "Revenge. And he started it."

"So it was self-defense? You were defending yourself against this man?"

Boardham sat up straight, excited. "Yeah! Yeah, I was defending myself. He come at me first."

Callahan nodded. "You *could* go to jail for a very long time."

"But you said—"

"I'm interested in hearing more about this captain." Callahan puffed casually. "These were Irish immigrants, you said?"

"Yeah." Boardham's heart was pounding.

"We are a city overrun with Irish immigrants." Callahan eyed him. "You're not Irish, are you?"

"No," Boardham spat. "English as they come."

"You look Irish, though. Small and flinty. Drink like an Irishman, obviously."

"Boardham's my name." Two red spots appeared on the steward's cheeks. "It's an English name. Not like Callahan."

The police captain's eyebrows went up. "Very good." He nodded approvingly. "Very deft. Yes, you're quite right. Callahan is an old Irish name, and I am descended of Irishmen, though my family has lived in this country for two generations now."

Boardham said nothing, unsure of his ground, then decided to hedge his bet. "My mother's name was Ceallachan," he offered.

"So you *are* Irish." Callahan looked pleased.

"My father was English. I grew up in Liverpool. I consider myself an Englishman."

"And I consider myself an American." Callahan set down the cigar. "The Irish coming off the boats these days are all riffraff, beggars and thieves, drunkards and spoilers. And they come in droves. Dumped into the city every day, an embarrassment frankly to those of us who've made something of ourselves."

Boardham glimpsed the path to redemption. "It's the captains bring 'em in for profit," he said. "Close 'em down and—no more Irish."

"Yes." Callahan nodded. "They are certainly part of the problem, especially if they're bringing in criminals. He's wanted for murder, you said—what's his name?"

"Donnelly." Boardham couldn't get it out fast enough. "Missus Grace Donnelly."

"A woman?"

"A bitch," Boardham spat. "Come at me with a knife, she did."

"You seem to attract that." Callahan flashed a quick smile. "Know where she's living?"

"No. I'm looking, though."

"Good." Callahan closed his notebook. "When you find her, I'd like you to tell me first. Before you do anything. In the meantime, I'll look into this Captain Reinders and his immigration trade."

"Is that all?" Boardham asked carefully.

"For now. But I may want to see you again. I may charge you with killing poor Mister"—Callahan checked his notes again—"Dean."

Boardham gritted his teeth.

"How would you like a job?" Callahan asked point-blank. "Working for me."

Caught off guard, Boardham pretended to consider. "What's it pay?"

Callahan laughed. "You'd do any job for the right price, is that it, Mister Boardham? That makes you a man worth hiring. My partners and I own a few buildings up in the Five Points district. One on Little Water Street, two on Orange. You know the area?"

Boardham nodded. It was a rough place—saloons and whores; he went up there quite a bit.

"It's overrun with Irish. And they don't pay their rent. I need a man who'll make them pay or make them move." He leaned forward. "You'll get your room for free and two dollars a week, plus part of all the rent you collect."

Boardham sat back in surprise. "That's a good deal."

"I'm a fair man. As long as I get what I want. Occasionally I will call in a favor." He paused. "Do we understand one another?"

"We do."

"Good." Callahan wrote something down, then handed the piece of paper over. "Here's the address. Come back tomorrow and we'll talk a little more."

"Thank you, Mister Callahan, sir." Boardham stood to go. "You won't be disappointed."

"No." Callahan smiled and leaned back in his chair. "I never am."

Twenty-three

THE first day of April was surprisingly cold, a steady rain beating against the roof, and Grace listened as she tidied their rooms under the eaves. In the corner, Mary Kate played with her doll bed, a gift from Liam for her fourth birthday in February; he'd made it himself out of a small crate Dugan had tossed in the alley. He had cleaned it up and painted it white, spelled BLOSSOM on the headboard. Grace had stitched together a doll quilt and stuffed a tiny pillow, and Mary Kate kept it next to her own bed. She'd been given a picture book from Sean, a dress and apron from the Ogues, an apple from Mister Marconi up the block, a hair ribbon from Sean's friend Marcy Osgoode, a pair of new boots and a bar of chocolate from Grace. The new four-year-old had eaten her cake, opened her gifts, and then burst into tears, overwhelmed with it all. But today she was wearing the dress, playing with the toys, and sharing her breakfast with Liam, whom she adored.

Grace eyed the boy sitting by the window, looking at the picture book. He was filling out now, getting big, and she knew he'd need new clothes come spring. And boots. He'd settled in so bravely with them all, and never let down his guard, though he slept with Alice's hair comb and Siobahn's sock under his pillow. He was devoted to Mary Kate, teaching her draughts and rope skipping, and even playing dolls when he thought no one was looking; Grace was so fond of him.

She was tired this morning, echoes of last night's stimulating conversations swimming in her head. Sean had taken her to the Livingstons' for dinner and she'd met his friends Jay and Florence—Jay was a terrible flirt, but she took no offense as he flirted equally with every young woman there; and Florence was kind and funny, her eyes blazing with intelligence, much like Julia's.

Grace had been seated next to the American author Herman Melville who'd written a book about Polynesians that Florence said was scandalous, but that had earned him so much money he was writing another. He'd confided in Grace at dinner, though, that what he really wanted to write was a book about whale hunting. It haunted him, he'd said after several glasses of wine: man and beast alone, the raw elements of nature. He was sure it would be his best book ever, and he promised her a signed copy. She had liked him very much. Another writer, Edgar Poe, had also been invited but had not come, and Jay had speculated privately about opium dens, though Florence said his wife had just died and to have some pity. The governor had also been there, a singer, two bishops, Florence's abolitionist ladies, and Jay's publishing friends. Grace had found herself tongue-tied, but had watched with admiration as her brother held his own in this dazzling crowd; he had come so far in America, and she was proud of him.

"Grace!" He called from the bottom of the stairs now, interrupting her thoughts. "Gracie! Will you come down a minute?"

She glanced at the children, playing happily, then went to see what all the urgency was about.

"They've found him!" Sean took her arm and led her to a bench against the wall. "Liam's da. They've an address for him over at the Irish Emigrant Society."

Grace's heart fell. "Sure and there are a thousand Kelleys in the city. Are they sure? Seamus Kelley from Dublin?"

"Aye. They sent a man round. Wife called Alice, two children. They told him what happened on board, and he wants to see the boy right away." He took her hand. "I know how you feel, Grace, but it's his very own father."

"He never speaks of his da. Alice told me he was a drinking man, and I promised to be careful."

"We'll go together," Sean reassured. "The three of us."

"When?"

"Today," he said as gently as he could. "Go and tell him now—it should come from you—and get him ready. Dugan'll drive us."

"Today?" She couldn't believe it. "Can it not wait until to-morrow, then? Go over in the morning?"

Sean shook his head. "They've told him we're coming, and what if he's a good man, Grace? What if he's been waiting all this time for word of his boy?"

She understood. She was waiting so anxiously for word of her own. "All right, then. I'll tell him."

"That's a good girl. I'll go help Dugan."

Grace climbed the stairs wearily, then stood in the open door-way for a moment, looking at the boy she considered family.

"Liam!" She forced excitement into her voice. "Liam, we've had some news. About your da!"

He looked up at her then, his eyes wide.

"He's alive," she added quickly. "He's alive and he wants to see you right away. Today."

"Today?" He glanced at Mary Kate, who was staring at him.

Grace crossed the room, picked up her daughter, and sat on the bed; she patted the spot next to her, and Liam came at once.

" 'Tis a bit of a shock, I know. Sean's been checking regularly, but I'd begun to think that maybe your da was . . ."

"Dead," Liam finished.

"Aye, and I'm sorry for that." She put an arm around his shoulders. "Because here he is, alive and well, and looking for you all this time, he was."

"He was?" Liam looked doubtful.

"Well, of course he was because haven't we all found each other now, and isn't it grand that we have, that we've found him, and he's found you?" *I'm rambling,* Grace thought.

Mary Kate looked at her mother and frowned. "I don't want Liam to go." She took hold of his shirt in her fist.

Grace sighed. "Nor do I. I'd be lying, if I said otherwise."

"Do I have to go?" Liam looked up at her so longingly that she squeezed him tight so as not to see his face.

"Aye, Liam, you do. He's your da, and he loves you. You're all he has left now."

He pressed his head into her shoulder for a moment, and then he stood up. "All right then," he said, her brave boy. "I'd best get my things. Is it far? Will I be far away?"

"No," she assured him. "Not far a'tall. Dugan'll drive us in the cart today as we'll have your trunk and it's raining so hard, but Sean says we can do it in a walk. You'll be seeing us all the time."

Relief flooded his face. "I can walk, then."

Grace nodded. "Anytime. All the time."

He had more questions, none of which Grace could answer, but it filled the half hour it took to gather his few things together, and then they went downstairs.

Dugan had brought up the Kelley trunk from the basement, and Liam set his small pile inside.

"Well, boy." The big man put his hands on his hips. "You won't be forgetting your old friends here at the Harp and Hound, will you now?"

"No, sir." Liam put out his hand stoically, but was yanked instead into a giant bear hug.

"Ah, you daft beggar." Dugan nuzzled the boy's neck, making him giggle. "What'll I do without all your mischief round here? Who's there to drop the tray, spill the drinks, bring back the wrong thing from the grocers, ask me a million questions? Eh?" He blew a big raspberry and Liam laughed out loud.

"Mary Kate!" He looked over his shoulder. "You'll drop his trays for him, won't you?"

"No." Mary Kate stamped her foot, and Grace looked at her in surprise. "I won't."

Liam wriggled away from Dugan and came right over to the little girl, whose arms were folded in a huff.

"Ah, now, don't be mad," he said, going down on one knee.
"I'll be back to see you plenty and we'll play jump rope and tag."

She shook her head, eyes filling with tears.

"Ah, now." He put his arms around her and whispered something in her ear, then kissed her cheek.

"Promise?" she asked.

He crossed his heart and spat, and she did the same.

Sean came in from the back. "All set, son?"

"Aye." Liam took a long look around the place, then winked at Mary Kate. "See you later."

Grace looked over his head at Dugan, who just shrugged.

They left Mary Kate to play in Tara's room, then headed north toward Five Points. The rain had stopped, but mud splattered up from the cart wheels; the neighborhoods grew progressively worse until at last they reached Orange Street, where pigs—turned loose from their corner pens—ambled through the muck, and already men leaned against the walls waiting for anything to happen.

"Terrible place, this," Dugan muttered. "Gets worse every day."

"How much farther?" Grace asked.

"We're here." He stopped the cart in front of a narrow brick building, behind which rose up a wooden barrack. "I better go first."

Grace noticed a loose gang of young men eyeing the cart. "You better stay here." She tipped her head in the direction of the men. "We'll take him up."

Carrying the trunk between them, Sean and Grace picked their way through the piles on the sidewalk to the front door, then inside.

"Which is number nine?" Sean asked a tired-looking woman sitting with her baby on the rickety stairs. "Seamus Kelley."

The woman snorted. "Through the alley," she directed. "Back behind, then up three flights. Waste of time, if you ask me."

Sean and Grace exchanged a glance, then picked up the trunk again and left the building, turning down a narrow alley intersected by other suspect paths, their shoes sinking into the

muck. They came out into a small courtyard, the source of the
putrid, cloying smell that hung over the neighborhood and
could mean only one thing—bone boilers. Men and women
stood over the rank cauldrons, stirring a nasty stew of animal refuse collected from the streets and markets, the bones and in-
nards and scraps of skin boiled together. These were the new
masters of the "offensive trades"—bone-boiling, horse-
skinning, glue and self-igniting match-making—the jobs no one
else wanted, but the desperate embraced. Grace could not
imagine how horrible this would be in the hot summer months.
They skirted past ramshackle privies with a steady stream of
people going in and out, many with buckets they simply
dumped; the slime on the ground was shiny and greenish, its
smell adding to the suffocating air, and yet, not five steps away,
there was a cheap groggery, windowless and dark, with pools of
standing water and piles of decay in the doorway, where a man
leaned, arms crossed, watching them.

The wooden barrack was no more than an add-on to the back
of a brick building, and when they entered, Grace realized it
had been divided into such cramped quarters that many had no
windows. She could not see where she was going and touched
the wall, damp with mildew. She tried to stay in the middle of
the narrow hall, towed along by her brother. Doors cracked
open, faces peered out, and Grace caught glimpses of light from
candle stubs. This was no better than the worst lanes in Skib-
bereen, she told herself—no chairs, no beds, only piles of straw
or rags, piles of children or exhausted adults, the smell of sweat
and sickness. She could hardly breathe. Liam moved closer in
behind her, his hand gripping her skirt, until at last they came
to number nine. Sean set the trunk down and knocked. There
was a cough from within, the shuffle of feet, a thud and a curse,
and then the door opened.

"Who's that, then?" A man—old or young, Grace could not
tell for the greasy hair and the grime on his face—held out a
candle and looked them over suspiciously. "What do you want
from me?"

Liam pushed past Grace. "Da? 'Tis me, Da! Your Liam!"

The man's face brightened and his rheumy eyes watered. He reached out and pulled the boy into an embrace, dropping kisses on his head. "Ah, now, son, you're here! You're here! Oh, my own boy, come all this way and lost your poor mother, God rest her soul. Lost herself and your sister, as well. Oh, no. Oh, no!" He wept now, rocking the boy. "Oh, to have seen them one last time. Oh, son. My son."

Liam wept, too, overcome, and Sean and Grace looked at one another.

"Come in then, come in." Seamus wiped his face on his sleeve and opened the door wider. "You must be Mister O'Malley." He extended a dirty wet hand, but Sean took it.

"We're happy to meet you, Mister Kelley." He looked around the dark room, saw a pile of straw in the corner, a stool and a barrel. "Though we'll miss having your boy at our place."

Liam could not take his eyes off his father.

"The lady can have the stooleen." Seamus pushed it toward her, then set the candle down on the barrel.

"This is my sister, Grace," Sean said. "She's the one came over on the ship with your wife."

"Alice was a good woman," Grace volunteered. "She loved the children very much, and wanted me to make sure Liam had a home."

Seamus nodded soberly. "She died of the fever then. And the little one, as well."

"Aye. There was a service aboard ship. Liam and I came the rest of the way together, and he's lived with us ever since."

"I thank you for that. I've not been well myself, as you can see." He coughed something up, then spat into the corner. "The good Lord sent him just in time, for I'm out of money and the rent's gone due, but a strong one like himself can earn that and more."

Liam looked up at Grace, who kept her face neutral.

"Come here, boy, and give your old da a kiss." He put out his arms and Liam stepped dutifully into them, but he was stiff now, unsure. "Aye, we'll work it out now you're here, won't we, boy?"

"Are you sure you're well enough?" Sean asked carefully. "We'd be happy to keep him until you're back on your feet."

Seamus frowned. "Give him up now he's finally home? Never!" A fit of coughing overtook him and he reached behind the barrel for a bottle. "Me medicine," he explained and took a swig.

"Really, Mister Kelley, you don't seem . . ." Sean gestured helplessly.

"Maybe you'd better go now." Seamus pulled Liam closer. "Give us some time to get to know each other again. Thank you for all you've done, and sure you'll get your fine reward in Heaven. Say good-bye now, boy."

"Good-bye," Liam said softly, eyes going from Sean's face to Grace's.

Grace came over and kissed him, whispering in his ear, "You know where we are, Liam."

He nodded and Sean shook his hand, and then they left. Numbly, they felt their way back down the stairs, through the courtyard, down the path, and out into the street, where it had begun to rain again.

Dugan took one look at them and smacked his fist against the side of the cart. "I knew it. I just knew it. He's a drunken old sot, isn't he?"

Sean and Grace nodded slowly, unable to believe it.

"Well, we can't just leave him here." Dugan eyed the neighborhood. " 'Tis no place for him."

"It's all my fault," Sean said, dazed. "I can't believe I did this."

"No." Grace put a hand on his arm. "We had to look for his father. We didn't know it would be like this."

They rode home silently through the rain, out of the dismal district and back to the less dismal one, to the warm shining lights of the Harp and Hound with its familiar smell of ale and pickles, baking bread and potato soup, the bar already lined with customers, Danny Young standing behind and serving as if he did it all the time. Mary Kate had seen them park the cart in the back, and lead the mule to the lean-to. She came running down the stairs to greet them, her cheeks glowing.

"He'll be back," she said resolutely, when she saw their faces.

Grace picked her daughter up and buried her face in the curly hair, felt the solid weight of the girl in her arms.

"He will." Mary Kate held out Alice's comb and Siobahn's sock. "He promised."

Twenty-four

JULIA'S carriage left the rugged country lanes and took the more well-traveled road to Cork. She knew she was approaching the city by the proliferation of well-fed English soldiers—fifteen thousand more since January, thank you very much, Lord Clarendon. She had hoped for an end to the invasion when the Special Commission of Judges declared that in every case they reviewed, murder was related to land issues, particularly evictions that cast out already desperate families; according to Lord Chief Justice Blackburn, "The motive for all was the wild justice of revenge." Clarendon's response, of course, was that the condition in Ireland was one of servile war, that this was a rebellion of slaves and must be quashed. And then he'd sent in more troops, ten thousand in Dublin alone with warships anchored at the Cove of Cork.

Julia sighed and looked out the window. A misty June rain had left the hedges glistening, and fields of wildflowers swayed in the breeze. The trees were thick now with lustrous leaves, though there was still an absence of birds and wildlife, and in some of the smaller villages, bark had been visibly stripped during the winter. The soldiers of Ireland's rebellion remained a gaunt and ragged bunch, but at least they were no longer freezing. It had been a long winter and all around the world, it seemed, countries moved ahead—insurrection in Sicily had forced the king to concede a constitution, and the people of Piedmont had secured one, too. King Louis Phillipe of France had slipped off to England after a popular, nearly bloodless uprising; a Republic had been proclaimed with Lamartine, the poet, Minister of Foreign Affairs. The English papers downplayed any comparison with Ireland, but the Irish papers gloried in France's triumph, celebrating it by lighting bonfires all over the country. Mitchel had taken advantage of this, blasting away at the English with the full fury of his rhetoric while at the same time calling upon the new arm of Young Ireland, the Irish Confederation, to exert military pressure to force the British government to concede Repeal immediately; only Repeal of the Union and an Irish Parliament, he insisted, could save Ireland from ultimate destruction. Julia admired his passion.

He had been so terribly frustrated when the mass meeting of the Chartists in England—led by Irish Repealer Feargus O'Conner—had come to nothing: the marchers had been stopped at the bridge on the river Thames by nine thousand troops and batteries of field artillery, along with special constables. A compromise had been reached wherein the marchers canceled their mass meeting in exchange for a private one later on. Diffused and taken out of the public eye, support for the Chartist movement had diminished. Another blow.

Angry—always angry—John Mitchel had broken with the Young Irelanders to form with Fintan Lalor a party dedicated to armed rebellion, beginning with a strike against high rents; but it was a later article proposing a refusal to pay poor rates that ended his friendship with Charles Duffy. Duffy adamantly held that, miserable though they might be, poor rates were the only thing standing between thousands of destitute Irish and certain death, and he demanded John write a retraction. John refused and left to start his own paper, *The United Irishman*, in which he called unrelentingly for rebellion while simultaneously inflaming England with threats and insults—it was heady stuff, but Julia had to admit to a secret glee in his calling Lord Clarendon "Her Majesty's Executioner General and General Butcher in Ireland."

The others carried on, and Julia accompanied Thomas Meagher and William to the Music Hall in Abbey Street the night they solicited for service in the Armed National Guard, reminding the men that Americans were recruiting an Irish Brigade, and fully one-third of the British Army consisted of Irishmen. Within days, Smith O'Brien and Meagher had been charged with making seditious speeches. John had been charged, as well, for his articles, but all of them posted bail and went straight back to work. Thomas and William planned to go to Paris with a letter for Lamartine, who they hoped would lend support to the cause, and John continued to address the masses who turned out in droves to hear him yell, "Arm yourselves, for the love of God!" There wasn't much to arm themselves with, however; several ships sent over from America had been confiscated once guns were discovered aboard.

Julia was exhausted now the trial was over—and bitter about John's sentence—but knew she must go to Cork. Britain had applied intense pressure on Rome and Pope Pius IX, formerly the liberal pope, had issued a statement admonishing the Irish priesthood for their involvement in politics and forbidding any further political activity. Priests were transferred, religious orders disbanded, convents and monasteries closed. Her dear friend Father Kenyon was a strong and visible supporter of the Young Irelanders and many looked to him for leadership, but he had disappeared without a trace. Julia was worried about Barbara and what would happen to Patrick and the baby.

At last they started up the long, winding road to the convent, gray and crumbling on the hilltop. The gate was open—indeed the gate was off its hinges—and they drove directly into the courtyard. Julia climbed out unassisted and asked the driver to carry the supply box around to the kitchen. She knocked at the front door, then pushed it open.

"Hallo!" she called, unpinning her hat. "Barbara?"

Barbara came down the stairs, hands outstretched. "Julia! Thank God you're here! Come in, come in!" She took her friend by the arm and led her into the study. "Abban saw you coming up the road. He's making our tea."

Julia looked around the study, saw the cold grate, patched windows and water-warped sashes. Heard the silence. "Where is everyone?" She set her hat on the desk.

"Mostly they're with the Lord," Barbara said matter-of-factly. "We were hit hard with fever. There's only Sister James now and myself to run things. And Abban, of course, God bless him."

"What about Mister O'Malley? And the baby?"

Barbara turned and looked at her. "Did you not get my letter, then? About Patrick?"

Julia sat down. "No."

"He died just after Easter." She sighed and sat down, too. "I wondered why I hadn't heard from you," she added. "I thought maybe you were traveling again, maybe in England, with all that's happened."

"I haven't been home much," Julia apologized. "And the mail isn't reliable anymore."

"I should've written you again."

Julia shook her head. "It's not your fault. I . . . was it fever?"

"Aye. But he was right with God, and peaceful at the end."

"What about the baby?"

"Still alive, though how I don't know. We lost his nurse, but Abban went to town and stole a goat right out from underneath their English noses!" she said. "God forgive him," she added contritely.

"What do you hear from Grace? Does she know?"

"I've not written yet." Barbara looked down at her hands. "There's been so much here, one after the other. And we didn't hear from her for so long, only the one letter saying they'd made it, and that took months." She sighed. "But I know I must. Sure and she's worried sick."

"I wrote." Julia frowned. "I told her everything was fine, that I'd see you in the spring and send her father and son soon after that."

"I'll take him." Abban pushed a rough tea cart on wheels into the room. "And then I'll come back."

"You with your one leg cannot take a wee sickly, blind baby and a stubborn goat on a ship to America," Barbara argued.

"I can, woman, and I will!"

"You can't! He fusses and spits up his food, takes sick all the time. He won't survive it, Abban, and you know that! *You* might not survive it."

"Barbara's right," Julia interrupted. "You can't take him, Abban. It doesn't make any sense."

"What are we to do then?" he demanded. "Has she told you they're closing this place down and sending her away?"

"I was afraid of that." Julia looked grim. "It's happening all over. They're afraid of rebellion within the orders. You nuns are the worst," she joked ruefully. "Smuggling food and weapons, harboring fugitives . . . Can't be trusted, you know."

"But look at Father Kenyon!" Barbara exclaimed. "He speaks out everywhere!"

"Not lately," Julia reported. "Either he's been suspended, or he's gone into hiding."

"But priests have been involved in politics since the day the church was founded." Abban shook his head in disgust. "I been a good Catholic all my life. With all due respect, His Holiness is letting the loud voices of angry men drown out the quiet voice of God."

"And the clergy is listening," Julia pointed out. "No one wants to defy the Holy Father—they're afraid of being replaced."

"I doubt very much there's a waiting list of priests wanting to come to Ireland," Abban scoffed. "There's weak men and strong men, and that's all. Those who leave us to fend for ourselves weren't worth much to God in the first place."

"You should start your own Order," Julia teased.

"No, thanks. God's got other work for me. Here now"—he lifted the pot off the cart—"tea's getting cold." He poured out the cups and handed them round. "What can you tell us about the trials, Julia? Were you there?"

She nodded. "Ten thousand men marched William from his lodgings in Westland Row to the Law Courts. It was a packed jury, and everyone knew it, but he was defended by Isaac Butts."

"I know the name." Abban stood next to Barbara's chair, his hand on her shoulder.

"Brilliant man," Julia said with admiration. "Brilliant speech. He won a refusal to convict."

"What about Mister Meagher?" Barbara leaned forward. "Did he go free, as well? Wasn't he also defended by Mister Butts?"

"He was tried the very next day, and Isaac spoke more passionately than ever. Rotten jury again, of course, but there was a Quaker who held out, so no conviction."

"How did they get Mitchel?" Abban asked. "He had that old Robert Holmes defending him, and we thought sure he'd get off."

"They got him with the new Treason Felony Act," she explained. "Pushed through by the Whigs in Westminster for that very reason. He sat in Newgate a week before the trial. They weren't taking any chances with him—somebody had to pay for all the rhetoric thrown down. And of course, he didn't help himself by telling everyone that sedition was a small matter and he intended to commit high treason." She smiled ruefully. "There wasn't a single Catholic on the jury, even with thousands on the list."

"Transportation?"

"Fourteen years in Bermuda." Julia sighed. "You wouldn't believe the troops pouring into Dublin. Clarendon must think he'll be murdered in his sleep."

"Maybe he will." Abban tightened his grip on Barbara's shoulder.

"Not by you." Julia eyed him. "Clubs are forming in every district. William says fifty thousand men are drilling even now. Money, arms, and officers are expected from abroad, and Old and Young are reconciling their differences. John O'Connell—"

"Bah!"

"I know—the father brought millions to the cause and the son drove millions away. But he's still a powerful man, and William has agreed to discuss terms with him."

"Terms," Abban scoffed. "All I want to know is, when do we fight?"

Julia set down her cup. "Autumn. William says there's a place for you, if you want it."

"I do," he said immediately, then looked down at Barbara. "But what about herself and the baby?"

Julia bit her lip. "Do you know where they're sending you?"

"No. And I'm not so sure I'm going anyway."

"Barbara—"

"You hush." She put her hand over Abban's. "This is between you and me, and no one else." She turned toward Julia. "I'm not going anywhere without the baby."

"No." Julia looked from one face to the other. "I can see that. Are you prepared to leave the Order?" she asked carefully.

Abban and Barbara looked at one another, communicating silently.

"I see." Julia leaned back in her chair. And then she smiled. "All right, then." She clapped her hands together decisively. "I've got an idea."

They talked through the afternoon and into the evening, until the light was dim and their voices ragged. No one slept well, all rose at dawn, and when Julia left, she carried Morgan's son in her arms.

Twenty-five

"YOU can't keep running away." It was hot and Grace was tired and here was Liam standing before her *again*.

"I'll just stay the day," he pleaded. "I promise I'll go back tonight."

"Ah, Liam love, you always say that, and then you don't, and I haven't the heart to make you, and then your da comes storming down here and makes a terrible scene, and you know what he said he'd do the next time you ran off."

Liam hung his head. "Take me to the asylum for incorrigibles."

"Aye, and I've no doubt he'll do it." She sighed, then pulled him in for a hug. " 'Tis a mess, this. I don't know what to do. But I know I've got to take you home."

Mary Kate glared at her from her place on the stool.

"That's enough out of you, little miss," Grace scolded. "You think I want to take him up there? Well, I don't. 'Tis no place for a child, for anyone. No one a'tall should live like that. Have you eaten?" she asked the grubby little boy.

He shook his head.

"How many days?"

He looked down and shrugged.

"And do you have any water up there for washing?" She simply could not bear this. "Because you look just awful. Is that blood on your chin?" She smudged it with her thumb.

"Are you angry with me, then?" His eyes filled with tears.

"Ah, no, love." She hugged him again. "I'm angry with myself, is the trouble. Just taking it out on you this morning. Sit down, and I'll fetch you something to eat."

She stormed into the kitchen, smashing into Dugan, who stood around the corner checking his stock.

"Slow down, girl! Too hot to be running all over the place," he griped, then took a closer look at her face. "What's wrong?"

She wiped the sweat off her forehead. "Liam's here. He's hungry. He looks terrible. Been in a fight or something up there."

Dugan's face grew stony. "You think that bastard's beating on him?" His own hands curled into fists. " 'Tis high time I went up there and killed that son of a bitch. Excuse my language."

" 'Tis nothing I've not already thought." Grace yanked over a loaf and angrily sliced off a piece. "But there's nothing to be done. He hires that little boy out and makes a wage from him, keeps the old sot in drink—that's all he cares about."

"Hires him out." Dugan scowled. "You know where I found him last time? Out on the sidewalk hustling customers for a whore—she paid his da ten cents for every man Liam snagged. And I know he's out there running with that wild lot, clubbing the dogs."

Grace peered out the door to the alley, as if she expected to see one coming even now. "What if he's bit, or attacked? Those dogs are mad, half of them."

"That won't stop 'em. Not when they get fifty cents a carcass. I hate to see it myself, those little boys running after any dog without a muzzle, screaming and whooping and bashing its brains out for the reward." He shook his head. "Makes 'em as wild as the dog itself."

"He lookes terrible wrung out." Grace carved off a piece of ham and put it on the bread. "Here 'tis July and he's pale as winter, head full of lice, nose running, smells bad." She slapped down the knife. "I tell you what, Dugan. I can hardly stand it. Bad enough I don't know where my own boy is or what's happening over there, I can't even take care of this one!"

"Ah, Grace." His big face melted with concern. "I know you're worried. And you never say a word about it. You been so good to my Tara, and I couldn't run the place without you anymore we got so many coming in each night . . ." He stopped and reached into his pocket. "Made a little something in the betting last night. Here, you take half, buy something for the boy."

She looked at the money, then up at his face. "That's it!" she exclaimed. "Will you hire Liam with this money? He could work around the place, and we'll pay his wage to his da. Sure and it's more than he gets out of the boy in a week!"

"That's not a bad idea. We're doing real well now, and he's big enough to actually help me out." He grinned. "That's a great idea! That's what we'll do!"

Grace hurried into the saloon, Dugan right behind. She set the plate down in front of Liam, watching as he tore into it.

"Slow down, boy," Dugan said gently. "There's always a meal here for you."

Liam stopped and took a deep breath, nodding.

"We got us an idea." The big man straddled the next stool. "Grace and me, we're thinking we could hire you to work around the place. Pay you a wage. Pay it to your da," he amended.

Liam's eyebrows went up and he swallowed the chunk in his mouth. "Pay him to keep me here?" his voice squeaked.

"I wouldn't want to put it like that. More like you could make a better wage here than up on Orange Street, and we'd pay it to him direct each week."

"Would I still go back at night?"

Dugan shook his head. "We need you to live in because the saloon closes late. What do you think?"

His face lit up. "Aye! That's great! That's just great!" He threw his arms around Grace. "Thank you."

"Thank that one over there," she chided. "He's the one paying."

"Thank you, Dugan." Liam squeezed the big man.

"You'll have to wash, though, boy," Dugan said gruffly, moved. "Can't have you driving the customers off with that smell."

Liam laughed. "Yes, sir. When do I start?"

"Right now, so go on with Grace and talk to your da."

"Hurray!" Mary Kate threw up her hands and they all looked at her, then burst out laughing.

Liam and Grace made their way through the heavy heat, watching out for mad dogs and loose pigs, crossing the street to stay in the shade as much as possible. No rain had fallen for weeks, and hard bricks of horse manure lay piled against the edges of the street. Each alley they passed emitted the dizzying smell of raw sewage; heat was no friend of the tenement dweller. Ropes of laundry stretched from side to side; wilted women in sleeveless vests and men in their undershirts sat on the stoops, smoking or talking. Maybe work, maybe not—the only hope for entertainment was a buggy accident in the street or a good fight with the neighbors. All but the very youngest children had already disappeared in search of water or shade.

"Do you think he's at home, then?" Grace asked as they started up Orange Street.

"He's always home," Liam said grimly.

They passed a gang of half-naked children, some of whom hailed Liam and disengaged themselves long enough to follow Grace down the pathway to the squalid barrack in the back.

"Go on now," she shooed, and all scattered screaming but two little girls who hung back shyly; Grace fished a penny out of her bag and handed it to the bigger one. "For ice cream," she whispered. "Don't tell."

They climbed the dark stairs, Liam leading the way and opening the door to number nine.

"Where have you been?" his father cried, stumbling to his feet. "The rent man's come and . . ." He saw Grace. "*You.* I've told you—you can't have him. He belongs to me. He's a Kelley."

Kelley was drunk and Grace in no mind to argue with him.

She opened up her bag and poured the coins out on the top of his barrel. His eyes opened wide in surprise, then narrowed suspiciously.

"I'm not selling him," he growled.

"No," Grace said quickly. "Of course you're not. I have a business deal for you, Mister Kelley."

He touched the coins with his dirty fingertip, pushed them around. "Go on."

"Whenever Liam comes, he does a few jobs around the place," she lied, not daring to look at the boy. "He's a good worker and Mister Ogue has offered him a job. It'll pay that much every week," she added.

Kelley licked his lips, counting the money and thinking. "Every week, you say?"

"Aye. But he'll have to live in," she said firmly. "It's long hours and we can't walk him back up here each night."

"Who'll bring me the money?"

"I will."

"How do I know you're good for it?" He laid his hand over the coins.

"I'll pay ahead," Grace explained. "This is the money Liam will earn next week. Each week, I'll bring you the advance. That way, you can't be cheated out of his wage."

Kelley eyed his son. "I suppose you want to do this?" He spat into the corner. "Seeing as how you can't get enough of them down there."

"Aye, Da." Liam stepped forward. "I'll work hard, and you can have every penny."

"You taking his bed and board out this?"

"No. We'll feed him. It's all yours, what he makes." Grace resisted the urge to grab Liam and run. "Do we have a deal?"

He scraped the coins off the barrel and pocketed them. "We do. Say good-bye to me, boy."

" 'Bye, Da." Liam put out his hand and his father shook it.

"Come and see me once in a while."

"I will."

"Don't forget I done this for you."

"No, sir. I won't, sir." Liam looked at Grace.

"Good-bye, Mister Kelley," Grace said, suddenly sorry for the broken-down man. "I'll see you next Saturday."

"Yeah, get out of here." He turned his back on them and started coughing.

Grace and Liam fairly flew the long blocks back home, and were met with whoops of joy from Dugan, who'd been waiting in the doorway, a rough towel over his shoulder, a bar of strong soap in his hand.

"I knew the good Lord would see it our way," he laughed. "Tub's waiting in the kitchen. Nice cool water'll feel good on a day like this!"

Liam offered not a word of complaint, pausing only to tug Mary Kate's hair playfully on his way back.

"I've got to go back out for our supper," Grace told her daughter, giving her a kiss. "Want to come along?"

Mary Kate shook her head. "Too hot. And Liam's here!"

"I know." Grace grinned. "Have fun, then."

Feeling better than she had in a long time, Grace decided to ride the omnibus down to the waterfront, where there was bound to be a breeze. She loved the bus; despite a reputation for reckless drivers, it was a fast, easy way to get around the city. She dropped her fare into a box lowered by the driver, who sat up on top, and when her destination approached, she pulled the rope attached to his leg, letting him know she wanted off.

It was still a few blocks to the great wharves, and she walked them gladly, enjoying the brisk salty air in her face. Mister Hesselbaum would drive his cart down her street later in the day, but whenever she could, she liked coming herself and visiting Lily, who had become, if not a friend—for clearly she was a private person—at least a familiar face. Tara had introduced them, and in the beginning, Lily would never look directly at Grace, but off to one side. She'd brought Liam and Mary Kate along one morning, however, and that had broken the ice; Lily also had two, a boy and a girl—twins—and they talked about their children.

Grace made her way around the knots of people on the dock,

heading for Hesselbaum's stall; as she got closer, she saw Lily talking earnestly with the only other customer. Grace approached hesitantly, not wanting to interrupt what was clearly an important conversation. She stood back a polite distance, waiting her turn, wondering at the familiarity of the man speaking to Lily. And then she realized who it was.

"Captain Reinders?" she asked, stepping forward.

He turned, startled, then removed his cap. "Missus Donnelly! What a surprise! What are you doing here?"

"Well, I'm hoping to buy a nice piece of fish from my friend Lily Free." Grace laughed. "Are you doing the same, then?"

"No," Reinders said at the same moment Lily nodded her head. There was an awkward silence. "Missus Free is an old friend of mine. I just stopped by to say hello," he explained, then turned to Lily. "Missus Donnelly came all the way from Ireland on my ship."

"Heard about that." Lily nodded. "Didn't know it was your ship, though, Captain. She was looking pretty scrawny when she got here."

"Hard trip," he said shortly, looking from one to the other. "Why am I not surprised that the two of you have found one another?" He laughed. "How are you then, Missus Donnelly? Fully recovered, I hope?"

"I'm fine, Captain, just fine." Grace shifted the basket to her other arm. "And how's yourself, then? Home for a while, are you?"

"Leaving tomorrow, actually. Tobacco run—quick and painless." He glanced at Lily, who nodded imperceptibly. "I've been to see my mother, though, Missus Donnelly. Gave you full credit for the visit."

"And you weren't persuaded to farming life, by the looks of you."

He laughed. "No. Nor did she try, even though times are still hard." His face sobered. "It was the right thing, going to see her. She's old and unwell, and I'm ashamed I didn't do it sooner. Thank you."

"Ah, well, that's fine," she said.

"How's Liam?" He turned to block the sun from her eyes. "Did you ever find his father?"

"I'm afraid so, but it wasn't the best for him," she confessed, then brightened. "Good news today, though." She turned to include Lily. "We struck a bargain—Liam's to work for Dugan at the saloon and turn his wage over to Seamus, who's agreed to let him live with us."

"That's good," Lily said, picking out a piece of cod for Grace. "He's a nice boy, and Mary Kate likes him so much."

"I'm glad it's worked out." Reinders turned his cap in his hand. "Does he ever talk about the ship?"

"All the time." Grace grinned. "To anyone who'll listen and even if they won't. You're a giant of a man in his eyes."

"I'd better not go see him, then. The letdown might be too great."

"You come along anytime. He'd love to see you."

"I'd like to see him, too." He paused. "You haven't had any other trouble since we landed?"

"None," she assured him. "I'm just another Irish widow among thousands of Irish widows. But I can't go back to Ireland. Not yet, anyway. Have you been?"

"To Ireland?" He shook his head. "No. Nor will I. I never want to be responsible for that many people again as long as I live."

"I'm always hoping for news," she said by way of explanation.

"Your son," he remembered. "Not arrived yet?"

"Nor my da, nor have we had any word but one letter come from my friend Julia Martin." Her eyes clouded. "They say things are bad in Cork and that's where they are, the two of them."

"I'm sorry," he offered. "I wish there was something I could do."

"You could sail me back across the ocean," she said, only half joking.

"I wish I could. I would, if I could."

"I know." She felt foolish for having asked. "They'll be all right. They're in God's hands."

"As are we all, if I remember correctly," he teased gently. "Missus Free shares the same sentiment, I believe."

"They big hands, Captain." Lily handed the newspaper-wrapped fish to Grace. "I put in a couple of them shrimps," she said.

"Thanks, Lily." Grace tucked it into her basket. "Sean loves those."

"Your brother?" Reinders asked.

Grace nodded. "He's quite the man about town, you know—speech-making for Ireland most of the time, though lately he's become religious. That often happens to Sean," she added wryly.

"More religious than you?" Reinders pretended shock.

She laughed. "Oh, aye—he's joined these Latter-Day Saints. Do you know anything about them?"

"Not really," he admitted. "What's the draw?"

"A Miss Marcy Osgoode, to my way of thinking, but he claims spiritual stimulation."

"Ah," Reinders said. "No comment."

"You must come to the Harp one night and let me give you a glass of real Irish ale—Dugan makes his own, you know." She wiped her forehead with the back of her hand. "And maybe I'll fix you a plate of supper, as well. By way of thanks."

"I don't know if I could hold my own in a roomful of Irishmen," he said doubtfully. "Don't they frequently burst into ballads and jigs?"

"Aye, and fight!" She laughed. "But I've no doubt you could hold your own, Captain, and I wouldn't mind watching you have a go at a jig or two." Her eyes danced merrily.

He remembered those eyes, the color shifting even as he looked into them—blue to green to hazel to brown with flecks of gold—just the way the sun changed the color of the waves.

"I might be tempted to dance if you'd join me," he heard himself say, then stopped, color rising in his face. *For crying out loud, Reinders,* he chastised himself, *is this your sorry version of flirting?* He glanced at Lily, who kept her head down.

"I haven't danced since my husband died," Grace admitted. "But I know the day'll come when 'tis time to try it again."

"I leave tomorrow," he apologized. "But I will stop in when I get back . . . to see the boy." He glanced at the ships, at the sailors roaming the wharves, and his tone changed to one of urgency. "You remember Marcus Boardham, the ship's steward?"

"How could I forget?" Grace asked gravely.

"Right. I sailed up to Boston and dropped him there, but I have reason to believe he's back in the city." He hesitated. "One of my men—Tom Dean—turned up dead, and the description of the man who did it fit Boardham. If you ever see him, I want you to turn around and go the other way as fast as you can."

"I will," she said absolutely. "What about that doctor?"

"He won't be a problem. We roughed him up a little, then let him off with a warning. Anyway, men like him aren't in your neighborhood too often, but rats like Boardham are. No offense," he added. "I don't think he'd recognize you at any rate— you look different now."

"Do I?" She touched her face self-consciously.

"You were awfully skinny."

"Yes, she was!" Lily spoke up, then pretended to busy herself at the other end of the stall.

"Yes, you were," he said. "Skinny and pale with dark circles under your eyes and always that shawl over your head. You look much better now." He eyed her appreciatively, the full face scattered with freckles, the red in her dark hair. "Really. Much better. Your face and your . . ." His hands fluttered uncontrollably before his very eyes. "And you've really filled out." *Oh, God, Reinders,* he said to himself, *will you shut up?*

"Thank you." Grace bit her lip, trying not to smile.

The captain nodded, feeling like an idiot. He didn't trust himself to say anything more, nor did he trust his traitorous hands, so he put them to work removing his hat, fiddling with the band, settling it firmly back on his head, all the while avoiding those eyes.

"You must have a great deal to do yet to ready yourself for the voyage," she said then, helping him out.

"It is getting late." Reinders glanced at the sun's position in the sky. "I'm glad to have seen you, Missus Donnelly. Give Mary Kate and Liam my regards, and tell them I'll stop in when I get back." *If I have the courage,* he added silently.

"Ah, now, Captain, don't be afraid." Grace put out her hand, grinning. "Have a safe voyage, and watch out for icebergs."

Reinders laughed despite himself, and allowed one hand cautiously out of confinement to hold hers for a quick moment. "Always a pleasure, Missus Donnelly. Lily"—he turned to her—"I'll see you before I go."

He strode off down the boardwalk, people moving out of his way, glancing back over their shoulders at the tall, commanding sea captain who appeared to be cursing himself under his breath.

"He's not like other men," Lily said pointedly.

"No." Grace watched him disappear. "He's not."

Marcus Boardham loved his new job so much, he started rounds early each morning, and that was how he'd discovered the Donnelly woman coming out of rooms on Orange Street. Didn't she know this was a dangerous neighborhood? he'd asked himself, stepping back into the shadow at the end of the hall. Bad things happened all the time to women, he mused, his tongue flicking his lower lip—well, maybe not on Saturday mornings when everyone was sleeping it off, he allowed, but still . . . it was no place for a lady. He'd watched her knock and go in, only to leave minutes later. He considered following her, but there was always the risk of being seen, and he wanted to keep on his side the element of surprise. The drunk would know, Boardham decided. It'd be easy to make him talk.

"Hello, old man." He popped the door to number nine open with his fist, and laughed meanly. "I was just in the neighborhood."

"I've paid this month." Kelley scurried back into his corner, but not before Boardham caught sight of the bag in his hand.

"What's that you've got?" He crossed the room in two steps and snatched it away. "Money? Where're you getting money?"

"It's from my boy," Kelley whined. "Give it back to me!"

"Your boy, eh?" Boardham dangled it just out of reach. "What's he do, your boy, earns him a sack of coins like this?"

"Why do you want to know?"

"It's my job to know things."

"Works for a saloonkeeper, cleaning up and the like." He made a grab for the bag, but Boardham yanked it away.

"What saloon?"

"The Harp, down by the docks. Run by a boxer," Kelley added belligerently. "Mighty Ogue—huge man—won't like it you're taking my boy's money."

"I'm not taking it," Boardham said easily. "Just holding it for a minute. Now"—he leaned against the wall—"who's the woman what brings it to you?"

"I don't know," Kelley lied. "Just some woman works for Ogue."

"Wrong." Boardham opened the sack, took out a few coins and pocketed them. "Try again."

"All right, all right. Calls her Grace, Liam does. Grace Donnelly."

And suddenly Boardham knew. "Your son is Liam Kelley. Of course. And he lives with Missus Donnelly. You're Liam Kelley's father."

Kelley was sure Boardham must be drunk. One of them had to be. "I been sick," he explained. " 'Tis better for the boy, living there, earning his keep."

"And yours."

The old man said nothing.

Boardham stood perfectly still for a moment, then unexpectedly tossed Kelley the bag. "That's all I wanted to know," he said pleasantly. "Thank you for your time."

After closing the door, Boardham heard Kelley slump into his corner. He smiled and patted the coins in his pocket. He wasn't sure how he was going to use this information, but he enjoyed having it. He wouldn't tell Callahan just yet, he decided. First he'd pay Missus Donnelly a visit.

Twenty-six

GRACE came into the upper rooms with a dress over her arm.

"What do you think of this?" She held it up. " 'Tis the same one, but with a new collar and sleeves now the weather's cooler. Is it all right, do you think? For Florence's party Saturday night?"

Sean set down his paper. "Ah, Grace, I can't go. I'm out all day on Saturday, and then Mister Osgoode is holding a meeting I must attend."

Grace's face fell. "And just when were you going to tell me, Sean O'Malley? It's tomorrow, is it not?"

" 'Tis," he allowed, ruefully. "Ah, forgive me, now. I didn't know myself until this very morning. Marcy sent a message after breakfast."

Grace tried to hide her irritation. "Are you telling me, Sean, that you're going to pass on a fine party you've already accepted, to sit in on yet another meeting of the Saints? What about your friends?"

"The Saints *are* my friends," he said indignantly.

"Not the friends providing you with work, nor looking out for your future," she replied hotly.

"That's where you're wrong!" He jabbed a finger at her.

"They care about my future—my eternal future, which is more important, mind you. God says to lay up your treasures in Heaven, not on earth."

"If you're laying them up in Heaven, then why is it costing you so much down here?" Grace flung the dress over a chair in the corner and put her hands on her hips. "You leave with money in your pocket each time, and then come back with nothing."

Sean's face burned red. "You've no want, have you?" He stood, wincing as his hip caught the table edge. "Don't I bring home enough for food and clothes, even for the boy who's no relation?"

"Shame on you, Sean O'Malley." She shook her head, disgusted. "You know I'm grateful for all you do. That's not the point. Have you not been down this road before? Have you not been Protestant and Catholic both, Quaker and Freemason? What of your pals—Quinn and Cavan? Danny Young? Do you ever see them anymore?"

"Danny's the one brought me to the Saints!" he reminded her. "Don't you remember me telling you his uncle knew Joseph Smith himself, knew him as a Freemason back when he was transcribing the Book?"

"What book?"

"The Book of Mormon, girl!" He dug around in the piles on his desk and brought out a dog-eared book marked all through with scraps of paper. "What do you think I've been reading day in and day out?"

"The Bible," she said, confused. "There it is right there, and that's what I saw open on your desk."

"Well, I was reading it," he allowed. "And also the other, which takes up where the Bible leaves off."

Grace eyed him suspiciously. "What do you mean, leaves off?"

"It's the account of Christ's days here in America when He walked among the natives." Sean leaned forward in his chair, eyes blazing with what Grace recognized as his old religious zeal.

"Bah," she said. "The Bible is God's holy and inspired Word, and there's nothing at the end of it says, 'to be continued.' "

He laughed despite himself. "But isn't that how Jews feel about the New Testament? Just because *you* don't believe it, doesn't mean it isn't the inspired word of God."

"Or the inspired word of a charlatan," she argued. "I know about your Joseph Smith, Sean. He was a seer, digging for other people's lost treasure, guilty of fraud and forgery, and finally killed in a shoot-out from a jail cell, where he and his brother were waiting to be tried."

"He and Hyrum were martyred," Sean asserted indignantly. "Satan is always working to keep the truth from us."

"And just maybe he's succeeded by making sure your one became an instant prophet," she shot back.

"Grace!" He put out his hands, hurt. "Why are we arguing about this?"

She crossed her arms in front of her, but her shoulders drooped. "I don't know. It makes no sense to me. It scares me."

"But why?"

"I guess because you're smarter than I am, Sean—you lead, I follow. Only I don't want to go this way. This way feels wrong to me."

"Why haven't you said anything to me before now?"

Grace frowned, embarrassed. "I guess I didn't understand you were serious about it. I thought you were only serious about Miss Osgoode. Sure and she's serious about you, no doubt there."

"So you thought I was only going along with this as a way to court Marcy?"

"Aye," she admitted. "I thought in the end it'd be you persuading her away from that lot, rather than her bringing you in."

He shook his head and Grace was afraid he was about to become angry again, but instead he laughed.

"Well, you're half right. No girl ever paid me the kind of attention Marcy does, and I admit I like it. She doesn't even see this"—he shrugged his twisted shoulder—"or mind the brace on my leg. That means a lot to me, Grace. That a girl can see past this."

"I know it does," she said, contrite. "And if she truly loves you and you her, then I'm happy for you both."

"She does love me." He paused. "But I'm a Gentile."

"Well, of course you are! Isn't she?"

He shook his head. "God ordered Joseph Smith to make a new church because the old ones were corrupt and divided—if you're a true believer, then you're a Saint. All others, Jews included, are Gentiles."

"Ah Sean, you're scaring me again. Are you saying you can't marry Miss Osgoode unless you join the Latter-Day Saints? Is that it?"

He nodded hesitantly.

"Do you want to marry her?"

"I might. I think I'm starting to love her. But joining the church would be about my love for God, Gracie, not about finding a wife."

She looked at her brother's familiar face, glasses slid halfway down his nose. "I want you to be happy, Sean," she said carefully. "But I don't want to lose you in the bargain. I'm not ready to follow you into this, and what will happen if I never am?"

"The Saints take care of their own." He spoke with quiet assurance. "I'll not go off and leave you, no matter what."

"Is that a promise you can make?"

"Aye," he said. "Will you make me one in return?"

She nodded.

"Will you promise to think about it, to come to a meeting with me, get to know some of these people and see for yourself? Maybe even read a bit of this?" He held up the dog-eared book.

No, her heart beat. No, no, no. They stared at one another.

"All right," she said at last, afraid of losing him. "I'll think about it."

He sat down again and picked up his paper. "That's fine then, Grace. That's grand. And listen, you go on to Florence's dinner without me."

"Ah, now, I never could!" she protested. "Not alone!"

"Jay is coming straight from his club to give us a lift. He'll take you. It's good for you to get out and take your mind off things," he insisted. "Besides, I need you there to stop all that wicked talk behind my back." He winked.

She bit her lip, torn.

"Think of all the work you put into that beautiful dress," he wheedled. "The hours spent, the money into lace . . ."

"Oh, stop." She held up her hand. "I'll go. But not because of the dress. I'll go because I might meet a few of those Transcendentalists and Shakers, a couple of Masons and a Theosophist, and maybe between the lot of them I'll come to understand you."

"I hope you do." Sean laughed and pushed up his glasses.

"Bah," she said and left the room.

"I've a surprise for you," Grace told Liam and Mary Kate when she returned from Orange Street the following morning. "Dugan has given us the day off so that I might take you both to a birthday party!"

Their mouths opened wide in astonishment.

"You work alongside me this morning, so he's not left with it all, and then we'll go out on the town, and after"—she paused dramatically—"we're meeting Lily and her two children in the park for a picnic! It's them having the birthday. What do you say to that?"

They both let out a cheer and threw their arms around her, Liam's encircling her waist, Mary Kate's around her legs. She squeezed them both in return and her heart was warmed. They were good children.

They swept and washed, tidied up, and Grace made plenty of soda bread to go with the cheese and meat for a ploughman's supper to be offered at the bar that evening along with pickled eggs. She packed a basket for their picnic, tied a scarf around her head, and sent Liam and Mary Kate for warmer hats as it was October now and the wind chilly, despite a deep blue sky and trees vibrant orange, marigold, and red.

"Where will we go first?" Liam asked, marching along on one side.

He would need new boots soon, Grace thought to herself,

noticing how they bulged at the sides and were near worn through at the end. New boots, new pants, new winter coat. The same for Mary Kate, who was growing at an astounding rate. Custom would fall off in the winter, but she'd still need to pay Liam's father each week. And what about her father and the baby—not a baby anymore. She bit her lip.

"Mam?" Mary Kate pulled at her coat.

"Hmm?" She pushed away the thoughts that consumed so much of her wakeful nights. "Oh, aye. We're going along to Broadway to look in a room at daguerreotypes."

"What?" Liam squinted, puzzled.

"Likenesses taken by a man with a camera," she explained. "This is a famous man, an Irishman no less, Mathew Brady. Had his name in the paper and all. They call him 'Brady of Broadway' as he takes pictures of famous people."

She liked them to see important Irish, Irish with accomplishments as a foil for the prejudice that confronted them in a hundred subtle ways; but when she glanced at their faces, both were clearly deciding if this was to be a boring thing or not.

"It's something very new," she told them matter-of-factly. "And as we're adventurous people living in a great city, we ought not to be afraid of new things."

That cinched it for Liam, who pulled himself up to full height and threw back his shoulders.

"Who says I'm afraid?" he demanded. "I'm not afraid of pictures, for crying out loud! Let's go see 'em right now. Afraid of some old pictures," he muttered under his breath. "Sheesh!"

"Sheesh!" Mary Kate attempted to copy Liam's swagger.

Grace smiled as she shepherded the children down the smaller street and onto the wide avenue. There, she pulled them back against the buildings, out of the way of the dangerous horse cabs and private carriages, the tangled mess of city transportation.

Eventually, they came to Broadway and as they walked down the sidewalk, they saw photographs of glamorous and celebrated people in the windows of Gurney's, Edward's, and Anthony's.

"Those are some of Mister Brady's," Grace pointed out, and the children dutifully stopped to admire the portraits.

They came to a building at the corner of Broadway and Fulton, and went in, climbing the stairs to the top floor, which housed the Daguerrean Miniature Gallery.

"Absolutely no touching," warned the thin, fastidious clerk behind the desk, eyeing Liam in particular. "And no lingering," he sniffed. "Stay in line, move along."

Grace nodded, steering the children into the line, which was moving slowly toward a larger room. A poster, printed with a sketch of Brady and a few sentences about his life and work, was propped on an easel; Grace read this in a low voice to the children, who listened carefully even as they stole glances round the room. She skipped over the part that said Brady did not photograph ordinary working people, though he had done studies of the inmates of Blackwell's Island penitentiary for a book on reading heads. This reminded Grace too keenly of Doctor Draper, and her pride in the Irish Mathew Brady slipped a notch.

The photographs were very good, and Grace found herself drawn particularly to those of the women, to the confidence in their smiles, their spectacular clothing, their dramatic eyes. It was the eyes that captured her full attention—so alive, so real, yet guarded—and she leaned closer, peering into them, attempting to see down into the souls of these women, to see the truth of their lives and understand what it must be like to be them, to be American, living an American life. Her intense scrutiny penetrated some of these barriers, and she glimpsed who they really were.

This one, she saw quite clearly, this theater star—so fashionably dressed with jeweled earrings and ropes of pearls—had many lovers when she was young, many lovers and three pregnancies, which she'd ended with little thought. Older, she'd found at last the love of her life only to be unable to provide him with the children for whom he longed. The irony had not been lost on her and she'd grown bitter, driving him away. She was beloved by thousands of fans, but not by him; her pain betrayed itself in the darkest parts of her eyes, in the fine lines that ran down from her mouth even as she smiled confidently into the camera.

Next to her was a prosperous man who'd made millions buying and selling land, as finely dressed as anyone else, one hand in his pocket, the other atop an ornately carved cane. His face was hidden beneath a thick beard and side-whiskers, his eyes shadowed by heavy brows. Grace could barely see into those tightly guarded eyes, but she concentrated and there he was: a boy with his mother, turned out of their home, begging on the streets in the dead of winter. And there he was again, sitting in a dark alley as snow fell upon the still body beside him, trying to keep it from covering her face. He was a man now to whom riches meant everything, and he fed his terrible hunger with land—buying it, selling it—wanting only to have more, make more, save more, so that on winter nights when the snow fell, he could breathe; he could sit inside by a warm fire, drink his brandy, eat a fine meal, and tell himself that this was who he was, and not the other. He did not think about beggars in the snow, never looked in their faces nor met their eyes; he hated them, the young boys most of all because they reminded him of things he'd done in desperate times to earn his next meal. There was more, but Grace had no wish to see it.

With the children behind her, she stepped back out of line and viewed the photographs from farther away, but even from there she saw who they really were—orphans, prostitutes, gamblers, liars, cheats, prophets, scholars, uncomplaining workers, saints, too; the wealthy older man and his wife who looked off to the side as if embarrassed privately funded a hospital for young women in need, girls who were about to give birth and had no place to go. They not only gave money, but took an interest, visiting the girls and talking with them, placing their babies in good homes, quietly handing out packets of money so that a new start might be made more easily. Grace could not resist and returned to the line to look in the woman's eyes—ah, there it was: a daughter whose suitor they had refused, a daughter whose anguish they had ignored, a daughter who disappeared because she was with child. It was all there.

Grace moved down the line, knowing better than to look too closely at church bishops and court judges, though the hardest and most grave had the faintest halo round his head. She had not known that this making of images could capture so much of the soul, and she wondered what her own image might reveal to those who looked.

"I think we're done now." Liam and Mary Kate were swaying on their feet with the close warmth of the room and all the staring eyes. She led them to the foyer and down the stairs, pausing to button their coats and secure their hats before going out again.

"What did you think of that, then?" The sharp wind revived her.

"Are they all rich?" Liam asked. "They look rich."

"Ah, well, they're famous enough, and fame often brings riches."

"What are they famous for?"

"Some are brilliant singers or act upon the stage," she told him. "Some are sportsmen or politicians. Authors of books or inventors. They've made tall buildings or discovered things. Others made lots of money in business."

"You can be famous for making lots of money?"

Grace shrugged. "Making money is a gift as well as any other thing, and people are interested in that."

As they walked toward the park, Grace realized that Mary Kate was gripping her hand more tightly than usual, her face grim.

"And what did you think of all that, wee girl?"

"Sad," was the faint answer.

Grace halted and bent down to look at her. "Why?"

"I don't know. Do they really look like that?"

"Not all the time. They're all dressed up for the camera."

"I mean their faces." Mary Kate looked directly at her mother. "Their eyes."

"Ah." Grace understood. "Some were not as sad as others."

"No?"

"No. And when you're older, I'll tell you what it means so it won't be a burden to you."

Mary Kate's face relaxed, and she patted her mother on the cheek. "Let's go to the park, now."

Grace took her hand and Liam's, and they strolled along the sidewalk, past Chambers Street toward Reade. They slowed in front of a five-story building sheathed in white marble, supported by giant Corinthian pilasters, its huge plate-glass windows reflecting the bright sun.

"Who lives here?" breathed Liam in awe.

Grace laughed. " 'Tis a shop."

"A shop?" he squeaked. "What kind of shop?"

"All kinds. Many kinds." She glanced in the window. "Clothes, boots, hats, scents, toys . . ."

"Toys?" he interrupted.

"Aye." She laughed again at the look on his face. " 'Tis called the Marble Palace. Do you remember the first picture we saw, of the big man sitting in a velvet chair?"

Both children nodded.

"Well, that was Mister Stewart, Alexander T. Stewart, and he's the man who built this place and runs it. People come from all over to look at it. It's meant to be beautiful inside."

"Can we go in?" Liam asked hopefully.

Grace bit her lip, painfully aware of their patched clothing and muddy boots. "We've no time today. But another day, I promise."

They moved off again, Liam stretching his neck, unable to tear his eyes away from the magnificent building. When they came to the corner, the street was crowded with carriages, private rigs, and omnibuses, and they were forced to stand and wait for a lull in the snarled traffic.

While the children looked for a break, Grace glanced warily at the bookseller's corner stall. She had approached one or two of these stalls eagerly soon after arriving in hopes of finding a penny novel for her brother or maybe even herself, but had been overwhelmed with such lurid titles as *Confessions of a*

Lady's Waiting Maid, Life of a Butler, Her Own Diary. Not to mention the papers—*Crime Street, Famous Criminals, National Police Gazette,* and *Life of the Town*—all cheaply printed. When she had asked confidentially if there might not be something else, something a little more interesting for her brother, who was a young man and particular about his reading, the bookseller had eyed her shrewdly and offered a book bound securely in yellow paper—only ten cents, he'd said, and just the thing all fashionable young men were reading. She'd carried it home proudly under her arm—her first gift for her brother— mistaking the glances from men she passed for admiration of her sophisticated purchase. Her embarrassment had been acute when Sean burst into laughter at the sight of the wrapper, took it gently from her, and proceeded to explain that cheap and exotic novels and thrillers were primarily a cover for the corner bookseller's more lucrative trade—pornography. He then attempted a delicate explanation of pornography, which left her mortified and angry. He recommended the secondhand bookshops on Nassau and Pearl Streets, or uptown along the canal, but never the corner stalls. She avoided these now like the plague, steering the children well away from them, and glaring at those she saw perusing the books or papers.

At last they were able to cross the street, stepping quickly but carefully around muddy ruts and piles of horse manure. They entered the park and immediately slowed their pace. The day was spectacular despite the cold, and Grace gloried in the vibrant color of the trees against the solid blue of a cloudless sky, the pink cheeks and sparkling eyes of everyone she passed. Men and women, arms linked, strolled the walkways; nurses pushed prams or sat on the benches drowsily rocking their napping charges; shop girls walked in groups, laughing and talking, eyeing the young men, who eyed them in return or boldly stopped to say hello. And there were the dog walkers, who captured Mary Kate's attention as she was particularly fond of dogs—all dogs, no matter the size—and always hoped for an invitation to pet one.

Grace let the children run on ahead, and they had covered

nearly half the park by the time they arrived at the duck pond. Tired now, she sank onto a bench and watched as the children stood at the water's edge, calling the ducks, then finally giving up in favor of gathering sticks and rocks. Lily was not here yet, so Grace pushed her shawl back and tipped her face up to the sun.

Lily had chosen this end of the park, and Grace could see why; most of those walking here were servants, working people, tradesmen taking shortcuts. There was another pond with a gushing fountain near the entrance, and she supposed this was where the better families went to air themselves. She watched as people came down the path or cut across the field, and at last she saw the one she was waiting for striding swiftly across the field with a child's hand in each one of hers.

"Lily!" She stood and waved her arm.

"I thought that might be you," Lily said upon arrival. "I saw the children down by the pond."

Grace nodded. "And this must be Samuel and Ruth."

"How do you do?" they said simultaneously, and Grace laughed.

"Well, aren't you fine-looking children?" She smiled first at the tall boy with long lashes, then at the girl, who was shorter but whose eyes were just like her brother's. "Your mother's told me all about the two of you. We're happy to come out for your birthday."

"Why don't you run down and play awhile?" Lily loosened her scarf. "We'll call you when it's time to eat."

They kissed their mother, then ran down to the edge of the pond and said something to Liam, who nodded gravely and looked back up at Grace. She waved to him, and he waved back, then handed Samuel a stick to throw. Mary Kate was looking up at Ruth in wonder, never having been so close to a person whose skin was so different.

"And now they're friends." Grace slid over on the bench to make room. "Did Mister Hesselbaum give you the day off, or have you been to work already this morning?"

"Day off. He thinks we need to have some fun." She sat. "Jakob's a good man. We been lucky that way."

"And you know Captain Reinders as well."

Lily hesitated. "I suppose he told you about me."

Grace shook her head, confused, then remembered the look that had passed between the two of them. "Is he your man, then?"

"Lord, no!" Lily laughed. "I got enough of that. He doing me a favor, is all. A mighty big favor, though, and I been waiting to hear from him. I thought maybe he was *your* man."

It was Grace's turn to laugh. "Ah, no, I'm just a grateful passenger wanting to give him supper one night by way of thanks. He did a favor for me, as well. What's he doing for you, then?"

Lily's face closed down and she turned away.

"I'm sorry," Grace said quickly. "You don't have to tell me. 'Tis your own business, that."

Lily frowned, thinking, and finally she moved closer on the bench. "I got me two more children. They still slaves." She watched Grace carefully. "I tell you this 'cause I know you left one of yours behind, too."

Grace nodded stiffly; it always hurt to think of that.

"He's nearly a year old. Called Morgan for his da."

"My oldest is Solomon," Lily said quietly. "Mary's my other girl."

"So you're a runaway, then?" Grace considered this.

"I am. Me and the younger ones. But I got papers says we free."

"The other two, they're still on the place you left?"

"Maybe Sol is." Lily paused. "Mary, though, she been sold away."

"Sold," Grace repeated, the full weight of the word tearing into her heart, and her eyes sought Mary Kate.

Lily, too, watched the children. "One morning, she go out to the field just like she always do, but January—that my husband—he come home without her. That's how they do it," she explained. "It easier that way, they say—no crying and carrying on, begging to stay together."

Grace turned to look at the woman beside her, but Lily kept her eyes on the children.

"He sell her off across the river, act like he done right by us, she gonna be a house slave instead of breaking her back in the fields. We see her Sundays, maybe, if she be good." She frowned. "Big house not so good if you pretty. Tall, too, for her age."

"How old?"

"Twelve," Lily said, then corrected herself. "Fourteen now."

"And Solomon?"

"Two year older. He a big boy, like his papa." She sighed. "Hated being a slave—hated slave life, everything. January told him to be strong, don't cause no trouble and just get along. But he get tired of hearing that, and run off. They beat him bad, but after he heal up, off he go again." Her eyes squinted in pain. "Third time, they cut him—he can still work, just can't run no more."

"Holy Mother of God," Grace gasped.

"They watch him all the time—can't squat to do his business 'out somebody standing over him. Can't sell him off—nobody buy a slave like him, nothing but trouble. So next time, they say, they just hang him. That's when we know we got to go."

Grace nodded.

"January set it up so a guide be waiting, but he don't wait long. When the signal come, we can't get Mary and Solomon out in the sheds to work all night." Her eyes searched Grace's for understanding. "Jan say maybe we never get another chance, better to save two children than lose four. Tells me go on, he bring Mary and Sol soon as he can." She stopped. "Been two years now."

"Maybe they escaped," Grace said hopefully. "Maybe they just haven't found you, yet. 'Tis a big place, this."

"Not so big he wouldn't find the Black quarter. No, most likely they beat him after we left—beat him bad to keep the others from running. I know. Seen it all the time. Best for them if they hobble ol' Jan up so he can't follow us, set a good example."

"Ah, Lily." Grace was stricken.

"I try not to think on it too much. I'm doing all I can." Lily's voice was fiercely resolved. "They in God's hands. And the captain's."

"How do you know him, Lily?" Grace asked. "Really."

"I saved his life," she said simply. "One day I'm down on the docks after dark and I see gang a negra boys working over a white man, beating him with a club and kicking at him, grabbing at his pockets. I tell myself just walk away, white man no business of mine, and them boys got plenty reason to hate. But I hear God's voice say clear as day, 'Help that man.' I carry a knife, you know, and I pull it out, screaming, swinging it like a crazy woman." She laughed, remembering, while Grace stared open-mouthed. "They just boys, turns out, but big and tough— they run off and I see he's hurt bad, blood all up in his face. He try to stand and talk, just fall over again, so I get an arm around him and somehow we start walking. That Mackley come running then, ask what happen, and give me money for my trouble." She paused. "But Jakob. He's a smart man, and when the captain come round to thank me himself, saying he owe me his life, we make a deal."

"Is that what he's doing then? Is he buying your family out?"

Lily shook her head. "Can't no Northerner buy up slaves. They're on to that, they got a system. He got to ask around, go to slave markets, auctions, find where everybody is. Then we got to hire us a broker, a man in the middle. Then we got to get them out of Georgia."

"Has he found anything?"

"We thought for a while Mary might be up for sale, but we lost out on that. I keep hoping for word of January or Sol—that's where he was going this time, the captain."

"I wish I could say I knew when he was coming back."

"Me, too." Lily leaned forward. "You can't tell no one about this. He'd get in a mess of trouble—lose his ship. Go to jail."

"I won't," Grace promised. "You can trust me."

Lily smiled then and nodded, lighter for having shared the burden of her story. They stood and stretched, and called the children, who came running, more than ready to eat. They spread a blanket on the ground and laid out their bread and meat, cheese, apples, nuts, cider for all, and little cakes made specially for the ten-year-old twins, who laughed with shy delight and shared them round. Leaves drifted from the oldest of the trees and swirled in an autumn dance, squirrels chattered up and down gathering winter nuts, geese rose as one from the rippling pond and climbed into the sky in perfect formation; they watched this as the last of the sun shone down upon them all, and for a little while at least, they knew peace.

Twenty-seven

SEAN and Jay Livingston stood elbow to elbow at the bar, taking a pint of Ogue's Mighty Irish Ale against the chill of the night air. They spoke quietly, Jay chastising Sean for skipping tonight's dinner in favor of a religious lecture, and Sean replying that the man who neglected his soul in favor of his belly jeopardized his place at the only table that mattered. Jay frowned; he hated it when Sean took this self-righteous tone— there was no arguing with a man who held up an invitation from God in answer to an invitation from Florence Livingston, even if she was the most intelligent, forthright woman in their circle.

Dugan listened intently as he dried the same glass over and over. He agreed with young Mister Livingston that Sean was spending too much time with these new fanatics, getting all tied up with them and their work while forgetting his own. Sean's place was out there beating the drum for Ireland, stirring hearts with his silver tongue. He was Irish, by God. If he felt a need for more religion, why not join the Catholics? There was religion enough for any man! Dugan shook his head, unable to fathom the draw of golden tablets and no drink—no drink, by God, and Christ Himself not hesitating to turn water into wine! He slapped the glass down with a bang, about to enter into Sean's business despite his vow not to, when the room suddenly hushed, those at the front tables now staring at the side door.

"Evening, Missus Donnelly," they murmured respectfully.

"Don't you look lovely tonight . . ."

". . . the rose of Eire, herself . . ."

"O, if I were a younger man . . ."

"A sight for poor Irish eyes . . ."

Dugan grinned proudly as she floated across the room. "I believe she's ready, Mister Livingston."

Jay, whose back had been turned to the stairs, now glanced over his shoulder, then choked on his drink. Taking the handkerchief Sean held out, he dabbed quickly at his mustache, touched his black satin cravat, smoothed the brown velvet waistcoat, cleared his throat, wet his lips, and turned smoothly to greet her.

"Ah, Gracelin, you are indeed a vision of loveliness." He took her hand and kissed it, bowing elegantly.

"You're looking none too shabby yourself tonight, Jay," she teased "Will you give me a hand with this?"

She held out her burnoose, then turned and waited, unaware that he now stood momentarily frozen by the sight of her shoulders beneath the sheer material. She turned slightly, and saw the look on his face.

"Surely now, Mister Livingston, a man-about-town like yourself can manage a lady's cloak." She made her eyes innocently wide. "But if not, I could ask Mister Ogue over there to show you how it's done."

Dugan laughed, and the men within earshot guffawed and slapped their knees or punched each other fondly—wasn't their Grace a grand girl? Sean joined in, enjoying the spectacle of the urbane Jay Livingston unnerved by a poor Irish widow.

"I'm sure he could," Jay said gallantly to the room at large. "But I believe the honor is mine." He stepped forward and arranged the long, hooded cloak expertly over those lovely shoulders. "You look magnificent," he murmured, his mouth close to her ear.

"You're too kind, I'm sure." The warmth of his breath on her neck flustered her, and she turned imploring eyes on her brother. "Won't you change your mind and come with us? You know you'll enjoy yourself."

"Ah, now, Grace, we've settled this, but I'll walk out with you. 'Tis time I made my way over to the Osgoodes. They'll be waiting for me."

"Shall we go, then?" Jay offered Grace his arm, and she took it—a little nervously, he thought, which pleased him.

From the moment they'd met, Grace had been a challenge, had always managed to unsettle him, whether slopping around the saloon with a bucket and a mop, her apron damp, hair flying around her face, children pulling at her skirts; or standing alone at a party, her best dress fashionably out of fashion, gorgeous hair swept back from her face as she listened to the conversation swirling around her. But Jay was the kind of man who appreciated challenge, especially when it came in the form of a desirable woman.

They said good night to Sean outside—he was going the opposite way and wouldn't hear of a ride—then got into Jay's handsome carriage.

"He's an odd duck, your brother," Jay said as they pulled away.

"Ah, well, he only seems odd when he's out with you swans." Grace eyed Jay's fine evening dress from the top of his perfect hat to the tips of his gleaming leather boots. "Put him in his own pond and he's not so very different."

Jay snorted. "You're as quick as he is. Maybe I won't miss him tonight, after all."

"You most certainly will," she replied. "For I've not half his mind."

"Twice the charm, however. And a thousand times the beauty. I'll enjoy looking at you all evening even if you have nothing to say!"

He laughed as the carriage rocked down the avenue, his knee now resting firmly against hers.

"Ah, but your sister will miss him." She shifted her position deftly while she spoke.

He raised his eyebrows ever so slightly, acknowledging the physical countermove in their little game.

"True," he admitted. "They never run out of things to talk about, those two—freedom fighters and abolitionists share a great deal of common ground. Florence is *particularly* fond of him, you know."

Grace looked up, surprised. "Is she?"

"Very." He leaned back, his leg once again touching hers. "She only hopes they can continue their friendship despite his courtship of the popular Miss Osgoode."

"He likes Miss Osgoode, true enough," Grace allowed. "But I don't know that he's courting her."

"I have jumped to a conclusion," Jay pronounced. "Please forgive me. Born of frustration, I suppose. He's so often unavailable now, and when he is, he talks of nothing but this . . . group." He waved his hand vaguely. "Anyway, we miss him. Florence especially, as he was a regular at her afternoon soirees and she so enjoyed him. All that stimulating conversation, you know. Gives one ideas."

"Was he . . . did he . . ." Grace hesitated. "Are you saying there was an understanding between them?"

"Absolutely not," Jay said quickly. "He's an honorable man, your brother, and his intentions were always quite clear, even if—and I take you quite into confidence here, my dear—even if Florence hoped that his feelings might have increased in the course of their mutual admiration."

"I see." Grace pulled on the fingers of her gloves. "I like Florence very much."

"And she likes you."

She allowed herself a brief look into his eyes and was glad to see he was sincere.

"He's not been himself," she confided, then bit her lip, the desire to understand her brother conflicting with the anxiety of betrayal. "It's not like him to turn away from a friendship like your sister's. Or yours."

"Any of ours!" Jay exclaimed. "Though we may be somewhat responsible. He's had to take a good deal of ribbing about all this. Everyone simply got fed up with his constant spouting off, and perhaps we were not as tactful as we might have been."

"Ah." Grace wove her fingers together to keep them still.

"We did humor him at first. Because he's got such an incredible mind, and he's so persuasive. But really, it's just too much to ask any reasonable person to believe. All you have to do is dig into Joseph Smith's background and . . ." He shrugged defensively.

She turned to look out at the damp streets, gaslight shadows looming large across dark buildings.

"Oh, I say—you may well think as your brother does, and then I have insulted you." When Grace made no reply, he added, "I do apologize."

"If Sean says it's the truth"—she struggled to remain loyal—"then I can only think I'm not seeing it because I've not looked hard enough."

"Or perhaps it is not there," he posited. "These new religions can bind one up with so much high emotion that reason is no longer as logical as it might seem." He glanced out the window. "We've arrived."

The carriage followed a circular drive, coming to a halt before the front entrance. Jay got out, gave Grace his hand, and escorted her to the door, which opened immediately. A butler helped with her burnoose, then took the young master's hat, gloves, and overcoat.

"Ah, there you are at last!" Florence came sailing into the foyer to greet them. "Don't you look lovely tonight, Grace! Where's Sean?"

"Unwell," Jay lied smoothly. "He wanted to come—made a great fuss about it—but I said absolutely not, not looking as he did."

"How ill is he?" Florence's eyes clouded with concern. "Will we send a doctor?"

"A long night's rest and he'll be good as new," Jay assured her. "But I insisted Grace come out anyway, and she kindly consented."

"I'm so glad you did." Florence was too gracious a woman to let her disappointment show, and now she took her guest's arm companionably. "Come, let me introduce you around. Going to be a talky bunch tonight. I'll miss your brother," she confided in a low voice.

"Aye." Grace nodded. "He's never without an opinion."

Florence laughed, and Grace allowed herself to be escorted into the main drawing room, where people stood or sat in small groups, already engaged in conversation. Florence made a number of introductions, pausing on the edge of a clique of young people comparing minstrel shows. Florence rolled her eyes and was about to move on, when one of them plucked at her sleeve.

"Oh, Miss Livingston, do give us your opinion," he implored, though his tone was not sincere. "You're more familiar with darkies. Who does them best—Christy Minstrels or the Kentucky Rattlers?"

The group as a whole appeared to be holding a singular breath, and Florence eyed them shrewdly.

"They do themselves best," she said pointedly. "I have seen many outstanding negros play their own music, tell their own jokes, and perform their own dances. And it was a far more rewarding entertainment than a stageful of white men who paint their faces black."

The young man persevered. "But surely, Miss Livingston, you understand that the minstrel show *celebrates* the life of the dar . . . negro? We see how they live, we understand them better, we are better able to accommodate them in civilized society—isn't that right?" he asked the group, pleased with his own pomposity.

Grace bit her lip, noting Florence's sudden high color.

"I had not thought you so dense, Mister . . . Tweedle, is it?"

"Tweedham, actually." His smile faltered.

"Well, Mister Tweedle, far from *celebrating* the culture of a people brought over so forcibly from their homeland and treated so abominably, minstrel shows *mock* what is good and decent about them and makes light of their suffering. It seeks to convince us that they are too stupid and ignorant to mind what has happened. It is an insult, Mister Tweedle, a further affront to the many whose lives have been brutally subsumed in the creation of wealth for a comparative few."

The faces of Lily and her children came before Grace, and she regarded Florence with renewed admiration.

"I hope that answers your question, Mister Tweedle?" Florence stared him into submission.

"Tweedham," the young man stammered. "Thank you."

"Anytime." Florence took Grace's arm once again and propelled her to the edge of the room. "I simply can't abide that kind of ignorance. I'm sorry if you were uncomfortable."

"Not a bit." Grace grinned. "It put me in mind of a woman I've come to know, of her life."

"Was she a slave?"

"Aye. Free now, but she left people behind."

"I know many who've had to make that choice," Florence said grimly. "Slavery is an abomination, a blight on the soul of this nation."

"You're an abolitionist."

"A negrophile, according to not a few here tonight." Her eyes twinkled darkly. "But they'll catch up. It's all coming to a head, you know, and there'll be war over this if nothing is done. I dread that." She shuddered. "The cost of freedom is so often paid in buckets of blood."

"Aye," Grace said, and the two shared a look of understanding.

"I must excuse myself," Florence apologized. "May I leave you on your own for a moment?"

"I'll be fine. I like to hear what's being said."

"You might sidle up to that group over there." Florence pointed to a tight circle of men standing at the far end of the great hearth, obviously in the middle of a heated discussion. "You know Mister O'Sullivan from the paper. Most likely the topic is Ireland."

She left then and Grace make her way over to the circle on the pretext of warming herself by the blazing fire.

"Duffy should never have issued an ultimatum in the first place," argued a distinguished man in glasses. "Never divide loyalties."

"Just shows how unstable the Young Irelanders really were." This from a round man in side-whiskers, who jabbed his finger with each point he made. "Mitchel's a hothead. They're all hotheads. They thought nothing of dividing loyalties when they broke from O'Connell's group!"

"They gave it a great deal of thought," O'Sullivan interjected. "Old Ireland refused to take up arms. The oppression was worse than ever. If it weren't for Mitchel and Smith O'Brien, they'd still be—"

"Starving to death?" Whiskers interrupted. "Dying like flies from disease? Emigrating by the thousands? Bah! I don't see one drop of difference made by the Young Irelanders."

"Moot point now, gentlemen," Glasses intoned. "Mitchel's been transported—fourteen years in Bermuda. John Martin, ten years. Smith O'Brien sentenced to hang, and Meagher—"

Grace stepped away from the fire and into their midst, unable to stop herself. "Are you saying, sir, that the sacrifice of these men means nothing to their country? That the lives given up were for naught?"

Mister O'Sullivan cleared his throat. "Gentlemen, this is Missus Grace Donnelly, sister to our own great orator, Sean O'Malley."

The men nodded dutifully, though some were clearly irritated that their intellectual debate would now be diminished by female emotionality.

"What we're saying, Missus Donnelly," Whiskers spoke carefully, as if to a child, "is that it has been too much sacrifice for too little gain, and had the Young Irelander movement stayed within the dictates of Old Ireland, that sacrifice would have been very much less."

"Aye, because O'Connell's group refused to fight!" Emotion made Grace's accent more pronounced. "Because in the end, they were more concerned with their own politics than with feeding their people!"

"That's hardly an accurate portrayal, Missus Donnelly." It was all Whiskers could do not to jab his finger at her. "The Young Irelanders were led by coddled idealists, men who lacked the experience needed—nay, *required*—to negotiate the terms of Ireland's independence. Just look at who they put in charge of carrying out the raids, no offense to your brother, madam," he said. "He's a brilliant man and probably the only reason they achieved as much as they did. But this McDonagh—an uneducated peasant, barely literate from what I gather, who had no choice really—was expected to organize armies out of ill-fed, ragged men like himself! What in God's name were they thinking? Were there no better men than that?"

Grace felt the heat of her blood spread across her chest, her neck, her cheeks. She willed herself to calm down, to resist slapping the maddeningly smug faces of these well-fed, well-dressed imbeciles.

"McDonagh had more courage and conviction in the look of his eye than all of you put together," she said in a voice that belied her rage. "He could've left Ireland. He had that choice. He could've come here to be with his family, the wife he loved . . ." She made herself stop. "But he didn't. He stayed and rallied his countrymen, spoke for them, fought for them." She looked at each of their faces, caught O'Sullivan's nearly imperceptible nod, and went on. "In the middle of the worst hunger we've ever known, he gave us hope—he gave us something to live for! You support Irish independence by laying down your wallet. He supported it by laying down his life." She jabbed her finger at Whiskers. "Who's the better man?"

Whiskers put his hand to his chest, feigning incredulity at such an attack. "My dear woman, we're all of us familiar by now with the legend. I'm talking about the sad reality of a man unprepared for the burden placed upon him, used as a sentimental pawn by those in charge."

Grace was nearly blind with fury. "Truly you must be out of your mind to say such things. Morgan McDonagh was the finest man I have ever known in all my life."

"He's the finest man every Irishman has ever known, my dear." Whiskers turned to his companions, chuckling. "And they *all* know him. Every Irishman fresh off the boat has a personal story about himself and 'The Great One.'"

"If Missus Donnelly says she knows the man, then she does."

The voice behind Grace was serious and commanding, and it wiped the smirk right off Whiskers' face.

"Captain Reinders. You misunderstand me, sir. I was not doubting the truth of Missus Donnelly's claim."

"It's no claim—it's fact," Reinders stated. "You owe her an apology."

"Of course." Whiskers frowned, then attempted to arrange his face in a show of contrition. "Please forgive me, Missus Donnelly, for any affront. I certainly have no doubt that McDonagh was indeed of your acquaintance."

"And a great man," she added. "Better than you. Now if you'll excuse me, gentlemen. Captain Reinders. Mister O'Sullivan."

"Give my regards to your brother, Missus Donnelly." O'Sullivan made a small bow away from the others, then lowered his voice. "Well done."

Grace crossed the foyer, shaken, and ducked inside the library. There was a low fire burning in the hearth, and she knelt on the rug in front of it, head down, eyes closed, pushing from her mind the words of that stupid, stupid man. Minutes passed in which she did nothing but listen to the steady tick of the mantel clock, the sigh of crumbling embers. She was startled from her solitude by the sound of pointed throat-clearing, but pulled herself together in that instant, composing her face before turning around.

"I've brought reinforcements." Reinders held up two crystal cups of dark punch. "May I come in?"

He stood in the doorway, smiling awkwardly, and she realized he was wearing evening clothes. He looked different without his cap.

"I'm afraid you've caught me hiding out."

"Don't get up on my account. You look very comfortable sitting there." He handed her a cup.

She took it gratefully and they both drank, Reinders finishing his in one long gulp, then frowning into the empty cup as if it had betrayed him.

"Guess I was thirsty," he commented. "These cups are small, though. Punch cups are always small. Or maybe I was just thirsty." *Oh, God,* he thought, *here I go again.* He smiled weakly, wishing he had his cap.

"I almost didn't know you without it, but I was never so happy to see your face," she said gratefully. "You saved me from myself, and that's the truth of it."

"Nonsense." He put his cup on the mantel. "It's just too bad Florence didn't hear it. You'd be her new hero."

"Oh, Lord." Grace covered her face with her hands. "I believe I was about to punch that man."

"Yes, I believe you were," he said, oddly happy. "He deserved it and I should have let you."

"Ah, no." She waved him off. " 'Twould've been shameful, that—the Livingstons so good to my brother and all."

"So that's how you know Florence."

"Aye. Sean was meant to come tonight, but"—she hesitated—"he couldn't. So Jay brought me on my own."

"Jay Livingston is your escort?"

She understood at once. "I know he's a bit of a ladies' man."

"A bit." Reinders snorted. "I'm surprised your brother would send you out alone with him."

"I'm perfectly capable of taking care of myself now, Captain."

"I know."

They looked at one another for a long moment, until Grace shifted her gaze to the fire.

"What's the news from home?" he asked.

"Not a word." She looked up into his face and he caught a flash of panic, but then it was gone. "I've written many times over, but we hear nothing. Not from anyone, and now the weather's changed or wouldn't I go after them myself?"

"Don't even consider it," he ordered. "All signs point to a long stormy winter, which as you know is much worse at sea."

"Aye." She sighed. "I couldn't put the children through that again."

"How are they? I've been . . . busy," he apologized.

"Mary Kate's grand, and Liam's doing better now he's back with us. He's a fine boy, full of wanting to make his fortune and lead the country someday."

"President, huh?" Reinders tried to hide his disappointment.

"Only after he's been a great American sea captain like his hero, sailing around the world a few times, discovering new places."

Reinders grinned. "Always liked that boy. Knew the minute I met him, he was a born seaman."

"So when do you think you'll be able to come, Captain? He'd be so happy to see you. He's always tearing up and down the wharf, looking for your ship." And then she remembered. "You must see Lily first, though."

"Why Lily?"

"Well, she's worried, isn't she? About her family, and all." Grace saw the guarded look on his face. "She told me what you're doing for her."

He studied her for a long moment. "You understand I can't afford to have this get out?"

"She only told me because she hadn't heard from you and thought maybe I had."

"You?"

"Aye. She thought we were, you know"—Grace felt herself beginning to blush—"keeping company. Or something."

His mouth fell open and he laughed. "Why would she think that?"

"I don't know," she said defensively.

"I don't believe I ever mentioned you."

"She never said you did."

"Then why would she think we were seeing each other?"

"I don't know," Grace repeated, rising to her feet. "Misunderstanding, I suppose. I made the same mistake myself."

He stared at her, baffled. "*You* thought I was seeing you?"

"Don't be daft," she scolded. "I thought you were seeing *her*."

"You did?" He felt foolish now, his face heavy and hot. "Why?"

"I don't know," she said for the third time, exasperated. "We were talking about you, is all. 'Twas a mistake. We had a good laugh about it."

"A good laugh." He had lost complete control of this conversation.

"Well, sure," she exclaimed. "Can you see either one of us stepping out with you, Captain?"

"No." His voice was sharper than he meant it to be, and it stung her, he could see that.

"Well, of course not," she said, and looked away.

The silence was incredibly awkward, and he suddenly felt empty and much too old. "Maybe I'd better go."

"Aye, they'll all be wondering what kept you here so long, and you wouldn't want there to be a misunderstanding now, would you?"

He opened his mouth as if to speak, then closed it again, and left the room.

She sank immediately into the closest chair, furious with him, but angrier with herself. Here he'd come to her defense, then sought her out for conversation, which she'd truly enjoyed until she apparently said the wrong thing and insulted him. But how? She wasn't interested in romance, nor was he. Why had he gotten so angry? Why had she? It made her tired to think about it—she just didn't understand men, she decided. Especially American men. They never really said what they meant. But it wasn't his fault, it was hers, and she wished she could do it all over again.

A voice harrumphed in the doorway, and she looked up relieved, words of apology already on her lips.

"Captain, I'm . . ."

"Ready for dinner, I hope." Jay arched his eyebrow, amused. "I've been looking for you everywhere, Missus Donnelly. How naughty of you to deprive us of your delectable company."

"I'm sorry, Jay." She pressed a cool hand to her hot cheek, then smoothed the front of her gown. "Shall we go in?"

"With pleasure." He offered his arm, and when she took it, he covered her hand with his, pulling her snugly against his side. "We'll be one less at dinner tonight," he confided intimately. "Poor Captain Reinders has gone home ill."

Twenty-eight

JULIA wasn't sure she could stand another month of disastrous trials and cruel sentencing. John was exiled to Bermuda, and William sentenced to hang; that had been the hardest, especially as the prosecution had given him an out—all Smith O'Brien had to do was admit that Duffy's "diabolical temper" had been a mitigating factor in taking such extreme action. But William—good William—had refused, not wanting to prejudice the public mind against a man who still awaited trial. Tom Meagher's had just ended; he'd been tried with MacManus and O'Donohoe, who were given death by hanging, though the consensus was that Meagher would escape by reason of his youth. But—following in Smith O'Brien's footsteps—Tom had refused, telling the court he regretted nothing and retracted nothing, his ambition only to lift Ireland up, to make her a benefactor to humanity instead of the meanest beggar in the world. Meagher said that he understood his ambition was also his crime, but that the history of Ireland justified it and he looked forward to standing before a higher tribunal, before the Judge of infinite goodness, who would most certainly overturn the wrong judgments handed down.

Julia sighed deeply, remembering the passion and eloquence

she had witnessed. She did not go out anymore, had not been out for weeks. Her anger had been spent, all her tears shed, and the ink in her pen had run dry. There was only one thing forced her out of bed in the morning, one thing that held back black despair. She checked on him now, asleep in his little bed in the corner of her room.

He was beautiful to her, though others turned their faces away when she showed him off. His eyes troubled them with their thick, milky stare, the crust that clung to his lashes from the oozing. But to her, he was the dearest thing, and she had come to love him with all her heart, no matter those who said he would not be in the world for long. She refused to believe it and took every day as it came, holding him for hours when he wheezed, painstakingly spooning hot cereals into his mouth, getting him to sip a little milk each hour. He was nearly a year old, young Morgan McDonagh, and he now called Julia "Mam."

"Hallo." Her father poked his head into her room. "How's the boy, then? Napping, still?"

She nodded.

"I'll stay with him." Mister Martin came all the way in. "Why don't you get out for a while? Take a walk along the river, or up to the college?"

"I'm fine, Father, really."

He moved a pile of books and sat cautiously on the end of her desk chair. "It's a beautiful day," he said, to entice her. "Lovely blue sky, the last of the autumn leaves. Lots of new things in the shop windows."

"I don't care about that." She frowned.

"Well, you're so changed, my dear, I wasn't sure." He leaned forward. "Are you all right, Julia?"

"It's not like last year," she told him firmly.

"No?" He looked around the small room with drapes drawn, plates of uneaten food, spilled ink, stacks of dusty books.

"I just don't like going out anymore. Too depressing."

"Ah, yes. Depressing." He nodded. "But you're not depressed being stuck in all the time?"

"Of course not." She looked over at the baby. "I much prefer his company to anyone else's."

"He's a grand boy," Mister Martin agreed. "And you know how well I think of him. But it's not good for the two of you to be so cooped up—babies need fresh air, sunlight, the stimulation of new people, new things to look at."

She eyed him suspiciously. "And just when did you become such an expert on babies?"

"Well, do you think you just sprang from your mother fully formed as you are?" He laughed. "Your mother was a busy woman, and I got to spend a lot of time with you, for which I've always been grateful. She knew when to stay and when to go, and look how well you turned out!"

"Are you saying I'm not a very good mother, then?"

"Of course not!" Mister Martin shook his head, then leaned forward. "But if truth be told, you're not really a mother at all. Have you forgotten that he has one of his very own, because I worry you have."

Julia fidgeted with her pen. "How could I forget a thing like that? But we've not heard a word from her, have we? How do we even know she's alive?"

"We don't," he granted. "But what of Barbara? She loves the boy, and he's her own flesh and blood."

"She's gone to Galway with Abban—you know that. To work in the children's schools." She put the pen down. "He's got a doctor here, and we've enough food. I promised her I'd take good care of him."

"Until she comes back."

"Yes," Julia told him. "Of course."

Mister Martin regarded her with his great kind eyes. "I just don't want you to be disappointed again, my dear. You've borne a lot for being so young. And I know how lonely you are."

She refused to look at him, to let him see the tears in her eyes and, to give her a moment, he stood and went over to the crib.

"So you think the little fellow's with us for a while?"

"Yes." She wiped her eyes before he turned around. "I do."

"Well, then." He gave her a smile. "What do you say we strike a bargain, you and I?"

"A bargain?" She tried to sound wary, but laughed instead. "Have I been set up again?"

He shrugged. "Maybe just a little."

"I suppose it involves fresh air and sunshine."

"There's my clever girl." Mister Martin opened the curtains and a shaft of sunlight cut across the room. "I've not wanted to get your hopes up, but I've been in contact with a very interesting, very progressive young physician in London."

"England?" She shook her head. "I'm not going back there, Father, ever." And then her eyes widened. "You're not having me committed to a sanatorium or something, are you?"

"You have enough commitments, my dear." He laughed, stacking plates and cups on an empty tray. "This is about Morgan, actually. I've been following a trail of sorts and it has led me to Doctor Nigel Wilkes." He paused. "Doctor Wilkes is an eye surgeon."

She sucked in her breath.

"He's agreed to take a look at our boy, but you'd have to be willing to leave the house, you know. Willing to go back to England."

"Oh, Father." Her eyes filled with tears again, but this time she didn't mind. "Thank you. Thank you. I'll start packing." She got up and moved a stack of books. "Right now."

He smiled, relieved to see her back in command. "I can get passage for you the end of this week, but before you go"—his tone grew serious——"you'll need to send word to Barbara, and you must get off a letter to Grace. They have to know what's happening . . . in case . . ."

"I will," she promised. "I'll do it this afternoon."

"After you take himself out for a walk." He picked up the tray.

"Right." She grinned. "After our walk."

"That's my girl." He kissed her cheek and left the room, the crockery rattling all the way down the stairs to Missus Geelan's kitchen.

Julia went over to Morgan's crib and looked down at the boy—her boy, she thought. She must write to Grace—she knew she must. She'd promised Barbara she would, but instead had let day after day slip by until Barbara had been gone for months and still Julia had not written.

Barbara had stayed in Dublin only a few days, afraid of running into Father Sheehan, who was often there on church duty, and who might try to change her mind. They'd charged Sister James with telling Father Sheehan the news of Barbara's abandonment, because the girl planned on going back to her old mother herself if she found the nerve; she would only be on her own for a few days until the presiding priest arrived. And so Barbara exchanged her robes for trousers and a cap, and dressed like a laborer, she and Abban made their way north. They hadn't been in Dublin long when they realized how dangerous it was; the city swarmed with troops, guards on the lookout for treasonous criminals, and Abban noted for his missing leg. Julia, by then so fond of Morgan, had begged to keep him, had pointed out the quality of his care here, the regular food and certain shelter, the doctor's clinic nearby, and after hours of anguish, Barbara had finally agreed. She and Abban decided to go to the west, to volunteer where the suffering was worst, promising to stay in contact and to see the boy when they could.

Julia looked down at him now and he awoke, his little arms flailing as he struggled to roll over and sit up. He cried out, and she picked him up, held his damp, sweet-smelling head against her breast and prayed that God would forgive her this.

Twenty-nine

OUTSIDE the windows of the Harp, snow fell steadily from a black sky, swirling through halos of lamplight, gusting into doorways, blanketing the grimy, littered sidewalks and muddy alleys, piles of muck freezing now into ruts that made the streets dangerous for horse and carriage. The city was strangely silent, muffled by the downpour of thick flakes. Traffic had dwindled to nothing, and the few pedestrians still braving the sidewalks slipped and slid, and clung to one another for balance. It was a beautiful, treacherous night.

Grace pressed her warm forehead against the frosty glass, and prayed for the sound of Dugan's heavy boots pounding up the stairs, midwife right behind. He'd gone out three hours before, when Tara's discomfort had proved to be labor; now Grace realized she might well have to deliver this baby herself. She glanced around the room, hoping it contained everything she would need. Her own births were still fresh in her mind, and it was the memory of these she relied upon to guide her; she could hear the voices of both Brigid Sullivan and Barbara telling her what to do, could see in her mind's eye the steaming kettle of water, the basin for cleaning the baby, the pile of fresh linens, the newspapers and extra sheets for underneath. She knew enough to put on a clean apron, roll up her sleeves, and wash her hands, and she knew about the pushing . . . just not when. Formal prayer had been abandoned an hour ago with Tara's first real groan, and now she just left the way open for steady communication, trusting Him to guide her in His own way.

Tara was such a small woman, her thin body easily overwhelmed by pregnancy, and she'd lost a great deal of strength from the long months in bed. Although Grace was, by now, very anxious, Tara was terrified and so Grace tried to remain outwardly calm and steadfast, as if she knew exactly what lay ahead.

"Ah, no." Tara panted from the bed. "No, no, no. Sure and I'm too old for this! I'll never make it!"

"Stop that!" Grace ordered. Best to be firm—she remembered that much. A laboring woman needed every drop of strength; pity did her no good. She strode purposefully to the bed, picked up Tara's hand, and patted it briskly. "You'll birth this baby, and do a jig the same day. Aren't you the very picture of health?"

Tara's eyes searched Grace's for some reassurance that this might be even remotely true, a weakly hopeful smile replacing her look of fear. But then the smile contorted and her eyes pinched shut as she began the climb up yet another hill of mounting pain, her forehead oily with sweat. She clenched Grace's hand in both of hers, back arching.

"Hold on to me, now." Grace's own body ached in response to Tara's agony. "Hold on!"

The pains were so close together that Tara had only a minute or two between each and she was exhausted, labor wearing heavily on her now. She lay still, her breathing shallow.

"Take the baby, Grace. There's no one else. And Dugan . . . Dugan . . ." Tears streamed down her cheeks into the sweat-stained pillow.

"Open your eyes!" Grace demanded. "Haven't I got family enough to keep track of, scattered as they are?" She forced anger into her voice. "You *will* bring this child into the world, Tara Ogue, and you *will* live to raise it because I won't do it for you. Now get ready."

This time, Grace had Tara bend her knees, sliding her heels up toward her hips. The desperate woman screamed.

"I see something!" Grace shouted, her hands firmly around Tara's ankles, keeping them in position. "It's the head, Tara! The baby's head!"

Tara thrashed and groaned, then gripped the iron bars of her bedstead, her face purple with exertion.

"That's right!" Grace cried. "Push, then! Push!"

To her utter amazement, the baby's head emerged, followed by its tiny shoulders—a seemingly impossible feat—and then the door burst open and the midwife rushed in.

"It's come!" Grace called over her shoulder. "Hurry!"

The midwife glanced toward the bed, then went to the basin to scrub her hands. "No need to hurry now. Hard part's over. Go on," she urged softly, drying her hands on a clean cloth. "Pick him up."

Grace stared in wonder at the little thing, now screaming and writhing on the bed, still connected to the womb. She picked him up carefully and the midwife severed the cord.

"Put a blanket round him and hand him to his mother," the midwife directed. "We'll let him have a feed, while I look at your handiwork here. Another push now, missus." She patted Tara's leg, and Grace watched, fascinated, as the afterbirth was delivered. "Nice work all round, girls," she commended. "You brought a strong, lusty boy into the world tonight."

Still stunned by the miracle of it all, Grace wrapped the baby in a clean, soft blanket, and carried him around the bed to Tara, who lifted up her arms, wordlessly. She took her son and peered with wonder into his tiny face, overcome with emotion. As his mewling grew louder and more insistent, she turned anxious eyes to her friend.

"He's only hungry after all that. You can take care of him well enough." Grace untied the top of Tara's shift and helped her settle the child to breast. He stopped crying immediately, shuddering now and then, as his mother cradled him with an aching tenderness, unable to take her eyes off the beautiful face of her very own baby. And then he fell promptly asleep, worn out from the journey.

The midwife took charge of the groggy baby, cleaning him up with practiced efficiency; he was inspected, washed, diapered, and bundled securely back into gown and blanket without ever fully waking. Grace turned her attention to the childbed, rolled Tara gently from one side to the other to remove the soiled linen and newspaper, then remade it with fresh, tucking in the blankets and plumping up the pillow.

When mother and child were resting quietly together, the midwife washed her hands, rolled down her sleeves and announced that she would be in the kitchen, partaking of the glass of ale and smoked ham Mister Ogue had assured her would be waiting. She thought two glasses might even be in order as all had gone so well, and wouldn't she be spending the night after all, no way to get home so late in this weather? Grace thanked her profusely and urged her to go down; she would finish settling the room.

Tara appeared to have fallen asleep, her arm at an odd angle around the baby; Grace gently lifted the warm bundle and was placing him in the wooden cradle when Dugan peeked around the door.

"Well, I wondered when you were coming to meet your new son," Grace teased.

"Aye," he whispered sheepishly, stepping into the room. "The midwife said 'twas a boy. A fine-looking boy. And Tara . . ." He looked at his shockingly pale wife, her eyes closed, mouth slightly open.

"She's fine," Grace reassured. "Resting now, is all. He was a lot of work, your one, though he came fast in the end. Say hallo to him, then, why don't you?"

The big man tiptoed across the room and bent awkwardly over the cradle; the baby's eyes opened at that very moment, and father and son regarded one another in amazement. He touched the bundle with a single finger.

"She did this for me."

"I did it for the both of us." Tara's voice was hoarse. "But I don't know that I'll be doing it again, if it's all the same to you."

He came and sat down gingerly on the edge of the bed, taking up her hand and smiling tenderly into her exhausted, contented face.

"One is miracle enough for me," he told her. "What will you call him, then?"

"Well, I'm partial to Dugan, as you know."

"Ah, now, one of those in the world is more than enough, don't you think?" He laughed, and then his face fell serious. "What I was thinking, down there by the fire . . . I mean, if it's all right by you . . ." He glanced at his wife. "What I thought is . . . I thought we might call him Caolon. You know. After your one."

Tara stared in disbelief, then covered her face with her hands. Dugan looked up at Grace in alarm, then moved closer to his wife and took her up in his arms.

"Ah, Tara, forgive me," he murmured. "You married a right eejit, you did. I'm sorry, girl—sorry for bringing it up. On this of all days."

She pulled back and wiped her tears, regarding him with no less wonder than she'd regarded the first sight of her son.

"You're the best man I've ever known, Dugan Ogue." Her mouth trembled. "What other would choose such a name for his own firstborn son, I'd like to know?"

"And why not?" he replied. "Wasn't he your husband and didn't he take fine care of you while he could? I'm grateful to him for that. 'Tis a shame he died and you suffering all those years. I thought maybe calling the boy after him . . . maybe 'twould make up for the loss in some way."

Tara put her hands on either side of that big, dear face. "You." She searched his eyes. "You made up for that the day you said you loved me. You, Dugan," she repeated. "The baby, he . . ." She had to stop, tears thick in her throat. "He's extra— a wonderful thing on top of it all. But you . . ." She broke off again, shaking her head.

He kissed her then, as tenderly as a man ever kissed the woman he loved, and held her against his mighty chest. "So it's settled," he stated. "We'll call him Caolon. Caolon Ogue."

"*Mighty* Caolon Ogue," she corrected, and they laughed,

holding on to one another so tightly that they didn't hear Grace's quiet leaving.

She slipped unnoticed from the warm room into the chilly hall. It was dark, but she had no trouble navigating the stairs that led down into the Harp, empty now, but smelling as it always did of ale and tobacco. The stairs directly across from those she'd just descended led up to her own rooms and she climbed them, opening the door at the top, grateful for the lamp Sean had left burning low. She sat down near the window, too awake yet to sleep, wanting a quiet moment by herself. From the cots came the soft, openmouthed breathing sounds of the children, the rustle of their shifting about; from the back, Sean's low snores and occasional mumblings, his dream life as vivid as the life he led by day.

Outside, the snow still fell and she was heartened somehow by the sight of it drifting along the windowsills. Quiet, it was . . . so quiet, and she felt warm and safe, wrapped up and hidden away from the cold, from hunger, from sadness. The baby had lived, and Tara had lived. There was hope in that, and Grace took hold of it. This baby lived, and her own still lived, and she would hold him again—no matter that he was one year old now and crawling, no doubt. She smiled, imagining her father down on the floor, creeping after the child, who was sure to be the world to him. What did he look like, this boy, their boy? What did he look like now?

She caught her reflection in the frosty glass, and lifted a hand to touch it. Lamplight glanced off her wedding band, and she touched that instead, turning it on her finger. "Ah, Morgan," she whispered, but that was all she said aloud, returning silently to the memory of his handsome face, the laughter in his voice, the way her heart leapt when he put his arms around her and whispered against her hair that he loved her, loved her. And then she closed the door on those memories—gently, but firmly—knowing that any more than this would be too much, grateful for the moments she could have that did not kill her. She brought her hand to her lips and tenderly kissed the ring he'd placed there the last night she'd seen him, and then she let it go. Tired now, she slipped off her shoes, turned down the lamp, and went quietly to bed.

What Boardham liked most next to drinking, whoring, gambling and dogfights—he realized, standing across the street from the Harp—was watching Missus Donnelly. He had even come to feel a certain affection for her and, just as a farmer takes pride in the pig he's fattening for winter, he kept track of the little changes in her appearance—her hair, a new skirt, the weight she'd put on.

It was very late and all the customers had long since gone home, but lights still burned inside the saloon and it appeared that someone had borne a baby on this cold night. Not Missus Donnelly, though; he would have noticed that change in her appearance with some interest. No, Missus Donnelly was up and around, quite busy tonight, anxiously peering out first one window and then another, looking out for that giant clod of an Irishman, who finally came slip-sliding down the walk with an old midwife in tow. Must be *his* wife bringing a new Irish brat into the world, just in time for Christmas; probably had a manger all ready for him, the wife robed and serene like the Virgin Mary herself, ignorant Papists.

Boardham laughed meanly—the rum tonight was still warming his belly. He took out a cigar butt and placed it between his lips, looking up at the window. And there she was, touching the glass, her hair falling down. She looked tired, he thought. Time for bed. He wouldn't mind helping her get ready for that, but he was a patient man. He struck a match and cupped one hand around the other as he lit the cigar, releasing puffs of smoke, the end glowing red in the dark.

It was Reinders he really wanted, though—Boardham shook out the match—Missus Donnelly was just the bait. He knew they still saw one another, had witnessed their little discourse on the wharf, Reinders standing out in front of God and everyone, talking to Irish and black—man had no sense of decent society. Thought too highly of himself, he did—Boardham narrowed his eyes—but all that was about to change. Paybacks for the long walk from Boston, every breath agony around a chest full of broken ribs.

Boardham's dreams of revenge were the sweetest things in his life, and he took them out often to compare their merits, consider their possibilities, admire their brilliance. And of course, anything was truly possible as the law was on his side—or in his pocket, rather. He was extremely loyal to Callahan, had carried out every job to its desired end—blackmail, extortion, beatings, thievery—with no questions asked, only helping himself to the spoils now and then, after Callahan was taken care of, when no one would know any different. And because of this, Boardham was a big man now; a big man in all the low places. Everyone was his friend, falling all over themselves to buy him the next drink, to take him into their confidence, even ratting on their own to earn his favor, to stay on the right side of Mister Boardham from Liverpool. Nightly, he picked over the gleanings of the underworld, offering up to Callahan those most ripe and worthy of plucking, and now Callahan owed him, it was true. Boardham could do whatever he liked in regard to Captain Reinders, and no one would look into it very far, any more than they had looked into the death of Tom Dean.

Yes, Boardham could do as he liked in this ward, but he couldn't do it if the captain was gone. Again. Another run down the coast, and that both frustrated and interested him. He could wait; he had the bait. Upstairs, the lights went out and the windows were black.

"Sweet dreams, Missus Donnelly," he growled, grinding out the last of his black cigar in the clean white snow.

Thirty

REINDERS awoke in a sweat and, for a moment, could not remember where he was. Charleston. He was in Charleston. Again. Though he'd been dreaming of Georgia—Georgia in the summertime with the sun so hot in that field, he'd felt sure the heat would kill him. Why it didn't kill the others, he'd never understand; they worked in those fields from dawn to dusk, pulled into the shade of bushes when they fell over, only to rise again and continue working as soon as they'd come to. They didn't dare complain to the overseer; Reinders had seen the answer to that: the woman, heavy with child, stripped down and lashed in front of her other children; the young man with shackled feet and an iron collar, the flesh worn away where it rubbed day and night; the branding marks; the missing limbs or eyes; the crippling, the maiming. And those were only the physical scars.

When he'd first come to Charleston, he'd been impressed to see free blacks going about their business, the independence of bondsmen hired out to work the factories or fields, slaves coming and going; everyone appeared to move around pretty freely—they wore decent clothing, dressed well, in fact; they had money in their pockets to buy food and goods, operated small businesses, had their own church. They had to negotiate a complex social system, true enough, but everyone seemed to understand the rules and to comply willingly. It wasn't such a bad life for them here when all was said and done—he'd seen far worse in the New York tenements, where starving blacks lived in filth and disease—at least here they were fed, clothed, and sheltered. Clearly slavery, he told himself, was not the evil Northerners made it out to be. But going to Georgia had changed all that forever.

Reinders got out of his bunk and dressed resolutely, knowing he'd sleep no more tonight. He lit his lamp and set it on the desk, unlocking the drawer and withdrawing a locked metal box; from that, he withdrew a sheath of papers, which included runaway notices and auction flyers. He smoothed the flyer, thinking of the tobacco broker he'd come to know and respect, one who secretly despised the family business and insisted Reinders not be blind to its true nature. Most of the buying and selling was done privately, the broker had explained, sometimes initiated by the slaves themselves in order to work for different masters. This was the preferred method, out of the public eye, but auctions did exist and were used to move quantities of stock. He took Reinders to one of these, and it had been a shock—despite Florence's attempt at educating him—to learn that families were divided. He'd watched a man, his wife, and five of their children sold away to different owners even though their master had requested they go in one lot, even though the man and woman begged to be kept together; he saw sisters separated, young children sold away alone, old men offered for twenty dollars and the promise of a few more years' good work still in them. Reinders was never the same after that afternoon, the flame of outrage burning steadily within him.

He supposed this was why Lily's request had felt like a chance to redeem something beyond her children, though that was reason enough to agree. He'd told Lars immediately—they were partners, after all—and the man had given his blessing with one caveat: Don't lose the ship. Lars had other ventures, other means of income, but he'd still tied a lot of his capital into this business, built on the tobacco trade, and Reinders did not want to jeopardize that. Neither one had ever considered too deeply the labor force used by the men with whom they traded—or *chosen* to consider, he amended, Florence's voice ringing in his ears. It had been she who put them in contact with a scout, a Southerner who tracked family members of former slaves under the guise of bounty-hunting. Florence had many contacts like this, and had also arranged free papers for Lily and her children, with three more sets standing by.

"Excuse me, Captain." Mackley opened the door, breaking Reinders' reverie. "I saw your light. Need anything, sir?"

"I wouldn't know where to begin," Reinders answered dryly.

"You should try to sleep, sir. Got a long day ahead of us."

"Why are you up? Isn't the new man on watch?"

"Nickerson. Yes, sir, he is."

"Nickerson," Reinders repeated, and then he sighed. "I wish Dean were here. I can't believe he's dead."

The muscle in Mackley's jaw flinched. "Should've killed that bastard when we had the chance."

Reinders would never forgive himself for that.

"We'll get him," the captain promised. "One day soon he'll stick his ugly head out, and then we'll cut it off and send it to Dean's wife."

"I'm all for cutting it off, Captain, but I'd rather feed it to the fish than send it to Laura." Mackley stepped in farther. "Are you sure you're all right, sir?"

Reinders stood up, his hand over his gut. "A little nervous, I guess. Worried that they just took off with the money like last time. Or that the boy ran again. We've missed him twice now, you know."

"Only by a couple of days, sir."

"Missed is missed. Next time they'll kill him." He massaged the tender spot. "And I don't know where the hell January is."

"But didn't the scout say he'd been sold down Mississippi, Captain? And that he knew we were coming for him?"

"Must've been more than he could stand." Reinders held out the notice. "He ran again."

" 'Wanted,' " Mackley read. " 'January. A runaway slave owned by Charles Beaustead. About forty, gray in the hair. Tall, strong, raw-boned man, very black, marked by the lash and a brand on his right cheek. Missing his left arm . . .'" Mackley's voice faltered. "I didn't know he was missing an arm."

"He wasn't," Reinders said grimly.

"Those bastards. 'Last seen wearing an iron collar. May be headed for Westerfield Plantation, Georgia.'" Mackley looked up. "They're offering a two-hundred-dollar reward."

"It's not good news. Any of it." Reinders glanced at the clock on his desk. "They should've picked up the boy by now. If everything went according to plan. Couple more hours, then we'll know."

"What about his sister, Captain?"

"The message was delivered last night." He paused. "Now it's up to her."

Mackley glanced out the window. No sign yet of dawn. The captain would pace his cabin the entire time. He needed to get off the ship, out into the cool night air, clear his head, calm himself.

"Excuse me, sir. What if we left now for the warehouse? Walk'd do us both some good, and it's still plenty dark."

Reinders nodded, pleased with the idea. "Mister Mackley," he said, grabbing his cap, "you do earn your pay."

Thirty-one

IT was a year since Grace had last seen her son, and as Christmas approached, she harbored a desperate hope that Patrick and Morgan would arrive any day now—surely, God owed her this much. She did not allow herself to think of the hardship they'd endure sailing this time of year; she and Mary Kate had survived the voyage and so would they. She spoke of this hope to no one, and so it grew unchecked until she'd begun to believe that their arrival was imminent.

Secretly, she stored extra food and tobacco for her da, determined where he would sleep, stuffed a pillow for his head; she sewed a shirt and trousers for her son, who would be walking now, bought him a small bowl and a cup, and bartered for a set of wooden blocks, which she hid in the corner beneath her bed. At times throughout the day, joy would rise like a bubble and catch in her throat, the giddiness nearly lifting her off her feet.

"Aye, you're full of secrets, aren't you?" Sean caught her as she came in from the market, cheeks red, boots soaked through with slushy snow. "You can't hide it from me."

"Only getting ready for Christmas, is all." She busied herself with the things in her basket.

" 'Tis but a part of the truth you're telling me now." He sized her up playfully. "But I'll let you off easy, providing there's a grand present for me on Christmas morn."

She laughed. She did have his present, the fourth book in the *Leatherstocking Tales* by Mister Cooper; Sean was enthralled by these stories of the frontier and now he'd have *The Pathfinder* to complete his set.

"What will we do at Christmastime?" She hung her heavy cloak near the fire to dry. "Will we go to services? Dugan's invited us to Mass at St. Patrick's, or we could go round to Grace Church if you like."

A look of annoyance flashed across Sean's face. "That's all just empty worship to me now—you know that."

"Will you go with Miss Osgoode, then?" She tried to keep her own annoyance from showing.

"You could come, as well," he offered. "I wish you would, Grace. We could bring the children. You'd enjoy it."

Grace struggled with her reluctance. "How many Irish in that lot?"

Sean eyed her, disappointed. "You know the answer to that— not many. But it doesn't matter. We're all Americans there, all of us Saints."

"Well, I like being just Irish myself." She came away from the fire and sat down opposite him. "And I miss being with our Irish friends. We hardly see them anymore."

"What in the world are you talking about? Aren't you surrounded by Irish every night in this place?"

"You know what I mean. What's happened to your friends from the papers, Mister O'Sullivan and them? Where are the boys from the Irish Society? No one calls for you but Danny Young." She lifted her chin defiantly. "Are you quits with the Irish, then—are we not good enough for you anymore?"

Sean banged his fist on the table, and Grace had a sudden vision of her father doing the very same thing the night he announced her betrothal to Bram Donnelly—Patrick had said he was Irish, by God, that was his religion and Sean would make it his, as well, if he had any sense a'tall.

"Have you lost your mind?" He sounded just like their father. "There's no being quits with the Irish! I'm reminded just how Irish I am every single day when I see yet another drawing of some monkey-faced ragpicker with a bottle in one hand and a potato in the other— 'Irish in America,' it says, 'happy as the pigs they sleep with.' Or of the serving girls—all called Brigid or Colleen, mind you, as if we've no other names for our women—asking the madam a question any child would know."

He shook his head in disgust. "But they bring it on themselves, you know. Playing the happy-go-lucky Paddy. I'm sick to death of the Irish buying off as ignorant and stupid, letting the rest of us pay for it," he said angrily. "When I walk into the shops, they look first at my face and then at my leg, and they point out the sign that says, 'No Irish Need Apply.' 'I don't need the work,' I say to them. 'I'm buying.' 'Buy it next door,' they tell me. 'We don't trade with Irish.' "

Grace sat back, stunned. She was well aware of the city's harshness toward the Irish, but had thought Sean oblivious to all that, had assumed he walked in a world of ideals far above the bitter ignorance of the street.

"Are you ashamed, then?" she asked quietly.

"No. I'm not ashamed. I'm angry," he declared. "And I'm tired of it. Tired of the Irish rolling over instead of standing up. Tired of watching them get beaten down at every turn, demanding respect but never fighting back—or fighting back too late with too few. Fighting losing battles. Always losing. It's as if we were born to be the mats other men wipe their feet on." He slapped his hand on the table. "All the work we've done. All the lives sacrificed—for what? When the raid failed and they all got arrested, one after the other like that . . ." He stopped, defeated.

"But they're starving, Sean." Grace leaned forward. "They can barely march across a field, let alone fight a battle. That's the truth of it, and maybe we should've waited."

"Waited for what?" he asked bitterly. "For the end of hunger? We've always had hunger in Ireland, and we always will. Wait for the fevers to end, for men to get strong, for weapons and food? Bah. We send money and arms, it's confis-

cated at port. We send food, it disappears before a mouthful
reaches those who need it."

"Are you saying we should give up after all we've survived?"
Grace argued. "Think about it—Elizabeth I, Cromwell, constant invasion and subjection to fevers, famines, terrible
poverty. We've not done this to ourselves, you know. 'Twas cen-
turies in the making!"

"We *have* done it to ourselves!" he snapped. "We let them
plunder our land, cut down our forests, make paupers of our
kings, slander our religion—all the while tipping our hats and
offering them a drink of our best *batha usaige*. The Irish are ignorant and bull-headed, Grace, and that's the sorry truth of it.
Even crossing an ocean, we can't escape it."

Grace stared at him, outraged. Bull-headed? Maybe. But ignorant? "I don't believe it," she scolded. "You've got your head
so wrapped up in this new religion of yours, you've lost sight of
who you really are—who *we* are! Don't shake your head at me,"
she warned. "You're just feeling sorry for yourself. Irish need
not apply? When did you ever have to apply for any job here,
a'tall?" She didn't wait for an answer. "Never! You were handed
a job right off the boat, at a newspaper for pity's sake—and
why? Because you're Irish! Because you're intelligent! And are
there no other intelligent Irish working there? Working anywhere, for that matter? Are you the only Irishman worth his salt
in the entire world?" She pushed back her chair and got up. "I'll
tell you what, brother. As far as I'm concerned there's only one
ignorant, bull-headed Irishman in this city and I'm looking at
him. I never felt ashamed of any Irish ever in my life, but I am
now. One day Ireland will be free, and you'll regret those
words."

"Ireland will never be free. She's no fight left in her, and all
the decent men are dead or gone." He looked up at her. "And
even if she were free, I wouldn't go back. Not ever. I was no one
in Ireland. A cripple earning his keep doing piecework by the
fire, and no chance of anything better. I can make something of
myself here, despite . . ." He stopped himself. "I'm an American, Grace. That's what I've become."

272   Ann Moore

"Aye." She crossed her arms over her chest. "And that's all you are." Did she know him at all anymore? she wondered.

He closed his eyes, and she saw the weariness in the sag of his cheeks, the heaviness of his mouth. "I'm sorry." He looked at her then. "I don't want to argue with you. I shouldn't have said all that."

She frowned, wanting to forgive him but not quite able to.

"Truth is," he began, then hesitated, steeling himself. "If you want to know the truth, the men who employ me have begun to question the value of their commitment to Irish revolution. Abolition is occupying their thoughts, these days—never mind there's half as many slaves in the South as in Ireland." He sighed. "I didn't want to tell you, to burden you with it, but there just isn't much work for me lately."

Grace's arms fell to her sides and she sat down again.

He kept his eyes focused on his fingers, splayed on the table. "So I've recently been made very aware of just how many windows display the sign 'No Irish,' and I began to realize that in the normal way of things, my face and my speech stand in the way of making a living."

She put her own hand on the table, fingertips touching his.

"But I'm serious about not going back to Ireland. As hard as it might be here, at least I have a chance." He looked at her. "I've come to believe that God has answered my very desperate prayers lately, by cutting me off from the past and forcing me to consider why I'm really here." He paused, thinking. "You ask why our friends don't come round anymore. Well, it's because they're still clinging to the past—to being Irish, to saving Ireland—when they should be building a future here in America, a future dedicated to serving God in a new way. They shun me now because I'm part of something they can't understand, and I accept that. But I don't want it to happen to us, Grace."

She pushed her fingers into his, entwining them.

"I don't pretend to understand God's will," he continued. "But clearly He's brought me to America for a reason, and now He's led me into this. I think it's what He wants for you, as well."

She searched his face, his wounded eyes, and oh, how she

loved him—her impassioned, fanatical brother. She thought of the hope carried in her heart; could it be that God had not answered her prayer because she had not prepared herself, had not listened to her brother? She closed her eyes and saw the grizzled, lined face of her father, the smooth face of her baby son. She'd followed Sean in so many things for all her life, had always given him the lead because he walked so closely with their Lord; and he'd never steered her wrong.

"All right, Sean." She opened her eyes. "I'll come with you."

It was more like a prayer meeting, Grace thought, with Mister Osgoode clearly in charge. In an hour, it had not so much ended as disassembled into a general discussion about attacks made on the Illinois colony. Sean had told Grace about Nauvoo, the mission city and model town, governed by Saints, its laws dictated by the teachings of Smith and his determined successor, Brigham Young. There had been trouble, however, and the town was under siege by outsiders, who felt threatened, jealous of Nauvoo's prosperity. Some had remained in the original settlement, and Young had taken another group out West to build an even greater community in the forsaken wilderness of Utah.

This was the topic of greatest excitement tonight; worshipers spoke of selling off their worldly goods, turning the money over to the church, and joining the sanctioned wagon train in the spring. It sounded to Grace as though many had relatives or friends already there, and she listened as parts of letters were read aloud, interested in descriptions of the wilderness, how much building had been done in readiness for winter, what the farming was like, and which supplies were most wanted from the East. She glanced over at Sean, who was engrossed in conversation with Danny Young; when at last he did look up, it was to smile warmly at Marcy Osgoode, who sat next to Grace.

And then they all rose to their feet and pushed back their chairs, men drifting to one side of the room, women gathering at the other. Marcy linked arms with Grace and led her to a group of women her own age, though a couple of matrons were also present—smiling indulgently as they straightened wayward collars or tucked up bits of stray hair, tidying the girls discreetly while keeping an eye on the young men.

"Ladies," Marcy announced in her calm, steady voice. "This is Missus Donnelly, widowed sister of our own Mister O'Malley."

The others regarded her now with keener interest, and she was offered refreshment, which she took gratefully, glad to have something to occupy her hands.

"So young to be a widow," Missus Bishop pronounced, speaking first. "And your brother says you have children."

Grace was never sure how to explain her family—did she mention Morgan back in Ireland? Or Liam, who wasn't really hers? "I do," she replied weakly.

"Very hard to bring them all this way alone." Missus Bishop's voice was full of grave concern. "So kind of your brother to take you all in."

"He's such a good man," Marcy declared, then blushed. "He's been so happy since you arrived. And hoping so much that you'd join us."

"We've been praying about it," volunteered a young woman who then covered her mouth with her hand, shy in front of a stranger.

"Yes, and for your children, too," Missus Bishop added.

All the women nodded in agreement.

"Children are the future of eternity." The young woman removed her hand long enough to reveal a rapturous smile.

"Do you have children of your own, then?" Grace inquired politely.

"Not yet. But I hope to have many. As many as God gives me," she added quickly. "I'm to be married next month. To him." She pointed out the fellow standing next to Sean.

"Danny? You're going to marry Danny Young?"

"Oh, yes!" the girl sang, then blushed bright red, her hands flying again to her face.

The other women laughed affectionately and touched her arm; she was a favorite and not a little prayer had gone into the Lord's granting her a husband.

"Ellen and Danny are just recently engaged," Marcy told Grace. "We're all so very happy for them."

Ellen's eyes sparkled with joy. "It happened so fast, but if we marry now, we can travel with my brothers and their wives on the wagon train this spring, rather than waiting to come out later."

Grace bit her lip. Danny moving to Utah was not good news, not considering how much influence he had over her brother.

"How many are going, if you don't mind my asking?"

"Almost all," Missus Bishop announced proudly. "My husband and our eldest son were part of the group that went out with Brigham Young. And now the rest of our family shall join them at last. A few of our number will stay behind—not everyone has raised the funds yet, you see."

Grace breathed an inward sigh of relief. If it took money to travel with this group, then Sean would not go. Not yet, anyway.

"And of course, there is important work to do that calls for some to remain," Missus Bishop continued. "But eventually, we'll all be together in the new community, where God's work can begin in earnest. This city is a hard place for Christian women, don't you find, Missus Donnelly?"

Grace considered that. "When I left Ireland, people were starving alongside the roads or dying in the workhouses. I'd have to say, Missus Bishop, that I find it a blessing to be in a place where I can work and buy food, clothe and shelter my children. City life is hard, true enough, but I believe that has more to do with being poor than being Christian."

"Oh, my." The matron's face froze in a mask of studied politeness. "I see you have the gift of forthrightness that is also your brother's."

"Ah, no." Grace chose to misunderstand. "Sean's the brilliant one. The head of our family."

"And you are the hands, I suppose." Missus Bishop's tone was subtle. "Doing all the labor?"

"No," Grace said carefully. "We share the labor. Maybe I'm the heart," she added, thinking of the children.

"Oh, that's beautiful," Marcy exclaimed. "Women truly are

the hearts of their homes, aren't they? That's very insightful, Grace. Isn't it, ladies?"

The women all nodded their heads, smiling at Grace with warmth and encouragement; Grace said nothing, only smiled in return, sensing she'd passed some sort of test but having no idea what it meant. It felt like hours before Sean came with her cloak, saying they'd better start back or the sidewalks would only get more icy.

He was in good spirits all the way home, chatting about what a fine man Mister Osgoode was, how powerful the leadership that had inspired the entire community to relocate to the Utah Territory. Always the romantic, he was taken with the idea of people banding together to make a new life in the wilderness; Grace recognized this and her anxiety grew.

"I met the girl Danny Young's got himself engaged to," she said, interrupting Sean's flow of ringing praise.

"Ellen LeVang," he confirmed. "Nice girl. Good family, and lots of hardworking brothers. They really like Danny."

"She says they'll join the wagon train."

"Aye, he's a man for the future, Danny is, and it'll be a comfort for him having a good wife and all. He's got no one here, you know, and he'd grown tired of struggling in the city." They walked on, mindful of the ice. "I'll miss him, though."

"You're not thinking of going, then?" Grace held her breath.

Sean stopped in his tracks and looked at her. "Of course not! Why would I be going all the way out to Utah of all places?"

"You said yourself you've found a life in the Saints and I know you, Sean O'Malley—going west with them has all the ring of adventure. And weren't you always a fool for that kind of thing?"

"Not a fool." He paused. "I admit, though, there's a part of me wants to go, wants to be part of it."

Her heart fell.

He linked his arm through hers and they walked again. "But we're not going anywhere till Da and young Morgan come, and that's all there is to it."

She nodded, not trusting herself to speak.

"Besides," he went on. "Mister Osgoode is staying to oversee the conversion of goods to cash, and he's asked me to work for him. 'Tis paid work, and plenty of it."

"Is Marcy staying, then?"

"Of course! Are you daft? She wouldn't go without her father. And he's got work for her to do, as well."

"I see." She grinned.

"Ah, you see nothing." He squeezed her arm and laughed. "I like Marcy—you know I do. But we have a lot to learn about one another before we ever talk of marrying."

"Sure and you'll be learning all kinds of things, working so close with her father and all," Grace teased.

He laughed again, and Grace was glad to see him so light-hearted.

"Thanks for coming out tonight. I wanted you to hear for yourself, and I want you to know Marcy. I care what you think, Grace. You're my sister."

"I think you're getting a little soft in the head, Sean O'Malley, but I *am* your sister and you're my brother, and haven't we always looked out for each other?"

"We have." He kissed her red cheek and she slipped her hand into his big coat pocket, drawing near to him.

They made their way across a town barely familiar beneath the blanket of white, beneath a clear, dark sky lit up with a million stars. Horse bells jingled as the great beasts snorted and tossed their heads, their hooves muffled as they trotted down the street; couples out for an evening stroll stood before festive window displays, pointing out wonders, laughing softly behind gloved hands; candlelight from inside churches spilled out onto the sidewalks as parishioners came and went with their baskets for the needy; and Sean and Grace passed them all as they headed for the lights of home and the people who would be waiting up.

Thirty-two

"MAMMIE, 'tis Christmas!"

Insistent hands shook Grace, and Mary Kate's breath was warm against her cheek.

"Get up, get up!"

"What do you mean, get up?" Grace pulled her daughter into bed and tickled her. "You naughty girl, waking your poor old mam on the wrong day! Christmas is tomorrow and you know it!"

Mary Kate stopped laughing and sat up, her lower lip beginning to tremble.

"Ah, now." Grace hugged her quickly. "What a terrible trick to play and I'm sure to get coal in my stocking for it!"

" 'Tis then?" Mary Kate asked tremulously.

"Aye, Merry Christmas, love." Grace kissed her. "Do you think St. Nicholas found us, all the way over here?"

Mary Kate nodded, eyes wide, and Grace slid out of bed, pulling on her cold underwear beneath the warm tent of her nightgown, abandoning that for the green woolen dress she'd made especially for today. Today. She held her breath and prayed quickly—please let them come.

"Ready?" She held out a hand, then noticed her daughter

was crookedly buttoned up, her hair ribbon askew. "And who dressed you this morning, might I ask? Was it yourself did such a fine job?"

Mary Kate shook her head. "Liam. But he was cross and said, 'Hold still, hold still.' "

Grace laughed and quickly redid the buttons, smoothing Mary Kate's new collar and tucking her hair—longer now and curling at the ends—behind her ears. "Well, and where is he then, your manservant?"

"Down. I'm to bring you."

"How on earth did you all get up and me not hearing a thing?" She put her hands on her hips.

"Uncle Sean set us to dress by the fire." Mary Kate lowered her voice and glowered in imitation of him. " 'Shush now, you hooligans, shush!' " She paused. "What's a hooligan?"

"Sure and I don't know, myself." Grace laughed. "Wait!" She went to her trunk and took out a small box, offering it to Mary Kate. "Would you like to wear the pretty ring Aislinn gave to you? 'Tis Christmas, after all. A special day."

Mary Kate's eyes went wide. "Oh, aye," she breathed, opening the box and taking out the band with the Connemara stone. She put it on carefully and showed it to her mother.

"It's almost as lovely as you are, wee girl," Grace said. *Blessed Christmas, Aislinn,* she prayed. *We're thinking of you over here.*

"You have to come now, Mam." Mary Kate giggled and pulled Grace by the hand, leading her out the door and down the stairs.

When they emerged below, there was a great burst of "Merry Christmas!" and Grace saw the long table near the fire was set with a lovely breakfast and herself given place of honor.

"Since you'll be spending the rest of the day cooking and waiting on all of us here, we thought we'd treat you to breakfast," Sean announced, looking very pleased with himself. "Tea?" He held up the pot.

"Thank you." She sat down, eyes shining. "How grand. Merry Christmas to all of you—Merry Christmas, Tara . . . Dugan. And happy first Christmas to you there, wee Caolon."

The Ogues beamed, and Liam kissed her cheek, then shyly handed her a clunky, carefully wrapped package.

"Are we passing round our presents, then?" she asked, and everyone shrugged good-naturedly.

"Well, now, that's a special gift," Dugan revealed in his growly voice. "Why don't you open it? He worked plenty hard on it, didn't you, boy?"

Liam nodded, his smile tight with anxiety. Grace patted his cheek, then untied the string and gently pulled away the butcher's paper.

It was a small wooden box with a fitted lid, sanded and oiled so that the grain glowed. In the center of the lid was carved the rough outline of a masted ship sailing on uneven waves, and on the front of the box were painstakingly carved letters that spelled out MOTHER.

"Sean and Dugan thought it would be all right, seeing as how you've cared for me all this time." Liam held himself stiffly. "Is it, then?"

Grace set the box carefully on the table as though it were the finest thing in the world, then stood and put her arms around him, holding him until she felt his arms go round her waist.

"Aye." She smiled down into his dear face, then covered it with kisses until he grew embarrassed and tried to squirm away. "No, no, son," she scolded lightly. " 'Tis a mother's right to kiss her boy whenever she pleases. Do you wish to change your mind, then?"

He stopped wriggling and shook his head, then raised his chin stoically and presented himself to her.

"That's better." She kissed him once more on either cheek. " 'Tis a beautiful gift, Liam. I'll treasure it always. Thank you."

Mary Kate pounded the table with her spoon. "Let's eat!"

They all laughed at her enthusiasm, then dished up the eggs and sausages, Christmas bread and butter, and ate and laughed and laughed and ate until all the food was gone.

After breakfast, Grace carried the cherished wooden box back upstairs, setting it on the table by the window. She had been near tears all day, but had not given in—there was much to do still to prepare for Christmas dinner. Sean had gone off with the Osgoodes, and Dugan had taken the children to Mass, leaving Tara to rest with the baby; Grace had the kitchen to herself.

Going back and forth between the cupboard and the long table, she listened for the sound of a knock upon the door, knowing it was sure to come. Had she not attended Sunday meetings with Sean? Had she not read what they'd given her to read, heard what they wanted her to hear, said what she was supposed to say? The women were always warm and kind, offering clothes for the children, advice on how to raise them, bottled preserves and medicinals; they'd done everything in their power to make her feel welcome, a part of the group—the fault lay within her, not them, but not for lack of trying. Her daily talks with God were full of pleas and promises; she had been patient and obedient, she had trusted and believed— surely God would not disappoint her yet again.

The table today would be filled with family and friends—the Ogues, the Osgoodes, Lily and her children. Liam's father could not be persuaded to join them, so Liam had tacked a message on the sailor's board inviting Captain Reinders if his ship was in. All would be in attendance when Grace's father came striding through the door with young Morgan in his arms, and Grace would rush to embrace them both, holding her boy again after so long—she could see it, she could hear it, it would be.

Thirty-three

IT was cold up here, bitterly cold; dirty snow lay in clumps all over the wharf and the sky threatened more. The ship had been secured, paperwork submitted, cargo unloaded, but Reinders was still tense.

Mackely was below even now, checklist in hand, keeping the crew away from the two large, padlocked trunks in the back; these belonged to Reinders, as everyone knew—he often took one or both on short runs to the South to haul back personal stores of rum or molasses, cigars, cloth, the odd antiquity for Lars' wife, Detra. The crew thought nothing of the presence of these trunks, and no longer bothered to ask what treasure he'd come by this time. He was grateful for the lack of curiosity, as this trip he'd come by the most precious treasure of all.

He thought of this now, and fought the urge to go down and check. They'd made it this far, he told himself. It wouldn't be too much longer; he mustn't do anything out of the ordinary.

"All done, Captain." Mackley presented the checklist to him.

Reinders looked it over, thanked his crew for a good voyage, and dismissed them, wishing them all a Merry Christmas and he'd see them in the new year. Only when the last man had gone, did the captain and his first mate breathe a sigh of relief.

"How is everything down there?" Reinders asked. "Any problems?"

"The girl coughed a couple of times, Captain. Once real hard, poor kid, but I don't think anyone heard. The sooner we get her out of there, the better."

Reinders couldn't agree more. "I'll do it. You go over to the market and look for Lily. If she's not there"—he handed over a piece of paper with an inked symbol—"post this on the sailor's board."

"Yes, sir. Then what?"

"Frankly, I have no idea. I didn't anticipate arriving unannounced on Christmas Day."

When Mackley had gone ashore, Reinders pulled up the gangplank, mentally reviewing his actions of the last few weeks. He'd been meticulous about his log, knowing he might have to give an accounting of his whereabouts on any given day, maybe any hour. He had alibis, he had witnesses, and the only real pieces of evidence against him were about to be delivered to their mother. The plan had always been to let her know the minute he arrived, wait for nightfall, then load them into Hesselbaum's wagon, cover them with straw, and smuggle them past the slave catchers who haunted this area, looking for stowaways. Lily was always on the docks—every day she was on the docks. Just not Christmas Day. She hadn't even been expecting them. He hadn't told her how close he was, just in case; there had been so many disappointments, and it was Christmastime. He was an idiot.

Grimly, he secured the ropes and went below. Even before he got to the hold, he heard the soft, distressed cough of someone trying to be quiet. He was worried about Mary; she hadn't looked well in the warehouse, and then she'd been stowed in a trunk and carted to the ship. Days of cold and damp with little food and terrible stress certainly hadn't helped. Solomon wasn't any better off; he could barely walk on legs whose tendons had been severed, whose feet had no toes, but Reinders had seen the fury in the boy's eyes and knew his will to live was fueled by pure rage. He hadn't said a word to the captain before climbing into his own trunk, hadn't spoken at all during the trip, Mackley said.

"He'd just as soon cut my throat as look at me," the first mate had reported. "Hates white men, that's for sure."

"Can you blame him?" Reinders had asked.

"No, sir." Mackley still couldn't get over the boy's feet. "I don't."

Reinders unlocked the first trunk and lifted the heavy lid. Her eyes were wide in the gloom, her face ragged with fatigue and strain. He opened the other, this time meeting the bristling defiance of the boy. The two stepped out, legs stiff from little use, shoulders and necks aching from long hours in one position. The girl began to cough again, bending over with the force of it. Reinders put an arm around her, supporting her until the spasm ended.

"I know it's been rough," he apologized. "We're here now. Crew's dismissed. Stretch your legs a bit. Then we'll go up to my cabin."

Brother and sister walked the length of the hold, stopping at the far end for a hurried, whispered exchange, which Reinders could not hear.

"Watch your step," he admonished when they returned. "I didn't bring a lantern."

He led the way out of the hold, then down the corridor and up another short ladder to the narrow hall leading to his cabin. Once they were all inside, he closed and bolted the door, then lit the lantern and hung it on its hook. In better light, they looked even worse. The girl was exhausted, her teeth chattering.

"Put this on." Reinders handed her a thick fisherman's sweater, then tossed the boy a woolen shirt. "You, too. Sit down."

They pulled on their garments, then sat gingerly by his desk.

"I've sent Mack to find your mother—she works on the dock. It's Christmas, though. I don't know if she'll be there."

"What then?" Solomon's voice was a low rumble. "We go out looking?"

Reinders shook his head emphatically. "Not you two. You might as well have a sign on your back that says, 'Runaways.' "

"New York ain't free?" Fresh anxiety came into Mary's eyes.

"It's free," Reinders assured. "But we've got more than our

fair share of bounty hunters waiting to knock you over the head and drag you back. The abolitionists keep an eye on things, but there's not much anyone can do if they decide to snatch you. It *is* a free state," he repeated. "But you're definitely on your own."

"How we going to find her then?" The young man frowned.

"There's a sailor's board on the wharf. Your mother checks there for messages from me."

"She can't read." Mary looked at Solomon.

"I know. It's a symbol. She'll recognize it."

"She all right?" The girl's eyes suddenly filled with tears, and Reinders realized he hadn't told them a thing.

"She's fine. Really, she is." He racked his brain for details. "She works in the fish market for Jakob Hesselbaum. He's a good man. He cares for your mother. Your brother and sister are fine. Samuel," he remembered. "Samuel and Ruth. Both fine."

The girl leaned forward, hungry for every word, disregarding the tears spilling over her cheeks. The young man listened, too, but his emotions were more carefully guarded.

"They live up in Five Points. It's not that far from here. Pretty rough, though," Reinders added.

"But they free, right?" Solomon checked again.

The captain nodded. "They're free. She carries papers. You'll have them, too."

Mackley whistled from the dock.

"There he is," Reinders announced, and they all rose at the same time. "Stay here. If he's got her, I'll bring her in."

He went up on deck, then strode quickly to the other side, but the first mate was alone. He pushed out the gangplank.

"Here, Captain." Mackley handed over a small envelope. "I went to post the message and found this instead."

Reinders tore it open.

Dear Captain,
    Please come to Christmas dinner if you can. Lily's coming and them. Please come.

                                 Your friend,
                                 Liam Kelley

"Hah!" He crumpled the page. "She's at the Harp!"

"What do you think, sir? Should we chance it?"

Reinders took a good look around. The wharf was nearly deserted, just the odd sailor moving about, and across the square, a ragged bunch sharing a bottle and smokes at the edge of one of the warehouses; they didn't look like slavers, their ferretlike attention focused on a loaded cart left unguarded in front of an open door.

"Go out to the avenue and hire a closed carriage. Wait for us at the end of the alley. We won't be more than five minutes behind you."

"Right!" Mackley sprang toward the gangplank, then turned back. "How about them coming home to their mother on Christmas Day?" he wondered. "That's something, isn't it?"

"That's coincidence," Reinders stated. "Now get going."

Mary and Solomon had no belongings to gather and, he realized, no shoes to speak of. The girl was wearing thin cotton slippers and the boy was barefoot. As he explained the situation, Reinders quickly dug out an old pair of mud boots, thrusting them into the young man's hands before picking up the lantern and going out into the dark passage, then into the dank space where the crew slept. He went directly to the cook's locker—Cook was a small fella—and rummaged around until he found a pair of boots for the girl. Back in the cabin, he wrapped his own cape around Solomon's shoulders and pulled a hat down firmly over the young man's head, low over his eyes; Mackley's cape went around Mary, a watch cap over her cropped hair.

"Keep your heads down," he ordered. "Don't look up no matter what. Solomon, you'll take my arm so we can move quickly." He glanced at the boots. "How do those feel?"

"Hurt." Solomon gave up a ghost of a smile.

"No doubt." Reinders winced at the thought of those toeless feet banging against that stiff leather—socks, he should've gotten socks. "They'll get you to the carriage, though."

Solomon nodded, tugging the hat down even lower, hunching into the cape so that his neck was covered.

"Mary." Reinders turned to the girl. "You'll walk directly behind. Long strides now, head down. If I run, you run, and don't
stop until we get to the carriage."

"Yes, sir." Her eyes widened in alarm as she watched him
take a pistol out of the drawer, load it, and slip it into his jacket
pocket.

"Ready?"

They nodded.

"Let's go."

On deck, the two took their first quick look at freedom. The
snow surprised them, and the biting cold, but they said nothing,
intently focused now on following Reinders carefully across the
gangplank. At the bottom, Solomon linked his arm with the captain's and moved as quickly as he could across the slippery
wharf. Mary was right behind, eyes on the heels of Reinders'
boots. Heads down, they strode purposefully through the last
bit of afternoon light, ignored by others in a rush to get home.
The unattended cart had been rescued by its driver, who was
now warily eyeing the rough group of sailors; his voice, urging
the horse to giddap now, echoed in the stillness with a bravado
Reinders was sure he did not feel. The captain glanced up, then
lowered his head again, aware that the sailors' attention had
shifted to him.

With a curt nod to his fellows, Boardham stepped away
from the group, pulled his jacket more tightly around him,
and trailed Reinders into the alley. How nice of the captain to
present himself like this on Christmas, Boardham chuckled.
He'd seen that dog Mackley spring across the wharf and back
again, then down the alley toward the avenue. And who
should come right behind but the noble captain, a couple of
odd ones by his side. He followed them, hanging back, watching as they slipped directly from the dark alley into a waiting
carriage.

Mackley rapped on the roof of the cab and the carriage
jolted forward, Solomon and Mary nearly sliding off their seat.

They braced themselves, glancing at one another, but no one said a word and the cab filled with anxious silence. They leaned to one side and then the other as the carriage turned corners, and finally Mackley lifted the edge of the flap and looked out. He recognized the area; they were well away from the waterfront now, and he turned back to them, smiling and rubbing his hands together briskly.

"Hah!" he barked delightedly. "We did it!"

Solomon squeezed Mary's leg. Reinders took off his cap and ran a hand over his tangled mat of hair.

"Well done, Mack. Good work." Reinders clapped him on the knee, relief evident in his voice.

"Good work yourself, sir." Mackley grinned, then glanced again out the little window. "I'm getting out here, Captain, if you don't mind." He knocked and the carriage pulled over. "Got friends in this part of town be glad to trade a plate of Christmas dinner and half a bottle for a good sea story."

"Not this one, though," Reinders cautioned.

"Oh, no, sir. I earn my pay, remember? Besides"—he winked—"I always got a few yarns saved up for when I need them."

Reinders laughed and put out his hand. "You're a good man, Mack. I mean it. Thanks for everything, and Merry Christmas."

"Merry Christmas to you, too, sir." He shook the hand warmly, then got out of the carriage, pausing before he closed the door. "Good luck," he said to Solomon; then to Mary, he added, "All the best to you and say hello to your mother." Then he was gone.

It was quiet again as the carriage swayed once more down the street, its wheels thumping over icy ruts. Outside, the young lamplighters were hard at work, moving cautiously down the sidewalks, stools tucked under their arms. Snow had begun to fall; it clung to the manes and tails of the big working horses, white steam billowing from their nostrils. Another couple of days like this, Reinders thought, and the carriages would be garaged, the horses harnessed to sledges instead. He had to admit that he loved the sight of the steaming horses pulling

loads of fur-bundled passengers, the icy swoosh of runners glid-
ing over packed snow. And the silence. Best of all, he liked the
silence of a snowbound city. It was as if everyone were at sea, as
if time had stopped and the world was at rest. Suddenly, the carriage stopped. Reinders looked out.

"We're here." He climbed down, paid the driver, then
helped them onto the sidewalk.

The Harp appeared dark, but then he saw the warm glow of
a hearth fire in the back, heard the muted sound of conversation, soft laughter. He nodded at the two young people by his
side, reassuring them, then knocked loudly on the front door.
Inside, conversation stopped. Heavy footsteps drew near and
the door was opened by a powerfully built Irishman with a
squashed nose.

"We're closed," he growled. "But Merry Christmas to you
anyway."

"Ogue?" Reinders asked quickly. "Mighty Ogue?"

"Aye? Do I know you?"

"Captain Reinders." He removed his hat. "Liam invited us."

Ogue's face spread into a great grin, and he practically
scooped the three of them into the warm room.

"Liam!" he called over his shoulder. "I believe God Himself
has appeared."

The boy came barreling across the room and hurled himself
into the captain's arms before remembering his dignity and
pulling himself up straight. His face beamed.

"You came," he said, then announced to the others, "He
came! I knew you would," he added confidently.

Reinders reached down and ruffled the boy's hair, unable to
meet that wide grin with anything less than one of his own.

"Wouldn't have missed it," he replied. "And I didn't come
empty-handed, either."

"Captain Reinders!" Grace wiped her hands on her apron,
her face flushed from the fire and the ale, her eyes taking in the
two young people standing hesitantly beside him. "Who've you
brought with you, then?"

But in that instant she knew who they were, and so did Lily, who'd come up quietly and now moved first to her daughter, then to her son, touching their faces with her fingertips as if they were made of glass.

They reached out and touched her, too, touched her hair, her face, her shoulder, her arm, until she put those arms around them both and pulled them to her. A perfect silence fell over the room as they held each other, eyes tightly shut, and then Mary whispered, "Mama."

"Mama," Solomon repeated, the word catching in his throat.

Lily gripped them even tighter, then opened her eyes and turned to the other two children standing behind her.

"Ruth." She beckoned gently. "Samuel. Come here."

They came forward shyly, and all five looked at one another.

"You big." Mary smiled through her tears, touching the ribbon at the end of Ruth's braid.

"How you, Sam?" Solomon put his hand on the boy's shoulder, feeling him through the cotton shirt, how real he was.

"Good, Sol. Real good." Samuel tried to look behind his older brother, eyes hopeful. "You got Papa?"

The two older children stared at him, then hung their heads.

"That's all right," Lily said immediately, chasing away her own pain. "It's enough you here, you two." She put a hand on the side of either face, then raised their chins with her fingertips until she could see their eyes clearly. "More than enough."

She took her children—all of her children—into arms that seemed long enough, strong enough to hold them all; she rocked them, soothed them as they wept, murmured words of comfort, of love, of thankfulness. They didn't have to hold on anymore, she would do the holding on.

Grace watched, unable to tear her eyes away, her own heart aching, until Dugan cleared his throat and said, "Will you join us at the table, Captain, and we'll give this family a bit of time to themselves?"

Reinders nodded and looked at Grace, watched as she struggled with her own longing, saw how she put it carefully aside and replaced it with joy for her friend. He was moved by this, but knew any words of comfort would be her undoing. He offered her his arm instead, and she took it, Liam clinging to the captain's other hand, and together they followed Dugan back to the table.

"Sean O'Malley, Captain. Grace's brother. A pleasure to meet you at last, sir." He grinned congenially, pumping Reinders' hand.

"Pleasure's all mine." Reinders liked him instantly, this charismatic young man who looked like Grace around the eyes.

"I'm happy for the chance to thank you properly, Captain. For bringing my sister and the children safely across the sea to me here."

"Again—my pleasure." Reinders glanced at Grace. "Your sister is quite an amazing person."

"Aye, and you should taste her cooking," Sean confided.

"He never will if you don't shut up, now," Dugan interrupted. "Sit here, Captain, please." He motioned to the head of the table. "We're honored to have you, sir."

"Thank you." Reinders sat and nodded at the others, all watching him with interest. "Hello, Mary Kate," he greeted the wide-eyed little girl sitting by her mother. "Remember me?"

She nodded, then gave him a heartbreaking grin, complete with a missing tooth. "Aye, aye," she said and waved.

"Aye, aye." He waved back.

Dugan poured a full glass of dark frothy ale and set it before the captain. "Best wet your whistle now," he warned with a wink. "We're expecting to hear some of those tales of giant fish and icebergs and the like. Grace," he admonished lightly, "will you make up a plate of food for the poor man before he wastes away on this cold night?"

Grace laughed and went immediately to carve him thick slices of beef, ladling rich gravy over a plate piled with potatoes, cabbage, carrots, and parsnips. Mary Kate grabbed a big chunk of soda bread from the board and tossed it onto the mountain of food.

"Look how much!" she cried.

"Smells delicious." Reinders suddenly realized how very

hungry he was. "But shouldn't you feed them first?" He tipped his head toward Lily, now sitting and talking earnestly with her children, then lowered his voice so only Grace could hear. "It was hard on the ship."

"We've enough to fill them up and more." She patted his hand. "Go on now, enjoy your dinner."

She and Mary Kate began making up plates for Solomon and Mary at the end of the table, and Reinders had just put a forkful of tender beef in his mouth, when Sean interrupted.

"Captain, I'd like to introduce you to Mister Franklin Osgoode and his daughter." He indicated the two people seated at his right.

"How do you do?" Reinders inquired around the food in his mouth.

"Captain Reinders is a very famous seaman," Sean explained to the Osgoodes. "Full of brave and daring deeds. Young Liam here will gladly tell you all about him, even if you never ask."

"Oh, aye." Liam nodded enthusiastically, then blushed and turned his attention to the last potato on his plate. Mary Kate giggled.

"And today it appears you have added to your reputation as a do-gooder," Mister Osgoode declared. "Reuniting family members."

"I just gave them a ride," Reinders improvised, not sure about the Osgoodes. "From . . . Boston."

"Domestics?"

"Not anymore." Reinders thought quickly. "Their employer is going West, so they've come home. To be with their mother. It's a surprise," he added. "She wasn't expecting them until the spring."

"A touching scene," Mister Osgoode commented. "I gather it's been some time since they were last together."

"Maybe they'll eat now." Grace glanced quickly at the captain before leaving the table.

"And what is it you do, Mister Osgoode?" Reinders changed the subject, giving Grace time to brief Lily.

"I'm a solicitor," Osgoode said importantly. "And also an elder with the Church of Jesus Christ of Latter-Day Saints."

Aha, Reinders thought, *so this is* the *Miss Osgoode.*

"Are you familiar with us, Captain?" Osgoode laid his fork aside.

"No sir, not really. Religion is not my . . . strong suit."

"Captain Reinders is a man of reason." Grace had returned, eyes sparkling with mischief. "A logical man. Not entirely convinced of God's existence."

"An atheist!" Osgoode exclaimed, interested now.

"Ah, well, he does have the occasional lapse in our direction, particularly during sea storms," Grace teased. "But in general he prefers to captain his own ship, you might say."

"And what of your mortal soul, sir?" Osgoode warmed to the task of conversion. "Do you captain that, as well?"

Reinders frowned; he'd had enough of these conversations to last a lifetime. "I've studied many books of anatomy, Mister Osgoode, and I have yet to see one that illustrates the seat of the soul."

"Therefore it doesn't exist?"

Reinders saw that the man was full of weak argument and easily dismantled, but he had no desire to do so on this day at this table.

"I suppose the idea of a soul is like that of love—if you choose to believe in it, then it exists." He smiled politely at Osgoode, then turned to Grace, who stood nearby. "This is delicious," he complimented her. "Best I've ever had."

"Let me get you more, then. Anyone else?" And she began a flurry of dish passing that overrode any further religious discussion.

Lily and the children rejoined the others, Solomon and Mary eating silently while their mother watched. At last the Osgoodes said they must be going, and to Grace's surprise, Sean got his own coat, too.

"But it's Christmas," she implored privately.

"Mister Osgoode's invited me to stay in their guest room. I'd have to go in the morning, anyway. And you don't really need me, do you?"

"I guess not. But I'm sorry to see you go like this."

He kissed her cheek. "See you tomorrow night. Thanks for a grand dinner. And I love my book!" He pulled it out of his pocket.

"Ah, go on now." She gave him a playful shove.

The Osgoodes said good night to everyone, and Grace noticed that Sean had taken Marcy's arm before they stepped out into the snow. When the door was closed and locked again, Dugan brought out tobacco and more ale, setting both down resolutely before Captain Reinders. "I can smell a good story a mile away," he declared.

Reinders glanced at Lily, who glanced at her children, then nodded.

"All right. But it goes no further than this room."

Bathed in firelight, the faces around the table nodded in agreement.

"Solomon and Mary are slaves. *Were* slaves," he amended, raising his glass to them. "We'd been trying for a long time to bring them north, but nothing worked. Then we got another chance, but I had to leave immediately. I didn't tell Lily because, well . . ."

"It was getting hard," she admitted quietly.

"Yes. But lucky for us, there they were in Charleston at the same time." He took a sip of his ale. "Mary had been brought along to help with the children while her master's wife visited family in the city."

Mary leaned forward now, listening carefully.

"Solomon was working out in the rice fields, just a couple of hours away. Our scout paid a couple of slave catchers to go out and take him at night. A risk—we'd been cheated before—but we promised twice the asking price if they delivered him unharmed. We had to pay a bonus, however." Reinders grinned. "Your boy there put up quite a fight."

Solomon allowed himself a guarded smile, now it was all over.

"The same night they went for Sol, we paid the free Black who did laundry for Mary's family to carry a message to Mary, saying she must get out of the house at dawn to meet her brother." Reinders looked at her. "Obviously, she succeeded."

Mary smiled bashfully, but her voice was proud. "I tell Missus Hayes I got a sister in the city just have a baby and can I go see it. She say all right and give me a note, some baby clothes even. I dropped them, though. When they grabbed me."

Lily put an arm around her daughter.

"I see her from up the warehouse window." Solomon forgot himself and took up the story. "I point her out and they go get her. She pretty scared, till she see it me."

"There wasn't any time to talk," Reinders continued. "I needed them in those trunks and stowed on board so we could get out of there."

"I was scared," Mary admitted. "Might be a trick, slavers selling us off somewhere else. If so, I just as soon stay put."

"When they open the trunks to feed us, we talk a little. We worried how long it was taking."

Mary nodded. "But we made it."

Lily's eyes welled with fresh tears. "You did," she whispered.

Everyone else around the table looked from face to face, their mouths hanging open in amazement.

Dugan pounded his fist onto the table. "By God in Heaven, isn't that the most incredible story you've ever heard in all your life?"

"We were very lucky," Reinders conceded.

"Ah, no, Captain." Dugan shook his head adamantly. " 'Twere no luck in any of that. Could only be the Lord's hand delivered you all."

"Aye," Grace added, almost to herself. "A miracle."

"What of your husband, then, Lily?" Tara spoke up from her place by the fire, where she sat rocking Caolon. "Do you know where he is?"

Lily shook her head. "Do you?" she asked the captain.

Reinders reached into his pocket and took out a folded piece of paper, which he passed to Lily, who carefully unfolded it, then laid it out on the table, smoothing the creases.

"I can't read this," she said. "But I know what it is."

"I'm sorry, Lily. He's on the run, and they're looking for him. But we'll keep looking, too."

She nodded, eyes still on the printed notice. "He's a strong man, and he trusts in the Lord. I'm counting the blessings I got right here." She forced a smile onto her face, then looked at her children, all of them nodding off right there at the table. "I best be taking them on home now, get them to bed."

"Don't be daft, woman—there's no going back out tonight!" Dugan waved his hand at the row of windows covered with thin sheets of ice. Behind them, snow was still falling. "You'll all be my guests and welcome. That is, if you don't mind bedding down in the front room."

"It's got a rug," Tara offered.

"I'll go see what's at hand in the way of blankets and the like." Dugan stood up. "Captain, you'll stay?"

Reinders thought of his cold rooms an icy ride across town. "I will," he decided, "if it's not too much trouble."

Dugan and Tara led Lily's family up the stairs to their beds for the night; then Dugan returned with a couple of thin blankets and a pillow, which he handed the captain.

"Best I can do. But you can stretch out on the bench there by the hearth and you'll not freeze to death—I promise you that."

"I've slept rougher than this, Mister Ogue, but thanks."

"I'm sure you have, Captain." Dugan laughed. "And you can leave off the 'Mister' when talking to me. You're a friend of the family now."

Reinders shook the big man's hand, said good night, then began readying his makeshift bunk.

"Ah, now, let me help with that," Grace offered, coming out of the kitchen, where she'd deposited plates and cups. "Liam, take Mary Kate up to bed. There's a good boy."

Liam stood rooted to the spot as if he hadn't heard.

"C'mon now, it's not a dream and he'll still be here in the morning." She winked at the captain.

Reinders came over and picked up the boy in one arm, Mary Kate in the other, and carried them to the stairs. "Aloft, maties," he ordered, depositing them on the first step. "Meet you in the galley for breakfast." He swatted their behinds gently and they started up.

"See you in the morning then, Captain." Liam's eyes were clouded with fatigue, but he mustered a last grin for the man he so admired, the man who had arrived with Lily's children and the fantastic tale of their rescue. *Oh*, he thought, his head spinning with it all, *what a wonderful Christmas this has been.*

Thirty-four

THE room was quiet with everyone gone out, and Grace was conscious of being alone with the captain. She busied herself shaking blankets and plumping pillows until there was nothing left to do, and then she turned and found herself looking directly into eyes brimming over with amusement.

"Now you know why I disappeared so suddenly from Florence's party. I told Jay I was ill—I'm sorry if you were worried."

"I wasn't worried," she replied. "I . . . I hadn't thought about it, really."

Reinders' smile faltered. "No. Of course you weren't. Didn't."

They stared at one another, then looked away, once again caught in an awkward silence.

Grace was the first to break it. "What a night this has been, eh, Captain? You coming through that door with Solomon and Mary . . ." She shook her head. "I can hardly believe it came true. That they're all together." To her horror, hot tears spilled down her cheeks.

"Grace." He took a step toward her.

"No." She stopped him. "I'm happy for them. I'm overjoyed. It's what they deserve after all they've suffered."

"It's what you deserve, too," he said quietly. "I know you were thinking of your father and your son. I could see it all over your face."

"Then truly I'm ashamed, thinking of myself and my own wants when God was in the midst of granting such a blessing. Is it any wonder He no longer hears me, I'm so selfish?" She forced herself to smile.

"He hears you."

"Ah, now, Captain, you don't believe that," she chided. "Don't I know more than most where you stand on the subject of God?"

"Yes! And thank you so much for exposing me to religious fanatics at dinner tonight."

She laughed a little and wiped her eyes.

"I'll let you in on a little secret if you promise not to hold it over my head." He waited until she nodded. "Well. After all that's happened to me these past two years, I'm willing to consider—to consider, mind you—that there just might be . . . *might* be . . . a higher power at work somewhere in the world. Perhaps. Maybe."

Grace stared. "Why, Captain, that's two miracles I've witnessed here tonight! But your secret's safe with me and don't worry—I see little chance of your conversion in the near future, even at the hands of the very persuasive Osgoodes."

He laughed and she laughed, too, and in the next moment, he took another step and put his arms around her, holding her to his chest, her cheek pressed against the rough cloth of his shirt. She didn't move and he didn't either, afraid to break whatever spell this was, hardly daring to take a breath, though the scent of her filled his head. And then—quite suddenly—he was aware of his own scent, of the sour sweat and sticky salt that clung to his clothing, made stiff his tangled hair and unkempt beard. Oh, Lord, he must be rank with oil and grime and dirt, and he'd sat at her table like this! He was rubbing her nose in this! *Step back,* he told himself, but then he felt her arms go gently around his waist, and his heart began to pound so loudly he was sure she could hear it. *Let go,* he ordered himself now, but instead pressed his mouth against the top of her head. Clearly his body no longer obeyed his mind. Sweat broke out on his forehead. *Oh, Lord,* he thought, *I'd give anything for a bath.*

She looked up at him. "Now?" she asked, confused. "Tonight?"

"What?"

She stepped back, breaking their embrace. "A bath?"

"A what?"

"Oh." She was flustered now. "I . . . I misunderstood. I thought you said . . . did you say? You wanted a bath?"

He felt his face grow hot. "Did I say that out loud?"

She bit her lip.

"I mean, my head's in a cloud," he improvised, raising a hand to his forehead. "It's been a long day, and I guess it's just all catching up to me. I'm more tired than I thought, and it's been a long day . . ." *Stop babbling,* he ordered himself. "Are you offering me a bath?" he finished weakly, now completely undone.

"Well, no." The corners of her mouth twitched. "But I could boil up some water and you could have a wash in the kitchen, if you like."

"No. No, that's fine. I'll just, um . . ." He motioned to the bench by the hearth. "We should go to bed now. *I* should go to bed . . . now."

"You must be exhausted." She touched his arm.

"Yes. Exhausted. I am."

"Good night then, Captain." She kissed him lightly on the cheek, then moved away. "See you in the morning."

"Morning," he repeated, watching her go, already missing the warmth of her in his arms.

He thumped himself on the forehead. This woman, he agonized, this woman turned him into a blithering idiot in mere seconds. He was a logical man, by God—a man with superior reason, able to stay calm even in the midst of life-threatening crisis, but she reduced him to a mass of quivering emotions every time they were together! He snapped back the blankets in frustration and crawled into bed, lying back and examining the corners of his logical mind for the answer, instead of listening to his quiet heart. For of course, his heart knew the truth, had known from the first moment it had glimpsed eyes the color of the sea and a heart as noble as itself; and now it simply waited patiently for sleep to blur the hard lines of reason so that it might enlighten the man who housed it, the man who now stretched his tired bones out on the hard bench and pulled the rough blanket up to his chin, closed his eyes and dreamed of those final moments the way they *should* have gone had he listened to his quiet heart. Finally, in a sleep as deep as the sea, he relaxed, her name on his lips. And his heart was glad.

"Get up!" a voice hissed and Reinders awoke to a cold blade held against his throat. "On your feet. Where are they?"

It was the ugliest man the captain had ever seen, but also one of the biggest, and then he knew—slavers.

"Run!" he yelled as loudly as he could before the ugly man's fist smashed into his face. He dropped to his knees, blood pouring out of his nose; the ugly man's boot connected with his chin and he was out.

Moments later, he surfaced to the sound of muffled chaos. He groaned and rolled over, saw the ugly man and three others hustling Lily and the children—gagged and bound, knives to the throats of the youngest—down the stairs, Ogue trailing them helplessly. He struggled to his feet and stumbled forward.

"Wait." Ogue caught him, held him back. "They'll kill them."

"Yeah," Ugly growled, backing up slowly, the knife biting into Samuel's neck. "We got nothing to lose here."

"We'll pay." Reinders' voice sounded far away in his ears, and his vision was blurred. "Let them go. We'll pay what they're worth."

The man holding Samuel laughed. "Five strong Blacks fetch us way more in the market than you got."

Lily's eyes were wide with terror.

The men dragged their hostages out the back door, which had been taken off its hinges and propped quietly in the alley, next to the waiting wagon. Reinders and Ogue followed them out, but not too closely, Ogue picking up a piece of firewood.

"Put that down, old man," Ugly menaced. "I swear to God I'll kill this buck right here. I can afford the loss. The girl'll more than make up for it." He licked the side of Mary's face.

She moaned in fear and Solomon struggled, earning himself a punch in the gut and a bootheel ground into his stub of a foot. He slumped, eyes rolling.

Reinders was afraid now. Once they got everyone into the wagon and covered with a blanket, they'd disappear on any of a hundred back roads leading south; or worse, they'd ride hard to the docks and load them on a ship while the captain looked the other way, his hand held out for the payoff. They had only minutes to figure this out.

"How much?" he offered, his head clearing. "I've got money."

They ignored him, in the alley now. Ruth was tossed roughly into the back of the wagon, then Lily.

"I'll give you a thousand dollars."

That stopped them.

"You ain't got that kind of money." The driver spat tobacco juice over his horse into the snow.

"I might," Reinders hedged. "Is it worth it to you?"

Ugly narrowed his eyes. "We get six hundred for these right here." He jerked his head at the three still standing.

"Maybe. But it costs you to deliver, doesn't it?" *Keep talking,* he told himself. "You got food, drink, bribes all along, fresh horses . . ."

The slave catchers glanced quickly at one another.

"I'm offering you a thousand dollars. Right now. Tonight."

Ugly licked his lip, thinking hard.

"You can walk out of here with a thousand dollars in your pocket. Easiest money you ever made." Reinders paused to let it sink in. "We got a deal?"

"Let's see it," the driver challenged.

"It's in my wallet, in my jacket pocket, on the long table next to the fireplace."

"I'll give you till the count of ten," Ugly granted. "And then we're gone."

Reinders turned and ran back into the saloon, dark now, the fire gone out. He felt his way to the back of the room, then picked up his jacket and retraced his steps. Grace stood in the shadows of the stairwell, the carving knife in her hand.

"Put that down," he hissed, racing past.

"Ten." Ugly laughed. "Where's the money?"

"Right here." Reinders reached in the pocket and withdrew a leather billfold stuffed with cash. "That's one thousand dollars." He showed it to them before putting it back. "Profit from my last venture."

"Hand it over," Ugly demanded.

"Not until you untie them."

"I think we'll just take it from you then." He sniggered, the other men joining in. "Christ Almighty, you're a dumb bastard."

"But armed." Reinders pulled his hand out of his pocket and this time he held the pistol. "It's loaded, gentlemen, and at this point, I'd have no problem pulling the trigger 'Nothing to lose'— isn't that right?"

Ogue watched, dumbfounded by the whole thing but still in the game. He stepped closer to Reinders.

"Here's what we're going to do," the captain announced, trying to buy himself some time. "First, untie the little girl and the woman in the wagon and let them go."

Ugly crossed his arms defiantly, and Reinders aimed the pistol at his face.

"You can die tonight," he stated calmly, "or go home a rich man."

"Do it," Ugly barked over his shoulder.

The driver climbed down into the wagon, cut the ropes off Lily and Ruth, then booted them out the back, jumping out after.

"Now him." Reinders tipped his head toward Solomon.

"I think maybe I'll just kill him."

"I think maybe I'll just kill *you*. Not a fair trade, but I'll sleep better."

It was a standoff; Reinders felt sweat trickle down his back.

"Ogue," he ordered without turning his head. "Take one hundred dollars out of that wallet and hand it to the driver."

Dugan moved quickly.

"That's good faith money. Now cut him loose."

The man holding Solomon slipped his knife between the boy's wrists and sliced off the rope. Solomon hobbled over to where Reinders stood, and pulled down his gag.

"Another hundred," Reinders ordered, and again Dugan handed it over. "Now the little boy."

Again they stared at one another until a commotion at the far end of the alley caused both men to glance that way; two big figures were silhouetted against the lamplight, weapons raised.

Dugan took advantage of the momentary distraction to move in and box Sam's captor one, two, three in the face, snapping the man's head back with each blow. With surprising dexterity, he swung Sam out of the way, shoved the man over, then started toward the driver.

Ugly backed toward the cart, furious, his knife under Mary's chin. "Get back," he snarled. "Back!"

"Behind you!" Reinders yelled, and Ugly actually turned his head. "Dumb bastard," he muttered as Dugan wrenched the knife out of his hand and Mary out of his grasp.

Grace darted forward and grabbed the girl, pulling her back toward the doorway, cutting off her ropes.

The other two men were running down the alley now— friend or foe, Reinders had no idea, but he braced himself, thankful for the big man at his side. The slavers piled into their cart, whipping their horse until she'd raced to the other end of the alley, sliding around the icy corner and out into the street.

Reinders and Ogue turned to face this new set of attackers, but then Dugan lowered his fists and started laughing.

"By God if it isn't Karl Eberhardt and Mister Marconi!"

The butcher and the grocer skidded to a stop, Liam right behind.

"I got help!" The boy jumped up and down, tugging on Dugan's arm. "I went through the tunnel! Grace sent me!"

"Tunnel?" Reinders blinked.

"Runs from my basement to Eberhardt's," Ogue told him. "We never use it. Just for storage." He was breathing hard.

"Well, the boy come yelling up the stairs, screaming about murder, banging on the door." Eberhardt was breathing hard, too. "I think maybe everybody's being killed over here."

"I hear it, too," Marconi declared. "I'm up at night, by the window, and I see Karl running out the door with that." He pointed to the meat cleaver. "I think he fall on the ice and kill himself. The boy, too. I gonna help, but all I got is this." He held up an old hammer. "Is my papa's from Italy. So what'sa matter?" He looked around at the dazed group. "They robbing you?"

"Slave catchers," Dugan said disgustedly. "Came in bold as you please, and tried to take them."

Marconi looked at the children, incensed. "You a poor slave family! That a terrible thing. They terrible men. We call the police!"

No one said anything and Marconi eyed them.

"Maybe we don't," he amended. "Maybe we say nothing to nobody."

"They be back, I think." Karl wiped the sweat off his forehead, shook the snow from his hair. "Just wait. You have to be careful."

Reinders looked at Lily and the children. "How'd they know she was here?" He thought for a moment, and then his face grew stony. "We must've been followed. They were tipped off." *Boardham.*

"That's what I think," Grace replied. "She can't go home, Captain. 'Tisn't safe. And they can't stay here, either, now."

"I know where to take them. But we'll have to leave while it's still dark." He looked up at the sky. "Can we take the cart, Ogue?"

"Aye." The big man nodded. "But I better come along, Captain. In case they're still out there. Waiting, you know."

"And I will come." Karl folded his strong arms across his chest.

The grocer held up his hammer. "Nobody messes with Mister Marconi!"

Grace gathered all the blankets from the house, and covered Lily and the children, who lay down in the back of the cart; Dugan and Captain Reinders up front, Karl and Marconi in the back. The snow was falling heavily now, and bravely they set out.

Thirty-five

ABBAN and Barbara had traveled west with grim determination until they found themselves, at last, in Galway. The schools Count Strzelecki had organized all along the hard-hit western fringe were closing down now, as the British Association's resources gave out, but there were volunteers attempting to carry on. These schools were primarily feeding stations for destitute children, enabling them to get at least a daily cup of broth and a piece of rye bread, estimated at a cost of one-third of a penny per child per day—at the end of one year, the Association had spent over six hundred thousand pounds with no end in sight. Strzelecki had refused to take any pay himself, living off a modest income from his family's property on the Polish-Russian border, donating most of this to the cause. The remarkable count was one of Barbara's heroes; she came to volunteer in whatever way she could, and Abban—seeing no viable way to help in Dublin—had followed, crutches and all.

It was the day after Christmas, and Ireland was entering her fourth year of famine. The previous year's emigration had taken away thousands of promising farmers, those with larger holdings and small bank accounts, a working class that Ireland could ill afford to lose. And yet they were encouraged to leave; the

economic designers of a new Ireland were convinced that con-
solidation of small farms was the only way to induce landlords
to sell off portions of their estates to buyers willing to invest
capital, arriving eventually at something resembling a settlement—a new beginning for Ireland.

Tramping west, Abban and Barbara had witnessed the dismal failure of this kind of thinking—land was for sale everywhere, most of it simply abandoned by farmers desperate to cut
their losses and get out. No one wanted to invest in a country
that was now basically a giant poorhouse, packed to the rafters
with the miserable and degraded. Towns had emptied as shops
closed their doors; even on the finest streets in Dublin, shutters
were up and broken windows stuffed with rags. Trade was at a
standstill. There were plenty of goods, but even at cut-rate
prices, the paupers could not afford to buy. And it was the paupers who remained, as cheap passage could no longer be had
and any benefactors were now leaving the country themselves.

In Dublin, Abban had been astounded at the thousands
being transported for criminal activity; so many young people,
he bemoaned. Julia had explained that jail was the final refuge
for those with nothing, that these people committed crimes
purely to be caught and transported—they *begged* to be transported. Even shackled on a ship headed for Van Diemen's
Land, they could count on shelter and food. Seven years' sentence was a blessing now, and not a curse. The prison wardens
were complaining, however, she told him—more prisoners
transported in the past months than in the past three years, and
what were they to do with people clearly too decent, too well-
behaved and considerate, to be mixed in with the hardened
prison population? And what were they to do with the *children*,
some as young as ten, come all that way alone? No one had any
answers, and so the steady stream out of the country continued.
After yet another crop failure, the people of Ireland were sin-
gularly depressed and most believed that the land was cursed.
Abban feared they might be right. Cholera had reared its ugly
head.

"They burned down Martin Eady's house today," he reported

to Barbara as she brought his bowl of soup to the bench in the schoolyard.

"Aye." She sat down beside him. "Third house in the village this week. All dead inside, and why risk going in only to burn them later?" She sighed and looked down into her bowl. "Hard, though, watching them all go up like that."

He heard the weariness in her voice. "Do you want to go back, Barbara? See Julia and the boy?"

She shook her head quickly. "I'd be afraid of taking the sickness with me. Sure and it's all over the country, though, and I only hope they stayed in London. Julia would have sense for that. She'd not risk it."

"No," he agreed. "She loves that little boy as if he were her own. What if it works, then?" He looked at her. "What if they're able to cure his blindness?"

"Just the fact that he's survived all this is miracle enough for me," Barbara told him. "But if he could see, as well?" She thought for a moment. "I'd fall on my knees and thank God every minute for the rest of my life."

"Do you miss the life you had before?" he asked gently. "In the convent, so close to God and all?"

"I'm closer to Him here." Her voice was strong and absolute. "I do wonder sometimes if I should go back, but I can't bring myself to do it."

"If that's what you truly wanted, I'd take you," Abban vowed. "Even though 'twould break my heart."

"And mine." She laid her hand on his thigh.

He felt the warmth of it there, and covered it with his own rough hand. "Barbara," he began, then hesitated. "Barbara, do you not think we should be married?"

"You know we can't." She frowned. "I may have abandoned my calling, but I've not abandoned God and am I not already His bride?"

"Well, I've been thinking about that." Abban took a deep breath. "And what I think is that God won't really mind so very much. I mean, why should He?"

"I've not been released from my vows. And there's no divorcing God, Abban!" She put her hand to her chest, aghast. " 'Tis a sin, even thinking that."

"Well, I said nothing of divorce, did I?" he objected. "But you know I was tallying them up the other night—our sins, I mean, and there's no small number, by reckoning of the Church—so the way I see it is, what's one more?" He sought her eyes. "No, really, Barbara. Are we not people living in hard times, people who love the Lord despite everything, who serve Him with devotion? You, most of all!" He squeezed her hand. "If you're not a saint, then they don't exist, and surely God will judge us with mercy when we finally stand before Him!"

"Abban . . ." She tried to pull her hand away.

"If I could find a priest who'd marry us—knowing the whole story, of course—would you have me as your husband?"

"No priest worth his salt would agree to that."

"Answer the question, love. And if it's no," he added soberly, letting go of her hand, putting his arm around her shoulders, "I'll never bring it up again. We'll just go on as we are and that's all right."

She looked over the desolate landscape, her breath like fog in the cold afternoon air. The sun was pale in the gray sky, and rooks called from their roosts high in the bare trees, swooping low over the stubbled fields. A band of children came racing by—ragged, dirty, some sick and soon to die—but still they raced and still they laughed, living as they did in the very moment of their lives.

"Yes," she whispered then, and felt his arm tighten around her. "I will," she promised and laid her head against his heart.

Thirty-six

REINDERS paced in front of the fireplace. "They're at Florence's right now, but tonight we leave for Boston."

"But she has an army of people who do this sort of thing," Lars Darmstadt protested from behind his desk. "Why do you have to go?"

"Because it's my fault." Reinders stopped in his tracks. "I never should've let that bastard live. It's me he's after."

"All the more reason to let someone else drive Lily and her family," Darmstadt pointed out. "Although I do think getting out of town for a while is a good idea." He shoved a letter toward Reinders. "Came this morning. Delivered by two policemen."

Reinders glanced at the signature. "Who's this Callahan?"

"A hard-nosed ass. Hates Italians, Jews, Blacks, Irish. Poles, too, I think. Gypsies."

"Isn't Callahan an Irish name?"

"Hates *poor* Irish," Darmstadt qualified. "An embarrassment to the old families already established in decent society, apparently."

"One of those."

"One of those with a badge," Darmstadt said pointedly.

"Views the steady flow of immigrants into this city as a river to be dammed, and is particularly loathing of Blacks, whom he considers something less than human. If he had his way, they'd all remain in slavery or be shipped back to Africa, which is where he thinks they all come from."

"How do you know all this?" Reinders quit his pacing and sat down.

"I make it my business to know. If one is to succeed in this town, one had best understand who the lawmen are—which wards are honest and which are corrupt. His is one of the worst," Darmstadt noted. "And it includes our moorage."

"Why didn't you tell me this before now?"

Darmstadt shrugged. "It's your job to run the ship, mine to run the business and grease the wheels. However, we have now come to his personal attention, and I want you to understand what that means."

"But I haven't broken any laws. Up here."

"No *written* law," Darmstadt corrected. "Callahan is one of those officials who works hand in glove with the slave catchers. No doubt, it's quite lucrative for him." He lit a cigar, puffing vigorously to get it going, shaking out the match. "He's established a rapport with many of his fellow lawmen down the coast, and they would not be happy to know one of their most frequent commuters is also smuggling slaves to the North."

"Where's his proof?" Reinders demanded.

"Read the letter, dear boy. This is not accusation, but intimidation. He has a report of suspicious activity aboard the ship, and mentions a later altercation in an alley with two men."

"Five. And how would he know if he wasn't involved?"

"Well, of course. Exactly. Have you guessed who this reporter of suspicious activity might be?"

Reinders slammed his hand down on the desk.

"Right again. And now we know why Boardham gets away with murder. He works for Callahan." Darmstadt leaned forward. "If this were just a money game, I could play. But it's more than that." He paused. "If Callahan notifies the port authorities along our route, we'll be barred from entering. Slavery is their right and they resent anyone who interferes. They don't need our business that badly."

Reinders understood. "I'm sorry, Lars. The ship . . ." He hesitated. "You'll have to find someone else to captain her."

Darmstadt held up his hand. "We're in this together, and no one sails her but you. Besides, we're not there yet. That's why I want you to get out of town for a little while. Make yourself unavailable to further scrutiny, and maybe he'll find a bigger fish to fry. Detra and I are going to take a trip ourselves," he added. "I'll put Mackley in charge of the ship. Maybe have him harbor down the coast a ways. In a few weeks this might well have turned to nothing."

Reinders thought it over. "All right," he decided. "I'll go. But I really am sorry, Lars, about dragging you into this."

"You and I make a good living dealing with men who make their fortunes off the backs of these slaves," Darmstadt replied. "It eases my conscience—only slightly, mind you—to know two came to freedom on the very same ship."

"It was worth it for that," Reinders allowed. "For the sight of Lily's face when she saw Mary and Solomon standing there."

"Remember that while you're gone." Darmstadt smiled fondly at his partner. "And don't lose your sea legs."

"Never." Reinders grabbed his cap. "I've got to go out for a while. Then I'll pack up."

"Is that wise, do you think? Is it necessary?"

Reinders looked out the window at the snow on the trees, everything so clean and brilliantly white. "Yes," he said finally. "It is."

" 'It' meaning the Irish widow?"

Reinders' mouth fell open.

"Hah!" Darmstadt grinned and stubbed out his cigar. "Detra has been saying for months that you're in love. She always wins," he added.

"I'm not in love!"

"Ah, well, we men are often the last to know." Darmstadt laughed. "Does she return your—what shall we call it, then— your regard?"

"No! I don't know." He faltered. "I don't think she's over the death of her husband. And she's got other concerns—a daughter here, a baby she had to leave in Ireland because of a . . . some trouble."

"Many things to overcome," Darmstadt acknowledged. "Only you would be drawn to such challenges in a wife."

"A wife!"

"Do you know how often you've mentioned her, Peter, in the course of the last year?" Darmstadt came around from behind his desk. "How often the subject of Ireland emerges in your conversation? And what about that rather large donation to the Irish Emigrant Society?"

Reinders looked askance.

"Don't forget I keep the books."

"But she makes me feel like an idiot!" Reinders protested. "Whenever I'm around her I can't put two sentences together, and we always seem to have misunderstandings. And she teases me. I hate to be teased."

"I like her already." Darmstadt grinned.

"It's just that we're not well suited. It wouldn't make any sense." He shook his head. "She is attractive, though," he admitted reluctantly. "And a devoted person—to her children, her brother, her friends—and she's brave," he said, remembering the ship. "And kind. Definitely kind."

"I see. But you're not in love, and you don't wish to marry."

"Yes."

"She is just a friend. A good friend."

"Yes," Reinders insisted weakly.

Darmstadt eyed him with amusement. "I think, Peter, that you've spent a little too much time at sea." He tucked a fresh cigar in Reinders' coat pocket, then patted it affectionately. "To smoke when you get to your mother's house."

"I'm not going to my mother's house."

"Of course you are," Darmstadt said confidently. "Where else would you go? And one afternoon while you're there, I want you to stand out on the porch, look over the bleak winter countryside, and be honest with yourself about this woman.

You're not a young man anymore, my friend. It's time to think about the future."

Reinders frowned, stubbornly.

"Detra's going shopping for our trip. Ride with her in the carriage, and let her drop you. Can you find your own way back?"

"But I've lived here for years!"

"No, Peter," Darmstadt said affectionately. "I don't think you really have."

Grace was exhausted. She and Tara had not been able to sleep after the terrible events of Christmas night, and so they'd lit a fire in the great room and sipped cup after cup of hot coffee until Dugan came home after dawn.

They'd taken Lily and the children to the Livingstons, he'd reported. Miss Livingston—so kind and gracious, not a'tall like that smooth operator of a brother—had immediately taken charge and bundled the poor, terrified family off to another part of the house, leaving Dugan and the other men with a bottle of brandy, which they managed to half finish by the time she returned. Lily's family would be transported secretly out of town, she told them, up north to what she called a safe house. They'd be looked after up there until they could decide what to do next.

It was afternoon now, and Dugan had gone upstairs to sleep before the evening customers arrived. He hadn't looked good, had complained of pains in his chest, and had a nasty cut on his arm from the swipe of the slave catcher's knife.

Grace did not mind being left downstairs alone—her own children were napping, even Liam, worn-out with excitement. She knew she was tired, but her heart continued to pound wildly throughout the afternoon, and dark specks floated in the air before her eyes. She was awash with emotion, and everywhere her mind turned it found no peace, only turmoil. The violence of last night had shocked her, even as she found a knife in her own hand once again; the rage that welled up within her was frightening, and even hours later she felt she had it barely under control. Her happiness for Lily was marred by jealousy and anger that her own child had not arrived last night, that her own family was not with her today—and she hated herself for those feelings. She was angry with Sean for not being here, for having been away when they needed him so. He still hadn't come back, had no idea what they'd all been through, would probably come home in a day or so, chiding her for worrying about him when wasn't he a free man and able to come and go as he pleased? And she was angry at Captain Reinders, though she didn't know why. What right had he to see into her heart that way, to take her in his arms when he knew she was not herself?

She shook her head, angry with herself and her swirl of emotions. There were times she thought she might be losing her mind with the waiting and wondering of it all, God help her. But He hadn't.

It was this reverie that Jay Livingston interrupted when he pushed open the door of the saloon and came exuberantly into the room.

"Grace! What an absolutely extraordinary night you people had!" He brushed the snow off his hat, shrugged out of his coat. "I've come to say that all is well. Florence has a driver taking them off to Boston tonight." He looked around the room, empty but for a few scattered drinkers in the back. "Where's that errant brother of yours? I'd love to hear his loquacious version of the events."

"He wasn't here," she replied shortly. "He went home with the Osgoodes after dinner, and we've not seen him since. He doesn't know a thing about last night."

"How very dull he's becoming! What a boor—to be there instead of here. And on Christmas, for heaven's sake! Really, I shall have to speak with him about this." He tossed his hat onto the table.

"Well, it's a job, isn't it?" she pointed out. "He's working for them all, setting up the wagon train that leaves soon and—"

"And his wedding to *Miss* Osgoode," Livingston added glibly.

"Ah, Jay, don't go telling me that."

He heard how tired she was and, peering more closely, saw

the fatigue in her eyes, the strain in her face. "Sorry. I'm out of line. As usual. Listen"—he set a leather satchel on the table— "I also stopped in because there's something in here I knew you'd want."

She glanced at it, puzzled.

"Sean's mail—it's been stacking up at the paper for weeks now. I meant to take O'Sullivan to lunch—he's always there, you know—and he asked me to deliver this instead. Maybe you'll want to have them sent here directly, if Sean's not going to come round the office anymore. Anyway . . ." He rummaged around in the bag. "Letters from Ireland. One with your name on it."

Her heart stopped and she could only stare at the bundle in his hands; he saw how pale she'd suddenly become.

"Let me find it." He paged through until he came to one that was less official than the rest, water-stained and smudged, and this he put in her hands.

She turned it over, and saw the address of the convent in Cork.

"Let's sit down." Jay pulled out a chair. "I think I'll pour us a drink." He went behind the bar, watching out of the corner of his eye as she slowly withdrew the letter and read it, then set it down and stared at nothing.

"Grace?" he called quietly; when she didn't answer, he returned to her side and put a hand on her arm. "Gracelin?"

She looked up, but her eyes were blank.

"May I?" He picked up the letter and perused it, his face sagging with the weight of the news it bore. He exhaled and sat down.

"This Father Sheehan says they'd all died by the time he got there. Is he talking about your father, Grace? Your son?"

She turned wide eyes to his and nodded slowly.

He glanced at the letter again. "Sister James was apparently the only survivor and had already returned to her mother. Your letters were unopened in a pile of correspondence he took back to Dublin with him." Jay looked up. "He confirmed the graves of the other nuns, and of your father and an infant."

Grace let out a low moan, then stood, knocking back her

chair, eyes frantically searching the room. She began to wail, and then to shriek, and finally she was screaming, pulling her own hair, clawing at her face. He leapt to his feet and grabbed hold of her, pinning her arms to her side so that she couldn't hurt herself, even as she fought him. He held her tightly, rocking her until the wailing stopped and she was left panting, desperate for air; until he felt her arms go around him, her hands clutching at his shirt, his shoulders, as if she were drowning in a raging sea and he the last bit of land. And he did not let go.

Thirty-seven

ON the final day of January, Captain Reinders left the warm kitchen of his mother's farmhouse and went outside to stand on the covered porch, Darmstadt's cigar clamped firmly between his teeth, though not yet lit. He leaned on the railing and looked across the bare yard to the small barn, his eyes sweeping over the shed and various outbuildings; the pens and fences, newly mended. The place still didn't look the way it had when he'd lived here as a boy, but it was in far better shape than when he'd arrived five weeks ago, and he knew his mother and brothers were grateful. They'd been surprised to see him again so soon after his last visit, but had asked no questions, and he'd volunteered only that business was slow, the ship needed repairs, he needed a rest. He smiled ruefully, for rest was clearly the last thing he did in those first weeks— rising early, roaming the countryside for hours at a time, entire days, taking only a rucksack and a rifle, returning with squirrel and rabbit, which his mother prepared for their evening meals.

He had hunted himself out, and had then poured his energies into the farm—mending, patching, clearing, cleaning, working until the sweat poured off his body despite the cold, until his limbs quivered from fatigue so deep he could hardly lift the shirt over his head at night.

His mother had said nothing, had simply let him be, had told Hans and Josef to give him work, then leave him alone. Sometimes he caught her looking at him, a question in her eyes, and finally she'd spoken one night when they were alone by the fire—she with her knitting, he with a rifle to be cleaned and oiled.

"Do sea captains ever marry, Peter?" she'd asked out of the blue.

He'd kept a straight face. "No, Mother, they never do."

"Ach, you. They *do* marry, and have families even. Little children."

"Do they?"

"Peter, I am serious now. And I want to know why you haven't found a nice wife."

"Well . . ." He had no ready answer. "I'm not in port long enough to meet anyone really. And even when I do, it's so awkward. I come and go constantly—we have to start over each time." He'd felt very irritated then, frustrated. "I'm used to rough men, Mother, to rough language and ordering people around. I'm not good at polite conversation, at making small talk. I am often misunderstood. Apparently."

She had stopped her knitting. "I see."

He'd returned the rifle to its rack, trying to end the conversation, but she'd refused to let it go.

"I will tell you something, Peter, that most men never learn. Women, they listen here." She put her hand on her chest. "More than here." She tugged her earlobe. "You understand?"

"I could say yes, Mother, but frankly most things about women baffle me these days."

She'd laughed at him, then. "Ach, Peter, you are a good boy, but so stubborn-minded like your father. You see what you want to see, not what God wants you to see. I will tell you something else."

"All right." He'd feigned weariness, sinking down on the step.

"A woman will guard like a bear the treasure of her heart. But it is a treasure she wants to share, if only you win the trust of the bear."

"Mother!" He'd been surprised. "I had no idea you were a philosopher."

"I am just an old German farm woman, but I know some things."

"Apparently so." And he'd blown her a kiss, which was so out of character that her eyes had opened wide in astonishment.

"You are changed," she'd pronounced. "It is good on you."

He'd gone to bed, and although they didn't speak of such things again, Captain Reinders felt closer to his mother than ever in his life and he knew she felt the same.

The final days had passed quickly, and he was grateful that she had not asked him to come home, find a wife, work with his brothers on the farm. She showed her acceptance of the man he'd become by presenting him with four pairs of woolen socks and a snug cap to pull over his ears when he stood out in all weather on his ship, determining his course.

He wished he could as easily determine his course standing here on his mother's porch, and he lit Darmstadt's cigar, mindful of his partner's last piece of advice. He thought again of the last time he'd seen Grace—the afternoon darkness, snow falling on his shoulders as he stood outside the Harp, Jay Livingston holding Grace in his arms. He'd almost gone in anyway—Livingston was such a seducer—but the look on the man's face had stopped him, had kept him frozen out there in the snow; the usual smug self-assurance had been replaced by an almost painful tenderness that only love could have revealed. Reinders had envied him in that moment, then had stepped back from the window and made his way home.

Here in the countryside, Reinders had tried to forget her, staying weeks longer than planned, but it was no good. He told himself that what he'd felt for her was not love, could not be love—but somewhere deep inside, he knew the truth. She had trusted him with her friendship and had never led him on; if he did not act like a complete idiot, he might still be able to enjoy that friendship, might still be welcome in her home. And would that be enough? Yes, he told himself, stubbing out the cigar—it would have to be.

When they mentioned it at all, they called it her "illness." Dugan and Tara had put her to bed, then broken the bad news to Sean, who sat up all night in the bar. They were amazed when she came down the next morning, dressed and ready for work. It had been a shock, she'd allowed, a terrible shock, and she was sorry for giving way like that. But she was fine now, really; she must've known all along in her heart—no word these many months, the baby so ill when she'd left him, her father wounded and alone. It was too much to have expected them to survive, she'd said, and though they could not understand it, they accepted this and let her carry on.

What they didn't know, as she pretended to carry on, was that she hated her heart for what it had known, and had banished it completely. Darkness now filled the place it had occupied, and at night, her sleep was plagued by terrors. In the morning, she'd awaken with an emptiness so deep she couldn't begin to fill it. But bitterness could, and it bound itself tightly to her very breath, making her resent the customers who sat and drank instead of going home to their families; resent Dugan and his sympathy, his insistence that she take the day off, go up, lie down; Sean's sudden presence after weeks of absence, his invitations to prayer meetings; and—most especially—Tara's apologetic eyes as she held her own living son in her arms, offering words of comfort, words that Grace accepted mechanically but did not take to heart because she had banished her heart.

Slowly, slowly, bitterness smoldered until it flared into anger—sharp words to the children or no words at all, pots slammed in the kitchen, meals slapped down without asking if hands were washed, the blessing said, and when it was done, making them go off to bed. Flare turned to fire, and she told Tara to take that crying baby back upstairs, out of her sight, wasn't she sick to death with the sound of it. She fought with Sean over his idiot religion and fanatical beliefs, over proud

Marcy Osgoode and her self-righteous father, over money and duty, selfishness and children—he didn't have any, she screamed, how could he possibly know?

Anger turned to rage when Liam sidled in late one afternoon and wouldn't say where he'd been. She'd grabbed him by his thin shoulders and shook him, shook him, shook him, shouting into his stunned face that he was no better than his drunken father and maybe that's where he belonged—shouting until he broke free of her and ran downstairs.

Rage had overtaken her then, had swallowed her up completely, and she'd smashed everything within reach upon the floor, ripped her own clothes, torn pages from books, flung chairs against the wall, kicked over the table, saw the baby's Christmas blocks and hurled them through the window. Dugan had burst into the room just as the knife tip pressed against her heart, the heart she hated so much. He'd pried it away, breaking two of her fingers, so strong was the grip of her despair; he'd flung the knife across the room and she'd attacked then, throwing herself at him again and again, kicking and biting, clawing, screaming, struggling furiously against him as he tried to restrain her without causing more pain than she already suffered.

The doctor had come—Liam ran all the way—and had poured laudanum down her throat while Dugan held her, one massive arm across her chest, his other hand on her forehead, tipping it back. The doctor had forced the liquid between her teeth, cursing when she kicked him, and at last she'd grown limp, held firmly in Dugan's arms while the great man wept.

Days had passed in an opium haze, and at night, she'd awakened and stared into the darkness, hearing voices from the past, whispering and just out of reach. At daybreak, her eyes had closed again, ushering in a black sleep that forbade all voices, all memories, all loss.

The Livingstons' physician had recommended commitment, but Dugan had declared he'd kill the first man tried to take their Grace to a place like that. The doctor had sighed and shaken his head, had left another bottle of laudanum, one that Dugan had carried to the alley and poured out, telling himself she might wake up and take too much, though the picture in his mind was of the knife at her heart.

The children had slept on cots in the Ogues' front room, where Tara could look after them, wounded as they were; Mary Kate rarely spoke, the tension in her small face easing only when Caolon was placed in her care. Liam stood often in Grace's room, looking down at her face, sometimes whispering her name or shaking her shoulder gently. Outside the room, however, he was sullen and stubborn, refusing to run errands for Dugan and getting into shouting matches with Sean, who had no idea how to handle the angry boy.

Sean continued to work with the Osgoodes, returning in the late afternoon to help Dugan serve the evening crowd. A girl had been hired to cook, but the food was bad and her outlook grim, and the old drinking men begged for the return of Missus Donnelly, please God. Sometimes, at night, Sean sat by Grace's side and read aloud or simply held her lifeless hand, more for his own comfort than for hers.

As the serving girl took over more duties, Sean began to stay at the Osgoodes for days on end. There was much to be done, he told himself, and he needed the money, now that Grace was too ill to work. Marcy had offered to visit her, but Sean declared his sister much too weak; really, though, he feared the sight of the young woman would send Grace into another fit, and he simply could not bear that. Marcy turned her attention then to the men in the house, bringing their meals to the study, fetching inks, pens, and paper from the stationers, sending Sean's clothes to be laundered, doing the mending herself. It was a relief, he had to admit, to be looked after once again.

At last, Grace began to awaken from her strange slumber, though she was exhausted and could barely sit up at first. When she realized how long she'd been ill and how badly this had affected the children—especially Mary Kate, who now reminded Grace painfully of the child she'd been in Ireland—she had forced herself to rise and sit in a chair by the window, to get up and walk around the room and, finally, to dress and come downstairs. She now did this each day, caring for her children and resuming her chores. The presence of Una, the dour serving girl, was worrisome, but Dugan assured her the job of cook was eagerly waiting as soon as she felt up to it, though they would keep Una a while longer; Grace should not take on the work all at once—she should rest, spend time with the children, get out into the light, go to the park.

It was good advice and Grace had taken her little family back to the duck pond, where they'd spent such a happy day last fall. She had thought they'd play as always, but they'd only sat quietly by her side, touching her, leaning against her and sighing as if resting now from a long, hard journey. At home, sometimes, one or the other would take her hand and urge her to sit; they brought her cups of tea, small bites of food, offered her little things they'd found—gull feathers, smooth stones, a leaf or new flower . . . look, they'd say, isn't it pretty? As if to convince her there was still beauty in the world, as if enticing her to stay.

And so to prove to them that she would not go away again, she traveled out into the world each day—out into its bustle, its oblivion, walking among the people, drawing strength from them, from their resilience and their very human nature, seeing that life went on. At times it was too much—too loud and boisterous, too celebratory—and she found herself drawn to the very edges of the city, to older neighborhoods, to parks, to peace and quiet. Sometimes she sat perfectly still, staring off at nothing, but never when Liam and Mary Kate were there, never when Sean might see.

That was why she stirred herself when she heard his foot on the stair, not wanting him to find her staring out the window. She opened the Bible in her lap to the place she'd marked, then looked up and greeted him warmly. He was so happy to see her looking well that he pulled up a chair and sat down to visit. Finally, after rattling on for most of an hour and sensing she had fully returned, he paused and raised the question she'd been waiting for him to ask.

"Can you tell me, Grace." He leaned forward in his chair. "Do you know why the death of this child hurt worse than the others? Did you love him more because he was Morgan's?"

"I loved the other two boys I bore just as much as this one," she told him honestly. " 'Twas Morgan himself I loved more than any other. All I had left of him in the world was his son, and I left that son behind. I couldn't forgive myself for that."

"But if he'd died in the crossing, you'd not have forgiven yourself for that either."

"Aye." She knew. "But at least it would've been in the arms of his mother who loved him."

"Da loved him. Barbara loved him."

"He was *my* son. Our boy. And I wanted him so much, to see his father in him." She stopped, her throat tight with emotion. "I wanted him to live."

"Grace." Sean leaned forward and took her hand. "You'll get over this, as well. You're strong, Grace. Stronger than all of us."

"I'm not strong a'tall, brother. That's where you're wrong. What I am is stubborn." She frowned. "I couldn't be grateful to God for what I had. No—I had to bargain with Him, instead."

"What?"

"I've been so angry with God," she confessed. "About everything that's happened. But I knew 'twas a sin and maybe that's why He wouldn't listen to me." She hesitated. "So I made up my mind to bargain with Him—I'd follow you into the Saints if He'd give me what I wanted."

Sean slumped. "But instead, they died."

"And then I hated God."

"But He doesn't work that way, Grace! You know that."

"Well, but I was stubborn, wasn't I? I wanted what I wanted. I wanted to hate God, and so I did. I pushed Him so far away that there was no comfort left for me. And then I went mad."

"It wasn't madness, Grace," Sean insisted. "You were exhausted. It was a terrible blow after so many blows."

"No, brother," she said firmly. " 'Twas madness. And a gift. It was God saying to me, 'Stop now. Stop and remember all the good. It's not Me causes the pain, but I'll help you through it if only you'll quit pretending you don't need Me.' "

Sean sat back, surprised. "God has revealed Himself to you, Grace. You must tell the others."

"No, I'm telling you and no one else. 'Tis a private thing be-tween us. And, Sean"—*Don't let me lose him,* she prayed— "I'll not be coming to services with you anymore."

His face fell.

"It's not the way for me," she added, as gently as she could. "I don't want to be lost anymore, now I've found Him again." She set her Bible on the table.

He saw the place she'd marked. *"I am the resurrection and the life, he that believeth in me, though he were dead, yet shall he live."*

"You read it to me one night. I could hear the sound of your voice and then . . . those words broke through."

"I remember." His face was pained. "I only wanted to com-fort you, Grace, to give you hope."

"You did."

"I wish you'd give them another chance. They're such good people. I feel Him in their midst, and I can't bear to give that up."

"I'm not asking you to." She held steady.

He nodded, struggling with his disappointment. "I'm sorry, Grace. I've been so caught up in my own life, I paid little mind to yours."

"It's time for me to find my own way, brother," she told him earnestly. "You were right about letting go of the past and looking to the future. I had one foot in Ireland and one in America—'twas a long reach and it finally wore me out."

He took her hands and kissed them. "Will you be all right, then?"

"I will." She smiled at him, this brother whom she loved. "I've not come this far for nothing."

Thirty-eight

As much as she despised the English, Julia had to admit that London was beautiful in the spring. All along the avenues, pink and white blossoms drifted from trees like a fragrant snowfall; banks of primrose, pansy, and daffodil lit up the parks; and the grass was tender and sweet and awash with new clover. The air was so intoxicating, she often came back to the hospital dizzy after her long walks, and her father would have been gratified to see how much she herself had bloomed these past months. Gone was the pale, defeated-looking woman who had barely been able to leave her room, who had despaired of ever finding a purpose in life again, who had made such impossibly poor decisions. When Julia looked in the mirror these days, she saw the person she used to be, the girl who got things done, whose eyes blazed and whose mind juggled a hundred details with joy.

"Ah, Doctor Wilkes! Is he awake, then?"

The tall, sandy-haired man in the hospital coat turned from his patient and smiled at the sight of his patient's guardian, her cheeks bright and pink from the sun and breeze, her eyes sparkling. He did love sparkling eyes.

"Yes, he is. Up and listening for you, I believe." Wilkes stepped aside so she could see the toddler standing in his cribbed, hands on the rail, bouncing and cooing now he'd heard her voice.

"Hallo, little Morgan." She swooped in and picked him up, so pleased with his sturdy bulk, the healthy weight of him in her arms. "Time for your drops, and then we'll have tea. I brought you a sticky bun," she whispered in his ear, and he giggled. "I brought *three* for you, Doctor."

"Oh, my." He laughed self-consciously. "I see you remembered my enthusiasm for sticky buns the last time we had tea. I'm sure I should be mortified." He peered into the bag she offered. "But apparently, I have no shame."

"Will we have him on the table, then? Or on my lap?"

"He's getting pretty good about this." Wilkes smiled warmly at the little boy. "Let's have the table."

Julia laid Morgan down, then pulled up his undershirt and kissed his round tummy, making him laugh that lovely belly laugh she never tired of.

"All right, old man." Wilkes smoothed the boy's dark hair off his forehead and began undoing the bandages. "How's it looking under there today, hmm?"

Morgan lay perfectly still, by now used to the routine.

Nigel Wilkes never hurried. He was a patient man—literally— and his patients all loved him for his kind consideration and gentle touch, his personal interest and dry humor.

Julia hovered down toward Morgan's feet, standing on tiptoe to see. "What do you think?" She bit her lip. "Any improvement?"

"Yes. A little less dry today, less irritated. Stand over here—" He made room. "See there, how the redness is nearly gone and moisture has gathered in the corners?"

She nodded.

"The tear ducts are working properly now, and eventually he won't need drops."

"Will he see clearly, do you think?"

"We won't really know for sure until he's older and can talk, what the exact range is. But"—he smiled encouragingly—"he'll be able to see *something*, even if it's blurred. He'll wear spectacles most likely, but that's no burden considering the alternative."

Julia shook her head, tears springing to her own eyes. "I can hardly believe it. That it's worked."

"You've done well by him, Miss Martin. Frankly, I thought he'd lose that battle with pneumonia over the winter, but he's a fighter, isn't he? And you kept his spirits up quite nicely. His mother would be grateful to know the kind of care you're giving him."

Julia felt a sharp pang of guilt as she watched Doctor Wilkes bend over the child's face, intent now on holding the eye open and getting the drops in accurately. She'd told him Morgan's mother had died, leaving the child in Julia's care; the same story she'd told everyone—his nurses, the staff—until she'd almost come to believe it herself.

There had been no letter from Grace or any communication from Sean, and Julia had held off writing, telling herself the boy might not survive the winter, or any of the following surgeries; they had been difficult, and Doctor Wilkes had told her quite honestly that many patients succumbed because of low thresholds for pain, which was why he used opiates both orally and as tinctures he put directly into the eye itself. Still, it had been touch-and-go several times, and Julia had told herself it would be cruel to write to Grace saying he was alive, only to write again saying he'd died; maybe Grace herself was no longer living, or maybe she'd made a new kind of life for herself and her daughter and didn't miss the boy so very much. She had repeated these excuses to herself over and over, trying to justify her actions, but then she had seen Aislinn and all those excuses had fallen to rot.

"All done." Wilkes bound Morgan's eyes again, sat him up, and ruffled his hair. "Such a handsome boy," he said, handing him over. "I have to tell you, Miss Martin, that I'm grateful for having been given the opportunity to operate on the boy. It's all very new and unproven. Not many patients would have risked this."

She looked at him, surprised. "I guess I didn't really consider the risk," she admitted, somewhat sheepishly. "Not after everything he's already come through. I only wanted him to have a chance to see his world." She smiled lovingly into the little boy's face.

"That's what I admire about you, Miss Martin—you have your sights set firmly on the future. You're willing to embrace a new and better way of living, and you do so with unshakable resilience."

"Do I, now?" She grinned. "Must be the fighting Irish in me."

He cocked his head. "I forget you're Irish."

"And how can you forget such a thing as that when my manner of speaking is so much more poetical than yours?" she teased, laying it on thick. "Or is it that you're in need of a hearing doctor?"

He turned around to pack his kit bag. "Well, actually, I think I'm in need of a heart specialist."

Julia's eyes went wide and she felt herself blush madly.

"Um, I suppose it's not proper protocol"—he faced her again, and pretended not to notice the change in color—"but I was wondering if we might not have dinner tonight? Away from all this." He waved his hand at the room. "I know a lovely nurse who'd be quite happy to sit with young Morgan here, and there's a place I'd like to take you. Quite respectable," he added quickly. "No low lights and all of that . . ."

"I don't mind low lights." The words were out before she could stop them.

"Don't you?" He laughed. "Well I suppose we could . . . um . . . yes, well, shall I call for you here at eight, then? Eight o'clock?"

"Eight would be fine." Julia bit her lip. "But I must warn you, Doctor Wilkes—I'm as Irish as they come and I make no apologies for myself or my countrymen. I don't like the English," she said, then wished she could slap herself.

"Well, thank you for the warning, but I believe I'll risk it anyway." He closed his kit, trying not to smile. "I appreciate your making an exception in my case, and I won't attempt to redeem myself, only hope that you'll see past my obvious shortcomings.

Good-bye, old man." He patted Morgan on the back, then leaned close to his ear. "I'll take good care of her for you."

Julia pretended not to hear.

He turned to her then, his eyes warm and full of good humor. "Eight o'clock then, Miss Martin. I won't be late."

Julia watched him go, Morgan in her arms, and when the door had closed she twirled the boy around gleefully.

"Well, what in Heaven's name do you think about that?" she whispered into his ear. "Your mam's having dinner out with handsome, brilliant Doctor Wilkes! Nigel," she tried it out. "Nigel Wilkes. Good evening, Nigel," she practiced, then laughed out loud.

Morgan laughed and patted her cheek; she caught his hand and kissed it, looked into his face and saw his father all over him, saw his mother written everywhere.

"They call me a saint for bringing you here," she said soberly. "But there's no truth in that."

She carried the little boy over to the tall window and looked down at the grounds, soft and blurry in the lovely afternoon light of spring. She'd done a terrible thing by lying to Barbara, by not writing to Grace—she loved this child with a full and open heart, but all the love in the world did not make up for what she had done. One day he'd grow up and want to know about his father, his real mother; would she be able to look him in the eye and lie to him as she had to everyone else, most of all herself? Aislinn had asked her that; she had been kind and gentle, not condemning as Julia had feared she might, but she had asked if Julia could live with this all her life and if she would make Morgan live with it, as well.

Julia looked down into his dear sweet face aglow with peace and contentment. No, she had told Aislinn. No, she had said, and knew that it was true, the first step toward truth. Even if it meant giving him up—she closed her eyes, her cheek on his head—she had promised Aislinn that she would write and tell Grace everything. And she had. She'd made a dozen false starts, but in the end she'd written a long letter and now it was on its way to America. To Grace, the mother of this boy she held in her arms. And she could only hope it was not too late.

Thirty-nine

LIAM sat on the edge of his cot, face flushed, boot angrily banging against the leg of Grace's chair.

"Stop that," she demanded. "What have you to say for yourself, young man?"

"I didn't do it," he answered sullenly.

"Mister Marconi says you did."

"Well, and he's only saying that because he knows it's my gang, doesn't he?" Liam insisted. "But I wasn't there! Ask any of the boys! Marconi's just out to get me because—" He caught himself and stopped.

Grace narrowed her eyes. "Because why?"

"Because I'm Irish and he's a stinking Italian!" Liam yelled, kicking Grace's chair again.

"Liam Kelley, I'll not have that talk in my house!" she yelled back, shocked. "We've no quarrel with Italians, and Mister Marconi is our own good friend!"

"He eats garlic," Liam mumbled. "He's a garlic eater."

"And you're a potato eater," she retorted. "For goodness' sake, Liam, what kind of talk is that coming out of you! I can't believe I'm hearing it!"

"He throws rotten vegetables at us!"

"Well, you boys've been nicking apples off the cart every day, calling him garlic eater and worse! You insult the man and steal his wares—you're lucky he's not called the police on you! We don't need that kind of trouble, Liam," she warned. "I'm at my wit's end with you, boy, and now he comes to me and says your ones kicked over his stand and ruined his nice fruit!"

"He's a liar!" Liam stamped his foot.

"He's not a liar! There's only one liar in all this, young man, and I'm looking at him!" she declared. "I've had enough of your running with those hooligans. You'll go to work for him every day until it's paid off—do you hear me?"

"I won't. He stinks!"

"Liam!"

"You don't care for me." Tears spilled down his cheeks. "You only care for money. And Mary Kate."

"Ah, now, Liam, that's just not true," she said wearily.

"Send me back to my da, why don't you? I'm just like him!" He began to sob in earnest.

She went quickly over to his cot and sat down, putting an arm around his shoulders.

"Liam, Liam. I'm sorry I ever said that. It wasn't myself talking. Can you ever forgive me?"

"No," he said, tears dripping from his chin onto the dark fabric of his pants. "No," he repeated, crying even harder, throwing his arms around her, burying his damp face in the warm place between her shoulder and her neck.

She held him tightly, cringing at the memory of her hard words, the way she'd shaken him, angry and out of control. Was it any wonder he was angry now, uncontrollable now? *Forgive me, Lord,* she prayed, hot tears prickling her eyes and nose— *forgive me forgive me forgive me for not looking after the one You placed in my care, this little boy You trusted to me. Forgive me for only thinking about the one that wasn't here.* And so she held him and rocked him, murmuring all the words of love she would have murmured to her own son, until his sobs subsided and his breathing grew deep and slow, his body slack; until he had fallen asleep, exhausted from the burden of holding himself together. She would hold him together now, she promised. She would make it up to him. Gently, she kissed the top of his hot, sweaty head, then lowered him onto the cot, untying his heavy boots and slipping them off, drawing a blanket up over his shoulders.

"Mam?" he murmured, eyes still closed. "I'm sorry, Mam."

"Shhhh," she whispered. "Never you mind, now. Go to sleep."

She sat a minute longer, brushing the hair back off his forehead, looking at his weary, tear-streaked face, thinking that she'd get up in another minute, go down and see to his supper. But in the end, she sat beside him the entire time he slept, unable to go, wanting him to wake up and see that she had not left him, but had remained by his side.

Boardham was counting his money when Callahan unlocked the door and walked in.

"Keeping that safe for me, are you?" He jerked his head and two henchmen closed the door, then stood before it, barring any quick exit.

"I don't know what you're talking about," Boardham replied, casually pushing the cash back into its bag. "This is mine. What I've saved." He glanced at the thugs. "From my pay, you know."

"Very industrious." Callahan straddled the chair opposite. "But I don't think so. What happened to the money you were supposed to pick up from Stookey last night?"

Boardham shrugged. "He didn't give it to me. He—"

"Says he did," Callahan interrupted.

"Not all of it," Boardham said smoothly, though beads of sweat had broken out on his forehead. "I'm getting the rest tonight was why I didn't bring it over straightaway. No sense making two trips."

Callahan eyed him calmly, noted the sweat, the tremor in the hands. "You've been cheating me." He let that sink in. "And you know what I do to people who cheat me."

"No!" Boardham held up his hand in protest. "I swear to you—"

"Stookey, Harriman, Jimmy Doyle, Big Dan." Callahan ticked them off on his fingers. "Apparently they've been paying out more than you've been turning in. Why is that, do you suppose?"

Boardham glanced at the two men by the door. Definitely trapped. He turned belligerent. "You're getting your price." He crossed his arms. "I'm not taking a penny out of yours. Where's the harm in me making a little extra?"

Callahan considered this. "That's what I like about you, Boardham." He smiled congenially. "You're a backstabbing double-crosser who makes no apologies to anyone."

Boardham licked his lips, unsure of the compliment.

"Here's what I've decided." Callahan put his hand on the table. "You're going to give me half of what's in that bag, and I'm going to let you keep your fingers, sticky as they are."

"Half!" Boardham snatched up the bag, indignant.

"Half right now, or all of it with interest. Boys?"

The two men took out their iron knockers and a small hatchet. It appeared to be stained.

Boardham immediately opened the bag and poured the money back out onto the table.

"Smart man. But then, you've always been a smart man." Callahan counted out his half. "Don't forget that I took care of your Captain Reinders. Remember that thorn in your side?" He arched his eyebrow. "Run off for good, I expect. House closed up, ship gone, partner, too." He pushed his money into the bag, leaving Boardham's on the table. "You should be looking for ways to pay me back, instead of stealing from me."

Boardham nodded contritely, though he felt oddly let down by how things had turned out. He'd dreamed of painful revenge for so long that merely running Reinders out of town left him feeling deflated, depressed. Graft had taken his mind off things, had been a welcome distraction.

"Don't do it again." Callahan stood up, pocketing the bag. "And I've got a job for you. I think you already know him—a Doctor Draper. New health inspector for our buildings. Make sure he's our friend. Pay him out of your share there." He laughed.

Boardham started to protest, then stopped, defeated.

"Do a good job," Callahan warned. "My patience is short."

He signaled his boys, who opened the door, and when it had closed Boardham slumped over the table and the remains of his day. Reinders was gone, half his money was gone, the other half as good as gone—life, he sighed, was so unfair.

Doctor Draper was an opium addict and strapped for ready cash, which was why Boardham's offer of a bribe was less distasteful than Boardham himself. He had taken the money—yes, he admitted it—and Callahan's rank, rat-infested tenements got clean bills of health. It was Missus Draper's fault really, the doctor rationalized; she was the one with the family money, he the one with the brains and a pauper's purse. She'd been thrilled to marry a physician on the rise, but sadly her expectations had not been fulfilled, and Draper seemed to be slipping ever backward on the professional ladder instead of nearing its highest rung. The opium probably didn't help, but he didn't think it hurt much either. Certainly, it left him animated and enhanced intellectually, while still relaxed—a man in his line of work, married to his line of wife, needed a place to call his own.

Missus Chang's over on Mott Street was Doctor Draper's private refuge. Downstairs, in the gambling rooms, games of *fan tan* and *pak ko piu* went on all day and night; but upstairs . . . upstairs was nirvana. He loved the ritual as much as he loved the drug itself—the sticky ball of opium paste skewered and warmed with precision over the flame of a candle until it was firm enough to stuff into the pipe, the pipe held delicately over the flame until just the right moment when smoke could be effortlessly drawn through the long ivory mouthpiece. An experienced smoker, Draper could draw in a good-sized ball of opium in a single breath—the effect: euphoria.

This little bit of Heaven in the evenings made somewhat easier his days in Hell—in and out of the worst neighborhoods in the worst parts of town, made completely intolerable by the smell of raw sewage, slaughterhouse offal, glue making, and human decay. He needed the solace of Missus Chang's on a regular basis now, required it, prescribed it for himself. But this took money, of which he had very little of his own. And so he'd sold his endorsement to Boardham—the devil himself—and now he only waited to be caught out and removed, for how long could it go on like this? he wondered. How long could he continue passing for healthy buildings with dead rodents in the walls, their decomposing carcasses visible through the chipped plaster; buildings with garbage piled into the street for the refuse carts that never came, not into those neighborhoods; buildings packed tight with the near-naked, the destitute, the insane. If this heat continued, there would be cholera, he had little doubt, and then he would quit if they had not the foresight to fire him, for even Missus Chang's sweet smoke could not save him from that horror.

He was no longer worried about the loss of income—Boardham's man Callahan had intimated that he had other work for the good doctor now he'd gotten himself in so very deep, now they owned his soul. And so he made his daily rounds and filled out his reports, collected his pay and then his bribes, and in the evenings he went to Mott Street, the quickest way to salvation.

Forty

REINDERS slipped in the back way of the big house, closing the door quietly behind him.

"Really, Captain, you mustn't slink in and out like a poor relation," the housekeeper scolded from the corner of the kitchen. "The front door does work, you know."

"I'm only here for a couple of days, Missus Jenkins," he explained. "And I'd rather not see anyone."

"Yes, sir." She pressed her lips together tightly.

"Any mail for me?"

"In your rooms, Captain. Excuse me, sir, but will the Darmstadts be returning anytime soon? I really should know," she insisted, "so that I might open the house back up. Mister Jenkins and I have been keeping to our own quarters and the kitchen, but I wouldn't want them to come home and find everything still in dust covers."

"They seem to like it in San Francisco, Missus Jenkins. But I'm sure they'll write and let you know when they're coming home."

She frowned; this was not the news she expected. "Will you want dinner tonight, Captain? Or will you be out?"

He thought for a moment. They were playing the new baseball out in Elysian Field and he wanted to take Liam Kelley to another game—the boy was mad about it, and they were anonymous enough in that crowd. But he'd been out of town a couple weeks again, and there would be a stack of correspondence from Lars. Baseball would have to wait, he realized reluctantly.

"I'll take it upstairs, Missus Jenkins, thanks."

The house was dark with the windows covered and the furniture draped, but it still felt good to be home and he took the stairs two at a time. His rooms were also closed, but he immediately pulled back the curtains and opened the window wide. It was stifling up here, hot already even for early morning. If the weather stayed like this, they'd be asking every man in the city to volunteer for fire duty, especially in the tenement districts, where those wooden rookeries went up like kindling, taking most of their occupants with them, unfortunately. He was glad Lily and the children were out of there and happily ensconced in Boston with Florence's friends. Lily was again selling fish on the wharf with—Reinders still got a kick out of this—Jakob Hesselbaum; the peddler had followed her up as soon as he heard the story and now they were full partners, with Solomon and Mary working alongside, Samuel and Ruth attending the Quaker school. Better than New York City in the summertime, he told himself, wishing for the sting of a salty breeze.

He went over to his desk and looked at the mail, shrugging off his jacket and unbuttoning his shirt. Sure enough, a packet from Lars. He slit it open and poured out all the information Darmstadt had gathered on timber transporting. It was a lot. The letter alone ran into pages, just like the others, urging his partner to hurry up, close out their accounts, and bring the ship around—there was a fortune to be made running timber up and down the coast. Reinders was two steps ahead this time—ready to sail in one week out of Boston with the finest handpicked crew he could muster, Mackley included. He couldn't wait to get out on the open sea again; it would be a new beginning, and he was ready.

But it was also an ending, and he leaned back in his chair, thinking about Liam. He had seen the boy as often as he could, whenever he'd been in town. Grace had brought him to Reinders on more than one occasion, leaving the boy for long afternoons. Grace had told the captain about losing her son and her father, and Liam had confided later that she'd been very sick. He'd been afraid she might die and what would happen, he'd asked the captain, if she did—would he return to his father? Reinders had asked if that was what Liam wanted and the boy had said no; he cared for his da and didn't mind seeing him now and then, but not to live. The captain had reassured him that Grace would not die, but if something ever happened and the Ogues did not claim him first, he could always come live aboard the ship. Liam had beamed all afternoon, more happy with the knowledge of that than with the sight of the circus elephants lumbering down the street. Reinders had mentioned this to Grace and she'd been grateful, had told the captain he meant the world to Liam.

Reinders had felt his way along cautiously with Grace; she seemed changed now, older than when he'd left her at Christmas, but they didn't talk of her illness. Nor did they talk about her relationship with Jay Livingston; Grace never brought it up, and he just couldn't. He found himself refusing dinner invitations from Florence for fear the sight of Grace with Jay would break the fragile bond he had managed to forge. It was good and he knew it, knew he needed to make a real life for himself. He would see them one more time, and then he would say good-bye with a promise to write the boy. It was the only thing that made sense.

He looked out the window at the early-morning sun on the rooftops. Off in the distance, he heard the fire bell clang as a wagon careened down the street. It was a good time to leave, he told himself; summer in the city was sure to be merciless.

Sean eyed the angry crowd from inside the courthouse, then glanced back over his shoulder at Mister Osgoode, who had posted his bail with the money Sean had delivered, and was now collecting his hat and coat.

Things had not gone well at the hearing and Osgoode would

stand trial for fraud, for attempting to bilk innocent families out of their life savings in the name of religious freedom. It was just another example of the persecution they suffered, Osgoode declared, brought about by angry families who didn't understand the commitment their relatives had made; another reason why they must go west, build their own community, their own self-governing country. But first he had to get out of jail.

Sean brought the money from Osgoode's safe as directed, reassuring Marcy that he'd be home soon with her father. She'd been packing since dawn; she and her father would leave immediately for Nauvoo, then try to catch the wagon train going west, and Sean . . . Marcy had begged him with tears in her eyes to come with them, to start a new life, and he'd loved her so much in that moment, loved her for loving him and wanting him with her. But Grace would never go, would never even consider it, and he had promised to never leave her. No, he'd told Marcy. He could not. But given time, he'd find a way.

Now all he wanted was to find a way through that crowd. They stood jeering, fists in the air, waving signs that read SAINTS OR SWINDLERS? and OSGOODE'S A CROOK! Sean looked again at Mister Osgoode, who'd joined him at the door, pale and shaken.

"There's Tom Bishop over there." Sean pointed to the carriage at the outer edge of the crowd. "He's got Richard and Harold with him. The minute we start out, those two will push their way in to us and lead us to the carriage."

"All right." Osgoode wiped the sweat off his forehead, then moved closer to Sean and lowered his voice. "Did you bring it?"

Sean opened his jacket just enough for Osgoode to see the butt of the pistol he'd retrieved from the safe along with the cash.

"Ready, then?"

"I'll go first." Sean moved out in front. "Stay right with me."

He pushed open the door and was hit with a blast of angry noise, the crowd surging forward as the culprits came down the stairs. Just before he descended into the mob, Sean looked out over the top and saw big Harold marshaling his way through, all elbows and jabs.

"Hang on!" Sean yelled above the shouts, and Osgoode grabbed hold of his jacket, pulling it back.

"Get him!" a man shouted, and the crowd closed in.

Sean's clothes were ripped as hands clawed at him, slapped and punched him. He took a blow to the face, which knocked his glasses off, and now he saw only angry blurs. He felt a hand at his waist, closing around the pistol, pulling it out—Sean reached down and grabbed the man's wrist, holding it tightly.

"Watch out!" someone screamed, and then it went off.

The crowd fell back, momentarily stunned, a man down and the pistol in Sean's hand. As one, they looked at the bleeding man, then back at Sean, behind whom Osgoode cowered. In the instant before they pounced, Richard and Harold scooped them up, driving them through the crowd to the waiting carriage. And then they were in, Tom whipping the horses until they galloped down the street, leaving the angry mob behind.

"By God, we were nearly killed!" Osgoode panted. "And the police! They just stood inside, watching the whole thing!"

"They saw me, then." Sean slumped with the realization. "They saw me shoot him. They know who I am."

The other men were silent.

"You'll have to come with us," Osgoode decided. "There's just no other way. If you stay, they'll arrest you for murder, and you see what prejudice there is against us. You wouldn't have a chance."

Sean looked at Harold, at Richard, and then at Mister Osgoode. "I can't," he said simply. "I won't leave my sister."

Grace pounded on the Osgoodes' door, pounded and pounded until at last it opened just a crack and Marcy's tear-stained face appeared.

"Where is he?"

"Quickly." Marcy pulled her in and shut the door, locking it firmly. "Back here," she said and Grace was left to follow her down the hall, and then into the study, where clothing, books, and papers were piled precariously, in a state of disorganized packing.

"What's going on? The police have been to the saloon, Marcy. I want to hear it from *you*." Grace grabbed the young woman's shoulder and turned her around.

"We're leaving," Marcy blurted, her eyes red and frantic. "It's only the housekeeper and me. I'm going to the Bishops' tonight, and leaving with Tom in the morning."

Grace's heart stopped. "Where's Sean, Marcy?"

The girl hesitated until Grace stepped closer as if to do her harm.

"He's with my father. They left hours ago. The police were here!" Her hands flew to her mouth in alarm. "They searched the house!"

"They searched our place, as well," Grace said grimly. "Are they hiding somewhere in the city, then?"

Marcy stared at her, wide-eyed, paralyzed.

"He's my brother. I'll not be telling the police, if that's what you're thinking."

"You never wanted him to go with us!"

"Nor do I want him in jail," Grace replied, exasperated. "Pull yourself together now, girl, and tell me where he is. I've brought his things." She shifted the basket on her arm.

Marcy shook her head. "He's gone, Grace," she confessed. "They're riding to Illinois, and from there—I don't know. Father and I are going on to Utah. We're going to try to catch up with the wagon train. But Sean . . ." She hesitated. "He said to tell you he'd wait in Nauvoo if it was safe. He'd stop and write to you from there."

Grace examined the face of the girl before her, heard in her voice a tone of ownership.

Marcy straightened her shoulders. "I love Sean," she declared. "And he loves me. We want to be a part of the new life out there. He wouldn't before, because he wouldn't leave you and he knew you'd never come. But he can't stay here anymore, can he?" She put her hands on her hips.

"No," Grace admitted. "He cannot."

"This is God's plan!" Marcy was defiant now. "God wanted this to happen so we could be together!"

"Well, I doubt the good Lord planned on shooting a man so you could run off to Utah with my brother. But I understand what you're trying to say."

Marcy softened just a little, her hands fell to her sides. "He refused to leave the city without seeing you first."

"Did he?" Grace felt as though her heart would break.

"They must've seen the police. And couldn't risk it."

"No, I'm glad he got away." She picked up the basket and held it out. "Will you take this to him? There's a brace he wears at night. He'll need that. And a clean shirt."

Marcy looked at it a moment, then took the handle.

"And will you tell him I love him, and that"—Grace hesitated, biting her lip—"I'll do whatever he says. Whatever he wants."

"I'll tell him, Grace." The young woman offered a tentative smile. "I'll take good care of him."

"See that you do," Grace said, and then she left the house.

Forty-one

REINDERS realized that Missus Jenkins was either not at home or not answering the door, so he crept down the stairs and peeked out the side window.

"Grace!" He started buttoning his shirt, tucking in the tail.

"Forgive me, Captain. I didn't know where else to turn."

"Is it Liam?" He stepped aside so she could enter. "Is he in trouble again?"

" 'Tis Sean," she said, still in shock. " 'Twas a riot down at the courthouse today and a man shot. Police come by our place looking for him."

"Oh, my God." Reinders stared. "Do you know where he is?"

"I've been to the Osgoodes'. Marcy's packing. Sean and her father left hours ago for Illinois. She's leaving tomorrow and they'll catch up to the group heading for Utah."

"Is Sean going, too?"

"I don't know. I think maybe he is." Grace paced the entry hall. "He's been working for Mister Osgoode, you see, handling the money for the wagon train folk, selling off their properties and the like for cash. Which all goes to the church," she said.

"I see."

"People complained, and Mister Osgoode was arrested. Sean

went to pay his bail, but there was a mob waiting when they tried to leave."

"And a man was killed?"

She nodded.

"Did Sean do it?"

"The police say he did."

Reinders sat down on the bottom step of the grand staircase. "This is pretty bad. What are you going to do?"

Grace sat down next to him. "Marcy says he'll stop long enough in Illinois to write me."

"And then?"

"I don't know," she confessed. "I don't even know where Illinois is." She buried her face in her hands.

He looked at her for a moment, then stood up. "We need a drink," he said, taking her hand and pulling her to her feet. He started into the drawing room, then considered how hot and musty it was in there, the decanters empty. "The house is closed up," he apologized. "Lars and Detra are in San Francisco, so I stay mainly in my rooms upstairs. It's nice, though," he offered. "There's a breeze coming through the window and I've got a fresh bottle of whiskey."

"I don't make a habit of drink in the afternoon." She bit her lip. "But the good Lord knows I'm about to fall over from trying to work this one out."

"Come on." He put out his hand.

"All right, then." She allowed herself to be led up the long staircase to his rooms, which were right off the landing.

He was right, it was nice in here, she thought, looking around at the orderly study, the charts and papers on the desk, two comfortable chairs, and through an archway, his bedchamber.

"You've more room here than on board," she commented.

"Yes, but I love that little cabin. Have a seat." He went to a sideboard and got out the whiskey, pouring a generous amount into each glass. "Drink it down," he ordered, handing it to her. "You'll feel better."

She did as she was told and felt, almost instantly, the effect on her empty stomach. "Are you only just home?" She settled back in her chair. "Or getting ready to go out again?"

"Out." He sat down, wondering if this was the time to tell her, then deciding he'd better. "Lars has set up a timber venture out in San Francisco. He wants me to bring the ship and a good crew."

Grace's mouth opened in surprise. "You're leaving for good, then, are you?"

"No, just for a year or two." He took a long drink. "It's going to take me quite a while to get there, and then we'll see how it goes."

Already shaky, Grace had no resistance left and didn't even try to hide how she felt. "Well, we're going to miss you, Captain. Liam'll miss you. We'll have no one left."

Reinders eyed her over the rim of his glass, puzzled. "You'll have the Livingstons," he reminded her pointedly.

"Oh, aye, they've been good to us, true enough. But aren't they really Sean's friends? I don't think we'll be seeing too much of them now he's gone." She took another swallow, then closed her eyes and let her head fall against the back of the chair. "Maybe I *should* take the children to Illinois," she speculated miserably.

"But what about Jay?" He couldn't help asking.

Grace opened her eyes and looked at him. "Jay Livingston? What's he got to do with going to Illinois?"

"Well, aren't you . . ." He frowned, unsure now. "I thought the two of you were . . ." He finished off his drink in one gulp. "Aren't you with Jay?"

Grace's lips began to twitch. "How d'you mean *with*?"

"Well, you know." Reinders was horribly uncomfortable now. "Together. A couple. Engaged."

"Have you lost your mind completely then, Captain?" She had to laugh. "Can you imagine someone like Jay Livingston ever marrying the likes of me?"

"Yes," he said helplessly, admiring her lovely face. "I can."

"Well, you're daft then, a right eejit." She finished off her drink, then frowned into the bottom of the empty glass. "And besides, I'd never marry a man like Jay. You old bachelors are the worst," she declared, "so stubborn and set in your ways."

"And you're not?" he asked, hurt.

"Aye." Grace laughed again. "I suppose I am. But why in the world would you ever think that about Jay and myself?"

Reinders shrugged sheepishly. "I've seen the way he looks at you," he lied. "And he talks about you all the time. And he's taken to drinking Irish whiskey."

"So have you." She eyed the bottle on the sideboard. "And maybe we've drunk all we should."

"Or not enough." He refilled his glass, his mind spinning: she was here, she didn't love Jay Livingston, she was probably going to Illinois, he was definitely going to San Francisco. He made up his mind and downed his drink. "Come with me," he urged. "Come with me out west. The children, too."

She stared at him. "What in God's name are you saying to me now, Captain? I can't just pick up and go off to sea!" She jumped to her feet and started to pace. "What about Liam's da, then—seedy, aye, but still the boy's father and he'd never agree to it nor should he! Liam likes to see him on Saturdays now, though he'd not want to live there and how could I ever leave him?" She stopped. "And what of my brother?"

"He's going west, too, you said."

"Well, but I don't know that for sure! I don't know where he's going or what's going to happen! I know he can't come back here. . . ." She shook her head. "And how could I ever leave Dugan and Tara, after all they've done for us—they saved my life, you know! And now they need me round there, and don't I owe them a boatload of money?"

"Ship," he corrected, drunkenly. "And I've got money—you could have it. All of it. Give it all to them. Do anything you like with it. I don't care." He got to his feet, slightly off balance. "Just say you'll come. Please, Grace."

"Ah, Captain." Her mouth trembled and her eyes filled with tears. "I never could."

"No?"

She shook her head sorrowfully, and the look on his face was so forlorn that when he opened his arms, she stepped instantly into them.

"I'm sorry," she whispered against his chest. "God knows I am."

"So am I." He rested his chin on the top of her head. "I've been a fool. A right eejit, as you so eloquently put it."

Her laugh was half sob, and when she tipped her head up to look at him, he gently kissed her mouth. She pulled back and started to speak, but he kissed her again, and it was so soft and warm and tender that he thought he might drown in it.

"Be with me," he murmured against her ear. "I need you, Grace."

She searched his eyes, then gently took his hand and led him into the bedroom. He watched, hardly daring to believe, as she began to undress, and then he moved her hands away, untying her blouse and pulling it up over her head, turning her around and kissing the back of her neck as she let down her hair, burying his face in the weight of it, cupping his hands around her breasts.

They kissed again, and he carried her to bed, tenderly setting her down on the top of the smooth sheets. Then he went to the window and lowered the shade, bathing the room in a dim glow. He undressed quickly and lay down beside her, running his hand over the lovely curves of her body, wanting her so much and afraid to begin.

"Is this all right?" he whispered, brushing the hair away from her face, looking into her eyes, those eyes that swallowed him like the sea.

"Aye." She reached up and pulled him down to her again.

He kissed her deeply then, and took her in his arms, folding her into him. A cool breeze blew across the bed from the open window, the curtain fluttered, and outside, birds soared toward home, calling their farewells through the delicate radiance of a twilight sky. *Peace*, he found the word at last—this was peace.

Later, she lay in his arms and he told her the story of his life—of leaving his family's farm and falling in love with the sea—only to be humbled when she told him the story of hers. He wrapped his arms more tightly around her, struggling to imagine this woman married to a cruel man, burying her infant sons, fighting for survival through starvation and illness, and finally marrying the one great love of her life, only to lose him forever. And then to lose his son. He pressed his lips to her cheek and tasted there the dampness of her silent tears.

"Marry me, Grace," he whispered, his heart pounding.

She wept harder then, turned and buried her face in his shoulder, and he knew that she could not, that her heart still belonged to McDonagh and that she was too honest to pretend otherwise.

"It's all right," he murmured, smoothing her hair—down now, loose on the pillow, heavy beneath his hand. "I can wait. I'll wait."

They drowsed against one another, and when he awoke, Grace was dressing. It was so late, she said, the Ogues would be worried, she had to go now. He got up quickly and pulled on his own clothes, then held her one more time by the window, kissed her and studied her face in the moonlight. Taking her hand, he led the way down the dark staircase, through the kitchen, and out to the stable, where he lit a lantern. She stood near the door while he saddled his horse, then climbed up, with him behind, his arm around her waist.

Slowly, the horse carried them through the hot summer night, down the lamp-lit streets, past the eyes of those who leaned out windows or gathered on rooftops to catch the breeze, past the open doors of noisy saloons, the dark alleyways, the quiet parks. Reinders wished he might always hold this woman against him, breathe in her scent, see the world through her eyes. He dropped his mouth to her neck and kissed her, lingering there.

They passed the butcher's shop, rounded the corner, then turned down the alley. Reinders pulled up outside the door and dismounted, lifting her down, but unable to let her go.

"You won't reconsider?" he forced himself to ask lightly. "Redeem me from the fires of Hell? This is your chance."

"Do you believe in Hell, then, Peter?" She stepped closer to see his face in the glow from the open door.

"I think I do." He was serious now. "Hell is what you lived through in Ireland. And Lily in Georgia. Hell is starvation and slavery and war."

"And what would Heaven be, then? In your mind, I mean?"

"Marrying you," he said simply.

She put her arms around him and laid her head against his heart.

"You're a good man, Peter," she whispered.

"Not good enough, though." He kissed the top of her head. "But two years is a long time. Things could change." He pulled back and looked at her. "Will you write to me, Grace?"

"Aye."

"And will you . . . think about it?"

She bit her lip, then nodded.

He kissed her, one last time, as long and as passionately as he dared, and then he just held her. *I won't lose this woman,* he told himself, *however long it takes, however many letters. I won't give up.*

"I hope not," she said, looking into his eyes, and then she let him go.

Forty-two

"WHERE are you taking me then, you old fool?" Barbara complained good-naturedly.

"You'll see soon enough." Abban led the way through the woods, managing his crutches on the trail as if he did this every day. "Have a little faith, why don't you, girl?"

It was a beautiful day for it, she had to admit; the wood was cool after a long afternoon's work in the hot sun, the ground a carpet of springy moss beneath her aching feet, the chatter of birds and squirrels—a bit of wildlife come back for now.

He was always full of surprises, her one, always doing the little things: bringing her something to delight in, to wonder over, to think about; fixing her a meal or a cup of tea; drawing buckets of water, then heating it over the fire—hours of work and all after dark—just so she could have a private bathe in the community tub. She didn't deserve it, she knew that to be true, not after what she'd done; but oh, how she'd come to love him and his familiar ways.

They emerged at last in a little clearing, then made their way through a patchy field full of wildflowers, and up a short rise to a deserted cabin, its door ajar. She was sweating now, the hair damp against her forehead, her shirt sticking to her back.

"Is this what you wanted to show me?" she asked, squinting against the light. "Whose is it, then?"

"Well, 'tis ours," he said, eyes twinkling. "If you want it, I mean."

"Ours?" She peered at him. "Are you daft? We've no money for cottages and land."

"That's where you're wrong!" he laughed. "Julia's just sent us some. As a wedding present," he added pointedly.

"What?" She was baffled. "Have you got heat sickness, then? We've never wed!"

"Not yet." He put his finger to his lips, shushing her. "You can come out now, Father," he called over his shoulder, and a priest disengaged himself from the shadow beyond the doorway. "This is an old friend of mine, Barbara. Meet Father Brown."

"I'm happy to know you at last, Miss McDonagh." Father Brown put out his hand congenially. "I married your brother, you know, to Gracelin O'Malley. Fine people, those two, none better. I admired your brother very much." Sorrow flitted across his heavily lined face. "I am honored to be here today."

"But do you . . ." She turned to Abban. "Does he know about . . ."

"Oh, aye." Abban grinned. "And you did promise to marry me if I found a priest willing to do it in light of the situation. You've not changed your mind, have you now?" He put his hand to his heart, pretending alarm.

"Well, no, but I . . ." She looked at the priest. "Are you sure, Father?"

Father Brown put an arm around her, leading her toward the house. "I'll hear your full confession first," he explained cheerily. "And then we'll have a wedding."

"Here?"

"There's a lovely little shrine next to the road over there." He pointed across the field. "I believe our Lord will be very pleased."

"Abban?" she asked, her eyes swimming.

"Go on now," he urged gently. "You first and then myself."

She followed the priest into the house, knelt before him, and poured out her heart, all her worries, all her doubts, all her sins. He listened carefully, and then he absolved her—in light of years of hard circumstance and endless struggle, their dear Lord would gladly forgive all trespasses. She wept with relief and when she came out, drying her eyes on her sleeve, Abban placed in her arms a bridal bouquet of brilliant wildflowers, plucked from the field while she'd unburdened her soul.

It was twilight when they stood before the little shrine, holding hands, the priest performing the ceremony; then it was over, both of them laughing through their tears, and Father Brown—before he disappeared back into the countryside—wished them a long and happy life, many children, and peace in the Lord until the very end of their days. Amen.

Forty-three

GRACE and Liam set out right after breakfast for Orange Street, Seamus' weekly pay in Grace's pocket. They were later than usual, and it was already hot, but Grace didn't mind. Despite Sean's absence and Captain Reinders' imminent departure, she felt more peaceful than she had in a long while.

Tara and Dugan had been waiting anxiously when she'd come home late two nights ago, worried that something else had happened. Grace had told them what she'd learned from Marcy, and then she'd confessed—hesitantly, though not shamefully—what had happened with Captain Reinders, except that she called him Peter now, and there was a protective tenderness in her voice. If the Ogues were shocked, they didn't show it. Dugan had proclaimed him an honorable man, good in a tight situation. Tara declared she'd known all along, and wasn't it about time the two of them did, as well. Grace insisted that she and Peter had no understanding, only that they would write to one another until he returned. He'd be coming round to say good-bye to Liam, she warned, and they were not to say one word about love and weddings and such. Though clearly disappointed, they'd given their word.

And then she'd asked if she and the children might stay, despite Sean having gone; she'd realized that Liam's father would no more allow his son to go to Illinois than to San Francisco, and she could never leave him. Tara and Dugan had said immediately she should stay, she could live with them all her life—especially as it appeared she'd never marry, they couldn't help adding with a nudge.

She laughed, remembering that. "Hurry up," she called to Liam, who'd paused in front of the candy shop. "I might find a penny for you on our way back."

They walked block after long block, Grace pressing a cloth to her nose and mouth as they drew close to Seamus' alley. Coming toward them was a health inspector and two policemen—trying to close down a building, most likely, or remove the children of a family too desperate to care for them anymore. She linked her arm through Liam's and reined him in closer.

Despite the filth in the courtyard, makeshift tents had been pitched on the ground—homes for newly arrived immigrants who couldn't find or afford even the lowliest rooms. They hovered over cooking pots too near the outhouses, their children playing barefoot in the slime.

Liam led the way up the stairs, then down the hall to number nine. How Seamus survived in that room was a mystery to Grace, and she harbored a hope he might pull himself together enough to move out, to do something other than drink himself to death, to finally know the boy who was his son.

When he saw Missus Donnelly come trudging up the street, Boardham broke away from Draper's group and trailed her into the wooden barrack, knowing she had money in her pockets. He'd had a disastrous week himself as there'd been no extra work—Callahan was cutting him off, he feared—and he'd lost what little cash he had on the dogs. He'd been looking out for possible shakedowns, but the few pennies he'd get from these bone-boilers didn't seem worth the effort. Now, however, his luck had changed. He stood in the hall, outside number nine, listening to the sound of their voices, and then he pushed the door open.

"Good morning, old man," he said meanly. "Morning, Missus Donnelly. Boy."

They said nothing, frozen, but their eyes reflected their fear.

"I've come to collect the rent." Boardham put out his hand. "Now."

"I already paid." Seamus' ragged voice quavered.

"Went up. Shortage of quality rooms, you know. Haven't you seen them camped out in the yard?"

"Give it to him," Seamus said wearily, already defeated. "There's nothing for it."

"We could call the police," Grace bluffed.

Boardham called her on it. "Be my guest. Inspector's right outside. That'd be your old friend, Doctor Draper. You remember him?" He smiled thinly. "The police with him work for me, too. So call all you like, no one'll come." He considered what he'd just said. "And no one'll interrupt us, either."

Grace glanced at the door behind him. Boardham turned and locked it, then leaned against it.

"Come here, boy, and bring me that money."

Liam looked at Grace, who hesitated, then nodded.

When Liam was within reach, Boardham grabbed him, his arm like a vise around the boy's neck. With his other hand, he pulled from his belt a long, thin blade.

"Let's have a little fun," he invited, licking his lips. "Been a long time since you seen a woman, eh, Kelley, you old drunk? Take off that dress," he barked at Grace.

"No," she retorted, her heart pounding.

Boardham narrowed his eyes and brought the point of the knife up to Liam's cheek. He flicked it and the boy gasped, a line of blood now trickling down his face.

"Leave him be," Seamus growled, moving forward.

Boardham flicked again, and Liam cried out. Seamus froze.

"Let's be reasonable," Boardham cajoled. "What's a little cunny compared to this sweet face?"

"All right," Grace said instantly. "I'll do it. But not in front of the boy. Let him go first. He'll wait in the hall. He won't make any noise, I promise."

"Oh, you *promise,* do you?" Boardham drew the blade delicately across Liam's throat. "I don't think so. More fun if he watches. Now take it off," he snarled.

Grace began to unbutton her vest, fingers shaking. Boardham laughed and put the knife between his teeth; then—still holding Liam tightly with one arm—he reached down and unfastened his own pants.

"Ready when you are," he snorted, the knife once more in position against the boy.

Blinded by tears of frustration and fear, Grace could not get the last buttons undone. Seamus watched her struggle, then sized up his son and the position of Boardham's knife. Giving a battle cry, he charged, crashing against them with his full weight, smashing them into the door and knocking Liam loose. Seamus locked his arms around Boardham, dragging him to the ground, the steward cursing now and fighting back.

"Run!" Seamus yelled to his son. "Run, boy!"

Grace didn't hesitate, but grabbed Liam, threw back the bolt, and opened the door. Out of the corner of her eye, she saw Boardham plunge the knife into Kelley's chest again and again, and heard the agonizing cry of the old man's last.

They ran full out, she and Liam, through the courtyard, down the alley and into the street, where they nearly collided with Draper and his escort. They all stared at one another, openmouthed.

"Murder!" Boardham shouted from behind. "Stop! Murderers!"

Grace grabbed Liam by the arm and they tore off in the opposite direction from home, careening through alleyways and the tangled labyrinths of the tenement district, unable to slow until at last they emerged down by the waterfront. There, they huddled in a doorway, sides heaving, trying to catch a breath. Grace looked down, saw her state of undress, and silently repaired it.

"I don't know where we are," she admitted then. "Are you all right?" She touched his bloody cheek.

"Aye." He winced. "And I can get us home from here."

She nodded and he led the way down the secret trails of little boys who roamed the city, coming out across the street from Eberhardt, the butcher. They watched until the shop was momentarily empty, then ran over and slipped inside.

"We have to use the tunnel," Liam called to Missus Eberhardt, not waiting for an answer but throwing open the cellar door and going down.

He moved the barrels and boxes out of the way, then ducked his head and led her through to the other side, into the dim coolness of Dugan's cellar.

"Stay here," she directed from the bottom of the stairs. "We don't know who's up there. If I yell, run as fast as you can to Captain Reinders. Tell him what happened and ask him to hide you."

She felt her way up the dark stairway, pushed on the door, and realized it was bolted from the outside. She had no choice. Banging as softly as she could with the heel of her hand, she called low and insistently, "Dugan! Dugan Ogue! Tara! Hallo!" Unexpectedly, the bolt slid back and the door opened.

"Good God Almighty, what're you doing down there, Grace?" Dugan was astonished. "I thought you were out with Liam?"

"Oh, Dugan!" She fell against him and began to sob.

"Here now, girl!" He patted her back. "What's all this, then? How long've you been stuck down there?"

" 'Tisn't that." She pulled herself together with a hiccup. "Have the police come?"

"Not since they ransacked the place looking for your brother."

"They'll be back." She looked up at him, stricken. "Seamus is dead. Boardham did it, but he's blaming it on me and Liam. We were there when it happened."

"Wait, don't move." He disappeared, then reemerged with Captain Reinders right behind.

"Peter!" Grace wept fresh tears. "Thank God you're here!"

He put his arms around her. "I came to say good-bye. What's happened?"

"Liam's hurt. We don't dare come up."

Dugan hooked a lantern off the table, then lit it and followed her down; he lifted it high until he spotted the boy sitting on a barrel, blood smeared across his right cheek.

"Who did this?" Reinders came immediately to his side, examining the cut carefully.

" 'Twas that nasty Mister Boardham from the ship," Liam declared angrily. "He told Grace to take off her dress and he cut me when she wouldn't." He stopped, the realization of what had happened sinking in. "I think he killed me da."

Reinders looked at Grace.

"He came into Seamus' rooms while we were there . . ." She turned away. "The boy's right."

"How the hell did you get away?" Dugan asked, astounded.

"Seamus fought him." She put her arm around Liam's shoulders. "He saved our lives, your da, didn't he?"

"Aye," Liam said with wonder, frowning against his tears. "He did."

"I'm sorry to bring more trouble on you, Dugan." Grace twisted her hands in her skirt. "I know the police'll come. Boardham's got them in his pocket. That Doctor Draper was there, as well," she told the captain. "He's the building inspector."

"Unbelievable." Reinders shook his head. "You're right about Boardham. He's Callahan's man."

"We're in for it then," Dugan set down the lantern. "Nobody gets around that bastard."

"He won't come round once we're gone," she reasoned. "We'll hide in the tunnel until we know where Sean is, and then we'll go there."

"Or you could come with me," Reinders offered, trying to sound off hand. "I hear San Francisco is a very exciting place. Not like here where nothing ever happens."

"I'm grateful to you, Peter, but if I left now—like this—I might not ever see my brother again."

"Will you take Liam?" Reinders put his hand on the boy's shoulder.

"Of course! I'd not leave him behind."

"What I mean is . . ." He glanced at Liam, who looked up at him, suddenly understanding.

"Would you take me, then?" the boy asked.

"I would." Reinders nodded soberly. "But it's not my decision."

Liam turned pleading eyes to Grace. "Could I go with him? Please, Mam?"

Grace looked down into that little face—*not so little anymore,* she thought, *twelve in another month*—and pressed her hand against the ache in her chest.

"Are you telling me you don't want to commit your life to working in the desert with the holy Saints?" She pretended disbelief. "You'd rather go to sea with Captain Reinders there?"

"Oh, aye," Liam breathed.

"You don't want to be president anymore?"

"No," he answered firmly. "I'm going to be a sea captain. Besides"—he smiled that endearing lopsided boy smile—"Sean says you have to be born in America, so it'll be my son who's president, then."

She considered the wisdom in that, and understood that he was right; for the children of immigrants come to America, anything was possible.

"All right," she granted and Reinders took her hand. "But it's not forever, mind you. You'll have to come home to me in a year or so."

Liam threw his arms around her and held on tight. "I love you," he said simply.

"And I, you." The words caught in her throat.

"Grace . . ." Reinders hesitated. "I'm leaving right away. Today. My buggy is outside. I only stopped in to—"

"Sooner the better," Grace resolved. "Dugan, will you bring down his clothes. And will you get Mary Kate?"

They were all silent for a moment at the thought of the little girl.

It happened so quickly—Liam's tearful, excited good-byes to Mary Kate and Tara and Caolon—that when he was gone,

Grace could hardly take it in. Peter had promised her over and over that he would take good care of the boy, guard him with his life, help him grow into a man Grace could be proud of. And Grace had known that this was true. Liam wasn't her child, after all, but God's—and God was putting him once again in the hands of Captain Reinders.

The murder of Seamus Kelley meant nothing to Marcus Boardham, but the thought of revenge slipping yet again through his fingers drove him mad.

Draper—the rat—had complained to Callahan, had insisted he could not be party to such obvious wrongdoing—a murder, for God's sake. Boardham could just hear the pompous whine in the doctor's voice. As if he wasn't party to murder every stinking day he allowed those sweltering, louse-ridden buildings to take in more tenants instead of boarding them up and burning them down. At least Boardham was honest about his work—he walked in, did a thorough job, walked right out again, no complaints. Like a man.

Killing Kelley had troubled him no more than killing the mad dogs that roamed the summertime streets, bashing in their brains for fifty cents each. The old drunk had surprised him, though, caught him off guard with that last ounce of courage. Very touching, what a man'd do for his boy if given the chance; Boardham hadn't minded in the least providing such an opportunity for glory, however badly misplaced.

What he had minded—and minded very much—was being unable to pin the murder on Missus Donnelly and the boy. Already wanted for murder in Ireland, she would've been found guilty hands down. It was so easy. And Reinders would've come riding back into town—hero that he thought he was—to stand for her, or if not for her then at least the boy. It was perfect. But Callahan hadn't wanted to hear it. No, not one word. He'd sent a couple of men to bring Boardham back to Stookey's private upstairs room; there, Callahan had unleashed his anger— Boardham had gone too far this time, was drawing too much unwanted attention to himself and everyone else. Callahan had not risen to this position only to be undone by a lowly snitch. There would be no police sent to Ogue's saloon, he insisted, no arrests made—Boardham had been seen by too many witnesses running from the building with the bloody knife in his hand. In broad daylight! Callahan had worked to calm himself, then had said between clenched teeth that Boardham should go home and wait for further instructions. No more trouble, he warned, or there'd be hell to pay.

Humiliated, Boardham slunk back to his hot little room at the top of the house and sweated there, growing angrier by the minute as he thought of the woman and the boy cowering somewhere in that old saloon: a closet maybe, a storage room— quivering like frightened mice, afraid to come out, easy pickings for someone wanting to finish the job. And oh, he wanted to fin- ish it. Once and for all. He paced the rotten floorboards, stop- ping only to pound his fist into the crumbling plaster of his wall, his clothes steeping in the sour sweat of fury. He looked out the window as darkness fell, watched families climb out onto half roofs and overhangs in order to escape the heat, while revelers claimed the streets, their raucous laughter and abrupt fistfights punctuated by the sound of the fire bell in the distance. Board- ham cocked his head, listening as the wagon drew near, horse hooves pounding, men shouting to one another, racing down the hill toward the fire. Smiling then, he stuffed a cap in his pocket and went out.

Grace awoke to the crack and crash of something heavy overhead, and then the muffled sound of breaking glass. She sat up and sniffed the air. Smoke. Hands shaking, she lit the lantern and lifted it, playing the light around the black cellar. Mary Kate still slept in the next cot, her doll clutched tightly to her chest. Grace shone the light toward the staircase and there it was— billowing down, beginning to fill the room now, and from above another explosion of glass. Someone was yelling up there, shouting to get out. She picked up her daughter and ran up the stairs, but the door opened only a sliver, then no more. Smoke poured in through the crack, and Grace realized a beam was blocking her escape. Mary Kate was awake now, her arms around her mother's neck.

"Blossom," she cried, and Grace scooped up the doll as they ran past the cot, heading toward the tunnel.

She splashed barefoot through the murky puddles, startling the rats, who disappeared into wall crevices, their long naked tails whipping behind them. It felt endless, but then they were out and Grace nearly slipped and fell as she rushed for Eberhardt's stairs. They pushed their way into the shop and Grace called out for the butcher.

"Fire!" she cried when he appeared on the stairs. "Fire at the Harp!"

In the distance, the brash sound of the bell rousted the volunteers from their beds yet again, sending them out into the street, where they jumped onto the passing wagons heading for the blaze.

"Karl!" Missus Eberhardt stood in the door, clutching a blanket over her nightgown, eyes frantic with fear.

Mister Eberhardt called to her in German and she nodded, then came down immediately.

"Stay here," he ordered, running out the door, calling for Mister Marconi as he raced down the street.

Grace stood there, staring after him. The police would be there. But Dugan . . . Tara . . . She handed Mary Kate to Missus Eberhardt and pointed to the boots in the corner.

"I've got to go." She slipped her feet into them, then kissed her daughter. "Be right back."

She tore down the block, turned the first corner, passed the alley full of smoke, and rounded the last corner to their side of the long block, then stopped, stunned. Snapping tongues of fire belched out of the lower windows, licking up toward the second floor and the rooms that had belonged to Grace and the children; black smoke poured out of those windows, the glass now shattered on the ground below.

A crowd had gathered across the street, some joining the team of firemen pumping water and passing buckets down the line.

"Dugan!" she shouted over the roar of the fire. "Dugan Ogue!"

He turned and broke away, running with giant strides, scooping her into his arms and off her feet, squeezing the very life out of her.

"Ah, thank God, thank God," he sobbed, his body shaking. "I thought you were done for. I couldn't get near that door."

"Tara?" she asked immediately.

"We're all out." He pointed to where his wife stood staring up at the fire, Caolon in her arms, the arms of other women around them both. She turned and saw Grace, relief flooding her face.

"Saints be praised." Tara embraced her. "How did you ever get out of there, and where's Mary Kate?"

"She's at the Eberhardts' shop. We came through the tunnel."

"Oh, Lord, of course you did! Thank God for that bloody thing. Karl!" Dugan shouted to the butcher. "Marconi!"

The grocer saw them, too, and pushed his way through the crowd. "It's a really terrible thing you got, Ogue." He shook his head sorrowfully. "But nobody hurt, no?"

"Una," Dugan told him. "Our serving girl." He turned to Grace. "She was sleeping in your room, since your things were all out and she thought you were gone. I told her she could." His voice broke.

"You mustn't blame yourself, Ogue," Karl consoled him. "We never know. Is summertime, and so hot. Every night, something goes up. How did it start, then, this fire?"

"In the alley, I think." Dugan and Grace exchanged glances. "It's worse back there."

There was a flurry of activity as another wagon pulled up and men jumped out.

"Police." Dugan nudged Grace, then turned to Karl. "Would you take Grace back to your place, Karl? Tara and Caolon, as well?"

"I'm staying," Tara said firmly.

"No, Mother." He put an arm around her. " 'Tis no place for the boy, all the glass and bad air. Go now, back to Karl's. I'm going to help on the line. There's Marconi, going up."

"Be careful," she warned her husband. "You're too big to climb those spindly ladders."

He didn't laugh, seeing her worry. "I won't do any climbing, Tara my love—promise."

Karl took the weary band back to his rooms above the shop, and then returned to fight the fire with all the other men in the neighborhood. A fire like that could spread from rooftop to rooftop, no telling where it might end, and every man was needed.

Missus Eberhardt put blankets on the floor and the children slept while the women talked. Fire was a terrible thing, they agreed in whispers, and what would be left in the morning? Finally, they drifted off—Missus Eberhardt with her head back on her chair, snoring lightly; Tara stretched out on the floor, the baby cradled in her arms. Only Grace remained awake, knowing the fault of this was all hers, yet unable to say how she might have done things differently. She watched out the window as the sooty orange sky lightened to dull gray, and she asked herself why she'd ever thought that her brother's life was more important than her own, why she hadn't understood that he could go his way and she could go hers, and they would always be brother and sister, no matter where in the world they ended up. She had told him she was letting go of the past, and yet she'd not been able to let go of him, had clung to him even as he went in a direction she did not want to go. It had taken an enormous blaze to help her see this, to make her realize that life was fleeting and the future now. When Karl and Dugan and Mister Marconi came tramping up the stairs hours later, she had made her decision.

"Well, it's bad," Dugan allowed. "But not as bad as it could've been. Wasn't old Dooley there at the crack of dawn, righting the chairs and pointing out that with the weather so nice no one would mind the breeze blowing through?"

"He just doesn't want to lose his place at the bar." Tara laughed, Caolon at her breast.

"And I don't want him to lose it, either. We're going to rebuild," Dugan announced. "I think we can, Mother. If you're up to it, that is."

"Dugan Ogue, when have I ever been afraid of starting over?" she chided, and he strode across the room to kiss her full on the mouth in front of God and everyone.

"I can help." Karl wiped the soot from his face with a towel. "I know some boys and they will help, too."

"Don't forget Mister Marconi," the grocer declared. "And my papa's hammer. All the way from Italia!"

"You can all stay here until is ready," Missus Eberhardt offered in her careful English. "We make room."

"Where's the boy?" Marconi looked worried. "Where's that Liam?"

"With Captain Reinders." Grace stood and took her daughter's hand. "I'll hope you'll forgive me, Dugan. You know we can't stay to help you." She paused. "Mary Kate and I are leaving today for Boston."

Tara's face broke into a grin. "That's my girl."

"Well, I'll be . . ." Dugan laughed. "All right, then. We'll have to get a move on if you're to catch them before they sail." His face clouded. "But, Grace, I've no way to do it. The cart burned, and the mule . . ." He glanced at Mary Kate.

"You can have my cart and my mule," Karl offered. "But the old thing will never make it to Boston."

"If you'll only take us to the Livingstons', Florence will know what to do next," Grace said thankfully.

"Marconi and I will pull your trunks through the tunnel," Ogue directed. "And Karl will bring the cart around front."

The men dispersed and Mary Kate tugged on her mother's hand.

"Are we going to sea with Liam and the captain, then?"

"I think so." Grace bit her lip. "Will you want to get back on that boat, then?"

"Aye." Mary Kate grinned. "And, Mam—'tis a *ship*."

Boardham sat in a chair by the window, waiting. He was anxious, but he controlled it with measured shots of whiskey. Callahan had sent a message—he had a job for the steward, which meant he hadn't connected Boardham to last night's fire. He allowed himself a tight smile of satisfaction. Burning the saloon had been nothing short of brilliant—Callahan would never be able to point the finger, Boardham had worked so quickly, had been so light on his feet, so very discreet. And even if Callahan did eventually figure it out—Boardham tossed back his drink—it had been worth it for the joy he'd felt watching that Irish bastard's watering hole go up in flames, seeing Missus Donnelly's body carried out and put in the death wagon, listening to that ugly giant blubbering out front as his life burned up in front of his eyes. Yes, it had been worth the risk of his own livelihood.

He had not waited around much longer than that, had hurried home before dawn and gathered his things, ready to fly if necessary. But moments after he'd arrived, the messenger had knocked. It was an important job, the messenger had emphasized, and if it went well, then all was forgiven. If not—Boardham had already decided—he would never return to this room but would head south to new friends and a new life.

It was quiet tonight, no fire calls yet, no brawls in the street. He poured himself another whiskey from the near-empty bottle. A sharp rap on the door jangled the silence, startling him, and he sloshed part of his drink out onto the table.

"Yeah," he growled, setting the glass down.

The door popped open and there stood his favorite Bowery B'hoy—Small John English, toughest man in the neighborhood. Callahan must have more faith than Boardham realized and his spirits rose. English was very select; he only worked with men who could get the job done.

"Whiskey?" Boardham offered congenially, the knot in his stomach easing now.

"No, thanks." The thug had a disarming smile. "Maybe later."

"I'll just finish this." Boardham drank it down. "Throat's a bit sore tonight."

"Better lay off the smoking then." English closed his jacket around the knife at his side. "Those things only get worse."

Forty-four

J AY sent a message, summoning his sister home from her meeting at once. "She's got all the contacts," he apologized. "I just throw the parties and pour the drinks. Speaking of which. . . ?"

"Thanks very much, but no." Grace stood by the window, looking out. "Best if I stay clearheaded."

He helped himself. "And were you clearheaded when you made this very rash decision to run off with the stodgy, passionless Captain Reinders?"

"Jay," she scolded absentmindedly, hearing Mary Kate's laughter from the kitchen, where she and the Ogues were being given a meal.

"I'm quite serious, Grace. He's a sailor, for God's sake! Gone for months, who knows where—foreign lands, exotic women, rum smuggling—"

"I thought you said he was stodgy and passionless?" She laughed.

"You could've had me, you know," he admonished lightly. "I just don't understand it."

"Jay!" She looked at him. "You never wanted to marry me!"

"Well, what if I did?" he argued. "What if I asked you now? Would you consider it?"

She shook her head.

"Why ever not?" he demanded.

"Well." She paused. "Because we don't love each other."

"Don't we?" he asked petulantly. "Because I was sure at least one of us did. Oh, there you are." His sister walked into the room. "She's running off with Peter and I can't talk her out of it."

"Good for you." Florence winked at Grace.

"I simply give up!" Jay stalked off to the desk in the corner, then lifted up a leather satchel. "This is your brother's. O'Sullivan dropped it by earlier—papers mostly, and some mail. What am I supposed to do with it *now*?"

"Well, it's no good her taking it to San Francisco," Florence told him. "Just keep it until Dugan hears from Sean, and then we'll send it to him ourselves."

Jay shrugged and set down the satchel. "All right. But I simply can't believe you're doing this, Grace."

"I am, though." Grace put out her hand. "Good-bye, Jay."

"I never say good-bye, and besides, you'll be back."

"Ready?" Florence asked, and Grace nodded, kissing Jay quickly on the cheek, then following his sister out into the kitchen.

Everyone stood and Mary Kate held out her arms for her mother, who picked her up and went out the back door to the waiting carriage. The driver finished loading the trunks and then it was time. Grace set Mary Kate down and smoothed her dress, then turned to their friends.

Tara held Caolon out. "He wants to say good-bye to his favorite wee girl."

Mary Kate kissed his little fists, then his round cheeks. " 'Bye, Caolon," she whispered, rubbing her face against his.

"You'll see him again before you know it," Tara assured her, but Mary Kate was resigned; she had said many farewells in her short life.

Grace held and kissed the baby, then handed him back to Tara, hugging her, as well.

"You send word now. Let us know what's happening. And, Grace, you've always got a place with us, you know."

"Thank you, Tara. For everything." The two women rested against one another.

"That's enough now, wife. Aren't they late enough already? And it's not forever, you know." Dugan picked up Mary Kate, swallowing her whole in his mighty arms. "You be a good girl for your mam," he said gruffly, and then his voice softened. "Ah, well, but aren't you always? Too good to be true." He kissed her and set her down, reached into his pocket, and brought out a little sack of candies. "For the trip. Share a few with Liam, now. When you see him."

"Aye, Dugan, thanks." She took the sack, biting her lip just like her mother.

"And give him this from Mister Marconi." He handed her a small pocketknife, its handle smooth and new. "For mumblety-peg."

She nodded soberly and put it in her pocket.

"All right, you." He turned to Grace. "I got something here." He handed her an old likeness of himself in his boxing togs, full head of dark hair, arms up in the fighting stance. "Don't forget your old friend Mighty Ogue, now, will you?"

Grace's face ached with trying to hold all the emotion she felt. "Never," she vowed. "Never, ever."

"I'll be on the lookout for Sean's letter, and I'll let him know where you've gone. Good-bye then, girl." He opened his arms.

She laid her head against his mighty chest, listening to the beat of his strong, steady heart. "Thank you, Dugan." She looked up into his eyes, both understanding what she meant. "Thank you for my life."

" 'Twas you delivered our Caolon over there, and we'll always love you for that." He kissed her cheek. "Off with yourselves now. God be with you," he pronounced, letting go. "We'll see you again."

She nodded and gave him a trembling smile, then climbed into the carriage, Mary Kate next to her, Florence sitting across. Grace stuck her hand out the window, and Dugan took it one last time.

"Go get him," he whispered.

The carriage pulled away and they watched until it had turned the corner, disappearing from sight, Dugan's arm firmly around Tara, who held the baby close.

"I love you," she said, leaning against her husband.

"And I love you," he said and kissed her lovely mouth.

From the upstairs window, Jay stood and watched the carriage go, then looked down and saw Dugan, his wife, and their child bathed in sunlight. And in that moment, he envied them more than he had ever envied anyone in his life.

Forty-five

"HE'S gone!" Lily cried out when she opened the door. "Lord Almighty, he left yesterday!"

Grace stared, then started to collapse, Florence and Lily catching her before she hit the ground. Each woman got her under the arm, then led her into the house.

"Sit her down," Lily directed. "I'll get you some tea. Mary!" Her daughter came in, wiping her hands on her apron. "We got company. Is there something we can give them to eat?"

"Yes, Mama." The girl smiled when she saw who it was.

Florence patted Grace's hand briskly and Lily fanned her with a piece of newspaper.

"Stop." Grace blinked and sat up. "I'm fine. Stop." She looked around for Mary Kate and found her hovering anxiously by the chair; she pulled the child onto her lap and hugged her.

"I just can't believe it!" Lily sat back.

"I knew we might be too late," Grace finally said wretchedly. "I just didn't want to think about it."

"He didn't know you was coming or he would've waited. I *know* he would've waited." Lily shook her head.

"It's not his fault. He asked me to come, but I said no. I told him I was going to my brother in Illinois."

Lily squinted at her. "You said no, but you love him?"

"I don't know how I feel," she confessed. "I can't trust that about myself. But I was willing to risk it. He has Liam, doesn't he? And I think he truly loves me."

"He does." Lily leaned forward. "And he's mighty fond of that boy. You, too, Mary Kate. He said so."

"Are they gone, then?" Mary Kate asked, bewildered.

The women looked at one another.

"Aye," Grace admitted, still not able to fully believe it. "We missed them."

Mary Kate's mouth fell open and she burst into tears. Grace hugged her fiercely, fighting her own terrible disappointment.

"Ah, now, girl, I'm sorry, I'm sorry. 'Tis my fault. But we'll think of something. We'll figure out what to do." She looked at Florence for help, and then at Lily.

"Ruth!" Lily called, and the shy girl Grace remembered appeared. "We got Mary Kate here to visit. Take her on out to the kitchen, will you, and show her the mama dog we got back there."

Mary Kate lifted her tear-streaked face at the mention of a dog, and allowed herself to be coaxed off her mother's lap, then taken by the hand and led out of the room.

"What are we to do then?" Grace asked in dismay. "I can't go out to San Francisco alone, and I can't go back to the city. I've not the least idea where Illinois is or how to find my brother once I get there." She had to laugh, it sounded so hopeless.

"You could stay here," Lily offered. "You could stay with us a while. We can make room."

Grace bit her lip. "Will I be able to earn my keep? Is there work?"

"Plenty." Lily got excited. "We got saloons and shops, factories, servant work . . . plenty of things you can do. You could even work with me and Jakob if you don't mind the fish. We doing real well up here! I could ask him."

"That's not a bad idea." Florence nodded. "You wouldn't have to decide anything right now. The Ogues will let you know when they hear from Sean"—Grace caught the note of sadness at the mention of her brother's name—"and Peter will write when he reaches San Francisco. You can take a little time, you know," she added gently. "Live peacefully for a while and rest. You've come so far already."

Grace took her hand, thinking about that.

They sat late into the evening, these women who led such different outward lives, but inwardly were much the same—each one of them had loved and lost, and carried bravely on, understanding that at every turn, life begins again.

When it was dark, Lily lit the lamps and took Grace to the room belonging to her daughters, the room they were happy to share with their mother's Irish friend, the woman the captain loved.

"You're going to be all right," Lily comforted her. "A lot of people, they care about you, Grace. They praying for you even now."

Grace's eyes filled with tears, and Lily set the lamp down, then wrapped her strong arms around those stalwart shoulders. "You sleep now. You'll know what to do come morning time."

Grace thanked her and kissed her, then crawled into bed and waited for Mary Kate, who came bounding in, face and hands clean, hair plaited, her little body swimming in one of Ruth's nightgowns with the sleeves rolled up.

"How are you?" Grace whispered.

"Good." Mary Kate snuggled in next to her. "They have puppies."

"Are they nice?"

"Oh, aye," the girl sighed. "Ruth says I can have one, but I said no."

"Don't you want a puppy, then?" Grace smoothed her daughter's bangs, smelling the child scent of her.

"Aye." Mary Kate turned to look at her mother in the dark. "But where do we live now?"

Grace's heart turned over and she wondered what to say to this child, who had traveled so far.

"Do you remember our house in Ireland?"

" 'Twas big," Mary Kate whispered. "But I liked Grandda's more."

"Aye." Grace saw the cabin clearly. " 'Twas best there."

"Why did we come away?" Mary Kate's finger traced her mother's chin.

"There was no food nor work to be had," Grace told her. "We came here to find a new life."

"And did we?"

Grace thought about that. "I think so. Almost." Peter's face drifted into her mind's eye and she smiled. "Mary Kate," she whispered. "We went west once, you and I. Shall we go west again?"

"What does God say?" Mary Kate asked drowsily.

"I've not asked Him yet," her mother admitted. "Good night then, love."

Mary Kate was instantly asleep, but Grace lay awake the whole of the night, watching moonlight inch from corner to corner. Hours passed and finally she eased herself out of bed, dressed quickly, then crept down the stairs and out the front door, stepping into the fresh, windswept air, the gentle darkness that comes before dawn.

She walked toward the harbor; it felt good to stretch her legs, to walk alone, her mind more clear with every step she took. At last, she came to the wharf and made her way carefully out to the very end of one of the docks, as far as she could go. Then she stood, peering at the horizon from which the sun was just beginning to emerge. East, she was looking east—to Ireland and all that had been left behind.

Which way? she asked finally, and in that moment the sun broke free, boldly spreading its light like angel's wings across the water, illuminating the world. It moved up through the sky—she watched its confident climb—and if she stood all day, it would turn her face from east to west, to all that lay before her, to all that was ahead.

She took a deep breath and then another, the clean, salty air filling her body, making her strong. She turned and walked back up the dock, across the wharf and all the way home with long, sure strides, the sun rising, the wind at her back. She pushed open the gate and strode up the path, opened the door and listened; they were all up now, in the kitchen chattering away, and when she came in to them, they stopped and looked up expectantly.

Mary Kate stood on her chair, biting her lip. "Jay's come!" she announced, as Livingston rose from the table, his hair and clothing stiff with dust from the hard, fast ride.

"This was in Sean's bag." He held out a battered letter. "It's for you, Grace—from Julia Martin."

Grace could only stare.

"I read it," Jay said gently, coming forward and placing it in her hand. "He's alive, your son. She has him."

"It's true." Florence touched Grace's arm.

Lily nodded, her own eyes bright, Mary's hand in hers.

Grace pulled the pages from the envelope and read, then clutched them to her heart, looking in amazement at the faces before her, seeking out the dearest—the little girl whose arms were already reaching for her. She swept up her daughter and held her tightly.

"He's alive," she whispered. "Your brother's alive."

"I came as fast as I could." Jay grinned wearily. "Thank God you were still here."

"Aye." Grace nodded in wonder.

"Hooray!" Mary Kate exclaimed, throwing her hands in the air, and everyone cheered with her.

Grace laughed and looked down into that lovely shining face; she covered it with kisses, then laughed again and danced her daughter round the room, the others close behind. Out the door they spilled, down the steps, over the grass, and into the middle of the beautiful garden, where flowers filled the air with sweetness and birds proclaimed the joy of life, where the sun shone down upon them all, and truly a new day had come.

Ann Moore was born in England and raised in the Pacific Northwest. She lives in Bellingham, Washington, with her husband and two children.

Leaving Ireland

✧

ANN MOORE

This Conversation Guide is intended to enrich the
individual reading experience, as well as encourage us
to explore these topics together—because books,
and life, are meant for sharing.

A CONVERSATION WITH ANN MOORE

Q. From the docks of Liverpool to the tenements of Five Points in Manhattan, you've vividly re-created the sights, sounds, and smells of a time so different from our own. How did you approach the historical research for this book?

A. This time period is really only 150 years ago, though it seems longer because civilization advanced so rapidly after the Civil War. Thanks to the historians of that time and to modern historians who have consolidated so much material, information is far more accessible today than ever before. With a little digging and diligence, one can read the diaries and letters of immigrants, peruse passenger and cargo lists, pore over maps, bills of sale, reward notices, and slave auction posters—and slowly one begins to get a feel for the language of the day, the rhythm of life in the midcentury, the hopes and concerns of those who took this enormous leap of faith in coming to a new land.

Sometimes I read through hundreds of pages until, at last, there appears a single paragraph that is of great value to the story; other times, valuable information drips from every page, and the difficulty is in choosing what to include and what to let go. I was particularly grateful for Edward Laxton's *The Famine Ships*, Edward Burrows and Mike Wallace's enormous *Gotham*, Tyler Anbinder's *Five Points*, Thomas Keneally's *The Great Shame*,

and—the book that has really been a light through the tunnel—
Cecil Woodham-Smith's *The Great Hunger*.

Q. *During her passage, Gracelin refers to America as the Land of the Young. Was her journey typical of the time? Did the reality match up with the dream?*

A. The dream for the Irish, coming from such extreme conditions—starvation, rampant illness, oppression—was fairly humble; they hoped for shelter and food, and were willing to work at the most menial jobs in order to secure these things for their families. Unlike many immigrants from other countries, very few Irish had trade skills; even their farming was limited to knowledge of a single crop. More than one million came into this country, most with no tools, no education, no money, few possessions; they took the lowest housing and the meanest work, and were subjected to great prejudice and scorn. But America offered two things that Ireland did not: opportunity and the freedom to take advantage of it.

Q. Leaving Ireland *continues the story of* Gracelin O'Malley, *yet stands fully as a separate novel. What were the challenges of writing a sequel that could be read on its own?*

A. I felt a great responsibility for maintaining the integrity of the characters in *Gracelin O'Malley* and for continuing their stories in a way that was true and honorable to the survivors of the Great Hunger. The response from those who have read *Gracelin O'Malley* has been so strong and emotional, that I was conscious throughout of holding to that standard. The greatest challenge was in figuring out how to weave Grace's past into this story in such a way that the plot was not bogged down by events that had happened in the first book, yet still provide enough information for new readers to have a clear understanding of all she had been through. The other difficulty was in picking up Grace's story right where it left off, even though, in real life, two years had passed. I found myself paying particular attention to the way in which my two years of additional life experience affected the way in which I now approached my writing of her character.

Q. *In writing about the immigrant experience, did you see any similarities to those who come to America today?*

A. The actual travel experience may be somewhat easier, but assimilation into this society is still very difficult. I think it's hard for many Americans to fathom the incredible poverty, despair, and religious or political persecution that forces people to leave their homelands and come here. We think them fortunate to get a chance to live in this country with all its opportunity, so it's easy to overlook the heavy emotional baggage they bring along with them after years of pain and struggle. The land of plenty can be enormously overwhelming to people who can barely speak English, let alone read labels and signs, who have never been faced with so much choice, who perhaps suffer loneliness, depression, regret, all the while trying to find living space and work, trying to find a way to fit into the community, to build a new way of life.

It's important to remember that the majority of Americans here today descended from immigrants—somewhere along the line, our ancestors made a decision to come to this country, to try for something better for their families. Writing about this experience has reminded me how much we've benefited from their choices, and I look around with eyes more open to the plight of others and a hand more ready, because—especially in a strange land—small kindnesses can make a world of difference.

Q. *What are you working on now? Have we seen the last of Gracelin?*

A. At the end of a story, I always ask the characters if they're done now, if they've anything else to say, and usually we're all quite satisfied. Gracelin, however, continues to whisper in my ear and show up in my dreams, so I think she wants to carry on a little further—you know how strong-minded she can be. She was a secondary character in what I had originally foreseen as a novel set in the Pacific Northwest around 1850; research led me to Ireland at the time of the famine and I realized it was her story I was meant to write. I thought this second book would take us, then, to the Pacific Northwest, but there was so much happening in Manhattan that we didn't make it! Perhaps the third book will take us across the country and Gracelin will, at last, find a peaceful life and a home by the sea.

QUESTIONS FOR DISCUSSION

1. In many ways, this is a novel of new beginnings. Have you ever had to start over in some essential way? Do you think that there are universals in the immigrant experience, regardless of culture or time? Do you think it's necessary to let go of the past in order to move forward?

2. The responsibility of motherhood is a theme that runs throughout the book. Was Julia's guardianship of Morgan different in motive from Grace's care of Liam? Did Grace make the right choice in leaving her son behind, and was it the same choice Lily made? Captain Reinders' mother also made a painful decision—what does she have in common with the other women?

3. Religion plays a central role in the novel, from Gracelin's Protestant faith to Barbara's Catholicism, Sean's fervor for the Latter-Day Saints, and Captain Reinders' god of Logic. Do you think people were more religious in the nineteenth century? How big a part did religion play in the daily lives of people then as opposed to now? Do people feel differently about God when life is more precarious?

4. The author makes reference to the Irish perception of themselves as slaves, and also includes the experience of American

slavery in the South. How does slavery affect the lives of the characters, both physically and emotionally? Do you think we tend to take our freedom for granted?

5. Grace and Sean faced glaring prejudice in America and were wounded by depictions of the Irish as ignorant, superstitious monkeys; African-Americans faced the same intolerance and blatant cruelty. Is our society more compassionate today? Have you ever been discriminated against because of your ethnicity or religion or economic background? Have you ever met someone who, like Callahan, turned against his own people? Do you think, fairly or unfairly, that the actions of one individual impact the perception of an entire group?